FREN

Short Stories

FRENCH
Short Stories

French Short Stories

Stories selected from
The Masterpiece Library of Short Stories, Volume III, French,
issued by Allied Newspapers Ltd., in association with
The Educational Book Company Ltd, London.

This edition published in 1995 by Senate, an imprint of
Studio Editions Ltd, Princess House, 50 Eastcastle Street,
London W1N 7AP, England

ISBN 1 85958 117 X
Printed and bound in Guernsey by
The Guernsey Press Co. Ltd

Contents

CONTENTS

ANTOINE DE LA SALE
1398–1470

THE CYNIC TESTAMENT

Now listen, if you please, to a thing that happened the other day to a simple village priest, who by his simplicity was amerced by his bishop in the sum of fifty good golden crowns. The good priest had a dog he had brought up from puppyhood, and that surpassed all the dogs of the parish in fetching sticks thrown in the water, or bringing back the hat his master forgot or purposely left behind him in any place. In short, all that a good and wise dog ought to know and do he was a champion at ; and for this reason his master loved him so much that he was quite besotted about his dog.

But it happened, I know not by what mischance, whether he got too hot or too cold, or ate something that hurt him, that the dog became very ill and died, and went straight from this world to the paradise that good dogs go to. But what did the good priest do ? Just below his presbytery was the parish graveyard ; and when he saw his dog had passed away from this world, he thought that such a good and wise beast had a right to a proper burial. So he dug a grave just outside his door, and there he buried him like a Christian.

I do not know if he erected a marble stone above the grave and engraved an epitaph on it, so I will keep silent about this part of the affair. But it was not long before the death of the worthy dog was known to the village of the neighbouring parishes and spread from there to the ears of the bishop, together with the rumour about the Christian burial that his master had given him. So the bishop summoned the priest to appear before him.

" Alas ! " said the priest to the lawyer who brought the summons, " what have I done that I should be brought before the bishop's court ? I am amazed at the summons, and cannot guess what I have done wrong."

" As for myself," said the bishop's man, " I cannot tell what they want you for, unless it is that you have buried your dog in holy ground in which the bodies of Christians are placed."

"Ha!" thought the priest, "so that is it!"

And for the first time it came into his head that he might have gone a little too far, and he thought to himself he would have to prepare for the worst. For his bishop was the most covetous in the kingdom, and the people around the bishop knew how to bring grist to the mill by ways God only could discern. And the priest knew that if he were condemned to prison he would be very heavily fined.

"Since I must lose my money," he said, "it is best to get it over."

So he answered the summons, and went straight to the bishop, who preached him a long sermon about the burial of the good dog. And it seemed, to hear him, that the priest would have committed a lighter sin if he had denied God. And when the sermon was ended, he ordered the criminal to be thrown into prison.

When the priest saw they wanted to shut him up in the stone box he was more terrified than a duckling, and begged his lordship, the bishop, first to hear what he had to say. And his request was granted. And you must know that at this trial there was a swarm of folks of many sorts, such as the official, the promoters, the scribe, notaries, barristers, procurers, and several others—and all of them together rejoiced over the case of the good priest who had buried his dog in holy ground. By way of defence the priest spoke but a few words.

"Truly, my lord Bishop, if you had known as much as I do of my good dog, you would not be amazed at the burial I gave him. For his equal was never found and never will be."

Then he began to praise his dog. "And just as he was most wise in his lifetime so was he more so in his death. For he made and executed an excellent testament, and knowing your necessity and your poverty, he bequeathed to you fifty gold crowns, which I now bring you."

And drawing the money from his purse, he counted it out to the bishop. His lordship gladly received the legacy, and then praised and approved the good sense of the worthy dog, and the testament he had made, and the burial that had been given to him.

A TUNE ON THE BAGPIPE

Antoine de la Sale

DURING the war between the Burgundians and the Armagnacs, there occurred at Troyes in Champagne a delightful adventure that is well worth relating. The people of Troyes had first been on the side of Burgundy and had then turned Armagnacs ; and among them was a half-witted fellow who kept with us. He had not quite lost his reason, but he inclined more to the side of madness than to that of sanity : yet at the same time he carried out by hand and mouth several tasks that wiser men than he would not have known how to manage.

This fellow was doing garrison work with the Burgundians at Sainte Menehoulde, and while talking one day with his companions he said that if they would trust him and help him, he would give them a good plan for capturing a great host of the rascals of Troyes. For he hated these townfolk mortally, and they did not exactly love him, but always threatened to hang him if he fell into their hands.

" I will go towards Troyes," he said, " and approach the outskirts of the city, and pretend to spy on the town and measure the moat with my lance. I shall be taken prisoner, and I am sure that the good bailiff will condemn me to be hanged, and none of the townsmen will object to it. For they hate me, all of them. So I shall be quickly led to the gibbet, and you will lie in ambush in the copse close by. And as soon as you hear me coming out of the gate into the field with my large following, you must spring out on the townspeople and make them prisoners and deliver me from their hands."

All the troops of the garrison agreed to help him if he were daring enough to undertake the adventure. So the game, gallant, half-witted fellow went to Troyes, and, as he wished, was taken prisoner, and the news of his capture quickly spread through the town. And there was not a man who did not wish to hang him. The bailiff, as soon as he saw him, swore by all his saints he would hang him up by the neck.

" Alas, my lord," said the adventurer, " I pray you have mercy on me. I have never done you wrong."

" You lie, scoundrel ! " said the bailiff. " You have guided the

Burgundians in their marches, and have harmed the good burghers
and merchants of this town. But you shall have your reward and be
hanged at the gibbet ! "

" For God's sake," said our good fellow, " since I must die, let it be
in the early morning and outside the town. For I cannot bear to
receive too public a punishment in this town, where I once had so
many friends and acquaintances."

" Very well," said the bailiff, " we will think about it."

At dawn the next day the executioner with his cart arrived at the
prison, and scarcely had he arrived than the bailiff came on horse-
back with his officers and a large number of people to accompany
him. Our man was taken and trussed and bound on the cart, and,
holding his bagpipe, on which he played continually, he was carried
to the place of execution. Though it was so early, a larger crowd
gathered to see him die than was usual at these scenes, so much was
he hated in the town.

Now you must know that the Burgundian troops had not forgotten to lie in ambush in the wood close to the place of execution.
They had come there at midnight, partly to save their man, though
he was not the wisest of creatures, and partly to get prisoners and
any spoil within reach. They disposed themselves ready for action,
and sent a man up a tree to watch and tell them when the townsmen
of Troyes were at the field of execution.

The watchman was placed so that he could do good duty. And
the people of Troyes came to the gibbet, and the bailiff ordered that
our poor fool should be despatched. He wondered where his
companions were, and why they did not attack the scoundrelly
Armagnacs. Ill at ease, he looked backwards and forwards, and
chiefly at the wood. But he heard and saw nothing. He lengthened
out his confession as much as he could, but he was taken from the
priest and pushed on the scaffold. There, God knows, he was pretty
well dazed, and he continued to stare at the wood. But all his
trouble went for nothing. For the watchman, who had been ordered
to start the rescue party, had fallen asleep on the tree.

So our poor fellow did not know what to do, and thought his last
day had come. The executioner made his preparations to fix the rope
round his neck to finish him. When our friend saw this, he thought
of a trick that might turn to his advantage.

" My lord," he said to the bailiff, " for God's sake, let me play one
tune on my bagpipe before your men lay hands on me. I ask nothing
more, and shall be content to die and forgive you and everybody for
killing me ! "

His request was granted, and his bagpipe lifted up to him. And
holding it as easily as he could, he began to blow, and played a song
that he companions in ambush knew very well. It was, " You stay
too long, Robin, you stay too long ! " And at the skirl of the bagpipe

the watchman awoke, and in his fear he let himself fall from the top to the bottom of the tree, and cried :

"They are hanging our man ! On ! on ! Quick as you can ! "

The troops were all ready, and at the sound of the trumpet, they sallied from the wood and fell upon the bailiff and all the folk round the gibbet. And in the tumult the executioner lost his wits, and instead of hanging his man told him to save his life. This our friend would willingly have done but it was not in his power. He did something better. Standing on the scaffold, he cried to his companions :

"Take that man ! Capture this man ! This one is wealthy, that one is worth nothing."

In short, the Burgundians killed a great heap of the men of Troyes, and took a large number captive, and saved their own man, who, never all the days of his life, was in such a state of terror as in that hour.

PHILIP THE GOOD, DUKE OF BURGUNDY 1396-1467

THE HONEST WOMAN WITH TWO HUSBANDS

IT is known not only in the town of Ghent, where the affair I am about to describe happened a few years ago, but by most folk of Flanders, that at the battle between the King of Hungary and Duke John, whom God absolve ! on the one part, and the Grand Turk in his land of Turkey on the other part, several knights and squires of France, Flanders, Germany, and Picardy were taken prisoners. Some were put to death by the Turk ; some were cast for life into prison ; others were condemned to the state and labour of slaves.

Among these last was a gentle knight of the land of Flanders named Messire Clayz Utenhoven. For several years he worked as a slave, and his labour was not light to him, but an intolerable martyrdom, seeing to what pleasure he had been bred and to what rank he belonged. For you must know that he had married at Ghent a very beautiful and good lady who loved him with all her heart. Daily she prayed to God that she might see him again, if he were still living, and that if he were dead he might be pardoned of his sins and placed amongst the glorious martyrs who, for the repulsion of the infidels and the exaltation of the holy Catholic faith, voluntarily abandoned themselves to temporal death.

This good lady, who was very rich, was continually urged by her friends to marry again. They assured her that her husband was dead. If he were alive, they said, he would have returned with the others ; if he had been taken prisoner, there would have been news of him in connection with his ransom. But no matter what they said, the good lady would not think of a second marriage, and did all she could to escape from it. Her efforts, however, went for little or nothing. For she was so constrained by her relatives and her friends that she had to obey them.

But, God knows it was with great regret, and after being widowed of her good and loyal husband for nine years and thinking him dead, as every one else did, that she married again.

But God, who guards and preserves his servants and champions, had not allowed Messire Clayz Utenhoven to die. He was still working miserably as a slave when his good lady married another knight. And about six months after this event some Christian gentlemen and merchants set him free, and took him aboard their galley and brought him back. And in the countries he passed on his return he met with several acquaintances, who were very joyful over his delivery. For in truth he was a very valiant man of virtuous character and high reputation. And the glad news of his deliverance spread into France and Artois and Picardy, where his virtues were not less known than in Flanders. It was not long before the rumour reached Flanders, and came to the ears of the good and lovely wife of the freed man. Greatly was she stricken by it, and so wrung with grief that she did not know her own face.

"Ha!" she said, when she was able to talk, "my heart never consented to do that which my parents and friends forced me to do. Alas! what will he think of it, my loyal lord and husband! I have not kept faith as I should, but like a frail, light, timid woman I have given up to another that of which he should have been the sole lord and master. I am not worthy to await his coming, and I dare not do it. I am not worthy that he should look on me, or have me in his company!"

And saying these words with great tears, her honest, virtuous, and loyal heart fainted away. She was carried on a bed, and her heart revived; but it was not in the power of man or woman to get her to eat or sleep. So she lived for three days, continually weeping, in the greatest sorrow of heart that ever woman knew. After some time she made her confession and ordered her end like a good Christian, praying mercy from every one, and especially from her husband. And soon after that she died, and great was the sorrow over her. I cannot describe the grief of her husband when he heard the news; and by reason of his sorrow he was in great danger of dying as his wife has done. But God, who had saved him from other great perils, preserved him also from this.

MARGUERITE DE NAVARRE
1492–1549

THE CRIME OF THE CORDELIER

THERE was in the dominions of the Emperor Maximilian of Austria a monastery of Cordeliers, held in high esteem, near which was the house of a gentleman. He was so infatuated with these Cordeliers that there was nothing he did not give them in order to have part in the benefit of their fastings and prayers. Among others, there was in this monastery a tall, handsome young Cordelier, whom the gentleman had taken for his confessor, and who was as absolute in the house as the master himself.

The Cordelier, struck by the exceeding beauty and propriety of the gentleman's wife, became so enamoured of her that he could neither eat nor drink, and lost all natural reason. Resolved to execute his design, he went all alone one day to the gentleman's house. Finding no one at home, the monk asked the lady whither her husband was gone? She replied that he was gone to one of his estates, where he was to remain two or three days; but that if he wanted him she would send an express to bring him back. The Cordelier told her that was not necessary, and began to go to and fro about the house, as if he had some affair of consequence in his head.

As soon as the monk had left the lady's room, she said to one of her woman (there were but two of them), "Run after the father, and learn what he wants, for I know by his looks that he is not pleased."

The girl, finding him in the courtyard, asked him if he wanted anything? He said he did, and, drawing her into a corner, he plunged into her bosom a poniard he carried in his sleeve. He had hardly done the deed when one of the gentleman's men, who had gone to receive the rent of a farm, entered the yard on horse-back. As soon as he had dismounted he saluted the Cordelier, who embraced him and buried the poniard in his back, after which he closed the gates of the château.

The lady, seeing that her servant did not return, and surprised at her remaining so long with the Cordelier, said to the other woman :

"Go, see why your companion does not come back." The servant went, and no sooner came in sight of the Cordelier than he called her aside, and served her as he had done the other. Knowing that he was then alone in the house, he went to the lady, and told her that he had long loved her, and that it was time she should obey him. She, who could never have suspected him of anything of the kind, replied:

"I believe, father, that if I were so unhappily inclined, you would be the first to condemn me and cast a stone at me."

"Come out into the yard," said the monk, "and you will see what I have done."

The poor woman did so, and, seeing her two women and her man lying dead on the ground, was so horrified that she remained motionless and speechless as a statue. The villain, who did not want to possess her for an hour only, did not think fit to offer her violence then, and said to her:

"Have no fear, mademoiselle; you are in the hands of that man in all the world who loves you most."

So saying, he took off his habit, beneath which he had a smaller one, which he presented to the demoiselle, threatening, if she did not put it on, that he would treat her as he had done the others.

The demoiselle, more dead than alive, made a show of obeying him, as well to save her life as to gain time, in hope that her husband would return. She took off her head-dress, by the Cordelier's order, as slowly as she could; and when she had done so, the monk, without regard to the beauty of her hair, cut it off in haste, made her strip to her shift and put on the small habit; and then, resuming his own, he set off with all the speed he could, with the little Cordelier, whom he had so long coveted, at his side.

But God, who has pity on the wronged innocent, was touched by the tears of this poor lady, and so ordered things that her husband, having despatched his business sooner than he expected, took that very road to return home by which the Cordelier was carrying off his wife. The monk, descrying the husband from a distance, said to the lady:

"Here comes your husband. I know that if you look at him he will try to get you out of my hands; so walk before me, and do not turn your head in his direction, for if you make him the least sign I shall have plunged my poniard in your breast sooner than he will have delivered you."

Presently the gentleman came up and asked him whence he came.

"From your house, monsieur," replied the Cordelier. "I left mademoiselle quite well, and she is expecting you."

The gentleman rode on without perceiving his wife; but the valet who accompanied him, and who had always been in the habit of conversing with the Cordelier's companion, named Friar John, called to his mistress, thinking that she was that person.

The poor woman, who durst not turn her head towards her husband, made no reply to the valet ; and the latter crossed the road that he might see the face of this pretended Brother John. The poor lady, without saying anything, made a sign to him with her eyes, which were full of tears. The valet then rode up to his master and said :

" In conscience, monsieur, Friar John is very like mademoiselle your wife. I had a look at him as I crossed the road. It is certainly not the usual Friar John ; at least, I can tell you that if it is, he weeps abundantly, and that he gave me a very sorrowful glance of his eye."

The gentleman told him he was dreaming, and made light of what he said.

The valet, however, still persisted in it that there was something wrong, asked leave to ride back and see to it, and begged his master to wait for him. The gentleman let him go, and waited to see what would be the upshot. But the Cordelier, hearing the valet coming after him with shouts to Friar John, and making no doubt that the lady had been recognised, turned upon the valet with a great iron-bound staff, gave him such a blow on the side that he knocked him off his horse, and springing instantly upon him with a poniard, speedily despatched him.

The gentleman, who from a distance had seen his valet fall, and supposed that this had happened by some accident, spurred towards him at once to help him. As soon as he was within reach, the Cordelier struck him a blow of the same staff with which he had struck the valet, unhorsed and fell upon him ; but the gentleman, being very strong, threw his arms round the Cordelier, and hugged him so roughly that he not only prevented his doing him any more mischief, but made him drop the poniard. The wife caught it up at once and gave it to her husband. At the same time she seized him by his hood and held him with all her might, whilst her husband stabbed him several times with the poniard.

The Cordelier, being unable to do anything else, begged for quarter, and confessed the crime he had committed. The gentleman granted him his life, and begged his wife to go for his people, and a cart to carry the prisoner away, which she did, throwing off her Cordelier's habit, and hurrying home in her shift and her cropped hair. The gentleman's retainers all hastened to help him to bring home the wolf he had captured ; and the culprit was afterwards sent by the gentleman to Flanders to be tried by the Emperor's officers.

He not only confessed the crime for which he was tried, but also avowed a fact, which was afterwards verified on the spot by special commissioners sent for that purpose, which was, that several other ladies had been taken to that convent in the same manner as this Cordelier had attempted to carry off the lady of whom we are speaking; and if he did not succeed, this was owing to nothing else than the goodness of God, who always takes upon Him the defence of those who trust in Him.

The girls, and the other stolen spoil found in the monastery, were removed, and then the monks were burned with the monastery, in perpetual memorial of a crime so horrible.

We see from this fact there is nothing more cruel than love when its principle is vice, as there is nothing more human or more laudable when it dwells in a virtuous heart.

THE UNHAPPY LOVER

Marguerite de Navarre

On the confines of Dauphiné and Provence there lived a gentleman who was much better endowed with the gifts of nature and education than with those of fortune. He was passionately enamoured of a demoiselle whose name I will not mention, on account of her relations, who are of good and great houses; but you may rely on the reality of the fact.

Not being of as good family as she was, he durst not declare his passion; but though his inferior birth made his despair of ever being able to marry her, nevertheless the love he bore her was so pure and respectful that he would have died rather than ask of her anything which could compromise her honour. He loved her, then, only because he thought her perfectly lovable, and he loved her so long that at last she had some inkling of the fact. Seeing, then, that his love for her was founded on virtue only, she deemed herself fortunate in being loved by so upright a man; and she treated him with such affability that he, who aspired to nothing better than this, was transported with delight.

But envy, the enemy of all quiet, could not suffer so innocent and so sweet an intercourse to continue. Some one told the girl's mother he was surprised the gentleman went so often to her house that people saw it was her daughter's beauty that attracted him, and that they had often been seen together.

The mother, who was thoroughly assured of the gentleman's probity, was greatly annoyed at finding that a bad interpretation was put upon his visits; but in the end, dreading scandal and malicious gossip, she begged he would for some time cease to frequent her house. The gentleman was the more mortified at this, as the proper and respectful manner in which he had always behaved towards the daughter had deserved very different treatment. However, to put an end to the gossip about him, he withdrew, and did not renew his visits until it had ceased.

Absence, meanwhile, by no means diminished his love ; but one day, when he was paying a visit to his mistress, he heard talk of her being married to a gentleman not richer than himself, and whom consequently he thought no better entitled to have her. He began to take heart, and employed his friends to speak on his part, in the hope that if the lady was allowed to choose, she would prefer him to his rival ; but as the latter was really the wealthier man, the young lady's mother and relations gave him the preference.

The gentleman, who knew that his mistress was a loser as well as himself, was so grieved at being rejected, that, without any other malady, he began by degrees to waste away, and became so changed that one would have said he had covered his handsome face with the mask of death, to which from hour to hour he was gaily hastening. Still he could not refrain from going as often as he could to see her whom he loved so well ; but at last, his strength being worn out, he was compelled to keep his bed, but would never let his mistress know of it for fear of distressing her. So entirely did he give himself up to despair, that he neither ate, drank, slept, nor rested ; and became so lean and wan that he was no longer to be recognised.

Some one made his state known to the mother of the demoiselle, who was very kind-hearted, and had besides so much esteem for the gentleman, that if the relations had been of the same mind as herself and her daughter, the personal merit of the invalid would have been preferred to the alleged wealth of the other suitor ; but the paternal relations would not hear of it.

However, she went with her daughter to see the poor gentleman, whom she found more dead than alive. As he knew that his end was near, he had confessed and communicated, and never expected to see any more visitors ; but on beholding again her who was his life and his resurrection, his strength returned, so that he at once sat up in bed, and said :

" What brings you hither, madam ? How come you to visit a man who has already one foot in the grave, and of whose death you are the cause ? "

" What ! " exclaimed the lady. " Is it possible we should cause the death of a person we love so much ? Tell me, I entreat, why you speak in this manner ? "

" Madam, I concealed my love for your daughter as long as I could ; my relations, however, who have asked her of you in marriage, have gone further than I wished, since I have thereby had the misfortune to lose hope. I say misfortune, not with reference to my individual satisfaction, but because I know that no one will ever treat her so well or love her so much as I would have done. Her loss of the best and most faithful friend and servant she has in the world touches me more sensibly than the loss of my life, which I wished to preserve for her alone. Nevertheless, since henceforth it can be of no use to her, I gain much in losing it."

The mother and daughter tried to comfort him. " Cheer up, my friend," said the mother ; " I promise you, that if God restores you to health, my daughter shall never have any other husband than you. She is present, and I command her to make you the same promise."

The daughter, weeping sorely, assured him of what her mother said ; but he, knowing that although God were to restore him to health he should not have his mistress, and that it was only to cheer him that these hopes were held out, replied :

" Had you spoken in this manner three months ago, I should have been the healthiest and happiest gentleman in France ; but this succour comes so late that I can neither believe it nor rest any hope upon it."

Then, as they strove to overcome his incredulity, he continued " Since you promise me a blessing which can never be mine even if you grant it, I will ask you to confer on me one much less, which I have never ventured to demand of you."

They both vowed that they would grant his request, and that he might declare it boldly.

" I implore you," said he, " to put into my arms her whom you promise me for a wife, and to bid her embrace and kiss me."

The daughter, who was not accustomed to such caresses, was on the point of making objections ; but her mother expressly commanded her to comply, seeing that there was no longer in him either the feeling or the power of a living man. After such a command, the daughter no longer hesitated, but going up to the bedside :

" Cheer up, my friend," she said, " cheer up, I conjure you."

The poor dying creature, notwithstanding his extreme weakness, stretched out his emaciated arms, embraced with all his might her who was the cause of his death, and, laying his cold pale lip to hers, clung there as long as he could.

" I have loved you," he said at last " with a love so intense and so pure that, marriage excepted, I have never desired any other favour of you than that which I now receive. But as God has not been pleased to unite us in marriage, I gladly surrender up my soul to Him who is love and perfect charity, and who knows how much I have loved you, and how pure my desires have been,

beseeching Him, that since I hold the dear object of my desires
within my arms, He will receive my soul in His."

So saying, he clasped her again in his embrace with such
vehemence, that his enfeebled heart, being unable to sustain the
effort, was abandoned by all his spirits ; for joy so dilated them,
that the seat of the soul gave way and fled to its Creator.

Though it was already some time since the poor gentleman had
expired, and could not retain his hold, the love she had felt for him,
and which she had always concealed, broke forth at this moment
in such wise that the mother and the servants had much difficulty
in detaching the almost dead survivor from the corpse.

The poor gentleman was honourably interred ; but the greatest
triumph in his obsequies were the tears and cries of that poor
demoiselle, who as openly displayed her feelings after his death
as she had concealed them during his life, as if she would make
amends for the wrong she had done him.   And I have been told
that for all they gave her a husband to console her, she never
afterwards knew real joy.

BONAVENTURE DES PERIERS
D. 1544

THE COBBLER BLONDEAU

THERE was a cobbler of Paris who was called Blondeau. He lived near the Croix du Tiroir, and there he mended shoes, taking life joyfully and loving good wine above everything. And he was ready to share it with all who came : for if the whole parish had come to him, he would have given them a glass and they would have wanted more of it. For it was good. All day long he sang and delighted his neighbours. He was never mournful but twice in his life.

On the first occasion, he found in an old wall an iron pot containing a large quantity of antique pieces of money, some of silver and some of gold. He did not know what they were worth, and he began to grow moody. His songs ceased, and he thought only of his iron pot.

" If the money is not current," he thought to himself, " I shall not be able to buy either bread or wine with it. If I take it to the goldsmiths, they will either betray me, and I shall lose the treasure-trove, or they will stick me for a large share of the find, and I shall not get half of what it is worth."

Then he became afraid that he had not hidden the pot properly and that some one would steal it from him. He was continually leaving his tent to go and see if it was safe. He was in the greatest trouble in the world, but at last he pulled himself together.

" What ! " he said, " I do nothing but think of my pot ! Every one who knows my ways must see that something has happened to me. Bah ! the devil take the thing ! It only brings me bad luck ! "

So he took the treasure up gaily, and threw it in the Seine, and thus drowned his melancholy with his pot.

On another occasion he was much upset by a gentleman who dwelt opposite to his shelter. This gentleman had a monkey that played a thousand tricks on poor Blondeau. For the animal watched him from a high window when he was cutting his leather, and noticed how he did it. And as soon as Blondeau went to dinner or left on some other business, the monkey came down and darted into Blondeau's tent, took his knife, and cut the leather about in imitation of the cobbler. And this went on every time that Blondeau went away.

The poor man at last dared not go out to eat or drink or leave his business without locking up all his leather. And if sometimes he forgot to shut it away, the monkey never forgot to cut it up in shreds for him. The thing angered him greatly, but he was not able to hurt the monkey for fear of his master. But, being greatly annoyed, he resolved to find a means of avenging himself.

He clearly saw in what way the monkey acted : this was to imitate everything he saw the cobbler do. If Blondeau sharpened his shoe-knife, the monkey sharpened it after him ; if he waxed his thread, the monkey also did it. If he soled some old boots, the monkey came and took a boot between his knees and tried to do the same. Having studied the matter in this way, Blondeau sharpened his shoe-knife till it cut like a razor. Then, when the monkey came out to watch him, he took up the shoe-knife and drew it backwards and forwards over his throat. And when he had done this long enough to attract the notice of the monkey, he left his booth and went to dinner.

The monkey came down in desperate haste. For it wished to try this new game that it has just been studying. It took the shoe-knife and put it against its throat, drawing it backwards and forwards as Blondeau had done. The animal, however, brought the knife too close, and cut its throat so badly that it died within an hour.

Thus was Blondeau avenged on his enemy without danger to himself, and he returned to his early habit of singing and taking life joyfully, and in this way he continued till the day of his death. And in remembrance of the glad life he had led, this epitaph was made for him :

> Underneath this stone is laid
> Blondeau, who plied a cobbler's trade.
> Hoarded wealth he held in scorn,
> And died as poor as he was born ;
> Yet now for him his neighbours pine—
> He taught them all to know good wine !

THE MISERLY FATHER

THE ancients thought so highly of neediness that they made a goddess out of it ; thereby signifying that in the pressure of need our spirit awakes and becomes brusque and lively, instead of being heavy and torpid, as often happens when a man's desires are fulfilled and he is profoundly happy and wrapped in comfort. If a man has little money, or if his affairs are confused and worrying, he will learn better how to make his way in the world than those who are born booted and dressed ; as was said of King Louis XI., the first prince who made his successors their own masters, and who best knew what his neighbours were doing.

Being in the bad graces of his father—oh, what a sweet thing it is to reign in absolute power !—he retired to his cousin, the Duke of Burgundy, and there learnt to eat small bread and make the most of a penny. This rendered him so admirable in the management of his affairs that he had few peers among all princes, and he was able to verify the prophecy of his father, King Charles VII., who told the Duke of Burgundy that he was feeding a fox that would eat all his chickens. For in the end King Louis carved up and parcelled out the estates of his host so well that he got most of the best pieces, which, he held, had been torn from his own property.

And with regard to fathers who are too rigorous with their children, there was seen but a little while ago in my country a man so grasping and peevish that he gave his son little or nothing for his keep. The boy, for his part, borrowed here and there all that he could, until he was riddled with writs by merchants, money-lenders, and other folk of seizure and interest. Very often he tricked them, and let his conscience sleep over the rest. All his defence was a reference to the avarice of his father ; and he would often say to his companions, who were running the same way of life for the same reason, that he wished to God his father would break his neck and take it with him to paradise ; with other imprecations and maledictions of the same import.

The father, whom it cost more than I know to spy on the actions of his son, was well informed of these things ; but he turned his deaf

33

ear to them, taking pleasure, which he esteemed profit, in keeping the young man in privations and calamities. Sometimes he threatened to marry again, or to give his property into such hands that he could not get a look at it. In this extreme necessity, the son thought of a good trick to play against his stingy father and restore the honour of his ancestors and his race, by getting enough money to take part in the King's wars, and thus strengthen his position that all brave and gallant men would side with him.

He went to a merchant and bought much black cloth on credit. You who do not pay your money down, judge of the loyalty of the vendor, and the acclamations and beating of the breast he made in connection with the price and the measuring! The young man had his mourning clothes made, packed them in his trunk, and whipped away towards Poitou, where his father had a fine, rich estate of great value. The farmer of it, a wealthy peasant, had in hand a year's revenue, ready to take it to his master. But he was saved this trouble. For the young gentleman, dressed in his mourning attire, and with a lackey sad and grim of face, alighted at the house of his father and told the farmer of the death of the old man.

" In his last words," he said, " he recommended you to me. He begged me, under pain of disobedience, not to make any change on the estate, because he had always found you a straight man and a good servant of our house. My father was a little hard and strict, but, farmer, my good friend, you can well understand that the niggardly way he managed things now means more money and profit to me."

" Oh, sir ! " said the Poitou farmer, all honey to keep the lease of the farm, " we must all pass through the door or through the window. Still it is a great solace that he has left an heir, who, unless I am much deceived, loves me, and from whom I can be sure of continuing to hold the farms that the rich man gave me in this district. I beg you to excuse me," bending, as he said it, first one knee and then the other, " if sometimes I have refused to give you money. For, on my conscience, I had a prohibition from the deceased—and I think I have it still in my pocket. No. It is in the place I keep my letters—just as if he suspected you. And you understand right well," bristling up and laughing like a bagpipe drone, " that since the boots of us fathers can serve our children, we are like cats, and do not want to see our offspring more than once a year, to hear of their fortunes. For we have put into their hands the tools and means to get a livelihood."

" There is one other thing," said the mourning son, " and then I have finished. You have heard of the wars in which the King is greatly worried. How reprehensible it would be of me, and what dishonour would come of it, if I failed to give my services to His Majesty ! For no matter how poor I have been, I have done my duty to him. And now that war has broken out, and I have done my part as a son to my dead father, whom God absolve ! I must in all haste go and find the regiment that is marching to the place where I must serve. Some of my men have already gone ahead. It would be a very great pleasure to me and pretty profitable to you to remain on my estate on the same conditions and charges as you held the farm from my father. And how much shall I have in addition if I renew the agreement ?

" Ho ! Pierre," added the young man to his lackey, " how much did that fat man offer me at dinner for the farm ? "

" Ah, sir," replied the pretended servant, " you don't know a man till you've buried him ! Never change your old servants. Your father, God keep his soul ! always had that saying in his mouth, but at each renewal of the farm he wanted a hundred crowns bonus and a year in advance. I do not know what you will require."

The farmer, who was full of fear that such a bargain should escape him, at once accepted the terms. Then the notaries got to work and a hundred crowns were given to the master and ten to Pierre who held he had well earned them. Then there were revenues for a year in advance, besides those due for the past year. Each thought he had got the best of the other. The farmer, reckoning on his fingers, thought he had gained a hundred per cent. The heir knew he might have obtained more by waiting, but he was well pleased with the plum that he was able to put in his pocket and he rode off with it.

He had been gone half a day when the trouble began, and the battle opened with a wild conflict of evidence. One of the father's men, an old notary, mounted on a mule and booted with straw, arrived with receipts ready to receive the money that had fallen due, and to make a new lease for the future. He showed the farmer his documents, his general and special power of attorney, properly drawn up and signed. The farmer, in turn, brought out his documents to prove that the new young lord had granted him a fresh lease. He said that the heir was in mourning, and that everything had gone well, and that the notary was a manifest liar who wanted to play double-or-quits with his mule.

The notary maintained that his old master was alive, and that the new lease was worthless. The judge, before whom the case was brought, could not come to a decision, and held that an inquiry should be made into the matter. And in the meantime the poor miserable miser of a father died of spite and rage and madness through losing such a mass of money, and being tricked by his own flesh and blood. And may the same fate befall those who burn the candle at both ends.

VERBOQUET LE GENEREUX
16TH CENTURY

THE THREE DRUNKARDS

THERE were three gossips in a little Normandy village, neighbours and great friends, who often told each other secrets of their household affairs. There was nothing done by one of their husbands but news was at once carried to the houses of her companions. In the end the three women all found themselves provided with husbands of equal stupidity, and they were often able to have a good time together in the market-place. There only remained one drawback in their lives ; but this they found almost insupportable. For on the days when the three friends set out to enjoy themselves together, their husbands went to a tavern, and there drank so much that they lost most of their good sense. Scarcely could they get back home, and when each of them met his wife there was no pot, platter, or stick that he did not use in greeting her.

So the good dames concluded one day to punish their men for their drunkenness. The husbands went as usual to the tavern, and their wives spied on them. While the men were drinking, three preaching friars came in and asked for alms. The jolly topers, who were sitting at the table with their backs to the fire, made room for the friars, and they all began to see who could drink the most. And each put such zest into the drinking that, when it grew late, they had much trouble in getting back to their houses.

The first wife, seeing her husband so profoundly asleep that it would have been easier to flay him than to wake him, took some scissors and tonsured his crown like a monk's, and dressed him in monastic garments which she was able to borrow. She then let him sleep on in his frock till daybreak, when, being accustomed to breakfast, he looked around for some food.

" How long you have slept, reverend father ! " said the woman in pretended astonishment. " Had you not better rejoin the other religious men of your order ? "

The husband, still dazed by his wine, did not look at his wife, and yet grew angry with her. But she, like a woman sure of her ground, went on in the same tone.

" Sir, out of pure devotion I gave you a lodging here for the night.

But I tell you that your companions have now departed, fearing that you would remain here alone, which would not be seemly and decent for a person in your way of life."

The husband, in utter astonishment, touched himself here and there, and, feeling his shaved head and his monk's frock, was terrified.

"Heavens! isn't this me? Isn't this Jean?" he cried.

His wife continued to call him "sir," and to treat him with great reverence, and she managed him so well with the flat of her tongue that, being still half-drunk, he could only remember he had been drinking with some monks, and seeing himself thus clothed, he thought that by the vengeance of heaven he had been transformed into a friar. And so strongly did this mad opinion take hold of him that he asked his wife to point out the road the other monks had taken.

His wife replied that he could scarcely catch up with the other friars, but that out of pity she would pay his mass for him if he wished to say it. As the parish priest was aware of the trick the women were playing, and was helping them to cure their husbands of drunkenness, poor Jean, reduced to utter stupidity, was led by his wife to the church and clothed in the ornaments proper to a funeral service, and then conducted to an altar.

The second wife, who did not wish to fail in her part of the enterprise, began to flatter her husband as soon as he awoke, and revive his spirits.

"You know, my dear, this is a festival day! Your gossip, Jean, so repents the time he has spent in evil ways that he has taken religious vows, and to-day he is saying his first mass, and by hearing it you will be infinitely benefited. Would you not like to confess your sins to him?"

Poor Guillaume, amazed and half-unwell from drinking too much, began to lament his faults, and in this frame of mind came to the church. There, seeing his crony, Jean, ready to say his office, he took a handful of candles and knelt down and offered them, begging pardon for his mistakes.

The third wife, who desired to carry the deception to its highest point, had at daybreak shrouded her husband like a corpse and placed him on a bier, which was borne into the church. As Guillaume presented his offering, the dead man opened his eyes a little and caught a glimpse of Jean in the garb of a preacher. He was ready to laugh at the folly of his two old cronies; but, feeling still the fumes of the night before and finding himself on a bier with lighted candles round him, he strongly doubted if he were alive. He dared not speak or move, and all three of them remained in this nightmare until the sun rising higher made them see more clearly what strange devotions can be produced by the fumes of good wine and the malice of women.

PAUL SCARRON
1610–1660

THE TWO JEALOUS LADIES

In the little town of La Flèche there were two most accomplished
gentlemen who were very backward in taking wives, as often
happens among persons of quality, according to the saying
" Between those we would have and those we would not, we never
marry." But the saying was at last crossed by both of these
gentlemen. One of them called Monsieur de Fons-blanche, married
a daughter of the family of Château-d'un, of humble origin, but
very rich. The other, whose name was Monsieur du Lac, married
a lady from the city of Chartres, who was not rich, but nevertheless exceeding beautiful, and of so good a family that she was
related to several dukes, peers, and marshals of France.

These two gentlemen, who could share the town betwixt them,
had always been good friends till after their marriage, when their
two ladies looking enviously on each other, it quickly occasioned a
rupture between the husbands. Madame de Fons-blanche was not,
it is true, handsome in countenance, yet she had nevertheless a
graceful mien, well shaped, had a great deal of wit, and was very
obliging. Madame du Lac, as beautiful as she was, yet wanted
address ; she had wit indeed a great deal, but so ill-managed that
she thereby rather rendered herself avoidable than acceptable. These
two ladies were of the humour of most women nowadays, who
never think they live great unless they have a score or two of
beaux after them. This caused them to employ all the arts they
had in making conquests, but therein du Lac succeeded much
better than de Fons-blanche, for she had subdued all the youth of
the town ; I mean among the quality, for she would by no means
suffer any others to speak to her. This pride and affectation
occasioned a great many murmurings against her, which at length
broke out into open detraction, but nothing harmed her, for it is
thought it rather contributed to than hindered her procuring new
lovers.

Fons-blanche was not so desirous of having a great number of
sparks ; she, nevertheless, had some, whom she managed with a
great deal of address, and whereof there was one, a very handsome

38

young fellow, that had as much wit as she, and was one of the bravest youths of his time.   This spark was her greatest favourite, but at length his diligence caused him to be suspected by the neighbours, and slander began to talk loud.   It was here the rupture began between these ladies, who before had visited each other very civilly, nevertheless with a little jealous envy.

Du Lac began at last to slander Fons-blanche openly, to pry into her actions, and do all that lay in her power to ruin her reputation, especially about the aforesaid gentleman, whose name was Monsieur du Val-Rochet.   This soon came to Fons-blanche's ears, who was extremely nettled at it, and said that, " If she had lovers, it was not by scores, as du Lac had, who every day gained new conquests by her impostures."

Du Lac hearing this, quickly returned her the like reflections. Whence you may imagine that these two women lived together in a town like a brace of demons.   Some charitable people did all they could to reconcile them, but this proved in vain, for they could never be prevailed upon so much as to see each other. Du Lac thought the only way to offend Fons-blanche to the quick would be to get away her lover du Val-Rochet from her.   She then caused Monsieur de Fons-blanche to be acquainted underhand that he was no sooner out of doors, which he was often, either hunting or visiting, but that du Val-Rochet called on his wife ; and further, that several persons of credit were ready to testify that they had seen him come out of her bedroom.

Monsieur de Fons-blanche, who had never yet had any suspicion of his wife, was nevertheless inclinable to reflect a little upon what he had heard, and in confusion, desired his lady to oblige him so far as to entertain du Val-Rochet's visits no longer.   She seemed all obedience, nevertheless insinuated so many reasons why she might safely admit him, that he gave her liberty, and suffered her to act as before.

Du Lac perceiving this contrivance of hers had not had its desired effect, resolved to get some opportunity to talk with Val-Rochet herself.   She was both fair and subtle, two qualities sufficient to surprise the wariest heart, though it had been never so much engaged.   De Fons-blanche was extremely concerned at being like to lose her lover, but much more when she heard that Val-Rochet had spoken unhandsomely of her.   This grief was augmented by her husband's death, which happened a little while after.   She went into close mourning 'tis true, but still jealousy got the ascendant of her outward concern.

Her husband had been scarce buried fifteen days before she had a secret conference with Val-Rochet.   I know not the subject of their discourse, but the event makes me pretty well able to guess at it, for in little more than a week after, their marriage was made public, so that in less than a month's time she had two husbands, a living and a dead. This seems to me to have been the most violent effect of jealousy imaginable ; for to deprive du Lac of her lover she both forfeited her modesty by marrying so soon, and forgave the unpardonable affront Val-Rochet had offered her.

Du Lac was almost ready to run mad when she first heard this news, and resolved forthwith to have him assassinated as he went on a journey to Brittany ; but which he being made acquainted with. she was prevented in that design.

Then she entered upon the strangest thought that ever jealousy could suggest, and that was, to set her husband and Val-Rochet together by the ears, which she brought about by her pernicious artifices. They quarrelled divers times, and at length came to a duel, which du Lac encouraged her husband in, being none of the wisest men in the world, that du Val-Rochet might have an opportunity to kill him, which she fancied no hard matter, and then she proposed to hang him out of the way for his pains.

But as fortune would have it, it happened quite otherwise ; for Val-Rochet, trusting to his skill in fencing, seemed to despise du Lac, thinking he durst not make a thrust at him, but therein he was extremely deceived ; for whilst he put himself out of guard, du Lac made a home thrust at him, and ran him through the body, whereof he instantly died.

This done, du Lac went home to his house, and acquainted his wife therewith, who was not only surprised, but concerned at so unexpected an accident. He after this fled away privately to a relation of his wife's, who, as I have told you before, had several persons of quality to her kindred, who laboured incessantly to obtain her husband's pardon from the King. Madame Fonsblanche was not a little astonished when she was first told that her husband was killed ; but coming afterwards to herself, she was advised to bury him quickly and privately, to prevent his body being arrested by the bailiffs.

Thus in less than six weeks' time Fons-blanche had been a widow twice. Du Lac not long after obtained his pardon, which was confirmed by the parliament of Paris, notwithstanding all the opposition the deceased person's widow could make.

This made her to entertain a wilder design than Madame du Lac had done before, and that was to stab du Lac as he walked in the market-place with some of his friends. For this purpose she provided herself a poniard, and marching up to him, attacked him so furiously that before he could get himself into a posture of defence, or have any of his friends turn about to help him, she had stabbed him mortally in two places, whereof he died three days after. His wife immediately got this virago seized and clapped up in prison. Her trial came on, and she was condemned to die, but her execution was respited by reason of her being with child ; nevertheless, not long after the stench of the prison did the work of the hangman, for she died of a disease caused thereby, after having been first delivered before her time, and her child, being baptized, died likewise soon after.

Madame du Lac began afterwards to reflect on what she had been the occasion of, and therefore forthwith resolved to turn a nun, which she did, after having put her affairs in order, in the nunnery of Almeneche, in the diocese of Sées, where she now continues, if she be not yet dead of her austerities, which she voluntarily inflicted on herself.

BISHOP FÉNELON
1651–1715

THE STORY OF ALIBEA

ABBAS, Shah of Persia, during his travels, left his court to wander through the country without being recognised, and see his people in all their natural liberty. Only one of his courtiers went with him. " I do not know," said the King to him, " the real manners of men. All that approaches us is disguised. It is art and not simplicity of nature that we see. I wish to view the country, and look at the country folks who are so despised, though they are the true support of human society. I am tired of seeing courtiers who study me in order to take me by surprise in their flattery. I must go amongst ploughmen and shepherds who do not know me."

He passed through several villages where the people were dancing, and he was delighted to find, far away from the court, tranquil pleasures without expense. He had a meal in a hut, and as he was very hungry after walking more than usual, the coarse food he ate seemed to him more pleasant than all the exquisite dishes of his table.

Wandering through a field strewn with flowers, with a clear brook running by it, he saw a young shepherd playing the flute in the shadow of a great elm, close to his grazing sheep. The Shah went up to the lad and found him pleasant of face, with frank and simple bearing, in which there was a certain nobility of grace.

The rags with which the shepherd was covered did not lessen his beauty. The Shah thought at first it was some person of noble birth in disguise ; but he learnt from the shepherd that his father and mother lived in a neighbouring village, and that his name was Alibea.

The Shah talked with him, and found he had a firm and intelligent spirit. His eyes were lively and had nothing fierce or fiery in them. His voice was sweet and insinuating with touching tones. There was no coarseness in his face, and yet it had no soft or effeminate beauty. The shepherd, about sixteen years of age, did not know how he struck other men. He thought he looked and talked and spoke like other shepherds of his village ; but, without

42

being educated, he had learnt all that a fine intelligence can teach those who listen to it.

The Shah, after a familiar talk, was charmed with the lad. He learnt from him in regard to the state of the people, all that kings never gather from the crowd of flatterers that surround them. From time to time he laughed at the ingenuousness of the boy, who was not at all tactful in his replies. It was a great novelty for the monarch to hear such natural speech. He signalled to the courtier not to reveal who he was ; for he feared that Alibea would at once lose his freedom and grace of manner if he learnt to whom he was speaking.

" I can see," he said, " that nature is not less beautiful in low conditions of life than in high conditions. Never has a son of a king seemed better born than this lad who looks after sheep. How happy should I be to have a son as handsome, as sensible, and as lovable ! He appears to me capable of filling any place, and if he is carefully taught he will surely be one day a great man. I wish to have him bred up by my side."

Alibea was taken to the court, and he was much surprised to learn that it was the great Shah whom he had pleased. He was taught to read and write and sing, and then he was given masters for the arts and the sciences that adorn the mind. At first, he was rather dazzled with the court, and his great change of fortune somewhat altered his feelings. His age and his favour joined together rather told against his wisdom and moderation. In place of his sheep crook and flute and shepherd's dress, he took a robe of purple, embroidered with gold, with a turban covered with precious stones. His beauty effaced that of the most handsome men at court. He learnt to handle the most serious affairs, and merited the trust of his master, who, knowing the exquisite taste of Alibea for all the magnificences of the palace, charged him at last with one of the highest duties in Persia. This was to watch over the jewels and precious articles of the crown.

Alibea wished to return to his village for a while. He lovingly roamed by all the places where he had danced and sung and played the flute with his companions. He helped his relatives and friends, and wished them, for their greatest happiness, never to leave their country life and never to know the unhappiness of an existence at court.

These unhappinesses he experienced. After the death of his good master Shah Abbas, his son, Shah Sophi, succeeded to the throne. Some courtiers of an envious and cunning nature found a way of prejudicing the new ruler against Alibea.

" He has abused the confidence of your father," they said. " He has massed immense treasures and stolen several things of high price entrusted to him."

Shah Sophi was both young and absolute in power. He did not need to be both to become a creature who was inattentive, credulous, and without caution. He had the vanity to wish to appear as a reformer of everything that his father had done better than he could. To get a pretext for deposing Alibea from his position, he asked him, following the advice of the envious courtiers, to bring him a sword adorned with diamonds of an immense price, which his grandfather had been wont to carry in his wars.

Shah Abbas had formerly taken from the weapon all its fine diamonds, and by good witnesses Alibea was able to prove that the thing had been done at the command of the late monarch, before the office of guardian of the royal jewels was given to Alibea. When his enemies found that this pretext would not serve to overthrow him, they advised Shah Sophi to order him to make, within a fortnight, an exact list of every precious thing entrusted to his care.

At the end of the fortnight the Shah demanded to see everything himself. Alibea opened all the doors, and showed everything that was in his keeping. Nothing was missing : all was right, well arranged, and preserved with the greatest care. The Shah was disappointed at finding throughout so much order and exactitude, and was almost inclined to take Alibea into favour again. But he perceived, at the end of a great gallery full of splendid articles, an iron door with three large locks.

" It is there," said the courtiers to him, " that Alibea has hidden all the costly things he had stolen."

" I wish to see what is behind this door ! " cried the Shah in sudden anger. " What have you put there ? Show it to me ! "

Alibea fell on his knees and begged him in the name of God not to take from him what was most precious to him in the world.

" It is not just," he said, "that I should lose in a moment all that remains to me, my only resource, after having worked so many years for your royal father. Take everything else away, if you will, but leave me this ! "

The Shah never doubted but that it was a treasure that Alibea had amassed by evil means. Speaking with still more determination he ordered that the door should be burst open. At last, Alibea, who had the keys, opened it himself. In the room there were found only the sheep crook, the flute, and the shepherd's dress which Alibea had worn in the old days, and which he often came to look at, for fear of forgetting himself in his new position.

" Behold," he said, " O great Shah, the precious remains of my ancient happiness ! Neither fate nor kingly power has been able to rob me of them. Behold my treasure, that I keep to enrich myself when you have reduced me to poverty ! Take all the rest : leave me these dear pledges of my early condition. Here are the true treasures that I shall never lack—simple innocent things, always sweet to those who know how to content themselves with the necessaries of life and are not tormented for the luxuries. Here are the treasures whose fruits are liberty and peace ! Here are the treasures that have never brought me a moment of care ! O delightful instruments of a simple and happy life, I love you only, and with you I would live and die ! What need was there that other deceptive glittering things should come and mislead me and trouble the quietness of my life ? I give them back to you, Grand Shah ! all these riches that I owe to your liberality. I will keep only that which I had when your father, by his favours, rendered me unhappy ! "

Hearing these words, the Shah understood the innocence of Alibea, and being indignant against the courtiers who had wished to overthrow him, he drove them away from him. Alibea became his chief minister, and was entrusted with the most secret affairs. But every day he came to look at his crook and flute and his shepherd's dress, which he always kept ready in his strong room to take up if inconstant fortune troubled his favour at court. He died in extreme old age, without having wished either to punish his enemies or to amass wealth ; and he left his relatives only enough to live in the position of shepherds, which he always believed to be the safest and the most happy.

THE ISLE OF PLEASURES

Bishop Fénelon

After having sailed for a long time over the Pacific, we saw in the distance an isle of sugar with mountains of stewed fruit, and rocks of candy and caramel, and streams of syrup flowing through the fields. The natives were very gluttonous ; they licked the paths as they walked along, and sucked their fingers after dipping them in the rivers. There were forests of liquorice and tall trees from which waffle cakes fell, and these the wind carried into the mouths of the voyagers, though their lips were scarcely parted.

As so many sweetnesses seemed to us insipid, we wished to go on to some other country where we could find food with a stronger taste. We were told that, ten leagues away, there was another island in which were found mines of ham, sausages, and peppered hashes. These things were dug out just as gold is dug from the mines of Peru. There were also brooks of onion sauce, and the walls of the houses were of pie-crust.

In stormy weather on this island it rains wine, and in fine weather the morning dew is a white wine like Greek wine. To reach this island, we placed on the shore of the land we were leaving a dozen men of prodigious fatness, who had been sent to sleep. They breathed so heavily in snoring that they filled our sail with a favourable wind.

Scarcely had we landed on the other island than we found on the shore a band of merchants who were selling appetites. For these were things the islanders often lost amid their pleasures of the table. There were also other persons who sold sleep. The price was regulated by the hour ; but some sleeps were dearer than others, in proportion to the dreams a man wished to have. The finest dreams were very costly.

I asked for the best that money could buy, and, feeling tired, I lay down to sleep. But hardly was I in my bed, when I heard a loud noise ; it terrified me, and I shouted for help. I was told that the earth had gaped open. I thought I was lost ; but the islanders reassured me, saying that the earth opened every night at a certain hour to pour out boiling streams of frothing chocolate and iced liqueurs of every kind. I rose in haste to get some : they were delicious.

Then I went to bed again, and in my sleep the world seemed to be made of crystal, and men nourished themselves as they pleased with perfumes. They could not walk without dancing, or speak but by singing : they had wings to travel the air and fins to sweep through the sea. These men, however, were like gun flints. You could not knock against them but they at once grew fiery. They were as inflammable as tinder, and I could not help laughing when I saw how easy it was to stir them up. I asked one of them why he was so touchy ; showing me his fist, he replied that he never gave way to anger.

As soon as I was awake, a merchant of appetites entered and asked me how much hunger I wanted, and if I would like to buy a relay of appetites that would enable me to pass the whole day in eating. I accepted the offer. For my money he gave me a dozen little bags of taffeta, which I fixed round me, and which were to serve me as stomachs to enable me to digest without trouble twelve great feasts in a single day. Scarcely had I put on the bags when I felt I was dying of hunger. I passed my time in a long delicious banquet. As soon as one repast was finished, hunger seized on me again, and I did not give it time to worry me. But, as I had a voracious appetite, the islanders remarked that I did not eat properly. They are distinguished by the exquisite delicacy and neatness of their meals.

By night I was tired of having passed the whole day at table, like a horse with his nose always in the manger. I resolved the next day to take a different course, and nourish myself only on fine fragrances. For breakfast I took some orange blossom perfume. At dinner a heavier nourishment was provided. I was given tuberoses to smell, and I had the scent of jonquils for collation. In the evening, I had for supper large baskets full of all sorts of fragrant flowers, to which were added some perfume stews. That night I had an attack of indigestion through having smelt so many nourishing odours. The next day I fasted as a relief from the fatigue of the pleasures of the table.

I was told that in the country there was a very singular town, and the people promised to take me there in a new kind of carriage. I was placed in a little wooden chair, very light and provided with great wings, and to this chair the people attached with silken cords four great birds as big as ostriches, but with wings proportioned to their bodies. These birds rose in their flight, and with the reins I turned them eastward, as I had been directed. I saw at my feet the high mountains, and we flew so rapidly that I could scarcely draw my breath as we swept through the waves of the air.

In an hour we arrived at the famous city. It is all of marble and three times as large as Paris. The whole town forms only a single house. There are twenty-four great courts, each of which is larger than the largest palace of the world. In the middle of these twenty-four courts there is a twenty-fifth, which is six times the size of each of the others. All the dwellings in this house are similar, for there is no inequality of condition among the inhabitants. There are no servants and no poor people. Everybody looks after himself, and has no one to wait on him. There are only the Wishes, which are little spirits, playful and fluttering, that give in a moment to each person all the he desires.

When I arrived I received one of these spirits, who attached himself to me and never let me want for anything. He scarcely gave me time to form my desires. I even began to be tired of the new wishes that this freedom of contenting every fancy excited in me. I understood by experience that it was better to do without superfluous things, than to be unceasingly full of new desires, without being able to stop and tranquilly enjoy a single pleasure.

The inhabitants of the city were polite and charming and obliging. They welcomed me as though I had been one of themselves. As soon as I wished to speak, they divined what I desired, and carried it out without waiting for me to explain in words. This surprised me, and I noticed that they never spoke among themselves. They read in each other's eyes all that they think, just as we do in a book. When they wish to hide their thought, they have only to close their eyes. They led me into a hall in which there was a music of perfumes. They arranged their perfumes as we arrange sounds. A certain assemblage of fragrances, some strong and the others weak, make a harmony that pleases the sense of smell, just as our concerts please the ear by the mingling of deep and high sounds.

In this country the women govern the men. They judge the lawsuits, and teach all sciences and carry on wars. The men powder and paint their faces and dress themselves up from morning to evening ; they spin and sew and work at embroidery, and are fearful of being beaten by their wives when they do not obey them. It is said that affairs were different a certain number of years ago. But the men, served by the Wishes, became so poor-spirited, so idle, and so ignorant, that the women were ashamed of letting themselves be governed by them. They met together to reform the evils of the commonwealth. They established public schools, where persons of their sex with most intelligence set themselves to study. They disarmed their husbands, who asked nothing better than to escape from fighting. They took away from them their judicial powers, watched over the public order, laid down laws and saw that they were kept, and thus saved the Republic, that otherwise would have been totally ruined by the frivolity and softness of the men.

Touched by this spectacle, and fatigued by so many feasts and amusements, I concluded that the pleasures of the senses, no matter how varied, how facile they are, degrade mankind, and do not make them happy. So I departed from these islands, so delightful in appearance, and, returning home, I found in a sober life, in moderate work, in pure manners, and in the practice of virtue, the health and happiness I had not been able to procure by a continuity of feasting and a variety of pleasures.

ALAIN-RENÉ LE SAGE
1668–1747

THE ADVENTURE OF DON POMPEYO DE CASTRO

FROM my boyish days, my passion was for a military life. Our own country being at peace, I went into Portugal; thence to Africa with the Duke of Braganza, who gave me a commission. I was a younger brother, with as slender a provision as most in Spain; so that my only chance was in attracting the notice of the commander-in-chief by my bravery. I was so far from deficient in my duty, that the Duke promoted me, step by step, to one of the most honourable posts in the service. After a long war, of which you all know the issue, I devoted myself to the court; and the King, on strong testimonials from the general officers, rewarded me with a considerable pension. Alive to that sovereign's generosity, I lost no opportunity of proving my gratitude by my diligence. I was in attendance as often as etiquette would allow me to offer myself to his notice. By this conduct I gained insensibly the love of that prince, and received new favours from his hands.

One day, when I distinguished myself in running at the ring, and in a bull-fight preceding it, all the court extolled my strength and dexterity. On my return home, with my honours thick upon me, I found there a note, informing me that a lady, my conquest over whom ought to flatter me more than all the glory I had gained that day, wished to have the pleasure of my company; and that I had only to attend in the evening, at a place marked out in the letter. This was more than all my public triumphs, and I concluded the writer to be a woman of the first quality. You may guess that I did not loiter by the way. An old woman in waiting, as my guide, conducted me by a little garden-gate into a large house, and left me in an elegant closet, saying : " Stay here, I will acquaint my mistress with your arrival." I observed a great many articles of value in the closet, which was magnificently illuminated; but this splendour only caught my attention as confirming me in my previous opinion of the lady's high rank. If appearances strengthened that conjecture, her noble and majestic air on her entrance left no doubt in my mind. Yet I was a little out in my calculation.

" Noble sir," said she, " after the step I have taken in your favour it were impertinent to disown my partiality. Your brilliant actions of to-day, in presence of the court, were not the inspirers of my sentiments, they only urge forward this avowal. I have seen you more than once, have inquired into your character, and the result has determined me to follow the impulse of my heart. But do not suppose that you are well with a duchess. I am but the widow of a captain in the King's Guards ; yet there is something to throw a radiance round your victory . . . the preference you have gained over one of the first noblemen in the kingdom. The Duke d'Almeyda loves me, and presses his suit with ardour, yet without success. My vanity only induces me to bear his importunities."

Though I saw plainly, by this address, that I had got in with a coquette, my presiding star was not a whit out of my good graces for involving me in this adventure. Donna Hortensia, for that was the lady's name, was just in the ripeness and luxuriance of youth and dazzling beauty. Nay, more, she had refused the possession of her heart to the earnest entreaties of a duke, and offered it unsolicited to me. What a feather in the cap of a Spanish cavalier ! I prostrated myself at Hortensia's feet, to thank her for her favours. I talked just as a man of gallantry always does talk, and she had reason to be satisfied with the extravagance of my acknowledgments. Thus we parted the best friends in the world, on the terms of meeting every evening when the Duke d'Almeyda was prevented from coming ; and she promised to give me due notice of his absence. The bargain was exactly fulfilled, and I was turned into the Adonis of this new Venus.

But the pleasures of this life are transitory. With all the lady's precautions to conceal our private treaty of commerce from my rival, he found means of gaining a knowledge, of which it concerned us greatly to keep him ignorant ; a disloyal chambermaid divulged the state secret. This nobleman, naturally generous, but proud, self-sufficient, and violent, was exasperated at my presumption. Anger and jealousy set him beside himself. Taking counsel only with his rage, he resolved on an infamous revenge. One night when I was with Hortensia, he waylaid me at the little garden-gate, with all his servants provided with cudgels. As soon as I came out, he ordered me to be seized, and beaten to death by these wretches. " Lay on," said he, " let the rash intruder give up the ghost under your chastisement ; thus shall his insolence be punished." No sooner had he finished these words than his myrmidons assaulted me in a body, and gave me such a beating as to stretch me senseless on the ground, after which they hurried off with their master, to whom this butchery had been a delicious pastime. I lay the remainder of the night, just as they had left me. At daybreak some people passed by, who, finding that life was still in me, had the humanity to carry me to a surgeon. Fortunately my wounds were not mortal ; and, falling into skilful hands, I was perfectly cured in two months. At the end of that period I made my appearance again at court, and resumed my former way of life, except that I steered clear of Hortensia, who on her part made no further attempt to renew the acquaintance, because the Duke, on that condition, had pardoned her infidelity.

As my adventure was the town talk, and I was known to be no coward, people were astonished to see me as quiet as if I had received no affront ; for I kept my thoughts to myself, and seemed to have no quarrel with any man living. No one knew what to think of my counterfeited insensibility. Some imagined that, in spite of my courage, the rank of the aggressor overawed me, and occasioned my tacit submission. Others, with more reason, mistrusted my silence, and considered my inoffensive demeanour as a cover to my revenge. The King was of opinion with these last, that I was not a man to put up with an insult, and that I should not be wanting to myself at a convenient opportunity. To discover my real intentions, he sent for me one day into his closet, where he said : " Don Pompeyo, I know what accident has befallen you, and am surprised, I own, at your forbearance. You are certainly acting a part."

" Sire," answered I, " how can I know whom to challenge ? I was attacked in the night by persons unknown : it is a misfortune of which I must make the best."

" No, no," replied the King, " I am not to be duped by these evasive answers. The whole story has reached my ears. The Duke d'Almeyda has touched your honour to the quick. You are nobly born, and a Castilian : I know what that double character requires. You cherish hostile designs. Admit me a party to your purposes ; it must be so. Never fear the consequences of making me your confidant."

" Since your Majesty commands it," resumed I, " my sentiments shall be laid open without reserve. Yes, sir, I meditate a severe retribution. Every man, wearing such a name as mine, must account for its untarnished lustre with his family. You know the unworthy treatment I have experienced ; and I purpose assassinating the Duke d'Almeyda, as a mode of revenge correspondent to the injury. I shall plunge a dagger in his bosom, or shoot him through the head, and escape, if I can, into Spain. This is my design."

" It is violent," said the King : " and yet I have little to say against it, after the provocation which the Duke d'Almeyda has given you. He is worthy of the punishment you destine for him. But do not be in a hurry with your project. Leave me to devise a method of bringing you together again as friends."

" Oh ! sir," exclaimed I with vexation, " why did you extort my secret from me ? What expedient can . . ."

" If mine is not to your satisfaction," interrupted he, " you may execute your first intention. I do not mean to abuse your confidence. I shall not implicate your honour ; so rest contented on that head."

I was greatly puzzled to guess by what means the King designed to terminate this affair amicably. But thus it was. He sent to speak with the Duke d'Almeyda in private.

" Duke," said he, " you have insulted Don Pompeyo de Castro. You are not ignorant that he is a man of noble birth, a soldier who has served with credit, and stands high in my favour. You owe him reparation."

" I am not of a temper to refuse it," answered the Duke. " If he complains of my outrageous behaviour, I am ready to justify it by the law of arms."

" Something very different must be done," replied the King : " a Spanish gentleman understands the point of honour too well to fight on equal terms with a cowardly assassin. I can use no milder term ; and you can only atone for the heinousness of your conduct by presenting a cane in person to your antagonist, and offering to submit yourself to its discipline."

" Oh heaven ! " exclaimed the Duke. " What ! sir, would you have a man of my rank degrade, debase himself before a simple gentleman! and submit to be caned ! "

" No," replied the monarch, " I will oblige Don Pompeyo to promise not to touch you. Only offer him the cane, and ask his pardon : that is all I require from you."

" And that is too much, sir," interrupted the Duke d'Almeyda warmly ; " I had rather remain exposed to all the secret machinations of his resentment."

" Your life is dear to me," said the King ; " and I should wish this affair to have no bad consequences. To terminate it with less disgust to yourself, I will be the only witness of the satisfaction which I order you to offer to the Spaniard."

The King was obliged to stretch his influence over the Duke to the utmost before he could induce him to so mortifying a step. However, the peremptory monarch effected his purpose, and then sent for me. He related the particulars of his conversation with my enemy, and inquired if I should be content with the stipulated reparation. I answered " Yes," and gave my word that, far from striking the offender, I would not even accept the cane, when he presented it.

With this understanding, the Duke and myself at a certain hour attended the King, who took us into his closet. " Come," said he to the Duke, " acknowledge your fault, and deserve to be forgiven by humility of your contrition."

Then my antagonist made his apology, and offered me the cane in his hand.

" Don Pompeyo," said the monarch unexpectedly, " take the cane,
and let not my presence prevent you from doing justice to your
outraged honour. I release you from your promise not to strike the
Duke."

" No, sir," answered I, " it is enough that he has submitted to the
indignity of the offer : an offended Spaniard asks no more."

" Well, then ! " replied the King, " since you are content with this
satisfaction, you may both of you at once assume the privilege of a
gentlemanly quarrel. Measure your swords, and discuss the question
honourably."

" It is what I most ardently desire," exclaimed the Duke
d'Almeyda in a menacing tone ; " for that only is competent to
make me amends for the disgraceful step I have taken."

With these words, he went away full of rage and shame ; and sent
to tell me, two hours after, that he was waiting for me, in a retired
place. I kept the appointment, and found his noblemen ready to
fight lustily. He was not five-and-forty ; deficient neither in courage
nor in skill ; so that the match was fair and equal.

" Come on, Don Pompeyo," said he, " let us terminate our
difference here. Our hostility ought to be reciprocally mortal ;
yours, for my aggression, and mine, for having asked your pardon."

These words were no sooner out of his mouth, than he drew upon
me so suddenly, that I had no time to reply. He pressed very closely
upon me at first, but I had the good fortune to put by all his
thrusts. I acted on the offensive in my turn : the encounter was
evidently with a man equally skilled in defence or in attack ; and
there is no knowing what might have been the issue, if he had not
made a false step in retiring, and fallen backwards. I stood still
immediately, and said to the Duke, " Recover yourself."

" Why give me any quarter ? " he answered. " Your forbearance
only aggravates my disgrace."

" I will not take advantage of an accident," replied I, " it would
only tarnish my glory. Once more recover yourself, and let us
fight it out."

" Don Pompeyo," said he rising, " after this act of generosity,
honour allows me not to renew the attack upon you. What would the
world say of me were I to wound you mortally ? I should be branded
as a coward for having murdered a man, at whose mercy I had just
before lain prostrate. I cannot therefore again lift my arm against
your life, and I feel my resentful passions subsiding into the sweet
emotions of gratitude. Don Pompeyo, let us mutually lay aside our
hatred. Let us go still further ; let us be friends."

" Ah ! my lord, " exclaimed I, " so flattering a proposal I joyfully
accept. I proffer you my sincere friendship ; and, as an earnest,
promise never more to approach Donna Hortensia, though she herself
should invite me."

"It is my duty," said he, "to yield that lady to you. Justice requires me to give her up, since her affections are yours already."

"No, no," interrupted I; "you love her. Her partiality in my favour would give you uneasiness; I sacrifice my own pleasures to your peace."

"Ah! too generous Castilian," replied the Duke, embracing me, "your sentiments are truly noble. With what remorse do they strike me! Grieved and ashamed, I look back on the outrage you have sustained. The reparation in the King's chamber seems now too trifling. A better recompense awaits you. To obliterate all remembrance of your shame, take one of my nieces whose hand is at my disposal. She is a rich heiress, not fifteen, with beauty beyond the attractions of mere youth."

I made my acknowledgments to the Duke in terms such as the high honour of his alliance might suggest, and married his niece a few days afterwards. All the court complimented this nobleman on having made such generous amends to an insulted rival; and my friends took part in my joy at the happy issue of an adventure which might have led to the most melancholy consequences. From this time, gentlemen, I have lived happily at Lisbon. I am the idol of my wife, and have not sunk the lover in the husband. The Duke d'Almeyda gives me new proofs of friendship every day; and I may venture to boast of standing high in the King of Portugal's good graces.

L'ABBÉ GRÉCOURT
1683–1743

THE LINNET OF THE POPE

To be a woman and keep a secret are two things that never go together, and the least womanly woman is better able to keep her honour than a secret. You will say this is putting it too extravagantly, but I have a tale that will support my theory.

There were some nuns in a convent at Fontevrault, to which Pope John XXII. used to go pretty often to grant indulgences by way of raising revenue. It was a convent of excellent fame, where Satan could do nothing but lead the holy women into some slight peccadillo when they came to talk at the grille. For, as you know, the enemy of mankind can only get hold of nuns through their passion for chattering. The Holy Pastor came to them one day on his mule—which they kissed—and heaven knows how many indulgences were brought out! Insatiable is the monastic tribe, and the nuns had got it into their heads to obtain the most fantastic of indults : they wished to obtain the right to confess each other, instead of going to a priest.

" Holy father," said the abbess, " speaking frankly as a woman, I must admit that there is little sincerity in the confessions we make to a man. With him we try to pass over a hundred little things, trifling mistakes, that we should blush to speak about to the other sex. For a man is often like to jest about the faults a nun accuses herself of."

" You want women confessors ! " said the Pope. " How can such a thing be possible ? I am sorry I must refuse your request, on one broad principle. This sacrament requires a great secrecy, and, as you know, the female race is over-talkative. Was it not a woman's love of chatter that first led to original sin ? Your sex cannot keep a secret. But if you like, I will test the matter and learn by my own experience if women have been defamed in this respect ? "

It was not the first time that the Abbess had worried His Holiness in regard to this affair, and he had made his preparations about the matter when he left Avignon. So he now took a little box, that he had carried on his mule, and handed it to the Abbess.

" Here," he said, " I will put this box in your hands to keep until I return to-morrow. Do not open it before I arrive, or you will not obtain the indult. If the box is intact to-morrow morning, I will grant your request."

He went away and all the nuns clustered round the mysterious box, crying :

" Let me touch it ! Let me see it ! "

They struggled to snatch it from each other, but happily no one attempted to open it, and the nuns went to bed, all worrying over what it was the box contained. Nobody slept very much, and the Abbess, especially, was almost sick with curiosity. At prayers the next morning everything went wrong. The convent was worried beyond bearing : for it does not take much to turn the head of a nun.

" Ah," said the Abbess to her anxious troop, " the Pope is trying to make us pine away in grief. What is this great secret he want to hide from us ? Why are we not good enough to have it revealed to us ? I must say he treats us nuns with no great honour ! Let us open the box just to be avenged on him. Who will be able to tell what we have done ? We can easily fasten it up again exactly as we found it."

At this speech every nun rejoiced. The Abbess opened the fatal box. What did she find in it ? A little linnet. The bird swiftly flew to the ceiling, and, singing, circled three times above their heads, and then flew out through a hole into the open air. The Abbess and her nuns heard a knock at the door, and the Holy Pontiff entered with a smile.

" Ah, there is my box ! " he cried. " Now we shall see if women can be trusted. For your indult was placed inside under seal. Oh, oh ! " he said, laughing, as he found the box open and peeped in, " your indult has flown away. Farewell, my discreet and trustworthy sisters ! There will be no woman confessor."

" So much the better," said one nun, softly. " I was not for the change. One man confessor is at least something."

COMTE DE CAYLUS
1692–1763

THE CHAUDRON GIRLS

" My son," said my father to me one day, " you will become
president of this salt granary, for nobody can tell who lives or
dies. I hear you hang about the house of Madame Chaudron.
She is a worthy woman ; I would not dispute it. It is not certain
that she threw her husband down a well, as some people say.
But though she has a good deal of society at her place, she has
no money. Of course you prowl around her daughters, and at
your age I should delight to flirt with the fair sex, especially as
the Chaudron girls are as pretty as flowers and conduct themselves
in a modest way. But money, my boy, is the main thing."

" I quite understand you, father," I replied.

And I went straightway into my study to consider things, thinking what I should do in the matter ; and, concluding that it was
necessary to take a definite course of action, I put on my wig and
went out.

I arrived at Madame Chaudron's ; as soon as I was seated and
began to make my compliments—

" On what footing have you entered my house for the last three
months ? " said Madame Chaudron, pointing to her three girls.

" I came here for a good reason," I said, somewhat astonished.

" Well," she continued, " you must be engaged to-day to her
whom you choose for wife. I am not a mother to let false rumours
get abroad about my girls."

Under this affront, I did not hesitate a moment.

" Madame," I said, " I am an honest man, and I will have no
other wife but your second daughter, Babiche, whose hand I now
ask of you in marriage. I told her I loved her when first I made
her acquaintance. Now I will see my father on the matter."

I went at a run to find him, and in all filial affection I told him
I had asked Babiche Chaudron in marriage. He looked at me
between the eyes for a while.

" Did I not clearly forbid you to marry any of the Chaudron
girls just about a quarter of an hour ago ? " he said. " They have

57

no money, and you know what money is, and what people will
say about her.   Still I am your father, and I will approve the
marriage.   Let us go to the mother.

So we went.

" My dear," he said, " my son is a fool, but I can't help having
the feelings of a father for him.   Since he wants to do this foolish
thing, I suppose we must arrange the articles."

This matter was soon settled.   We all had supper in the garden,
and by what happened there at the table you can see what pre-
destination is when the stars fight against a man.   I sat between
Babiche and her eldest sister, and talked about the betrothal.

" I shall not say what I think," said the eldest Mademoiselle
Chaudron, " but if you mean to marry my sister Babiche, may this
wine poison you, if I do not become your wife instead of her ! "

And she pleasantly tossed off a glass of red wine.

" You see, my son," said Madame Chaudron, " how the matter
stands.   She is the eldest of the family, and rather than let her
second sister marry before her, she would do anything.   What is
it that makes you prefer Babiche ?   Is it because you love her ?
After you have been married to her less than a year, you will be
complaining to me about her ! "

She was still speaking when—as by arrangement, though really
by chance—our notary, Monsieur Gandion, arrived.

" Your servant ! " he said.   " Here are the articles all drawn up.
But who is going to hold the handle of the frying-pan ?   In other
words, which of the young ladies is about to be married ? "

My father all this time had seemed to be doing nothing, but he
was enjoying the society of the youngest Mademoiselle Chaudron,
to whom he listened without saying anything, because she was as
witty as she was pretty.   Now he cried suddenly :

" She shall be my daughter-in-law, or I shall die through grief
at not being her father by marriage.   You see," he continued,
" she has just said to me like that, that if she had a husband, he
should never die but by her hand.   A pleasant wit like that can
only come from a fine intelligence, and I want her to marry my
son.   Yes," he said to me, " beg Mademoiselle Babiche to
excuse you."

And this I did, saying :

" Mademoiselle, I beg you to pardon me and excuse me.   It is
due to my not having reflected.   But if I marry your youngest
sister, I shall make it a veritable pleasure to be your brother-
in-law."

" Sir," she replied, " I do not know how to be a shrew, and since
you use me in this fashion, I shall not say a word."

And with that, she gave me a blow with one hand, and broke a
pile of plates with the other, and went away.

" All that is only a sign of joy," said Madame Chaudron. " Don't let us enjoy ourselves any the less for that. Master Gandion, make out the contract ! We will sign it to-morrow, and the wedding will take place on Sunday."

As we returned to spend the evening at my father's, we met on the road Sieur Bertrand's troop of play-actors, who were taking down their theatre. His eldest son, dressed up as a girl, took a violin and played us to the house.

" It is the custom," he said, " on an occasion like this, to kiss the young lady before we part."

And thereupon he embraced my betrothed. That put us all in a merry humour, and we invited him to come with his troop and dance with us. And this was done. About midnight, as I was going to dance the Forlande with my future bride—

" It is necessary for me to disguise myself," she said, " isn't it ? "

And she took the arm of young Bertrand and stealthily went away.

An hour afterwards, I asked myself where could she be. We all began to look for her. " Wherever has she got to ? We must find her ! " said everybody. We ranged the house. She was no more there than in my eye.

" It is some trick she is playing on us," said madame Chaudron, " that will make us laugh."

She called to her other two daughters, and hurried home ; but the youngest girl was not there. I went to bed. Next morning I awoke early, and leaving my father still snoring, for he had been overcome with wine at the ball, I went to the stable and took his mare and the road to Niort.

" They will know all the news there," I said to myself, " since the gazette is sold there."

On arriving, I saw in the market-place the theatre of Sieur Bertrand, and on the stage I recognised my betrothed. She was playing, I think, the part of Chiméne, for she wore a riding dress.

When the play was over, seeing Mademoiselle Chaudron leaving, arm in arm with young Bertrand, disguised as harlequin—

" Ha ! So I've found you at last," I said to her.

" Who is this insolent creature ? " she said. " I do not know you, my friend ! "

And with that, she made me a deep curtsey, and departed with the young actor.

THE LETTER

Comte de Caylus

Not being a newsmonger, Madame, and liking only old reports about the wars and about politics, because they seem to me more truthful, I must turn to the events and stories of the town in order to keep my word with you. I will not answer for the impression that this tale will make on you, but I can assure you of its truth.

You know all the bonds that unite us, Alcidor and myself, so you will not think it strange that he should take me into his confidence. But judge of the astonishment he caused me by confessing to me that he was jealous! He is the last man I should have suspected of this weakness. His natural gaiety, his carelessness, and his knowledge of the world would have led me to think that he was stronger than I am in this respect. Yet he was jealous, but he took it like a gallant man.

" Spare me," he said, " all the commonplaces with which I used to cheer up any husband in my position. I have employed them on other men, and I know what they are worth. Just listen to me, and do not interrupt by trying to lighten my view of my wife's position."

So I promised to hear him in silence, and he continued :

" I will admit I am no longer in love with my wife. So it is not passion that blinds me. But I have still some sincere feelings for her, and I am hurt by her conduct. It is the kind of man she has chosen that upsets me. I imagined she had better taste. If I flattered myself I could hinder a woman of twenty-four years from following the movements of her heart, after I had ceased to love her, I should be a fool. Never shall I be capable of such an injustice. But counting on her discernment and her fine taste, I thought she would choose somebody like a gentleman, who would not compromise her—some one with a mind and character that I could welcome to my house. You see I was the most reasonable of husbands ! "

" I agree with you," I answered, " though it might be objected that supposing your wife has made a choice, it will be difficult for her to suit your taste in the matter as well as her own."

"That may be," said Alcidor. "Still it is not so much her
choice of the Chevalier that angers me, as the affectation with
which he speaks to her in my presence, and the desire he seems to
have to wound me. The thing is got to such a point that many
times I have need of all my self-control not to break out and make
a scene. I am even pretty sure that my wife has noticed it. Yet
it makes no change in her conduct. Her head is so turned that
she goes out of her way to make things unpleasant for me."

My mouth was closed by the first words he had said to me. Still,
I should have liked to tell him how surprised I was over the
appearance of the Chevalier, whose vain and ridiculous character
you well know. But to talk in this way was only to increase my
friend's distress. He noticed how embarrassed I was, and saw the
reason for it.

"Don't attempt to talk to me," he said. "I want no advice
from you, though you would be better at it than any one else.
I have only wished to relieve my feelings by showing you, my dear
friend, the cruel situation in which I am placed. It is an insult
the young brainless fop does to me : it is my honour he attacks—
not the honour of the common mind—but that which even an
enlightened man of some gallantry cannot relinquish."

He went on talking in the same manner all through our first
conversation. That made it very embarrassing for me. After we
had finished our walk, for he had led me to the Allées du Roule
so as to make sure we should not be interrupted, you will guess,
Madame, that my first idea was to have an interview with his wife.
I wanted to tell her all I had learnt and warn her to be more
careful, and to think a little on what she owes herself as well as
her husband. But I could not find an opportunity. Alcidor
never left the room, while I was with his wife, and it would have
been worse than useless to speak to her in whispers in his presence.
He would have begun to suspect me.

But I was a witness to the truth of all he had said concerning
the conduct of the Chevalier. He was always at her side ; he
spoke to her always in a low voice, and leered at her in a scandalous
fashion. I do not know if Alcidor's admissions, and the fear I had
of seeing him get beyond himself, led me to find all that happened
before my eyes too much for any man to bear. But I know that
I left the house, not only convinced of his patience and the justice
of his complaint, but astonished at the indiscretions of the other
pair. But I was more than ever resolved to speak to his wife at
any cost. And I was about to call on her at noon the day before
yesterday, thinking I should then be sure to find her alone, when
my man brought Alcidor in to see me. His strange air—downcast,
dismayed, and triumphant all at the same time—surprised me and
disquietened me.

"What is the matter?" I said to him when my man had left the room. "I do not know what to think from your looks."

"I was right," he said in sorrowful satisfaction. "I can no longer doubt. The affair is settled and the Chevalier wins. I must admit," he continued, "that I did not think it had got beyond a flirtation. I thought a woman of character would have quickly been disgusted with a man of that sort. But he has won, and my wife will suffer for it. Affairs of this kind, conducted without any sort of brilliance, end in a clap of thunder. Read this," he said, giving me a letter, "and look at the address."

I saw that the name and address of the Chevalier were written without any attempt at secrecy.

"Heavens! what have you done?" I cried. "How did this letter get into your hands?"

I thought he had killed the Chevalier or murdered his wife.

"Don't be disturbed," he said, with great coolness. "Chance alone made me the possessor of it. I went out, about an hour ago, to see a man in the neighbourhood about some business. I did not use the carriage, but went on foot, dreaming and enjoying the fine weather, when a Savoyard asked me to look at the address on a letter he was carrying, and tell him where he would find it. Think what my feelings were when I recognised the handwriting of my wife! I told the Savoyard to follow me, and went into a café, where there were some writing materials."

"Well?" I said to him.

"God!" he said, "how I suffered in copying the letter—the most passionate a woman ever wrote! You can see how she is blinded by her mad feelings! She entrusted a letter of this importance to the first beggar that came her way! It was yesterday that the accursed Chevalier won her completely. Read it," he said, "read it, and see how I am attacked for entering my own house, and interrupting their courtship. But what I can't understand is that I did not perceive anything when they were talking together yesterday. They seemed to be continuing a dull sort of conversation that my arrival did not in the least interrupt. To finish my story," he continued, "I copied this terrible letter, kept the original, and gave the Savoyard some money to take the copy to the Chevalier. Now do you think my complaint is not well founded?"

It was then that I read the fatal letter, from which nothing that could wound the feelings of a husband was omitted. I did not want to give it back to him, and I was afraid to leave him in the condition in which he was. So I went with him to his wife. It was an awkward situation for me. Happily, we found her alone, and she greeted us with that frank and graceful air that you have remarked in her. But she did not keep it for long. For her husband overwhelmed her with the most offensive reproaches. The poor woman, trembling and amazed fell on the floor so stricken that she could not weep. I was sorry for her in spite of her faults, and went to her help.

"What, sir!" she said to me. "You stand by and see me treated in this way? Where am I? Were you not my friend?"

"I am willing that he should judge between us," exclaimed Alcidor.

I did all I could to arrive at some kind of compromise and put an end to the terrible scene. To some extent I succeeded. But an angry man will always continue to repeat himself, and Alcidor kept talking of the convincing evidence he had of the guilt of his wife. But she still protested her innocence with a firmness that astonished me; and, when the letter was mentioned, she still held to her position. So I began to think that, in spite of the difficulty, she had thought of some way of getting out of the matter: and then, as Alcidor pressed me more and more strongly, I was obliged to show the letter.

"This is not my writing," she said proudly, after she had looked at it. "How can Alcidor ever have thought so!"

Her husband was not struck by this reply. He regarded it as a confession of defeat on her part. And I will admit to you that I took the same view. Still I began to support her statement, having, it seemed to me, no other course. But I was quickly interrupted by her, and speaking to us both she said:

"I have always loved my husband. It was with much sorrow that I saw him grow cold to me. But with all his injustice he cannot say that I ever wearied him with any reproaches. I knew they were useless. The only fault I have committed is to have tried to win him back by the dangerous means of jealousy. I saw all the danger, but I thought I had avoided it by choosing a man who seemed to me incapable of wronging me in the minds of those who really knew me. The man himself, in fact, offered to carry out the plan I had formed. But when I saw yesterday what pain I was causing Alcidor, I told the servants I should not be at home if the Chevalier called again. I even gave this order in his presence, so that he should not pretend to be ignorant of my wishes. If your servants will deny that I gave this order, I will consent that you shall think me capable of having written this infamous letter. The handwriting, I admit, is like mine, but you," she said, looking with astonishing sternness at her husband, "should not have been deceived by so slight a resemblance. Do you mean still to tell me that this is my handwriting?"

"Oh, heavens!" said Alcidor, "I can see it now. You never wrote this!"

For some moments there was a silence, and as for myself I did not know where I was, when Alcidor, throwing himself at the feet of his wife, implored her to pardon him. And this she did, sweetly and nobly. I then wished to retire, but Alcidor begged me to stay for some time with his wife.

" This affair is not yet finished," she said to me with a smile. " Let him go on with it."

Alcidor went out in a quick, excited way, and as there was nothing to prevent me showing my curiosity, I begged his wife to satisfy it.

" To any one but you," she said, " I should not say anything of what I am about to tell you. Alcidor is still as much hurt in the depths of his soul as he was before he saw I had not written the letter."

" I do not understand it," I said.

" I will explain the mystery," she continued. " He is strongly attached to Céphise. You know how this woman always conducts herself ? Very well I It is she who wrote the letter. Our hand-writings slightly resemble each other, and it was only my husband's jealousy that prevented him from at once seeing the difference. The likeness of the handwriting, the address to the Chevalier, all seemed to him to relate to me, while in fact it was all connected with Céphise."

" Now I understand," I said.

" But that is not all," she continued. " The Chevalier is madly in love with the woman. He pretended to attach himself to me, simply to draw Alcidor away from his loved one ; and you know why I pretended to listen to him. For the rest," she added, " you must stay with us. A man has need of a friend when he has just discovered the unfaithfulness of a woman. In one way, Alcidor is calmed down, but the discovery he has just made is perhaps just as upsetting in another way."

Our conversation was easily sustained. It was far from languishing for want of matter when Alcidor returned.

" I went to Céphise," he said, " to give her back her letter and break with her. Will you believe ? They would not let me in. Yet she was at home. I even saw the Chevalier's carriage. He, no doubt, received my copy of the letter, and, alarmed by the handwriting, he hastened to her to warn and advise her."

" I am delighted," I said, " with the way they are acting. They will see you no more, and you are happier than you deserve."

The trouble, however, is too recent to convince Alcidor of the justness of my remark. He still affects at times a nonchalance he is far from feeling. In the meantime, I neglect nothing to lead him from scorn to indifference for Céphise. She is a woman of no merit. His wife is excellent. She does not seek for any advantage over her husband, and she has no resentment for the unjust attack he made on her. She has wiped his wild words from her mind. I admire her and I console him. This, Madame, is my present occupation which I especially wanted to give you an account of, as it seemed to me connected with an adventure singular enough to entertain you for a moment.

VOLTAIRE
1694–1778

JEANNOT AND COLIN

MANY credible persons have seen Jeannot and Colin of the village of Issoire in Auvergne, a place famous all over the world for its college and its cauldron. Jeannot was the son of a very renowned mule-driver ; Colin owed his existence to an honest labourer in the neighbourhood, who cultivated the earth with the help of four mules, and who, after he had paid the poll-tax, the military-tax, the royal-tax, the excise-tax, the shilling-in-the-pound, the capitation, and the twentieths, did not find himself over-rich at the year's end.

Jeannot and Colin were very pretty lads for Auvergnians : they were remarkably attached to each other, and enjoyed together those little confidences, and those snug familiarities, which men always recollect with pleasure when they afterwards meet in the world.

The time dedicated to their studies was just upon the eve of elapsing, when a tailor brought Jeannot a velvet coat of three colours, with a Lyons waistcoat made in the first taste ; the whole was accompanied with a letter directed to Monsieur de la Jeannotiere. Colin could not help admiring the coat, though he was not at all envious of it ; but Jeannot immediately assumed an air of superiority which perfectly distressed his companion.

From this moment Jeannot studied no more ; he admired himself in the glass, and despised the whole world. Soon after a *valet-de-chambre* arrived post-haste, bringing a second letter, which was addressed to Monsieur the Marquis de la Jeannotiere ; it was an order from Monsieur the father, that Monsieur the son, should set out for Paris directly. Jeannot ascended the chaise and stretched out his hand to Colin with a smile of protection sufficiently dignified ; Colin felt his own insignificance and burst into tears : Jeannot departed in all his glory.

Those readers who like to be instructed as well as amused, must know that Monsieur Jeannot, the father, had very rapidly acquired a most immense fortune by business. Do you ask how it is one makes a great fortune ? It is because one is fortunate. Monsieur Jeannot was handsome, and so was his wife, who had still a certain bloom about her. They came up to Paris on account of a law-suit, which ruined them ; when fortune, who elevates and depresses mankind at will, presented them to the wife of a contractor for the army hospitals, a man of very great talent, who could boast of having killed more soldiers in one year than the cannon had blown up in ten.

Jeannot pleased the lady, and his wife pleased the contractor. Jeannot soon had his share in his patron's enterprise ; and after-wards entered into other speculations. When once you are in the current of the stream, you have nothing to do but to leave your bark to itself ; you will make an immense fortune without much difficulty. The mob on the bank, who see you scud along in full sail, open their eyes with astonishment ; they are at a loss to conjecture how you came by your prosperity ; they envy you at all events, and write pamphlets against you, which you never read. This is just what happened to Jeannot the father, who quickly became Monsieur de la Jeannotiere, and who, having purchased a marquisate at the end of six months, took Monsieur the Marquis his son from school, to introduce him into the fashionable world of Paris.

Colin, always affectionate, sent a letter of compliment to his old school-fellow, in which he wrote his " *these lines to congratulate* " him. The little Marquis returned no answer : Colin was perfectly ill with mortification.

The father and mother provided a tutor for the young Marquis. This tutor, who was a man of fashion, and who knew nothing, of course could teach nothing to his pupil. Monsieur wished his son to learn Latin ; Madame wished him not : accordingly they called in as arbitrator an author, who was at that time celebrated for some very pleasing works. He was asked to dinner. The master of the house began by asking him :

" Monsieur, as you understand Latin, and are a courtier——"

" I, sir, understand Latin ? not a word," replied the wit, " and very glad am I that I don't ; for there is not a doubt but a man always speaks his own language the better when his studies are not divided between that and foreign languages : look at all our ladies, is not their vivacity more elegant than that of the men ? Their letters, are they not written with a hundred times the anima-tion ? Now all this superiority they possess from nothing else but their not understanding Latin."

" There now ! was not I in the right ? " said Madame : " I wish my son to be a wit : that he may make a figure in the world ; and you see if he learns Latin he is inevitably lost. Are comedies or operas played in Latin ? In a law-suit, does any one plead in Latin ? Do we make love in Latin ? "

Monsieur, dazzled by all this ratiocination, gave his judgment ;

when it was finally determined that the young Marquis should not
lose his time in becoming acquainted with Cicero, Horace, and
Virgil.   But then what was he to learn ? for he must know something : could not he be shown a little geography ?

" What would that serve ? " replied the tutor : " when Monsieur
the Marquis goes to any of his estates, won't the postillions know
which way to drive him ? They'll certainly take care not to go out
of their way ; one has no need of a quadrant to travel with ; and a
man may go from Paris to Auvergne very commodiously, without
having the least idea of what latitude he is under."

" You are right," replied the father ; " but I have somewhere
heard of a very beautiful science, which is called astronomy, I
think."

" The more's the pity then," cried the tutor ; " does any one
regulate himself by the stars in this world ? and is it necessary
that Monsieur the Marquis should murder himself by calculating
an eclipse when he will find its very point of time in the almanack,
a book which will teach him, moreover, the movable feasts and fasts,
the age of the moon, and that of all the princesses in Europe."
Madame was entirely of the tutor's opinion ; the little Marquis
was overjoyed ; the father was very much undecided.

" What must my son learn then ? " said he.

" To make himself agreeable : if," replied the friend whom they
had consulted, " he knows but how to please, he knows everything ;
that is an art he can learn from his mother, without giving the least
trouble either to that master or this.

At this speech Madame embraced the polite ignoramus, and said
to him, " It is very plain, sir, that you are the most learned man in
the whole world ; my son will owe his entire education to you :
however, I conceive that it will be as well if he should know a little
of history."

" Alas ! Madame, what is that good for ? " replied he : " there is
nothing either so pleasing or so instructive as the history of the day ;
all ancient history, as one of our wits observes, is nothing but a pre-
concerted fable ; and as for modern, it is a chaos which no one can
disintricate : what does it signify to Monsieur your son that Charlemagne instituted the twelve peers of France, and that his successor
was a stutterer ? "

" Nothing was ever better said," cried the tutor ; " the spirits of
children are overwhelmed with a mass of useless knowledge ; but of
all absurd sciences, that which, in my opinion, is the most likely to
stifle the spark of genius is geometry. This ridiculous science has for
its object surfaces, lines, and points, which have no existence in
nature ; ten thousand crooked lines are by the mere twist of
imagination made to pass between a circle and a right line that
touches it, although in reality it is impossible to draw a straw

between them. In short, geometry is nothing but an execrable joke."

Monsieur and Madame did not understand too much of what the tutor said ; but they were entirely of his opinion.

" A nobleman like Monsieur the Marquis," continued he, " ought not to dry up his brains with such useless studies ; if at any time he has occasion for one of your sublime geometricians to draw the plan of his estates, can't money buy him a surveyor ? or if he wishes to unravel the antiquity of his nobility, which rises to the most obscure times, can't he send for a Benedictine ? And it is the same in every other art. A young lord, born under a lucky star, is neither painter, musician, architect, nor sculptor : but he makes all those arts flourish in proportion as his magnificence encourages them ; and it is much better to patronise than to exercise them. Enough that Monsieur the Marquis has a taste ; let artists work for him : it is in this we have so great reason to say that men of quality (I mean those who are very rich) know everything without having learned any-thing ; because, in fact, they at least know how to judge of every-thing which they order and pay for."

The amiable ignoramus then took up the conversation.

" You have very justly remarked, Madame, that the great end of man is to rise in society : seriously, now, is it by science that success is to be obtained ? Does any man in company even so much as think of talking about geometry ? Is a man of fashion ever asked what star rose with the sun to-day ? Who wishes to know, at supper, if the long-haired Clodia passed the Rhine ? "

" Nobody, without doubt," exclaimed the Marchioness de la Jeannotiere, whose personal attractions had somewhat initiated her in the polite world ; " and Monsieur my son ought not to cramp his genius by studying all this trash. But, after all, what shall he learn ? for it is but right that a young lord should know how to shine upon occasion, as Monsieur my husband very justly observes. I remember hearing an old abbé say once, that the most delightful of all possible sciences was something, of which I have forgotten the name ; but it begins with an *h*."

" With an *h*, Madame ; it was not horticulture ? "

" No, it was not horticulture he meant ; it begins, I tell you, with an *h* and ends with a *ry*."

" Ah ! I understand you, Madame, 'tis heraldry : heraldry is indeed a very profound science, but it has been out of fashion ever since the custom of painting arms on carriage doors was dropped. It was once the most useful thing in the world in a well-regulated state : but the study would have become endless ; for nowadays there is not a hairdresser but has his coat of arms ; and you know that whatever becomes common ceases to be esteemed."

At length after having examined the merits and demerits of every science, it was decided that Monsieur the Marquis should learn to dance.

Nature, which does everything, had bestowed on him a gift that quickly developed itself with a prodigious success ; it was an agreeable knack at singing ballads. The graces of youth joined to this superior talent made him looked upon as a young man of the greatest promise. He was beloved by the women ; and having his head always stuffed with songs, he manufactured them for his mistresses. He plundered *Bacchus* and *Cupid* to make one sonnet, the *Night* and the *Day* for another, the *Charms* and *Alarms* for a third ; but as he always found in his verses some feet too little or some too much, he was obliged to have them corrected at twenty shillings a song ; and thus he got a place in the *Literary Year*, by the side of the La Fares, the Chaulieus, the Hamiltons, the Sarrasins, and the Voitures of the day.

Madame the Marchioness now thought she should gain the reputation of being the mother of a wit ; and gave a supper to all the wits in Paris accordingly. The young man's brain was presently turned ; he acquired the art of speaking without understanding a single word he said, and perfected himself in the art of being good for nothing.

When his father saw him so eloquent, he began to regret, very sensibly, that he had not had his son taught Latin ; for in that case he could have bought him such a valuable place in the law. The mother, whose sentiments were less grovelling, wished to solicit a regiment for her son ; and in the meantime the son fell in love. Love is sometimes more expensive than a regiment : it cost him a great deal ; while his parents pinched themselves still more, in order to live among great lords.

A young widow of quality in their neighbourhood, who had but a very moderate fortune, had a great mind to resolve upon putting the vast riches of Monsieur and Madame de la Jeannotiere in a place of security, which she could easily do by appropriating them to her own use and marrying the young Marquis. She attracted him, suffered him to love her, gave him to understand that she was not indifferent to him, drew him in by degrees, enchanted, and vanquished him without much difficulty : sometimes she gave him praise, and sometimes advice, and quickly became the favourite both of his father and his mother. An old neighbour proposed their marriage ; the parents, dazzled with the splendour of the alliance, joyfully accepted the offer, and gave their only son to their intimate friend.

The young Marquis was thus about to marry a woman he adored, and by whom he himself was beloved ; the friends of his family congratulated him, and the marriage articles were just about to be settled, whilst all hands were working at their wedding clothes and songs.

He was one morning upon his knees before the charming wife with whom love, esteem, and friendship were about to present him ; they were tasting in a tender and animated conversation the first fruits of their felicity, and were parcelling out a most delicious life, when a *valet-de-chambre* belonging to Madame the mother came up quite scared :

" Here is very different news," said he : " the bailiffs are ransacking the house of Monsieur and Madame ; everything is laid hold of by the creditors ; nay, they talk of seizing your persons ; and so I made haste to come and be paid my wages."

" Let us see a little," said the Marquis, " what all this means what can this adventure be ? "

" Go," said the widow, " and punish these rascals—go quickly."

He ran to the house ; his father was already imprisoned ; all the domestics had fled, each about his own business, but having first carried away everything they could lay hold on ; his mother was alone, without protection, without consolation, drowned in tears ; nothing remained but the recollection of her fortune, the recollection of her beauty, the recollection of her errors, and the recollection of her mad profuseness.

After the son had wept a long time with the mother, he ventured to say to her :

" Let us not despair ; this young widow loves me to distraction, and is still more generous than rich, I can answer for her ; I'll fly to her, and bring her to you."

He then returned to his mistress, and found her in a private interview with a very charming young officer.

" What ! is it you, Monsieur de la Jeannotiere ? what do you do here ? is it thus you have abandoned your mother ? Go to that unfortunate woman, and tell her that I wish her every happiness : I am in want of a chambermaid, and I will most undoubtedly give her the preference."

" My lad," said the officer, " you seem well-shaped enough, if you are inclined to enlist in my company, I'll give you every encouragement."

The Marquis, thunderstruck and bursting with rage, went in quest of his old tutor, lodged his troubles in his breast, and asked his advice. The tutor proposed to him to become a preceptor like himself.

" Alas ! " said the Marquis, " I know nothing ; you have taught me nothing, and are indeed the principal cause of all my misfortunes."

As he spoke this, he sobbed aloud.

" Write romances," said a wit who was present ; " it is an excellent resource at Paris."

The young man, more desperate than ever, ran towards his

mother's confessor, who was a Theatin in great repute, troubling himself with the consciences of women of the first rank only. As soon as Jeannot saw him, he prostrated himself before him.

" Good God ! Monsieur Marquis," said he, " where is your carriage ? how does that respectable lady, the Marchioness your mother ? "

The poor unfortunate youth related the disasters of his family and the farther he proceeded, the graver, the cooler, and the more hypocritical was the air of the Theatin.

" My son," said he, " it has pleased God to reduce you to this ; riches serve but to corrupt the heart ; God has therefore conferred a favour on your mother in bringing her to this miserable state.

" Yes, sir."

" Her election is thus rendered the more sure."

" But, father," resumed the Marquis, " in the meantime, is there no means of obtaining relief in this world ? "

" Adieu ! my son ; there is a court-lady waiting for me."

The Marquis was ready to faint : he was treated in pretty much the same way by all his friends, and gained more knowledge of the world in half a day than he did all the rest of his life.

As he was thus plunged into the blackest despair, he saw advancing an old-fashioned sort of calash or tilt-cart, with leather curtains, which was followed by four enormous waggons well loaded. In the chaise was a young man coarsely clothed ; he had a countenance round and fresh, breathing all the complacency of cheerfulness : his wife, a little brunette, fat, but not disagreeably so, was jolted in beside him ; the vehicle did not move like the carriage of a *petit-maître*, but afforded the traveller sufficient time to contemplate the Marquis, motionless and abyssed in grief as he stood.

" Eh ! good God ! " cried the rider, " I do think that is Jeannot."

At his name the Marquis lifted up his eyes ; the chaise stopped.

" It is too true, it is Jeannot," sighed the Marquis.

The fat little fellow made but one jump of it, and flew to embrace his old school-fellow. Jeannot recognised Colin ; and shame and tears covered his face.

" You have abandoned me," said Colin ; " but though you are a great lord, I will love you for ever."

Jeannot, confused and heart-broken, related to him with many sobs a part of his story.

" Come to the inn where I lodge and tell me the rest there," said Colin ; " embrace my little wife, and then let's go and dine together."

They all three set forward on foot, their baggage following behind.

" What is the meaning of all this equipage ? is it yours ? " says Jeannot.

" Yes, it is all mine and my wife's. We are just arrived from the country, where I have the management of a good manufactory of tin and copper ; I have married the daughter of a rich dealer in utensils which are necessary both to great and small : we work hard ; God has prospered us : we have never changed our condition ; we are happy ; and we will assist our friend Jeannot. Be a Marquis no longer ; all the greatness in the world is not to be compared to a friend. You shall go back into the country with me, I will teach you our trade ; it is not very difficult ; I will make you my partner, and we will live merrily in the very corner of the earth where we were born."

The astonished Jeannot felt himself divided between grief and joy, between affection and shame ; and said to himself :

" All my fashionable friends have betrayed me, and Colin, whom I despised, alone comes to my relief."

What an instruction. The goodness of Colin's soul elicited from the breast of Jeannot a spark of nature which all the world had not yet stifled ; he felt himself unable to abandon his father and mother.

" We'll take care of your mother," said Colin ; " and as to your father, who is in prison, I understand those matters a little ; his creditors, when they see he has nothing to pay, will make up matters for a very trifle ; I'll undertake to manage the whole business."

Colin quickly released the father from prison : Jeannot returned to the country with his parents, who resumed their former profession ; he married a sister of Colin's, who, being of the same disposition as her brother, made him very happy ; and Jeannot the father, Jeannot the mother, and Jeannot the son, now saw that happiness was not to be found in vanity.

BABABEC AND THE FAKIRS

Voltaire

WHEN I was in the city of Benares on the banks of the Ganges, the ancient home of the Brahmins, I endeavoured to gain some information. I understood Hindustani tolerably well ; I heard much, and noticed everything. I lodged with my correspondent Omri, the worthiest man I have ever known. He was of the religion of the Brahmins, and I have the honour to be a Mussulman ; yet we have never had high words on the subject of Mohammed and Brahma. We made our ablutions each on his own side, we drank of the same sherbet, and we ate of the same dish of rice, like a pair of brothers.

One day we went together to the pagoda of Vishnu. We saw there several groups of fakirs, some of whom were Janghis, that is to say, fakirs devoted to contemplation, while the others were disciples of the ancient gymnosophists, who led an active life. They have, as every one knows, a learned language, which is that of the most ancient Brahmins, and, written in this language, a book which is called the Vedas. It is undoubtedly the most ancient book in the whole of Asia, not excepting even the Zendavesta.

I passed in front of a fakir who was reading this book.

" Ah ! wretched infidel ! " cried he, " you have made me lose the number of vowels which I was counting ; and in consequence of that my soul will have to pass into the body of a hare, instead of going into that of a parrot, as I had good grounds for flattering myself would be the case."

I gave him a rupee to console him. A few steps farther on, having been so unfortunate as to sneeze, the noise that I made roused a fakir who was in a trance.

" Where am I ? " said he ; " what a horrible fall I have had ! I can no longer see the tip of my nose ; the celestial light has vanished."[1]

" If I am the cause," said I, " that you see at last beyond the tip of your nose, here is a rupee to repair the damage that I have committed ; so recover your celestial light."

Having thus got myself discreetly out of the scrape, I passed on to the gymnosophists ; some of them there were who brought me very nice little nails, to thrust into my arms and thighs in honour of Brahma. I bought their nails, and used them to fasten down my carpets. Others were dancing on their hands ; others were tumbling on the slack rope ; others again kept hopping continually on one leg. There were some loaded with chains, some who carried a packsaddle, and some who had their heads under a bushel ; yet they were all eminent for their virtues. My friend Omri brought me into the cell of one of the most famous of these philosophers, whose name was Bababec. He was as naked as an ape, and had a big chain round his neck, which must have weighed more than sixty pounds. He was seated on a wooden chair, neatly furnished with sharp little nails, which ran into him, and yet one would have supposed that he was sitting on a velvet cushion. Many women came to consult him as an oracle on family affairs, and it may be

---

[1] Voltaire has a note here : " When the fakirs wish to behold the celestial light, an aspiration which is very general among them, they turn their eyes towards the tip of the nose." Mr. Braid adopted a very similar process for inducing hypnotism.

truly said that he enjoyed the very highest reputation. I heard the important conversation that Omri had with him.

" Do you think, father," said the former, " that after my soul has undergone the probation of seven transmigrations, I may be able to reach the abode of Brahma ? "

" That depends," said the fakir ; " what is your manner of life ? "

" I endeavour," said Omri, " to be a good citizen, a good husband, a good father, and a good friend ; I lend money without interest to the rich when they have occasion for it, I give it away to the poor, and I maintain peace among my neighbours."

" Do you ever sit on nails ? " asked the Brahmin.

" Never, reverend father."

" I am sorry for it," replied the fakir ; " you certainly will not enter the nineteenth heaven ; and that is a pity."

" Very good," said Omri ; " I am quite contented with my lot. What does it matter to me about the nineteenth or twentieth heaven, provided I do my duty during my pilgrimage, and am well received at the last stage ? Is it not enough to be an honest man in this world, and then to be happy in the land of Brahma ? Into which heaven do you expect to go, Mr. Bababec, with your nails and your chains ? "

" Into the thirty-fifth," said Bababec.

" You are a droll fellow," replied Omri, " to expect a higher lodging than I ; that expectation can only proceed from an inordinate ambition. You condemn those who seek for honours in this life, why do you aim at such great ones yourself in the next ? Besides, on what do you found your expectation of having better treatment than I ? Let me tell you that I give away in alms more in ten days than all the nails upon which you sit cost you in the course of ten years. What does it matter to Brahma that you pass your days stark naked, with a chain round your neck ? That is a fine way of serving your country ! I reckon that man is worth a hundred times more who sows pot-herbs, or plants trees, than the whole tribe of you and your fellows who look at the tips of their noses, or carry a pack-saddle to show the extreme nobility of their souls."

Having spoken thus, Omri soothed, coaxed, persuaded, and at last induced Bababec to leave his nails and his chain there and then, to come with him to his house, and to lead a respectable life. They scoured him well, they rubbed him all over with perfumed essences, they clothed him decently, and he lived for a fortnight in a thoroughly rational manner, confessing that he was a hundred times happier than before.

But he lost credit with the people, and the women came no more to consult him ; so he left Omri and betook himself once more to his nails in order to recover his reputation.

L'ABBÉ BOURDELOT
17TH CENTURY

MONSIEUR OUFLE

A CHEERFUL man was M. Oufle, who loved a jovial evening with his friends, a glass of good wine, and a merry tale. A worthy man, too, was he, the most exemplary of husbands and the most indulgent of fathers,—but he had his weakness—which of us has not ?—and his weakness was weakness of intellect ; in short, he was a very good, a very respectable, a very kind-hearted man, but also a very silly one.

He regarded himself as a bit of a philosopher, and despised superstition, yet for all that he was fidgeted if the salt-cellar were upset, alarmed if the knife and fork were crossed, and he would positively decline to make the thirteenth at dinner.

It was Carnival time, and M. Oufle invited all his own relations and his wife's relations to dinner. A pleasant evening they passed ; they ate and they drank, and they talked and they sang,—they ate till they were more than satisfied, drank till they were very merry, talked themselves dry, and sang themselves hoarse. Far be it from me to assert that any of the party had drunk more than he ought, but they had all grazed the line of moderation, and M. Oufle, being naturally light-headed, had become exceedingly " jolly."

When the relations withdrew, the children went to bed, Madame Oufle took her candle and departed with her lady's maid, and M. Oufle, for the sake of a little exercise, festooned up and down his chamber, whistling a plaintive melody, and whistling it out of tune.

This gentleman's eldest son, who had inherited all his father's amiable qualities, and his empty-headedness into the bargain, had slipped off from the paternal house by the back door, as soon as the guests began to leave, in a masquerading dress, and had betaken himself, after the manner of scapegraces, to a ball.

M. Oufle, having wearied of describing curves in his own room, opened the door and went upstairs, a process attended with difficulties which would have proved insuperable but for the assistance of the banisters. Arrived on the landing, M. Oufle observed his son's door open, so he walked into the room, impelled either by

76

curiosity or by a desire for a little more conversation.

The son was, however, at that time dancing in the ball-room of a hotel two streets off.

M. Oufle, not finding the young man, sat himself down beside the bed, and began to overhaul the various masquerading dresses which his son had left out upon his chair. There was a neat suit of green and gold, intended as a forester's dress; there was a costume of the time of François I., covered with spangles; and last, but not least, there was a bearskin suit, so contrived that the wearer of it was covered with fur from head to foot, and looked precisely like a black bear escaped from a travelling caravan. M. Oufle turned this dress over and over, and its originality attracted his interest. He thought he should like to see whether it would fit his person; he therefore arrayed himself in the habit, and found that it suited him to a T. Just then the idea entered his head that the opportunity of disabusing Madame Oufle of her superstitions had now presented itself. Madame Oufle was nearly as great a fool as her husband, and that is saying a good deal. She was infected with the vulgar belief in witchcraft and demonology, and believed implicitly that warlocks could transform themselves into wild beasts for the purpose of devouring children.

" Now," mused M. Oufle, " is a chance for me to eradicate these baneful superstitions from her mind. If she sees me in this dress, and takes me to be a werewolf, and when I show her the deception, she will never believe in the supernatural again."

Accordingly he walked to his wife's door and listened. The servant was still with her mistress, so M. Oufle retreated downstairs to the dining-room, intending to wait till his good lady was alone; and that he might know when the maid was dismissed, he placed the door ajar.

Then, taking up a book, he seated himself before the fire. The book happened to be Bodin's *Dæmonomania*, and M. Oufle opened it at the chapter on Lycanthropy.

He read on, and the tales of werewolves floated in strange colours through his brain, till he fell asleep with his head on the table, and the book on his lap. And as he slumbered he dreamed of sorcerers being provided by the Evil One with wolf-skins which they were condemned to wear for seven years, and of Lycaon sentenced by Jove to run about in bestial form, till a piercing shriek and a crash brought him with a start to his feet.

The lady's maid, after having pinned her mistress's back hair into a heap, and fitted over it the nightcap, had left the chamber, and had come downstairs. As she passed the dining-room, she saw that there was still a light in it, and thinking that the candles had not been extinguished, she entered precipitately to put them out.

There in the dead of night she stood—and saw before her a
monstrous black bear fast asleep before the fire, snoring loudly,
with its head on the table and its snout up in the air, its hind paws
upon the fender, a silk pocket-handkerchief over one knee, and a
book on the lap.   No wonder that she dropped her candle and
screamed.

But the shriek which testified to her fear frightened M. Oufle
out of the few senses he did possess. He sprang up, bewildered
with his dreams, confused with the fumes of wine, and alarmed
at the suddenness of his *reveil*. Opposite him was a pier-glass. He
forgot entirely all the circumstances connected with the assumption
of the bearskin, and with the last impressions produced by Bodin,
and by his dream, stamped upon his brain, he jumped to the
conclusion that he was bewitched, and that he had been changed
into a werewolf. Full of this idea, he dashed past the terror-
stricken maid ; and his wife, who had rushed to the landing, saw
a frightful monster bounding down the stairs, uttering howls
sufficiently loud to awake the dead, heard it unlock the front door
and burst into the street. Thereupon, she fainted away.

M. Oufle, impelled by terror, ran along the street yelling for
assistance ; he was naturally provided with a deep and sonorous
bass voice, but his voice sounded hollow and fearful through his
hideous vizor.

A few terrified people appeared in their nightcaps at the windows,
only to run back and bury themselves trembling beneath the clothes.

A watchman who had started on his rounds came upon him
suddenly as he turned a corner, and dropping his lanthorn beat a
precipitate retreat.

In an adjoining street lived a fair damsel of considerable personal,
but superior pecuniary, attractions, who was loved to distraction by
a grocer's apprentice. The young man had made the lady's acquaintance as he served the shop, and had breathed his love over the cheeses
he sold. His addresses had been countenanced by the beloved one,
but were discouraged by the parents, who had not permitted the
devoted youth to set foot within their doors. The apprentice had no
other means open to him of testifying his devotion than by hiring a
band of street musicians to perform at the rate of two francs an
hour, during the silent watches of the night, below the window
of the adored.

On the present occasion the band was performing the " Descent
of Mars," when a discordant howl in their ears produced a sudden
pause in their music not noted in their score, and the apparition of
a monstrous bear running into the midst of them upon its hind
legs, with ears and stumpy tail cocked up, produced such a panic
among the sons of Orpheus, that they cast their instruments from
them, and took to their heels. Not so the grocer's apprentice.

True love knows not fear. He flew to the door of his beloved and cast himself before it, determined to perish in her defence.

But the monster, without perceiving him, ran on repeating its dolorous howls.

The grocer's apprentice rose from the doorstep, dusted his coat, collected the scattered instruments, cast an amorous glance at the window of the adored, and retired home.

A party of students from the University were that evening going their rounds, performing feats of heroism, of which they might boast among their companions. These feats were not attended with much danger, and yet the achievement of them was an object of considerable ambition. They consisted simply in breaking lamps, and wrenching the knockers off doors.

Some people might think that the smashing of a street lamp was an operation within the scope of the most infantile abilities, and that the wrenching of a knocker from a door was neither a hazardous nor a very heroic act. But these people are entirely mistaken. The police occasionally interfere and capture one of those engaged in these acts, and, if captured it costs the student several francs to bribe the officer to let him escape.

Consequently, the ringing of a street bell at midnight is regarded by University men as an achievement equal to the bravest deed of a tried general, and the breaking off of a knocker is supposed to rank very much on a level with the proudest trophy of a blood-stained field.

On the night in question four valiant collegians were engaged on the hazardous undertaking of screwing up the door of a worthy citizen, an act of consummate ingenuity and sublime originality. Suddenly a wild and unearthly yell ringing through the hushed night broke upon their ears. Instantly the four students paused and turned pale. In another moment they saw a diabolical object moving rapidly down the street towards them. The young men shrank against the wall, each endeavouring to get behind the other, and reversing the proverb of the weakest going to the wall, for in their struggle the ablest-bodied secured that position, whilst the feeblest was the most exposed, and served as a screen to the others.

The approaching monster stood still for an instant, and they were able to observe him by the wan light of the crescent new moon, and the flickering oil lamp slung across the head of the street. A fearful object ! In their terror the screw-drivers dropped from their fingers. The noise attracted the creature's attention, and it ran up the steps towards them, articulating words in a hoarse tone, which they, in their alarm, were unable to catch. Suffice it to say that the sight of this monster coming within arm's length was too much for their courage ; with a shriek they burst past it, tumbling over each other, and rolling down the doorsteps, picked themselves up again and fled, palpitating, in four separate directions, calling for the police, imploring the aid of that august body which they had so long set at defiance.

What tales they related on the following morning to all the old ladies of their acquaintance it is not for me to record.   One of the students broke his sword, and vowed that he had snapped it in his fight with the Daemon, another exhibited the bruises he had received in his fall as evidence of the desperate character of the conflict, a third wore his arm in a sling as though it had been broken in the encounter, and all agreed that the monster had fled from them, and not they from the monster.

The police ! " Oh, horrors ! " thought M. Oufle, "they have summoned the aid of the police.   I shall be captured, be tried and sentenced, and burned at the stake as a werewolf."

The fear of this urged him to retreat stealthily homewards, keeping as much as possible in the shadows, lest any of the agents of justice should get sight of him, and carry him away to trial.   If he could but reach home, he would implore his wife to stab him with a knife between the eyes, and draw some drops of blood, a sovereign cure for lycanthropy.

But poor M. Oufle's head was never very clear, and now it was in a thorough condition of bewilderment, so that he completely lost himself, and slunk about the streets in a disconsolate manner, vainly searching for his own domicile.   His bewilderment became greater with every step he took ; his confusion and alarm were not a little heightened by his stumbling over an elderly gentleman and leaving him apparently dead of fright on the pavement.

It did not mend matters when, hearing a *fiacre* drive by, he suddenly stepped towards it and asked the way of the driver,— for the coachman jumped off his seat in a paroxysm of terror, and the horses, equally frightened, ran away with the carriage, whilst the people inside screamed through the windows.

At last M. Oufle sat down on a doorstep and gave himself up to despair.   The stake was before him, and his imagination conjured up all the horrors of his position, chained about the waist and dancing in the midst of the flames.

All at once, a familiar voice smote upon his ear—the voice of his eldest son.   A ray of hope penetrated his breast.   He rose from his seat and walked to meet his first born.   That young gentleman was returning from the masquerade ball at which he had been figuring.   He had imbibed a considerable amount of wine before he left home, and he had absorbed a little more during the pauses in the dance.   He was accordingly scarcely sober, and as he returned home, he sang or talked to himself at the top of his voice.   But now he saw something which sobered him instantaneously.   This was nothing else than his own masquerading habit of bear's skin, which he had left hanging over the back of his chair, walking deliberately towards him, as though the spirit of the departed Bruin had retenanted his forsaken skin and was coming in the dead of night to demand a reckoning with him who had dared to use it as a Carnival habit.

He stood and looked at it with pale face and staring eyes, whilst a shudder ran through his frame.

If it had been within the limits of physical possibility, he would have sunk into his shoes. When he heard his own name articulated in hollow tones from the muzzle, he turned heel, and fled like the wind. In vain did M. Oufle call after him ; the louder he called, the faster fled the youth, and the distracted father was obliged to pursue his son.

The race was run with the utmost speed by both parties. The young man was urged on by terror lest the skin should overtake him, and M. Oufle dreaded losing sight of his son, lest he should at the same time lose all chance of regaining his home.

When M. Oufle le Jeune turned his white face over his shoulders, he saw the creature gaining upon him, and heard its hollow calls. He dodged from street to street, but he invariably saw the bearskin double the corner and rush after him, turn where he would. It was in vain for him to hope to throw it out, and at last he ran straight for his home. This he had left by the garden. It was his custom to leave the house by the back door, and clamber over the garden rails, whenever he went out on his night expeditions, and now he made for the garden, hoping to climb the rails and escape through the door and lock it before the skin could overtake him.

He reached the railings. It was a difficult and delicate matter to surmount them with time at his disposal, but now that it was to be accomplished in no time at all, it was hazardous in the extreme. M. Oufle, junior, had reached the top, and was preparing to jump down, when a furry paw grasped his ankle and held him as though in a vice, for the monster proceeded to climb the railings, holding on to his leg. The poor youth vainly endeavoured to break away, he writhed and strained to be free ; holding the iron bars with his hands, he vociferated loudly for help. The creature reached the top and clasped him round the waist, whilst the hideous snout was poked close to his ear over his shoulder. Both leaped together, and were brought up with a jerk.

The rails were topped with sharp dart-heads, and one of these caught in the hide, so that M. Oufle and his son were suspended from it in mid air, the latter in the arms of his father. Both cried together for assistance ; the young man louder than ever when he heard the sonorous howls of his captor in his ear.

Lights appeared in the lower apartments at the back of the house, and presently the garden door was opened by a troop of terrified male and female servants, provided with blunderbusses, swords, and pistols. In the rear appeared Madame Oufle, half-dressed, but with her nightcap on her head.

The young man called to his mother, and the moment she saw the hope of the family dangling in the grasp of the monster, she fainted away again. There was an old man, a servant of the house, who claimed and exercised supreme authority in the household. He walked forward with a pistol in each hand; and the youth cried to him to shoot the creature which clasped him through the head. In vain did M. Oufle shout to him to desist, his words were lost in the mask, and he would undoubtedly have received a couple of bullets through his head, had not the buttons of the dress just then given way with a burst, and slipped M. Oufle in a heap upon the ground, leaving the habit torn and dangling on the spike of the rails.

"Thank goodness!" exclaimed M. Oufle, sitting up; "the spell is off me."

"My father!" cried the flower of the family.

"My husband!" ejaculated the lady, recovering from her fainting fit.

"My master!" exclaimed the grey-haired servant.

"Let us embrace all round," said M. Oufle.

L'ABBÉ BLANCHET
1707-1784

THE DEAN OF BADAJOZ

THE Dean of the cathedral of Badajoz was the most learned man in Spain. He knew more than all the doctors of Salamanca, and those of Coimbra and Alcala. He understood every dead and living tongue, and he was master of all sciences, human and divine. But unhappily he did not know magic, and he was inconsolable over it. He was told that there was a very skilful magician in Toledo, who was named Don Torribio. At once he saddled a good mule, and set out for Toledo, and alighted at the door of a pretty miserable house in which the great man was lodged.

"Sir," he said to the sorcerer, "I am the Dean of Badajoz. The learned men of Spain do me the honour of calling me their master ; but I come to beg from you a title more glorious—that of being your pupil. Deign to initiate me into the mysteries of your art, and count on a gratitude worthy of the benefit and of its author."

Don Torribio was not very polite, though he plumed himself on the fact of living with the best company of the under-world. He told the Dean that he must look elsewhere for a master of magic. He said he was tired of a profession in which he had gained only compliments and promises, and that he would no more dishonour himself by prostituting the occult sciences to ungrateful wretches.

"Ah, the ingratitude of men !" cried the Dean. "What, Don Torribio, you have found some men without a sense of gratitude, and you would be so unjust as to confuse me with such monsters ! "

Then he poured out all that he had read about gratitude. With the sweetest of tones and the most honest air, he retailed all the virtuous sentiments that his memory could provide. He spoke so well that, after a moment's thought, the sorcerer avowed he could not refuse anything to a gallant man who knew by heart so many fine passages.

"Jacintha," he said to his servant, "put two partridges on the spit. I hope the Dean will do me the honour of staying to supper."

At the same time he took him by the hand and led him into

his study. There he touched his forehead, murmuring these three mysterious words, which I beg the reader not to forget :

" Ortobolan ! Pistafrier ! Onagriouf ! "

Then after other preparations, he began to explain to him with great clearness the prolegomena to the book on magic. The new pupil listened with such attention that he scarcely breathed. Then Jacintha entered, followed by a little man, booted up to the waist, who asked to speak to the Dean on a pressing matter. It was the postillion of his uncle, the Bishop of Badajoz, who had come to tell him that, a few hours after his departure, His Lordship had so violent an attack of apoplexy that his life was despaired of. The Dean swore with a good heart—softly, however, and without scandal —at the sickness, the sick man, and the courier who was taking up his time. He got rid of the postillion, telling him to return at once to Badajoz and that he would immediately follow. After that, he resumed his lesson as though there were not in the world either uncles or apoplexies.

Some days after, more news came from Badajoz ; but it was hardly worth while listening to. His uncle, the most reverend bishop, had gone to heaven to receive the reward of his virtues, and the chapter had elected the Dean to fill the vacant see. Don Torribio was present when the deputation arrived, and, as an able man, he profited by the occasion. Taking the new Bishop aside, he said he had a son, Don Benjamin, born with intelligence and good inclinations.

" But, my Lord," he said to his pupil, " my boy has no taste for occult science, and finding he would make a good priest, I let him study at the seminary. He is now one of the best of the clergy in Toledo, and I humbly entreat Your Lordship to resign the deanery of Badajoz to Benjamin, seeing you cannot keep it with the bishopric."

" Alas ! " said the prelate with an embarrassed air, " I shall always do all I can to favour you. But I must tell you I have expectations from a relative, an aged priest, who is only good enough to be a dean. If I do not give him this post, I shall upset all my family, for whom my love amounts to a weakness. But," he added in a more affectionate tone, " will you not come with me to Badajoz ? Will you have the cruelty to abandon me just at the moment when I am beginning to be able to help you ? Trust in me, my dear master, and let us go together, and think only of teaching your pupil. Rest easy about Don Benjamin. As soon as I can, I will do more for him than ever his father asks. A poor deanery in the depths of Estramadura is not a benefice that suits the son of a man like you."

So Don Torribio followed his illustrious pupil to Badajoz. He had splendid rooms in the episcopal palace, and he was respected by the whole diocese as the favourite of the Bishop as a sort of grand vicar.

Under the conduct of so skilful a master, the Bishop of Badajoz made rapid progress in the secret sciences. At first he gave himself up to them with an ardour that seemed excessive ; but little by little he moderated this kind of intemperance and managed it so well that his studies in magic never interfered with his duties as a bishop. He held strongly to a maxim—which is very important for ecclesiastic sorcerers and for philosophers and men of letters— that it is not sufficient for them to frequent witches' dances, and arm their minds with all the most curious things in human knowledge ; they must teach others the path of virtue, and make wholesome doctrines and sound morals flower in the souls of the faithful. It was by conducting his life on this wise principle that the learned bishop filled the whole of Christendom with the fame of his merits. And when he was thinking least about it, he was called to the archbishopric of Compostello.

The people and clergy of Badajoz grieved over an event that robbed them of so worthy a pastor ; and as a last mark of respect the canons of the cathedral asked him to appoint his successor. Don Torribio was not asleep on such a fine occasion for placing his son. He asked for the bishopric from the new Archbishop, and it was with all the graces imaginable that his pupil refused him. He had such veneration for his dear master ! He was so afflicted, so ashamed at having to refuse a thing that seemed quite simple ! But what else could he do ? Don Fernando de Lara, high constable of Castile, demanded this same see for his natural son. He had secret, important, and above all, long-standing obligations to the constable. So it was his duty to prefer an old benefactor to a recent one.

Don Torribio rather liked this equitable way of dealing with the matter. He saw by it that he would have to wait till his turn came, but that it would come surely on the first occasion. The magician was honest enough to believe in the tale about a long-standing obligation, and he rejoiced at being sacrificed to Don Fernando. There was nothing more to think about, except about preparing to depart, and they removed to Compostello. But it was scarcely worth the trouble, seeing how short a time they stayed there. For at the end of a few months, a messenger from the Pope came from Rome with a Cardinal's hat for the Archbishop, and with a letter in which His Holiness invited him to come and help him with his advice in the government of the Christian world. He was further permitted to bestow his mitre on any one he chose.

Don Torribio was not at Compostello when the courier from Rome arrived. He had gone to see his son, who was still the priest of a little parish in Toledo. But he returned quickly, and on his return he was not put to the trouble of asking for the vacant archbishopric.

The Cardinal ran to him with open arms.

"My dear master," he said, "I have two pieces of good news to tell you instead of one. Your pupil is a Cardinal, and your son is soon going to be one, or my position in Rome will be worth nothing. In the meantime, I should like to make him archbishop of Compostello, but wonder at his misfortune, or rather at mine! My mother, whom we have left at Badajoz, has written me a cruel letter that has upset all my plans. She wishes, at all cost, that I should take for my successor the archdeacon of my old church, Don Pablas de Salazar, her confessor and intimate friend. She threatens me she will die with grief if I do not obey her, and I cannot doubt for an instant that she will fail of her word. Put yourself in my place, my dear master! Shall I kill my own mother?"

Don Torribio was not a man to advise parricide. He applauded the nomination of Don Pablas, and did not keep a grudge against the mother of the Cardinal. This mother, if you want to know it, was an old dame, almost imbecile, who lived with her cat and her maid, and scarcely knew the name of her confessor. Was it really she who insisted that the archbishopric should be given to Don Pablas? Was it not rather a Galician lady, a relative of this arch-deacon, a young widow, very pious and very pretty, to whom the prince of the church used to go very assiduously in search of edifica-tion since he came to Compostello?

However this may be, Don Torribio followed His Eminence to Rome. And hardly had he arrived than the Pope died. It is easy to foresee where this event will lead us. The conclave was held, and all the voices of the Holy College were in favour of the Spanish Cardinal. So behold him the Pope! After the ceremonies of exalta-tion, Don Torribio was admitted to a private audience, and he wept with joy at the feet of his dear pupil. He humbly recalled his long and faithful services, and reminded his disciple of his promises—inviolable promises—that had been renewed just before the conclave. He touched on the scarlet hat that His Holiness had cast off on receiving the tiara, but instead of asking this hat for Don Benjamin he ended on a note of such moderation that few person will under-stand it. He protested that he and his son had lost all ambitious hopes, and that they would be well content if it pleased His Holiness to grant them, with his benediction, a little pension that would suffice for the modest needs of an ecclesiastic and a philosopher.

During this little speech, the sovereign pontiff was asking himself what he could do for his teacher. Could he not at length do without him? Did he not know as much magic as was needed by a Pope? Would it even be seemly for him to appear any more at the witches' meetings, with their unbecoming etiquette? All things considered, he judged that Don Torribio was nothing but a useless and even inconvenient man. This point decided, he was no longer troubled to find an answer.

" We have heard with grief," he said, " that under the pretext of occult sciences, you carry on an abominable commerce with the spirits of darkness and falsehood. This is why we exhort you, as a father, to expiate your crime by a penance proportionate to its enormity. We enjoin you to leave the lands of the Church in the space of three days, under pain of being handed over to the secular arm and the rigour of the flames."

Without disconcerting himself, Don Torribio repeated backwards the three mysterious words, which I hope the reader has not forgotten. And approaching the window, he cried :

" Jacintha! Only put one partridge on the spit. The Dean will not stay to supper! "

It was a thunderstroke for the pretended pope. He suddenly recovered from the kind of ecstasy into which the three magic words had thrown him when they were first pronounced. He saw that instead of being in the Vatican, he was still at Toledo in the study of Don Torribio. And he saw by the clock that it was not a complete hour since he had entered the magic room in which such beautiful dreams were woven. In less than an hour he had fancied he had become magician, bishop, archbishop, cardinal, pope ; and he found at the end of the affair he was only a dupe and a knave. All had been illusion, except the proofs he gave of the falseness of his evil heart. He went out without saying a word, found the mule where he had left it, and returned along the road to Badajoz without having learnt anything.

L'ABBÉ DE VOISENON
1708-1773

HE WAS WRONG

AND well! who is there that isn't? In this world we are surrounded by wrongs: they are necessary: they are the foundations of society: they make the mind lissom: they abate our self-love. A man who was always right would be insupportable. A man should be pardoned all his errors except that of being a bore: that alone is irreparable. When we bore our fellow-creatures we must live at home all alone. But I am wandering from my topic.

Let us pass to the story of Mondor. He was a young man with an unfortunate nature. He has a fine intelligence, a tender heart and a sweet soul. These are three great mistakes that are bound to produce many others.

In entering society he set himself chiefly to try to be always in the right. You will see how far that carried him. He struck up an acquaintance with a courtier and his wife: the lady found that Mondor had a fine intelligence, because he had a handsome figure; the husband found that he had but a poor intellect, because he never agreed with any of his opinions.

The lady made many advances for the sake of the fineness of his intelligence: but as he was not in love with her, he did not perceive that she was paying him attentions. The husband begged him to look over a treatise on war which he had written—so at least he claimed. Mondor, after reading the work, said quite frankly that he thought the writer would make a good negotiator for a treaty of peace.

In these circumstances, the command of a regiment fell vacant. A little abortive Marquis found that the writer of the book on war had a transcendent genius, and he treated the wife of the writer as though she were a pretty woman. He obtained the regiment: the Marquis was made Colonel. Mondor was only a true man: he was in the wrong.

This adventure upset him: he lost all idea of making a fortune, and came to Paris to live quietly, and formed a plan for making friends there. Good heavens, how wrong it was of him! He thought he found a friend in the person of the young Alcipe.

Alcipe was amiable, with a decent air and the opinions of a sound man.

One day he came to Mondor with a sorrowful face. Mondor at once felt sorry for him : for there are no persons so foolish as those who have both intelligence and a good heart. Alcipe said that he had lost a hundred pounds. Mondor lent the money to him without a written acknowledgment. He thought by that he had won a friend. He was wrong ; he never saw him again.

He took up with some men of letters. They judged him capable of examining their pieces : it was easier to obtain an audience from him than from the public. There was one man in whom Mondor thought he recognised talent : he seemed worthy of real criticism : he read his work with attention : it was a comedy. He cut out some unnecessary details, showed that it wanted more solidity, asked the author to connect his scenes and make them rise one out of the other, to give the actors always a good situation, to make the dialogue full of character instead of a diamond-paste glitter of cheap epigrams, and to build up his characters and shade them finely instead of making them crudely contrast with each other. Such was the advice he gave, and the author corrected the piece in consequence. He found that Mondor was a bad adviser : the actors said that the piece was not capable of being played.

This disgusted Mondor with giving advice. The same author, whom he had tried to help, wrote another piece which was only a scrap-heap of unshaped and disconnected scenes. Mondor did not dare to advise him not to have it played : he was wrong. The piece was hissed off the stage. This threw him into a perplexity. If he gave advice, he was wrong ; if he did not give it, he was still wrong.

He renounced all commerce with the wits of the town, and mingled with men of learning. He found them almost as dull as persons who tried to be witty. They talked only when they had something to say : they were mostly silent. Mondor lost patience, and seemed to be only a giddy-minded creature. He made the acquaintance of some women of beauty—another mistake. He thought he was in a country nearer to the tropics. It was a land of lightning in which nearly all the fruit was burnt before it was ripe. He remarked that most of these women had only one idea, which they subdivided into little, shining, abstract thoughts. He perceived that all their art consisted in cutting up a little piece of wit. He saw how wrong he had been in seeking their society. He wished to reason about things and appeared awkward : he wished to shine as a wit and appeared heavy. In a word, he displeased, and felt it would not do to say to a young man : " Do you wish to get on with women ? Read the classic authors."

Of all men of the world Mondor was the most reasonable, and

he did not know what was the reasonable side to take. He felt
that a man does wrong less from taking a bad opening than from
taking a good one in a clumsy way. He had tried to be a courtier
and had broken his neck at it : he had tried to make friends and
had been duped in friendship : he had mingled with the wits and
had wearied of them : he had been bored with men of learning, and
he had bored the ladies whose society he sought.

He heard some vaunt the happiness of the man and woman
who truly loved each other. He thought the most sensible thing
to do was to fall in love : he planned to do it : this was precisely
the way of failing to know what love was. He studied all the
women he met : he weighed the graces and the talents of each, in
order to determine to love her who had one perfection more than
the others. He thought that love was a god with whom he could
trade.

In vain did he carry out this review ; in vain did he force himself
to fall in love. It was useless. One day, without thinking about
it, he was seized with a passion for a most ugly and capricious
woman : he congratulated himself on his choice. He saw, however,
that she was not beautiful : he was glad of it : he flattered himself
he would have no rivals. He was wrong. He did not know that
the uglier a woman is the more she flirts.

None of her mincing manners, none of her glances, none of her
little speeches but has its intention. She takes as much trouble
to make the most of her face as a farmer does to get a crop off a
poor soil. It succeeds with her ; the advances she makes flatter
the pride of the other sex, and the vanity of a man almost always
effaces the ugliness of a woman.

This Mondor learned by sad experience. He found himself
surrounded by competitors. He was disquietened by it : he was
wrong ; it led him into a much greater mistake, which was to
marry. He treated his wife with all possible consideration ; he
was wrong. She took his sweetness of character for weakness, and
harshly lorded it over him. He tried to quarrel ; he was wrong ;
it led him into the further mistake of a reconciliation. During the
reconciliations, he had two children—that is to say two mistakes.
He became a widower ; here he was in the right ; but he made
an error out of it, for he was so afflicted that he retired to his
country estates.

In the country he found a rich man who lived in arrogant
fashion ; he visited none of his neighbours ; Mondor thought he
was wrong. He showed as much affability as the other did
arrogance ; this was a great mistake. His house became the
haunt of small gentry who overwhelmed him without respite. He
envied the lot of his neighbour ; he saw too late that the misfortune
of being beset with folk is far more disagreeable than the mistake

of being feared. A suit was brought against him in regard to some rights of land. He preferred to give way to this unjust attack than to plead his case. He bore himself like a good fellow, gave a dinner to the other party and made a disadvantageous compromise ; he was wrong. Such a good way of making money attracted the attention of the parish. All his little neighbours tried to profit by his easy ways, and laid claim without any title to some imaginary right over his estate. He had to fight twenty law actions to avoid one.

That disgusted him ; he sold his lands ; he was wrong. He did not know what to do with his capital ; he was advised to finance a concert hall in a neighbouring large town. The director was a fine fellow who had become a lawyer in order to learn to be a connoisseur of music. The musical affair went into bankruptcy at the end of a year, in spite of the charming manners of the lawyer. This event ruined Mondor. He left the nothingness of all things here below ; he wished to become nothingness himself ; he became a monk and died of boredom ; that was his last error.

DENIS DIDEROT
1713–1784

THE TWO FRIENDS OF BOURBONNE

THERE were two men here, who might have been called the Orestes and Pylades of Bourbonne. One was named Olivier and the other Felix ; they were born the same day, in the same house, and from two sisters. The same milk fed them, for one of the sisters died in child-bed, and the other looked after both infants. They were brought up together, and they always separated from other boys. They loved each other as a man exists, as a man sees, without thinking about it. They felt it at every moment, but they never spoke about it. Once Olivier saved the life of Felix, who prided himself on being a great swimmer, and was almost drowned : neither of them remembered the incident. Many times Felix got Olivier out of some sorry scrape into which his impetuous character had carried him. Olivier never thought of thanking him ; they returned home without talking, or, on the way, they chatted about something else.

When they drew lots for the militia, the first fatal ticket was drawn by Felix, and Olivier said, " The other is for me ! " They served their time together, and came back to their village, dearer to each other than they had been before. This doesn't often happen in similar cases. For if reciprocal benefits cement a friendship based on intelligence, on the other hand they often add nothing to what I might call domestic and physical friendships. In one of the battles of our army, Olivier was in danger of having his head split open by a sabre stroke ; mechanically Felix sprang in front of him and received the stroke, and came back with his face marked with a large red scar. Some pretend that he was proud of this scar, but I do not believe it. At Hastembeck, Olivier brought Felix from a heap of dead on the battle-field, where he had fallen.

When they were questioned, the two friends sometimes spoke of the help each had received from the other, and never of that which they had given. And they never praised each other. Some time after their return from the wars, they fell in love, and, as chance

92

led, they both loved the same girl. There was no rivalry between them. The first to see the passion of his friend retired from the wooing : this was Felix. Olivier married, and his friend, disgusted with life without knowing why threw himself into some dangerous trades. His last exploit was to become a smuggler.

You are not unaware that there are in France four tribunals at which smugglers are judged—Caen, Reims, Valence, and Toulouse—and that the most severe of the four is that of Reims presided over by Coleau, the most ferocious soul that nature has yet formed. Felix was caught with arms in his hand, and led before the terrible Coleau, and condemned to death, like five hundred other men who had preceded him. It was at night when Olivier learnt the fate of Felix. He rose up from the side of his wife, and without saying anything to her, went to Reims. He came before Judge Coleau, fell at his feet, and begged to be allowed to see and embrace his friend. Coleau looked at him in silence, and signed him to sit down. Olivier sat down. At the end of half an hour Coleau looked at his watch and said to Olivier :

" If you wish to see your friend while he is alive, you must make haste. He is on the way, and, if my watch is right, he will be hanged in less than ten minutes."

Transported with fury, Olivier leapt up, and with his cudgel caught Judge Coleau such a heavy blow on the neck that he stretched him out almost dead. Then running to the place of execution, shrieking, he struck down the executioner, attacked the police, and the populace, long indignant at these executions, broke out in riot. Felix was rescued by the mob, and got away. Olivier thought of following him, but a trooper of the horse police caught him on the flank with a lance. Olivier dragged himself as far as the gate of the town, but could not get any farther. Then some kindly waggoners lifted him on their cart and left him at the door of his house. The moment after he died.

" Wife, come and let me kiss you," he had just time to say. " I am done for, but Felix is saved ! "

Felix is still living. Escaping from the hands of justice, he threw himself into the forests of the province, the ways and by-ways of which he had learnt as a smuggler. Little by little he drew near to the house of Olivier, of whose death he was unaware.

In the depths of the wood was a charcoal-burner's hut that served as shelter to the smugglers. It was one of the places where they kept their goods and their arms. Here Felix came, not without running the risk of falling into an ambush, for the mounted police were following his trail. Some of his mates had brought news of his sentence at Reims, and the charcoal-burner and his woman thought Felix was a dead man when he appeared before them.

I will tell you the thing as it was told me from the charcoal-burner's wife, who died here a little while ago.

The children, wandering round the hut, were the first to see him. While he stopped to caress the youngest, who was his godchild, the others ran into the hut crying, " Felix! Felix! " The father and mother came out with joyful shouts ; but the wretched fugitive was so worn with fatigue and hunger that he had not the strength to reply, and he fell almost swooning in their arms. The good people helped him all they could, and gave him bread and wine and some vegetables, and he ate and fell asleep.

" Olivier! Children do you know anything of Olivier ? " were his first words when he awoke.

" No ! " they answered him.

He told the story of his adventure at Reims, and passed the night and the following day in the hut. He sighed and called on Olivier, and thinking he was in prison at Reims, he wished to go there and die with him. It was not without much trouble that the charcoal-burner induced him to give up this plan.

In the middle of the second night, he took a gun, put a sabre under his arm, and called in a low voice to the charcoal-burner :

" Friend ! Take your axe and come with me."

" Where ? "

" What a question ! To Olivier's house."

They set out together, but, just as they left the forest, they were surrounded by a detachment of mounted police. I can only go by what the wife of the charcoal-burner told me. But it is unheard of that two men on foot should have been able to make a stand against a score of men on horseback. Apparently the police were scattered out, and they wished to take their man alive. However this may be, the fight was very fierce. There were five horses lamed and seven horsemen brought down with the axe or sabre. The poor charcoal-burner fell dead on the spot, with a bullet through his temple. Felix regained the forest, and as he is a man of incredible agility, he ran from one tree trunk to the other, and while running he charged his gun, fired, and gave a whistle. The continual whistles and gun-shots from different places at different intervals made the horsemen think that they had to do with a horde of smugglers, and, fearing an ambush, they quickly retreated.

Felix returned to the field of battle, and took the body of the charcoal-burner on his shoulder and carried him along the path to the hut, where the man's wife and children were still sleeping. He stopped at the door, he laid the corpse at his feet, and sat with his back against the tree and his face turned to the entrance to the hut. Such was the spectacle that awaited the charcoal-burner's wife when she came from the hovel. She awoke, and

did not find her husband by her side. She looked around for
Felix. He was not there. She arose, she came out, and, at the
sight awaiting her, she fell to the ground. The children ran out
and cried at what they saw. They threw themselves on their
father, they threw themselves on their mother. The poor woman,
recalled to her senses by the cries and movements of her children,
tore at her hair and dug her nails into her cheeks. Felix, motionless at the foot of the tree, his eyes closed, his head thrown back,
said, in a broken voice:

"Kill me!" There was a moment's silence, and then the cries
and the moans went on; again Felix said:

"Kill me, children, out of pity kill me!"

Thus three days and three nights passed in grief. On the
fourth day Felix said to the woman:

"Take your wallet and put some bread in it and follow me."

After a long circuit over our mountains and through our forests
they came to Olivier's cottage, which lies, as you know, at the
end of the village, at the spot where the road divides into two
routes, one leading to Franche Comté and the other to Lorraine.
It was there that Felix found himself between the widows of two
men massacred for his sake.

"Where is Olivier?" he brusquely said to his friend's wife.
From the silence of the woman, her mourning clothes, and her
tears he understood that Olivier was dead. He felt sick, and he
fell and struck his head against a trough in which bread was
kneaded. The two widows raised him up: his blood ran over
them, and while they were staunching the wound with their aprons,
he said to them:

"You are their wives, and yet you help me!"

Then he swooned again, and when he recovered he said:

"Why did he not leave me? Why did he come to Reims?
Why didn't he let the thing go on?"

Then he lost his head and madness came upon him, and he rolled
about the floor and tore his clothes. Drawing his sabre, he tried
to kill himself, but the two women sprang upon him, crying for
help. Neighbours rushed in and tied him up with ropes, and he
was bled seven or eight times. His fury fell with the weakening
of his strength, and he remained like a dead man for three or four
days, and then recovered his reason. In his first movement he
looked around him like a man awaking from a deep sleep.

"Where am I?" he said. "Who are you, you women?"

"I am the charcoal-burner's wife," said one.

"Ah, yes," he said, "I know you. But who is that other
woman?"

Olivier's wife remained silent. Felix began to weep: he turned
his face to the wall.

" I am in Olivier's house . . . this is Olivier's bed . . . this woman, there . . . she was his wife ! Oh, my God ! "

But the women took such good care of him, they inspired him with so much pity, they prayed him so continually to live, they showed him in so touching a manner that he was their only resource, that he let himself be persuaded.

All the time he remained in this house he did not go to bed. He went out at night, wandering about the fields, rolling on the earth and calling out, " Olivier." One of the women always followed him and brought him back at daybreak.

There were several persons who knew that he was in Olivier's cottage, and among these persons were some who intended to betray him. The two widows warned him of the peril he was running. It was one afternoon ; he was sitting on a bench, his sabre across his knee, his elbows on the table, and his two hands over his eyes. At first he said nothing. Olivier's widow had a boy of sixteen to eighteen years, the charcoal-burner's wife a girl of fifteen.

" Go and look for your girl," he said to the charcoal-burner's widow, " and bring her here."

While she was away in the forest fetching her daughter, he sold some fields that he owned. The charcoal-burner's wife came back with her daughter, and the son of Olivier married the girl. Felix gave them the money he had got by his sale, and embraced them, and, weeping, asked them to forgive him. They went to live in a hut, where they still reside, and where they are now father and mother of children. The two widows lived together, and the children of Olivier had a father and two mothers. It is scarcely more than a year and a half since the charcoal-burner's wife died. Olivier's wife is still living.

One evening the two women were watching Felix—for there was always one of them who kept him in view—and they saw him burst into tears. He waved his arms in silence at the gate that separated him from them, and then began to pack his knapsack. The women said nothing to him, for they understood how urgent it was that he should depart. They supped together all three, without speaking. In the night Felix rose up ; the women could not sleep. He went towards the door on tiptoe. There he stopped, looked at the bed where the two women lay, wiped his eyes with his hands, and went out. The two women clasped their arms about each other, and spent the rest of the night in tears. No one knew where Felix had hidden, yet few weeks passed without him sending the widows some money. He has now gone to Prussia, where he serves in a regiment of the guards. It is said he is liked by his comrades, and that even the King has taken notice of him. Olivier's widow tells me he still sends her remittances.

THE
PLASTER OF DESGLANDS

DENIS DIDEROT

CLOSE to the house of Monsieur Desglands was a charming widow, who had several qualities similar to those of Ninon de Lenclos. Staid by intelligence, wanton by temperament, grieving in the morning for the folly of the night, she spent all her life in going from pleasure to remorse and from remorse to pleasure, without the habit of pleasure stifling her remorse, without the habit of remorse lessening her taste for pleasure. I got to know her in her last days, when she said she was finally escaping from her two great enemies. She never accepted the homage of a fool or a knave : her favours were always given to talent and worthiness. To say of a man that he had been one of her favourites was to say that he was a man of merit. As she knew her fickleness, she never promised to be faithful to anybody.

" I only gave one false pledge in my life," she said. " It was when I married."

If a man lost his feelings for her, or if she lost her passion for him, he still remained her friend. Never has there been a more striking example of the difference between probity and morals. You could not say she had any morals, and yet you were bound to admit it was difficult to find a more honest creature. The parish priest seldom saw her in church : but he always found her purse open to the poor. She said jestingly that law and religion were a pair of crutches that must not be taken away from those who had feeble legs. Women, who were afraid for her to meet their husbands, liked to see her among their children.

One day Desglands invited the lovely widow to dinner with some gentlemen of the country round about. The reign of Desglands was drawing to an end, and among his guests there was a man towards whom the fickle heart of the widow began to lean. They were at table, Desglands and his rival sitting side by side, opposite the lady. Desglands employed all the wit he had to enliven the conversation : he made the most gallant advances to the widow : but she was distracted and heard nothing, sitting with her eyes fixed on his rival. Desglands was holding an egg in his hand : a convulsive movement of jealousy took him : he clenched his hand and the lightly-boiled egg splattered on the face of his neighbour, who raised his hand to strike back. Desglands gripped him by the wrist and whispered :

" Sir, I will take it as received."

There was a deep silence : the fair widow felt unwell. The meal was gloomy and short. On leaving the table, she had Desglands and his rival taken alone into another room. All that a woman could do to reconcile them she did. She pleaded, she wept, she fainted : she shook the hands of Desglands, she turned her eyes flooded with tears to the other man.

" And you love me ! " she said to one. " And you have loved me ! " she said to the other. " And yet you both wish to ruin me ! You want to make me a byword, the object of scorn and dislike to the whole province ! No matter which of you two takes the life of the other, I will never see him again. He cannot be my friend. My hate for him will finish only with my life."

Then she swooned again, and in swooning she said :

" You cruel men ! draw your swords and plunge them in my breast. If, while dying, I could see you embrace each other, I should die without regret ! "

Desglands and his rival did not stir, but their eyes were wet with tears. However, it was necessary to separate. The fair widow went home more dead than alive.

Next day Desglands paid a visit to his fickle charmer : he met his rival in her house. Who was most astonished ? It was the rival and the widow at seeing that Desglands had his right cheek covered by a great round patch of black taffeta.

" What is it ? " said the widow.

" It is nothing," said Desglands.

" A slight inflammation ? " said his rival.

" It will go away in time," said Desglands.

After a little conversation, Desglands left, and in leaving he made a sign to his rival which was well understood. For he too left, and they strolled away in opposite directions, and made a round, and met behind the gardens of the fair widow. There they fought their duel, and the rival of Desglands was left on the grass, seriously, but not mortally wounded. While he was being carried home, Desglands returned to the widow's house. He sat down and they talked again about the affair at the dinner.

" And what is the meaning," she asked, " of this enormous and ridiculous plaster that covers your cheek ? "

Desglands rose and looked at himself in the mirror.

" As a matter of fact," he said to himself, " I do find it now a little too large."

Taking the lady's scissors, he detached the taffeta from his cheek and cut off an inch or two, and replaced the black plaster.

" How does it look now ? " he said.

" An inch or two less ridiculous than before."

" It is always something," said Desglands.

His rival got better. There was a second duel, in which Desglands again won. So it went on for half a dozen duels. And after each combat, Desglands cut a little edge off the large, strange, black beauty-spot he wore on his cheek. The end of this adventure was the end of the fair widow. The trouble of it ruined her health that had always been somewhat weak and tottering.

And Desglands ?

One day, as we were walking together, he received a letter, and opened it and said :

" He was a very worthy man, but his death is hardly an affliction for me."

And at once he pulled off his cheek the rest of his black plaster that had been almost reduced, by frequent cuttings, to the size of an ordinary beauty-spot.

FRIAR CÔME AND THE CORPSE

Denis Diderot

Here is an amusing little comedy that happened just outside my door. The scene of it is the hospital La Charité. Friar Côme, the famous surgeon of the Feuillants Order, had need of a corpse to make some experiments in cutting. He went to the Father attendant of the hospital :

" You have just come in time," said the attendant. " There you have, No. 46, a tall young fellow, who has no more than two hours of life left."

" Two hours ? " said Friar Côme. " That is not quite what I want. It is a bit too quick for me. I have to go to-night to Fontaine-bleau, and I shall not get back till to-morrow evening at seven at the earliest.

" Very well ! That does not matter," said the attendant to him. " You can go, and I will do all I can to keep him going for you."

Friar Côme went away, and the Father attendant called on the apothecary and ordered a good cordial for No. 46. The cordial worked wonderfully. The sick man slept for six hours. In the morning the attendant went to his bed and found him sitting up, coughing freely : hardly any fever, no more oppression, and not the least pain under the ribs.

" Ah ! Father," said the patient to him, " I do not know what you have given me, but you have put life in me again ! "

" Is that so ? "

" It is truth itself. Another dose like that and I am quit of my trouble."

" Yes. But what will Friar Côme say about it ? "

" What were you saying of Friar Côme ? "

" Nothing, nothing," answered the Father attendant, rubbing his chin with his hand, and looking somewhat disconcerted and disappointed.

" Father," said the sick man to him, " you look sulky. Are you angry because I've got better ? "

" No, no ! it is not that."

Yet from hour to hour, the attendant went to the bed of the sick man, and said to him :

" Well, my friend ! How are you getting on ? "

" Wonderfully well, Father."

" If this goes on," said the attendant, as he went back to his room, " I shall have done more than kept you going for Friar Côme."

And this was in fact what happened. In the evening Friar Côme came to make his experiments.

" Well," he said to the Father attendant, " where is my corpse ? "

" Your corpse ! There is not any ! "

" There is not any ! How's that ? "

" It is all your fault. Our man asked for nothing better than to die ; you are the cause that he has changed his mind. And now as a punishment you will have to wait. Why the mischief did you want to go to Fontainebleau ? If you had stayed here, I should never have thought of giving him the cordial that has cured him, and your experiment would have been carried out."

" Never mind," said Friar Côme. " It's no great misfortune. We must wait for another case."

CHARLES NODIER
1780–1844

THE LEGEND OF SISTER BEATRICE

NOT far from the high summit of the Jura Mountains, and a little way down on its western slope, you can still see the ruins of the Convent of Our Lady of the Flowering Thorns. It lies at the end of a deep and narrow gorge that is sheltered to the north, and there every year the rarest flowers of the country are found. Half a league away, at the opposite end of the gorge, are the remains of an ancient manor house. Little is known about it, except that the last of the knights that took their name from the manor died in the conquest of the Tomb of Christ in the Holy Land without leaving an heir. His mourning widow did not desert the wild beautiful spot where the happiest days of her life had passed, but devoted herself to good works, and the fame of her piety and her benefactions is still remembered by the peasants. Having forgotten her name, they call her still the Holy Woman.

On one of those days when winter, drawing to an end, suddenly relaxes its harshness under the soft influences of a sky of springtime, the Holy Woman was walking at the end of the gorge, and to her surprise she found one of the hawthorn bushes covered with blossom. She at first thought it was the whiteness of fallen snow, and she was full of wondering delight on seeing it was really an innumerable multitude of beautiful little white stars with scarlet rays that crowned the bush with splendour. She took one of the sprays of flowering thorn and carried it home joyfully, and placed it in her oratory before an image of the Virgin Mary. And she felt so strange a joy in her soul, after making this simple offering to the Mother of God, that she resolved to go every day to the flowering bush and bring a new garland for the altar.

One evening, however, her care of the poor and the sick detained her much longer than usual. In vain she hastened to her wild garden : the night fell before she arrived. She was beginning to grow afraid of the darkness and the solitude, when a calm pure brightness, like that which falls from the sky at dawn, showed her all the flowering thorns, gleaming just ahead of her. She stopped for a moment, thinking that the light came from the camp fire of some wandering robbers. But rather than return without her garland for Our Lady, she collected her courage and stole on tiptoe toward the bush of white flowers, and with trembling hand took a branch, and returned down the road to the manor house without daring to look behind her.

All the night she thought on the strange light without finding any explanation of it. The following evening she went in the darkness to the hawthorns, accompanied by her old servant and her chaplain. The soft clear radiance still shone from the bushes ; and as they approached it seemed to become brighter and deeper. They fell on their knees. For it appeared to them there was something miraculous in the strange lovely radiance. Then the good priest arose, and singing a hymn, walked to the flowering thorns and, moving them aside, saw something that struck him with such wonder that he was overwhelmed with joy and gratitude. Amid the bushes was an image of the Virgin Mary, carved with artless simplicity from a piece of wood, and crudely coloured and clad in rough garments. From this image came the miraculous radiance that lighted up the hawthorns. Reciting the litany, he took the statue in his hands, and, followed by the lady and her servant, carried it to the oratory in the manor house. But in the morning the statue was not to be seen on the altar where it had been placed. Everybody wondered what had happened. All day long the lady of the manor grieved over the loss of the miraculous image. In the evening she went with all her people to the flowering thorns, and there, in the darkness, the radiant statue was again seen. The Mother of God had returned to her wild green dwelling-place, fragrant with the sweetness of her favourite flowers.

" Queen of the Angels ! " said the lady of the manor, " we can all see now that this is your chosen home, and here shall your church be built ! "

And soon afterwards a beautiful glorious temple was built around the sacred image. Kings came with an offering of a tabernacle of pure gold, and great lords enriched the church with their gifts. The fame of the miracles of Our Lady of the Flowering Thorns spread throughout Christendom, and from many lands a multitude of pious women gathered in the valley and formed themselves into a religious order. The Holy Woman was made Superior of the Convent, and after a long life of good works and sacrifices, she died in the service of Our Lady.

For two centuries after the death of the Holy Woman some young maiden of her race ever acted as sister custodian of the sacred tabernacle. She kept watch over it, and she alone was allowed to open the tabernacle on the solemn festivals when the miraculous image was displayed to the pilgrims. It was her duty to dust it every day and gather the offerings of flowers, chief among which was the flowering thorn, and weave them into a garland for the sacred statue.

At fifteen years of age, Beatrice was appointed by her family to enter the convent and become the sister custodian. As pure as her flowers was the lovely maid when she took her vows and entered on her gracious duties.

But there is an age, happy or unhappy, when the heart of a young girl understands that it is created to love, and Beatrice reached it. This need of her being, at first vague and restless, only made her duties dearer to her. Incapable then of explaining the secret movements that agitated her, she took them for the instinct of a religious fervour that accuses itself of not being sufficiently ardent, and believes itself wanting in sincerity unless it carries its love to enthusiasm and frenzy. The unknown object of her transports escaped from her recognition ; and among those that fell under the torrent emotions of her ingenuous soul, the Virgin Mary alone seemed to her worthy of that passionate adoration to which her life could scarcely suffice. The worship of the Divine Mother became the unique occupation of her thoughts, the only charm of her solitude ; it filled her with dreams of mysterious languors and ineffable transports. She was often seen lying before the tabernacle, praying and sobbing and wetting the altar-steps with her tears. The Queen of Heaven smiled, no doubt, from the height of her eternal throne, at this happy and tender mistake of innocence ; for the Holy Virgin loved Beatrice, and was pleased to be loved by her. And perhaps she had read in the heart of Beatrice that she would always be loved by her.

But an event happened about this time that lifted the veil under which the secret of Beatrice had long been concealed from herself. A young lord of the neighbourhood was attacked by robbers, and found almost dead in the forest. Indeed he scarcely showed any signs of life when the servants of the convent carried him into their infirmary. As the daughters of noble ladies were then always instructed from early childhood in the art of dressing wounds, Beatrice was sent by the other nuns to the help of the dying man. She used all the knowledge she had learnt of healing wounded men, but she relied more upon her prayers to Our Lady of the Flowering Thorns. Her long weary vigils by the bedside of the young lord, and the prayers she offered for him, effected all that she had hoped for. Raymond opened his eyes and recognised her.

" Ah," he cried, " Beatrice ! Is it you that I see again ? You that I loved from my boyhood ! You that the forgotten agreement between my father and yours once allowed me to hope I should wed ! By what unhappy hazard do I see you again, chained to a life that is not suited to you, and separated for ever from the brilliant world

that you adorned ? Ah, if it were you yourself that chose this life of
solitude and abnegation, it was because you did not know your own
heart when you did it ! Beatrice, I swear to you, the vows you took
in your ignorance are nothing either before God or before men !
Heaven has brought us together again to unite us in love for ever-
more ! Beatrice, it is your lover who implores you and who will guide
you. You will become the wife of your Raymond as well as his
sweetheart. Do not turn away with your eyes full of tears. Do not
take your hands away that tremble in mine. No ! you will come with
me, and you will never leave me ! ''

Beatrice did not answer. Escaping from the enfeebled arms of
the wounded knight, she staggered—bewildered, troubled, and
panting—into the chapel, and fell at the feet of the Virgin, her
consolation and her support. There she wept as she had done before :
but it was no longer from a feeling unrecognised and without aim.
Her passion was now more powerful than her piety, more powerful
than her sense of shame, more powerful, alas ! than the Holy Virgin
to whom she called in vain for help. Her tears this time were bitter
and burning. The other nuns saw her lying for days outstretched
and suppliant, but they were not astonished. For everybody in
the convent knew her passionate devotion for Our Lady of the
Flowering Thorns. Beatrice passed the rest of her time in the
infirmary with the wounded knight, though he was now so far
recovered that he scarcely needed her attention.

One evening, when the church was closed and all the sisters were
retired in their cells, Beatrice came slowly into the choir and placed
her lamp on the altar. With trembling hand she opened the door of
the tabernacle, turning away as she did so, shivering and lowering
her eyes, as though she feared the Queen of Heaven would strike her
down with a glance. Then she threw herself on her knees and tried
to pray, but the words died on her lips, or lost themselves in sobs.
She enveloped her face in her veil and tried to calm herself, and in
a last effort she broke out in wild confused words, without knowing
if she were offering a prayer or a blasphemy.

" O, Heavenly Helper of my youth ! " she cried. " O, you that
I have loved alone so long, O Mary, Divine Mary ! why have you
abandoned me ? Why have you let your Beatrice fall a prey to the
horrible passions of hell ? You know how I have fought against
them, how I have struggled ! But now it is done with for ever.
I can serve you no longer, for I am no longer worthy of my office.
Far away from you must I go to hide my sin. Yet suffer me, O
Mary, to worship you still ! Take pity on my tears. My senses
have now betrayed me, but my soul at least still struggles against
my passions. Receive the last of my prayers, and if my ancient
service is worthy of any reward, send down death to the unfortunate
woman at your altar before she can leave you."

Beatrice rose and approached with trembling body the miraculous image. She adorned it with new flowers, and taking those that were faded, she pressed them on her heart, and placed them in the blessed receptacle of her scapulary, so that she should never be separated from them. Then with a last glance at the tabernacle, she cried with terror and fled.

In the night, a horse-litter carried the handsome knight far from the convent, and a young nun, unfaithful to her vows, accompanied him. The first year passed in an intoxication of fulfilled passion. The world to Beatrice was a new spectacle, inexhaustible in delights. Love multiplied around her all the means of seduction that could perpetuate her error and achieve her ruin. She came out of dreams of pleasure only to awake amid the joy of feasts, the music of minstrels, and the play of the dancers. Her life was a wild festival in which the voice of her conscience vainly tried to make itself heard amid the clamours of the orgy. Still she had not quite forgotten Mary. More than once, in the preparation of her toilet, her scapulary had opened under her fingers. More than once she had let a glance and a tear fall on the withered flowers of the Virgin. Prayers had risen to her lips like a hidden flame beneath the ashes, but they had been extinguished under the kisses of her lover. Yet in her wildest moments something told her that a prayer might have saved her.

It was not long before she learnt that there is no lasting love except that which is refined by religion : that the love of our Lord and of Mary alone escapes from the changes of our feelings, and grows and strengthens as time goes on, while other loves quickly burn themselves away in the ashes of our heart. Yet Beatrice loved Raymond still, but a day came when she saw that Raymond loved her no longer. On this day she foresaw the more horrible day when she would be utterly abandoned by him for whom she had abandoned the altar, and this dreaded day arrived. Beatrice found herself with no support on earth, and, alas ! with no support in heaven. In vain she sought for solace in her memories and for comfort in her hopes. The flowers of the scapulary were as withered as those of her pleasures. The source of tears and prayers was dried up. The fate that Beatrice had made for herself was accomplished. The unfortunate woman accepted her ignominy. The higher one falls from the path of virtue the more terrible is the descent, and it was from a far height that Beatrice had fallen. She was at first frightened by her infamy, but she ended by taking it as a matter of course, because the spring of her soul was broken.

Fifteen years thus passed, and oh, what pleasures these fugitive years carried away with them !—innocence, modesty, youth and beauty and love, the roses of life that flower but once. And she could not keep that which would have repaid her for all other losses—

her conscience. The jewels with which she had been adorned were a resource that was soon exhausted. She remained alone, derelict, an object of scorn to others as well as to herself, an example of shame and misery that mothers pointed out to their children to turn them from sin. She grew tired of living on pity, of receiving alms that even pious persons were often loath to give her, of being helped secretly by women who blushed at giving her a little bread. One day, wrapping herself in her rags, she determined to seek for food and shelter in some place where she was not known. She hoped to hide her infamy in her misery, and went away with nothing but the flowers she had once taken from the altar, and that now fell, one by one, in the dust beneath her dried lips.

Beatrice was still young, but shame and hunger made her look prematurely old. When her pale silent figure timidly implored help from passers-by, when her white and delicate hand was stretched out trembling to take their alms, there was no one who did not feel that she should have had another destiny on earth. The most indifferent persons stopped and looked at her with a glance that seemed to say, " Oh ! my daughter, how is it that you have fallen so low ? " But Beatrice never answered them : for she had long since lost the power to weep. She walked on and on ; her journey looked as though it would end only in death.

One day in particular she followed from dawn a hard and stony mountain-path, where there were no houses at which she could beg. She had for food only some roots torn from the clefts of the rocks. Her worn-out shoes tumbled from her bleeding feet. As, at night-fall, she felt that she would swoon from weariness and want of nourishment, she saw suddenly a long line of lights of a great building ahead of her. Collecting her remaining strength, she pushed forward. But at the silvery chime of a bell, that stirred in her heart a strange vague memory, all the lights went out, and around her were only night and silence. She still made a few more steps with outstretched arms, and her trembling hands struck against the closed door. There she leaned for a moment to take breath. She tried to hold on to the door so as not to fall. But her feeble fingers would not bear her ; they slipped under the weight of her body.

" Oh, Holy Virgin ! " she cried, " why did I leave you ! "

And she swooned on the doorstep. Such a night as this is an expiation for a whole life of disorders. The keen fresh air of dawn had scarcely begun to revive in her a confused and painful sense of life, when she saw that she was not alone. A woman knelt by her side, and raised her head carefully, and stared at her in an attitude of anxiety, waiting until she fully recovered her senses.

" Praise God for sending us so early such a case of misfortune and misery ! " said the good nun. " It is a happy augury to the glorious feast that we celebrate to-day. But how is it, my dear child, that you did not pull the bell ? The sisters would have welcomed you at any hour. Well, well ! do not try to talk now, poor lost lamb ! Drink this broth that I hastily heated as soon as I saw you. Taste this wine that will warm your body and remove the soreness from your limbs. Drink it all ; and now give me your cold little hands and let me warm them. Can you feel my breath on your fingers ? Oh, you will be well again soon ! "

Beatrice, touched with emotion, took the hands of the good nun and pressed them to her lips.

" I feel better already," she said to her, " and I am sure I am strong enough to go and thank God for his mercy in leading me to this holy house. But tell me first where I am ? "

" Where else could you be," said the nun, " if not at Our Lady of the Flowering Thorns. There is no other convent in these mountains less than five leagues away."

" Our Lady of the Flowering Thorns ! " cried Beatrice, with a look of joy, that at once gave way to signs of deep dismay. " Our Lady of the Thorns ! God have pity on me ! "

" What, my daughter ! do you not know our convent ? " said the nun. " You seem to come from a far country. I have never seen a woman wearing clothes like yours. But Our Lady of the Flowering Thorns does not limit her protection to the people of this land. If ever you have heard of her, you must know that she is good to all the world."

" I know her and I have served her," answered Beatrice. " But I come from a distant country, as you say, my Mother, and it is not astonishing that I did not at once recognise this home of peace and benediction. But there is the church, and there the convent and the hawthorns where I gathered so many flowers. Alas ! they are still blossoming. But I was so young when I saw them last. It was in the days," she continued, lifting her face to heaven with that resolute expression of self-sacrifice which comes of Christian remorse, " it was in the days when Sister Beatrice was the custodian of the holy chapel. Do you remember her, Mother ? "

" How could I forget her, my child, since Sister Beatrice has never ceased to be custodian of the tabernacle. She still lives among us to-day, and she will, I hope, remain for many years to come an example to all the community. After the protection of the Holy Virgin, we do not know a greater help to a holy life than she is."

" I was not speaking of her," said Beatrice, with a sad sigh. " I was speaking of the other Beatrice who occupied the same place sixteen years ago, and ended her life in sin."

" God will not punish you for your mad words," said the nun, drawing the beggar woman to her bosom. " Illness and distress have deranged your mind, and your memory is impaired. I have dwelt in this convent for more than sixteen years, and I have never known another custodian of the holy tabernacle than Sister Beatrice. And since you have decided to pray in the church while I prepare your bed, go, my daughter, to the altar. There you will see Beatrice. You will easily recognise her, for by Divine favour she has not lost in growing old a single grace of her youth. I will come for you very soon, and then I will not leave you until you are quite well and sound."

The nun went away into the cloisters. Tottering forward, Beatrice gained the church stairs, and knelt on the floor, and beat her head upon the stones. Then, growing bolder, she rose and stumbled from pillar to pillar, advancing as far as the rood screen, and there she again fell on her knees. Through the mist that covered her eyes, she had seen the sister custodian standing before the tabernacle.

Little by little the sister approached her, while making her usual round of holy duties, filling and trimming the dying lamps, and replacing the old garland of flowers by new blossoms. Beatrice could not believe her eyes. This sister was herself, not the woman that age and sin and despair had made her, but the girl that she had been in the innocent days of her youth. Was it an illusion produced by remorse ? Was it a miraculous punishment, anticipating those reserved for her by the anger of God ? In doubt she hid her head in her hand, and rested motionless against the bars of the screen, stammering the most tender of her ancient prayers. And yet the sister custodian continued to walk forward. Already the folds of her dress were brushing against the screen. Beatrice was so overpowered she dared not breathe.

"It is thee, dear Beatrice," said the sister, in a voice whose sweetness no human words can express. " I have no need to see thee to recognise thee, for thy prayers come to me now just as I used to hear them of old. Long have I waited for thee ; but, as I was sure of thy return, I took thy place on the day thou didst leave me, so that no one should perceive thy absence. Thou knowest now the worth of the pleasures and joys that seduced thee and thou wilt not leave again. What has happened will be known only to thee and me. Return then with confidence to the position thou hast among my daughters. Thou wilt find in thy cell, the way to which thou hast not forgotten, the habit thou didst leave there, and with it thou wilt clothe thyself again in thy early innocence, of which it is the emblem. This rare grace I owe to thy love, and I have obtained it on thy repentance. Farewell, sister custodian of Mary ! Love Mary as she has loved thee."

When Beatrice looked at her with eyes flooded with tears, when she stretched towards her her trembling arms in an act of gratitude broken by sobs, she saw the Holy Virgin mount the altar stairs, open the door of the tabernacle, and seat herself in heavenly glory, under her halo of gold and under her garland of flowering thorn.

Not without emotion did Beatrice come down from the choir. She visited her companions whose faith she had betrayed, and who, exempt from reproach, had grown old in the practice of an austere duty. She glided among her sisters, with bowed face, ready to humiliate herself at the first cry raised against her. In deep agitation of heart, she listened to their voices and heard nothing. As none of them had observed her departure, none of them remarked her return. She threw herself at the feet of the Holy Virgin, and it seemed to her that she was greeted with a smile. In the dreams of her life of illusions she had known nothing approaching such happiness as now was hers.

The Divine Festival of Mary—I think I have said that this happened on the Feast of the Assumption—was accomplished with a solemn calmness and intense ecstasy such as the community had never known before. Some saw miraculous lights playing around the tabernacle, others heard the songs of angels mingling in their chants, and stopped singing themselves to listen to the heavenly harmony. It seemed to the nuns that there was a great festival in heaven as well as in the Convent of Our Lady of the Flowering Thorns ; and by an event strange to the season of the year, all the hawthorns on the mountains burst again into blossom in the middle of August, so that, without as well as within, it was spring-time and fragrance. A soul had returned to the bosom of God, stripped of all the infirmities and all the ignominies of our condition, and there was great rejoicing in heaven.

Just for a moment the innocent joy of the nuns was obscured by one disquietude. A poor beggar woman, sick and weak and hungry, had been found at dawn at the door of the convent. The nun who saw her had tended her a little, and had then gone to prepare for her a warm soft bed, but when the bed was ready the woman could not be found. The unhappy creature had disappeared without leaving any trace. But it was thought that Sister Beatrice might have seen her in the church where she had gone to pray.

" Do not be disturbed, my sisters," said Beatrice, touched to tears by this tender solicitude, and pressing the nun who was looking for her to her bosom. " I saw the poor woman, and I know what has become of her. She is happy, my sisters—happier than she deserves, happier than ever you could hope she would be ! "

This answer quietened all anxiety ; but the nuns spoke of it a good deal, for it was the first harsh word that had come from the lips of the sister custodian. Thereafter, all the life of Beatrice passed like a single day, like the day promised in the future to the elect of the Lord, without tediousness, without regrets, or any

emotions except those of piety to God and charity to men. She
lived a century without seeming to grow old ; because it is only
the evil passions of the soul that age the body. A good life is a
perpetual youth. When Beatrice died, she fell asleep calmly
in that light slumber of the grave that separates time from eternity.
The Church honoured her memory by placing her in the ranks of
the saints.

STENDHAL
(MARIE-HENRI BEYLE)
1783–1842

THE PHILTRE

ON a sombre, rainy night in the summer of 1823 a young lieutenant of the 96th Regiment, garrisoned at Bordeaux, withdrew from the café where he had lost nearly all his money. He cursed his folly, for he was poor.

He was walking quietly down one of the loneliest streets of the Lormond district, when suddenly he heard cries, and from a door that was noisily flung open, a woman escaped and ran and fell at his feet. So thick was the darkness he could not guess what was happening, save by the sounds about him. The men who were pursuing the woman, whoever they were, stopped in the doorway, apparently on hearing the steps of the young officer.

He listened a moment. The men spoke in whispers, but did not come up to him. Though the affair only filled him with disgust, Lieven thought it his duty to lift up the woman who had fallen before him.

He saw that she had only a chemise on. In spite of the profound darkness of the night—it was then about two o'clock in the morning —he dimly saw her long, unloosened hair. So it was a woman. The discovery by no means pleased him.

She seemed unable to walk without help. Lieven had need to call to mind his ideas of duty towards one's fellow-creatures, in order to prevent himself from leaving her. He saw himself appearing the next morning before a police magistrate. There would be jests from his fellow-officers, and satirical stories in the newspapers of the town.

"I must put her against the door of some house," he said to himself, "and ring the bell, and then get away as fast as I can."

He was preparing to do this, when he heard the woman moan some words in Spanish. He did not know a word of the language. Perhaps that was why the two very simple words that Leonora spoke stirred in him the most romantic feeling. He saw no longer a police magistrate, and a girl of the streets beaten by some drunken brutes. His imagination soared away into ideas of love and strange adventures.

Having lifted the woman up, Lieven began to speak to her and tried to console her. " But was she ugly ? " he asked himself. The doubt on this point brought his reason into play, and made him forget his romantic ideas. Lieven wished to get her to sit down on a doorstep ; she refused to do so.

" Let us go farther on," she said, with a foreign accent.

" Are you afraid of your husband ? " said Lieven.

" Alas ! I have left my husband, a most worthy man who worshipped me, for a lover who has treated me worse than a savage."

Lieven again forgot the police magistrate and all the unpleasant sequels to a night adventure.

" I have been robbed, sir," said Leonora, a few moments afterwards, " but I see I still have a little diamond ring. Perhaps some inn-keeper will give me shelter. But, sir, I should be the talk of the place, for I will admit to you I have only a chemise on me. Sir, I beg you, in the name of humanity, to find me some sort of room, and buy any kind of rough dress for me from some working woman. As soon as I was properly clad," she added, encouraged by the silence of the young officer, " you could take me to the door of some small inn. There I would cease to rely on your generosity, and beg you only to leave a most unhappy woman."

All this, spoken in bad French, was rather pleasant to Lieven.

" Madame," he answered, " I will do all that you want me. The main thing, however, for you and me is not to get ourselves arrested. I am Lieutenant Lieven of the 96th Regiment. If we meet a patrol, and the men are not of my regiment, they will take us to the guardhouse, where we shall have to pass the night ; and to-morrow you and I, madame, will be the talk of Bordeaux."

Lieven felt Leonora shiver as she leant on his arm.

" This horror of scandal is a good sign," he thought to himself. " Please take my coat," he said to the lady. " I will conduct you to my room."

" Oh, sir, sir. . . ."

" I will leave you absolute mistress of my room, and I will not appear there until to-morrow morning. But my orderly comes at six o'clock, and he is a man who will knock until the door is opened. I am a man of honour, madame. But is she pretty ? " he asked himself.

He opened the door of his house. The unknown lady almost fell at the bottom of the stairs, where she could not find the first step. Lieven spoke to her in whispers. She answered him also in a low voice.

" How dare you bring women into my house ! " cried the shrill-voiced, pretty landlady, coming out with a little lamp.

Lieven turned quickly towards his unknown lady, saw an admirable figure, and blew out the lamp.

" Silence, Madame Saucède, or to-morrow morning I leave you ! This lady is the wife of the Colonel, and I am not sleeping here to-night. Here are ten francs for you, if you keep a silent tongue in your head ! "

Lieven had reached the third floor ; at the door of his room he trembled.

" Enter, madame," he said to the lady. " There are phosphorus matches just by the clock. Light the candle, and make a good fire, and bolt the door from the inside. I respect you as if you were my sister, and when I come in the morning I will bring a dress."

" Jesus Maria ! " cried the lovely Spanish lady.

When Lieven knocked at the door the next morning, he was madly in love. In order not to wake his unknown lady too soon, he had had the patience to wait for his orderly at the door, and to go into a café and sign the papers brought to him. He had taken a room close by, and he brought clothes with him and also a mask.

" Thus, madame," he said through the door, " I shall not see you if you so desire."

The idea of the mask pleased the young Spanish woman, distracting her from her deep melancholy.

" You are so generous," she said, without opening the door, " that I will be bold enough to beg you to leave the parcel of clothing outside. When I hear you descend, I will take it."

" Adieu, madame," said Lieven, going away.

Leonora was so charmed by the promptitude with which he obeyed her that she said to him in almost the tones of the most tender friendship, " If you can, sir, come back in half an hour."

When he returned, Lieven found her masked ; but he saw she had lovely arms, a beautiful neck and delicate hands. He was delighted. He was a young man of good birth, who still had need to force himself to act with courage with women he loved. His tone was respectful, and he did the honours of his poor little room with such grace, that, turning round after having arranged the screen, he stood motionless with admiration before the most beautiful woman he had ever met. The foreign lady had taken off her mask. She had black eyes that seemed to speak. There was so much energy in them that they might have appeared hard in the ordinary circumstances of life. Despair gave them a little sympathy, and nothing was wanting to the beauty of Leonora. Lieven thought she was from eighteen to twenty years of age. There was a moment of silence. In spite of her deep grief, Leonora could not help remarking with some pleasure the rapture of the young officer, who seemed to her to move in good society.

" You are my benefactor," she said at last to him, " and in spite of your age and mine, I hope you will continue to respect me."

Lieven answered as the most passionate lover can ; but he was sufficiently master of himself to refrain from the pleasure of saying he loved her. Besides, the eyes of Leonora were so impressive, and she had so distinguished an air, despite the poorness of the dress she had just put on, that he had less trouble in acting prudently.

" One might as well be a complete ass," he said to himself.

He gave himself up to his shyness and to the heavenly pleasure of looking at Leonora, without saying anything to her. He could not have done better. Little by little the beautiful Spanish woman regained her confidence. It was very droll, sitting opposite one another and staring silently.

" I must get a hat like that of a working woman," she said, " which will hide my face. For, unhappily," she added, almost laughing, " I cannot use your mask in the street."

Lieven found a hat, and then took Leonora to the room he had rented for her. She redoubled his agitation and almost his happiness by saying to him :

" All this may end for me on the gallows ! "

" To serve you," said Lieven, with the greatest impetuosity, " I would throw myself in the fire. I have taken this room in the name of Madame Lieven, my wife."

" Your wife ! " said the Spanish girl, almost angry.

" You had to appear under this name or show a passport. And we have no passport."

The " we " gave him a thrill of happiness. He had sold the ring, or at least he gave the lady a hundred francs as its value. Lunch was brought in. She asked him to be seated.

" You have shown yourself the most generous of men," she said after lunch. " If you like you can leave me now. My heart will preserve an eternal gratitude for you."

" I will obey you," said Lieven, rising.

There was the pain of death in his heart. The unknown lady was very thoughtful, then she said :

" Remain. You are very young, but I need help, and where shall I find a man as generous as you are ? Besides, if you have a feeling for me of which I am unworthy, the story of my faults will soon make me lose your esteem, and take away all your interest in the most criminal of women. For, sir, I have done great wrong. I can complain of no one, and least of all of my husband, Don Gutier Ferrandez. He is one of those unhappy Spaniards who sought a refuge in France two years ago. We are both of us from Carthagena. But he is very rich and I am very poor.

" ' I am thirty years older than you, my dear Leonora,' he said to me, on the eve of our marriage, ' but I have some millions of money and I love you to madness. Look at the matter and decide for yourself. If my age makes the marriage disagreeable to you I will make your people think I am responsible for breaking it off.'

"That was four years ago. I was fifteen. What I felt most keenly then was the profound poverty into which my family had fallen in the Revolution. I did not love him, but I accepted him. Sir, I have need of your advice, for I do not know the ways of this country nor your language, as you can see. Did I not need your help so badly, I could not support the shame that is killing me. Last night, when you saw me driven from a poor tenement, you must have thought it was a woman of evil reputation whom you were helping. Sir, I am still worse than that. I am the most criminal and also the most unhappy of women," added Leonora, bursting into tears. " One of these days you will perhaps see me brought before your judges, and I shall be condemned to some ignominious punishment. Scarcely was I married when Don Gutier began to be jealous. Ah, heavens! it was then without grounds. But no doubt he saw I had a bad charcter. I was so foolish as to be irritated by my husband's suspicions. Ah, unhappy woman ! "

"No matter what your crimes are," said Lieven, interrupting her, "I am devoted to you to death. But if we are likely to be pursued by the police, tell me about it quickly, so that I can arrange for your flight without loss of time."

"Flight ! " she said to him. "How can I travel in France ? My Spanish accent, my youth, my agitation, will lead to my arrest by the first policeman who asks for my passport. Doubtless the police of Bordeaux are searching for me at this moment. My husband will have promised them handfuls of gold if they succeed in finding me. Leave me, sir, abandon me ! I will speak more boldly to you. I adore a man who is not my husband—and what a man ! He is a monster. You will despise him. Yet he has only to send me a kind word, and I will fall, I will not say into his arms, but at his feet. In the depths of shame in which I find myself, I do not want at least to deceive my benefactor. I am an unhappy woman, sir, who admires you, who is very grateful to you, but never can I love you."

Lieven became very sad.

" Do not mistake my sudden grief, madame," he said in a feeble voice, " for an intention to leave you. I am thinking how you can avoid the pursuit of the police. Perhaps the best way is to remain concealed in Bordeaux. Later I can arrange for you to take the place of a woman of your age for whom I will book a passage on some ship."

The light died out of Lieven's eyes as he finished speaking.

" Don Gutier Ferrandez," continued Leonora, " became suspect to the party that tyrannises over Spain. He used to go for pleasure-trips on the sea. One day we found in the offing a French brig. We went on board, leaving behind all our property in Carthagena. My husband is still very rich. He has taken a fine mansion at Bordeaux and started in business again. But we live absolutely alone. He will not let me mix in French society. During the last year especially, under the pretext of political difficulties with the Liberals, I have not been allowed to pay two visits anywhere. My husband is the most generous of men, but he suspects all the world and takes a gloomy view of everything.

" Unhappily, he yielded a few months ago at my desire to have a box at the theatre. He chose the worst, and took a box just by the stage, so as not to expose me to the glances of the young men of the town. A troop of Neapolitan riders had just come to Bordeaux. . . . Ah ! sir, how you are going to despise me ! "

" Madame," replied Lieven, " I am listening to you with atten-tion, but I think only of my misfortune. Your love is fixed for ever on a happier man."

" No doubt you have heard of the famous Mayral ? " said Leonora, lowering her eyes.

" The Spanish circus-rider ! Yes, all Bordeaux went to see him. He is a very smart, handsome chap."

" Alas ! sir, I thought he was a man out of the common. He always looked at me as he rode. One day, passing under my box, from which my husband had just gone, he said, in Catalanian :

" ' I am a captain in the army of the Marquesito and I adore you.'

" To be loved by a circus-rider ! How shameful, sir ! And it was still more shameful that I could think of it without shame. For some days I did not go to the show. I was very unhappy. One morning my chambermaid said to me : ' Senor Ferrandez has gone out ; I beg you, madame, to read this letter.' And she hastened away, locking the door behind her. It was a love-letter from Mayral. He told me the story of his life, saying he was a poor officer forced by the direst need into a way of life that he offered to abandon for me. His true name was Don Roderigue Pimentel. I returned to the show. Little by little I believed in the misfortunes of Mayral : I received his letters with pleasure. Alas ! I ended by answering them. I loved him with passion—a passion," she said, breaking again into tears, " that nothing can extinguish, not even the saddest of discoveries. I desired as much as he did an opportunity to speak to him. Yet I soon suspected that he was no Pimentel or officer of the army of the Marquesito. He had no pride, and I sometimes saw he was afraid I would laugh at him for being merely a circus-rider in a troop of acrobats.

"About two months ago, as we were starting for the show, my husband received the news that one of his ships had been wrecked near Royan.

"'I must go and see it to-morrow,' he said.

"This was unlike him, for usually he did not speak ten words a day. At the show, I gave Mayral a signal we had agreed upon, and while my husband was in the box, Mayral went to our house and took a letter I had left with our porter's wife. I saw Mayral return full of joy. I had had the weakness to write to him that I would see him the next night in the hall by the garden.

"My husband left at noon. It was splendid weather, and the heat was very great. In the evening, I said I would sleep in my husband's room, which was on the ground floor by the garden. At one in the morning, having opened the window, I was waiting for Mayral, when there was a sudden noise at the door. It was my husband. Half way on the road to Royan he had seen his ship quietly sailing up the Gironde towards Bordeaux.

"In entering, Don Gutier did not perceive my dreadful anxiety. He praised my idea of finding a cool room to sleep in, and lay down by my side. Think of my disquietude! Unhappily, the moonlight was very clear. Less than an hour afterwards, I saw Mayral come to the window. After the return of my husband, I had not thought of closing the glass door of the study next to the bedroom. It was wide open, and so was the door that led from the study into the room.

"In vain I tried, by movements of my head, to make Mayral understand that something had happened. I heard him enter the study, and he was soon close to the bed. Think of my terror! Everything could be seen as clearly as in daylight. Happily Mayral did not speak as he drew near.

"I showed him my husband sleeping by my side. He drew a dagger. Horrified, I half raised myself. He leaned over and said in my ear:

"'I see I come at an awkward hour. You may have found it pleasant to make a fool of a poor circus-rider, but this handsome gentleman is going to have a bad time.'

"'This is my husband,' I whispered, while with all my strength I held his hand.

"'I saw your husband go on the steamer to Royan this morning! An acrobat isn't such a fool as to believe that. Come and speak to me in the next room. I insist!—otherwise I will wake this fine gentleman. I am stronger and quicker and better armed, and I will show him that it is not good to jest with me. I want you, and he shall not have you'

"At this moment my husband awoke."

" ' Who is that speaking ? ' he cried, greatly disturbed.

" Mayral, who was holding me and speaking in my ear, lowered himself quickly. I stretched out my arm as though my husband's words had aroused me : I said several things to him that made Mayral clearly see it was my husband. At last Don Gutier, thinking he had been disturbed by a dream, went to sleep again. The blade of Mayral's dagger continued to gleam in the rays of the moon, which were now shining straight on the bed. I promised Mayral all he wanted, and at the end of an hour he went away.

" Will you believe me, sir, when I tell you that though the foolish action of Mayral made me see what sort of man he was, my passion for him did not diminish ? My husband, never going into society, passed all his time with me. Nothing was more difficult than the second interview that I had sworn to Mayral I would grant him. He wrote letters full of reproaches, and at the theatre he would not look at me. At last, sir, my fatal love carried me completely away.

" ' Come from the Exchange, when you see my husband there.' I wrote to him, ' I will hide you. Then if by any chance I get a moment of freedom I will see you ; and if my husband goes to the Exchange to-morrow, you can see me. Is not this a proof of my love and the injustice of your suspicions ? Think what I am exposing myself to ! '

" He replied that he always feared I should choose some one in good society, and make a fool of the poor Italian acrobat. One of his comrades had told some absurd tale about the matter. Eight days afterwards, my husband went to the Exchange ; Mayral came to me in broad daylight, climbing the garden wall. We had scarcely been three minutes together when my husband returned. Mayral went into my dressing-room ; but Don Gutier had only come back for some papers. Unfortunately, he had also a bag with some valuables. In an idle fit, he would not go down to his strong room, but put the gold in one of my chests in the dressing-room, and locked it, and for extra precaution, as he is very suspicious, he took away the key of my room. Mayral was furious. I could only speak to him through the door.

" My husband soon returned. After dinner, he compelled me to go out for a walk. He wanted to go to the theatre, and it was very late when we got home. All the doors of the house were closed with great care every evening, and my husband took all the keys. It was by the greatest hazard in the world that, profiting by my husband's first sleep, I managed to let Mayral out of the room. I got him into a little attic under the roof. It was impossible to let him out through the garden. Balls of wool had been stretched over it, and two or three porters were set on watch. Myral passed all the following day in the attic. Think of what I suffered ! Every

instant I fancied I saw him coming down, dagger in hand, to murder
my husband. He was capable of anything. The least noise in
the house startled me.

"To crown my unhappiness, my husband did not go to the
Exchange. At last, without having been able to speak for a minute
to Mayral, I was able to let him escape through the garden, by
giving each of the porters something to do. In passing, he broke the
great mirror of the drawing-room with the handle of his dagger.
He was furious.

"Here, sir, you will despise me as much as I despise myself.
From this moment, I see now, Mayral loved me no longer. He
thought I had made a fool of him. My husband was still very fond
of me. Several times that day he kissed me and took me in his arms.
Mayral, sick with pride rather than with love, fancied I had concealed
him so that he could see these transports.

"He would not answer my letters ; he would not even look at me
at the show. You must be growing tired, sir, of this tale of infamies.
Here is the worst and the most dastardly. It is eight days since the
Neapolitan troop of riders announced its departure. Last Monday,
mad with love for a man who for three weeks had not replied to my
letters or looked at me, I left the house of the best of husbands, and,
sir, in going away, I, who had brought as dowry only an unfaithful
heart—I took the diamonds he gave me, and from his coffer I stole
three or four rolls of five hundred francs, thinking that Mayral would
be suspected at Bordeaux if he tried to sell diamonds."

At this part of her story, Leonora blushed deeply. Lieven was
pale and desperate. Each word of Leonora's pierced his heart, and
yet through the frightful perversity of his character, redoubled the
passion that burnt in him. Beside himself, he took the hand of
Donna Leonora, and she did not draw it away.

"What baseness it is in me," said Lieven to himself, " to play
with her hand while she openly speaks to me of her love for another
man. Only from disdain or absent-mindedness she lets me do it.
I am the least delicate of men."

"Last Sunday, sir," continued Leonora, " towards two in the
morning, after drugging my husband and the porter with laudanum,
I fled. I came and knocked at the door of the house from which
I was escaping when you passed. It is Mayral's.

" ' Now will you believe I love you ? ' I said to him.

"I was wild with happiness. He seemed to me, even from the
first, more astonished than loving. The next morning, when I
showed him my diamonds and my gold, he resolved to leave the
troop and fly with me to Spain. But heavens ! I saw from his
ignorance of the ways of my country, he was not a Spaniard. I was
uniting myself for ever to a circus-rider ! ' Well ? What did it
matter,' I thought, ' so long as he loves me ? I feel he is the master

of my life. I shall be his servant, his faithful mate. He will follow his trade. I am young, and if needs be, I will learn trick-riding. If we fall in poverty in our old age, well ! in twenty years, I can die by his side. I shall have nothing to complain of. I shall have had my happiness.' What a mad fool I was ! " she said, interrupting herself.

"It must be admitted you were dying of weariness with your old husband," said Lieven. " He would not let you mix with people of your own position. This justifies you in my eyes. You were nineteen and he was fifty-nine. How many wives live in high honour in my country who have really done worse things than you, and have none of your generous remorse ! "

Several phrases of this sort seemed to lighten the grief of Leonora.

" Sir," she continued, " I spent three days with Mayral. Yesterday evening he said to me :

" ' As the police may come and search my house, I will go and deposit your gold and jewels with a good friend.'

" At one o'clock in the morning, when I was frightened to death thinking he had fallen off his horse, he came in, gave me a kiss and soon left the room again. Happily I used a light, though he forbade me to do so. Some long time afterwards, as I was sleeping, a man got in the bed. I knew at once it was not Mayral. I took a dagger, and the coward was afraid and threw himself at my knees begging for mercy.

" ' There's the guillotine for you if you touch me ! " he said.

" The baseness of the appeal shocked me. With what people had I compromised myself ! I had the presence of mind to tell the man I had relatives in Bordeaux, and that I would have him arrested if he did not speak all the truth.

" ' Well,' he said, ' I have not stolen any of your gold or your diamonds. Mayral has left Bordeaux with all the spoil. He has gone off with the wife of our manager. He gave him twenty-five of your fine louis to get the woman. He has given me two louis, and there they are, unless you like to let me keep them. He gave me the money to keep you here as long as possible, so that he could get twenty or thirty hours' start.'

" ' Is he Spanish ? ' I asked.

" ' Spanish ? Him ? He comes from San Domingo, and he fled from there after robbing and murdering his master.'

" ' Why did he come back this evening ? ' I said. ' Answer, or my uncle will send you to the galleys ! '

" ' I hesitated to come here and keep you from going out. Mayral said you were beautiful. He said it would be easy to take his place, and it would avenge him for some trick you had played on him. Then, as I still did not dare to, he brought the postchaise to the door, and came up to kiss you, getting me to hide on the other side of the bed.' "

Leonora's voice was stopped by sobs.

"The young acrobat who was with me," she went on, "was frightened, and gave me true and desolating information about Mayral. I was in despair. 'Perhaps he made me drink a philtre,' I said to myself, 'for I cannot hate him.' Amid all his infamies, sir, I cannot hate him. I feel I adore him!"

Donna Leonora stopped and remained thoughtful.

"Strangely blind!" said Lieven to himself. "A woman with such intelligence and believes in witchcraft!"

"At last," said Leonora, "the young man, seeing I was sunk in thought, began to be less afraid. He left me, and came back with one of his comrades. I was obliged to defend myself. The struggle was serious. Perhaps they wished to take my life. Finally I gained the door; but if you, sir, had not been there, they would probably have pursued me down the street."

The more Lieven saw Leonora maddened with love for Mayral, the more he adored her. She wept, and he kissed her hand. As he was speaking in veiled words of his love:

"Do you believe me, my true friend," she said to him, several days afterwards, "but I think if I could prove to Mayral that I had never tried to make him a dupe or play with him, perhaps he would love me?"

"I haven't much money," said Lieven. "I gamble out of boredom. But may be the banker at Bordeaux, to whom my father recommended me, will not refuse me fifteen or twenty louis. I will do all I can to get it. Do anything! With this money you can go to Paris."

Leonora flung her arms round his neck.

"My God! Why can't I love you? What! You will forgive my horrible folly?"

"To such a point that I would marry you with rapture, and pass my life with you, the happiest of men!"

"But if I meet Mayral, I feel myself weak and criminal enough to leave you, my benefactor, and fall at his feet."

Lieven reddened with anger.

"The only cure for me is to kill myself," he said, covering her with kisses.

"Ah! do not kill yourself, my friend," said Leonora.

He was never seen again. Leonora has entered the convent of the Ursulines.

THE JEW

STENDHAL

" I WAS then a very handsome man."

" But you are still remarkably striking."

" With what a difference ! I am forty-five. Then I was only thirty. It was in 1814. All I had were an uncommon figure and a rare beauty. For the rest I was a Jew, despised by you Christians, and by Jews as well. For I had been for a long time excessively poor."

" Men are very wrong in despising——"

" Don't put yourself to the cost of finding pretty phrases. This evening I feel disposed to talk, and when I do talk I am sincere. Our ship is going well ; the breeze is delightful ; to-morrow morning we shall be in Venice. . . . But to come back to the story of the curse about which we were speaking, and of my travels in France in 1814. I was very fond of money in 1814. It is the only passion I have ever known in myself.

" I spent my days in the streets of Venice with a little box, on the top of which some golden jewels were displayed ; but in a secret drawer I had cotton stockings, handkerchiefs, and other contraband English goods. One of my uncles, after the burial of my father, said to each of us—we were three—that there remained a capital only of five francs. This good uncle gave me a napoleon—twenty francs. In the night my mother decamped with twenty-one francs ; that left me only four francs. I stole from one of the neighbours a violin-case I knew she had put in the garret. I went and bought eight handkerchiefs of red cotton. They cost me ten sous ; I sold them for eleven. The first day I sold out all my stock four times. I hawked my handkerchiefs among the sailors by the arsenal. The merchant, astonished by my activity, asked me why I did not buy my goods by the dozen. It was a good half a league from his shop to the arsenal. I told him I only had four francs in the world, that my mother had stolen twenty-one francs from me. He gave me a very hard kick that lifted me out of the shop.

" Still, the next day I was back again. I had already sold the eight handkerchiefs the evening before. As it was a warm night I slept out of doors. I had lived, I had drunk Chio wine, and I had saved five sous out of my trade. That was the life I led from 1800 to 1814. I seemed to work under the blessing of God."

The Jew uncovered himself with a tender air.

"I was so good at the trade that several times I doubled my capital in a single day. Often I took a gondola and went to sell stockings to sailors on the ships. But, as soon as I had put by a little money, my mother and my sister found a pretext for making friends with me again, and robbing me. Once they took me to a jeweller's shop, put on a necklace and earrings, and went out, as for a moment, and never came back. The jeweller wanted fifty francs from me. I began to weep. I had only fourteen francs on me. I told him where my box was. He sent for it; but, while I was wasting time at the jeweller's, my mother had also gone off with the box. The jeweller gave me a good thrashing.

"When he was tired of beating me, I explained to him that if he would give me back my fourteen francs and lend me a little table drawer, in which I could fix a double bottom, I could certainly pay him back ten sous a day. And this is what I did. The jeweller ended by trusting me with earrings worth twenty francs; but he never allowed me to gain more than five sous on each piece.

"In 1805 I had a capital of a thousand francs. Then I considered that our law orders us to marry, and I thought of accomplishing my duty. I had the misfortune to fall in love with a Jewish girl named Stella. She had two brothers; one of them was quartermaster-sergeant among the French troops, and the other cashier at the paymaster's. They often pushed her at night out of the room they occupied in common, on the ground-floor on the side of San Paolo. I found her there one evening, weeping. Mistaking what she was, I offered to buy her ten sous' worth of Chio wine. Her tears increased. Telling her she was a fool, I walked on.

"But she struck me as very pretty. Next night, at the same hour—ten—my sales in Saint Mark's Place were finished, and I passed by the spot where I had met her. She was not there. Three days afterwards I was luckier. I had a long talk with her. She refused me with horror.

"'She has seen me go by with my box filled with jewels,' I thought. 'She wants me to make her a present of one of my necklaces, and that's what I won't do!'

"I resolved not to take the street any more. But in spite of myself, and almost without admitting it, I gave up drinking wine, and each day I set apart the money I thus saved. I was still more foolish not to use this money in trade. In that time, sir, I tripled my capital every week.

"When I had saved twelve francs—the price of my cheapest necklaces—I went several times down the street where Stella lived. At last I saw her. She rejected my gallant advances with indignation. In our talk I told her I had stopped drinking wine for three months to save the cost of one of my necklaces and offer it to her.

She did not reply, but asked my advice on a misfortune that had happened to her since she last saw me.

" Her brothers worked together at clipping any golden coins they could procure. (They plunged the sequins and napoleons in a bath of *aqua fortis*.) The quartermaster-sergeant had been put in prison ; and for fear of rousing suspicions, the cashier at the paymaster's would not take any steps to help him. Stella did not ask me to go to the citadel ; and for my part I never mentioned the place, but I begged her to wait for me the next evening. . . ."

" But we are still very far," I said, " from the curse that overcame you in France."

" You are right," said the Jew, " but I promise to finish in a few words the story of my marriage, or be silent. I don't know why I like to talk to-day of Stella.

" At some trouble, I got the quartermaster brother out of prison. They gave me the hand of their sister, and brought their father to Venice—a poor Jew of Innsbruck. I had rented some rooms, happily paid in advance, and had collected some bits of furniture there. My father-in-law went among all his relatives in the city announcing he was marrying his daughter. At last, after a year of anxieties, on the eve of the marriage, he made off with six hundred francs he had collected from his relatives. We were going, his daughter and he and I, to eat a salad at Murano. That was when he disappeared. Meanwhile, my two brothers-in-law stole every bit of the furniture in my room, and unfortunately the stuff was not all paid for.

" My credit was ruined. My brothers-in-law, whom folks had always seen with me, had told the merchants with whom I dealt that I was at Chiozzia, where I was selling anything I wanted. In a word, by all kinds of trickeries, they had stolen more than two hundred francs. I saw it was necessary to fly from Venice. I placed Stella as nursemaid with the jeweller who had trusted me with the necklaces. Early the next morning, having given Stella twenty francs, keeping only six myself, I fled.

" Never had I been so ruined. For I now seemed a thief. Happily, in my despair, I had the idea, on reaching Padua, to write the truth to the merchants of Venice from whom my wife's brothers had taken the goods. I learned next day there was an order out for my arrest, and the police of the kingdom of Italy were not to be trifled with.

" A famous lawyer of Padua had become blind. He wanted a valet to lead him about, but his misfortune made him so ill-tempered that he never kept a man more than a month. But I wagered with myself that I would not be driven out of his house. I entered his service, and the next day, as he was bored that nobody came to see him, I told him my story.

" ' If you do not protect me,' I said, ' I shall be arrested one of these days.'

" ' Arrest one of my servants ! ' he exclaimed, ' I should soon stop that ! '

" At last, sir, I won his favour. He went to bed early, and I obtained permission to do a little trade in the cafés of Padua, from eight o'clock, when he went to bed, to two o'clock in the morning, when the rich people left the cafés.

" I made two hundred francs in eighteen months. I asked to go. He told me that in his will he was leaving me a considerable sum of money, but that I must never leave his house.

" ' In that case,' I thought, ' why did you let me trade ? '

" I decamped. I paid my creditors at Venice. This brought me much honour. I married Stella. I taught her to trade. Now she can sell better than I can. At last I come to the story of my travels, and after that to the curse.

" I had more than a hundred louis capital. I must tell you the story of a new reconciliation with my mother, who stole from me again, and then got my sister to rob me. So I left Venice, seeing that, as long as I was there, I should be the dupe of my family. I settled at Zara, where I got on wonderfully. A Croatian captain, whom I had furnished with part of the clothes of his regiment, said to me one day :

" ' Filippo ! do you want to make a fortune ? We are going to France. Learn one thing ; that is, without seeming to be, I am the friend of Baron Bradal, the colonel of the regiment. Come with us as sutler. You will earn a good deal. But this business will only be a pretext. The colonel, with whom I seem to be on bad terms, has given me all the provisioning of the regiment. I want an intelligent man. You will suit me.'

" Now, you see, sir, I did not love my wife any more."

" What ! Poor Stella, to whom you had been so faithful ? "

" The fact is, sir, I loved nothing but money. Ah, I was very fond of that ! "

I began to laugh ; there was such true passion in his exclamation.

" I was made sutler to the regiment. I left Zara. After a march of forty-eight days we reached the Simplon. The five hundred francs I had brought with me had become already fifteen hundred francs, and besides I had a pretty covered cart and two horses. At the Simplon our sufferings began. I almost lost my life. I spent more than twenty-two nights sleeping in the open air in the cold."

" Ah," I said, " you were compelled to bivouac ! "

" I made each day fifty to sixty francs, but every night I was in danger of being frozen. At last the army got over the frightful mountain, and we arrived at Lausanne. There I entered into part-nership with Monsieur Perrin. Ah, the worthy man ! He was

a brandy merchant. I knew how to sell in six different languages,
while he was good at buying. Ah, the excellent man! Only he
was too violent. When a Cossack would not pay for his drink, if
he was alone in the shop, Perrin thrashed him till he bled.

" ' But my friend,' I used to say to him, ' we are making a hundred francs a day. What does it matter if a drunkard does us out
of a couple of francs ? '

" ' I cannot help it,' he answered ; ' I do not like Cossacks.'

" ' You will get us murdered. Then, Monsieur Perrin, it will be
better to end our partnership.'

"The French vivandiers would not venture in our camp, for
no one paid them. We did splendid business. On reaching Lyons
we had fourteen thousand francs in our coffers. There, out of pity
for the poor French merchants, I went in for smuggling. There
was a great deal of tobacco outside Saint Clair gate. They came
and begged me to get it into the town. I told them to be patient
for a couple of days, until my friend the colonel was in command.
Then for five days I filled my covered cart with tobacco. The
Frenchmen at the gate grumbled, but did not dare to arrest me.
On the fifth day, one of them, who was drunk, attacked me. I
whipped on my horse, but the others stopped me. I was bleeding
all over, and demanded I should be led before the commander of
the guard. He belonged to our regiment, but would not recognise
me, and sent me to prison. While going to prison I gave two crowns
to my escort to lead me before my colonel. In the presence of the
soldiers he treated me very harshly and threatened to hang me.
As soon as we were alone he said :

" ' Cheer up ! to-morrow I will put another officer at the gate.
Instead of one cart, bring in two.'

"But I would not. I gave him two hundred sequins.

" ' What ! ' he said to me, ' do you take such a lot of trouble for
nothing ? "

" ' I am sorry for the poor merchants,' I replied.

"Our affairs—Perrin's and mine—went admirably as far as
Dijon. There, sir, in one night we lost more than twelve thousand
francs. The sales had been splendid. It was a grand review, and
we were the only vivandiers. We had a net gain of more than a
thousand francs. At midnight, when everybody was sleeping,
a cursed Croatian would not pay up. Perrin, seeing he was alone,
overwhelmed him with blows, and covered him with blood.

" ' You are mad,' I said. ' It is true this man has drunk six
francs' worth ; but if he has the strength to use his voice there will
be a row.'

"The Croatian tumbled like a dead man out of our shop, but he
was only stupefied. He began to shout. Some soldiers, bivouacking
close by, came up, and, finding him covered with blood, broke in

our door. Perrin tried to defend himself, and got eight sabre wounds.

" 'I am not guilty,' I said to the soldiers. 'He did it. Take me to your colonel!'

" 'We will not wake the colonel for you,' said one of the soldiers.

" In spite of my efforts, our unhappy shop was attacked by some thousands of soldiers. The officers outside the mob could not get through and use their authority. I thought that Perrin was dead: I was in a pitiable condition myself. At last, sir, they pillaged us of more than twelve hundred francs' worth of wine and brandy.

" At daybreak, I succeeded in escaping. My colonel gave me four men to rescue Perrin if he were still alive. I found him in a guard-room, and took him to a surgeon.

" 'We must separate, my friend,' I said. 'You will end in getting me killed.'

" But he insisted so much, that we started a second partnership, paying some soldiers to guard our shop. In two months we made twelve thousand francs each. Unhappily, Perrin killed in a duel one of the soldiers who were guarding us.

" 'You will get me killed,' I repeated, and I left him.

" I went to Lyons, where I bought watches and diamonds, which were then cheap. For I am well up in all sorts of business. If you dropped me into any country, with fifty francs in my pocket, in six months I would have lived well and tripled my capital. I hid my diamonds in a secret place I made in my cart. The regiment having left for Valence and Avignon, I followed it after staying three days in Lyons.

" But, sir, when I got to Valence at eight in the evening, it was raining and dark. I knocked at the door of an inn. I was told there was no room for a Cossack. I knocked again. They flung stones at me from the upper window.

" 'It is clear,' I said to myself, 'I shall die to-night in this accursed town.'

" No one would answer : and no one would act as guide. I saw that if I did not want to die, I should have to sacrifice some of my goods. I gave a glass of brandy to the sentry. He was a Hungarian. Hearing me speak his language, he took pity on me, and told me to wait until he was relieved. I was perishing with cold : at last his relief came. I treated the corporal and all the men, and they led me to the commander. Ah, what a gentleman, sir ! He called me in at once. I explained to him that, out of hatred to the king, no inn-keeper would give me a night's lodging for any money.

" 'Very well,' he cried, 'they shall lodge you for nothing.'

" He gave me a fine billet for two nights, and four men were told off to accompany me. I returned to the inn, where they had thrown stones at me. I knocked twice. I said, in French, I had four men

with me, and we would break in the door if it were not opened.
No answer. We found a great piece of wood and began to break
down the door. It was half broken through when a man opened it
angrily. He was a tall fellow—six feet high—with a sabre in one
hand and a candle in the other. I thought there was going to be a
row and my cart would be pillaged. So, though I had a lodging billet,
I cried :

"' I will pay in advance, sir, if you like.'

"' Ah, it is you, Filippo ! ' cried the man, lowering his sabre and
embracing me. ' What : don't you remember Bonnard, corporal of
the twentieth regiment ? '

" I embraced him in turn, and sent the soldiers away. Bonnard
had lodged with my father for six months at Vicenza.

"' I am dying of hunger,' I said. ' For three days I have been
wandering about Valence.'

"' I will awaken my servant and soon get you a good supper.'

" He embraced me again, and was never tired of looking at me
and questioning me. I went with him to the cellar, from which he
brought an excellent wine that he kept in sand. As we were drinking
while waiting for supper, a tall handsome girl of eighteen came in.

"' Ah, you have got up ! ' said Bonnard. ' So much the better.
Friend, this is my sister ! You must marry her ! You are a nice
boy, and I will give her a dowry of six hundred francs.

"' I am married already,' I said to him. ' I have a wife at Zara,
where she is in business.'

"' Let her go to the devil, with her business. Settle yourself in
France—and marry the prettiest girl in the town.'

" Catherine was really very pretty. She looked at me in wonder.

"' You are an officer ? ' she said, deceived by a fine pelisse bought
at the review at Dijon.

"' No, mademoiselle, I am a vivandier to the army, and I have
made two hundred louis. I assure you there are not many of our
officers with that money.' I had more than six hundred louis,
but I am always very prudent.

" At last, will you believe it, sir ? Bonnard would not let me go
any farther. He rented for me a little shop by the side of the guard-
room, near the gate, where I did business with our soldiers. And
though I did not follow the army any longer, there were days when
I still made my ten francs. Bonnard was always saying to me :
' You must marry my sister.' Little by little Catherine got into the
habit of coming to my little shop, and spending three or four hours
there. At last, sir, I got madly in love with her. She was still more
in love with me. But by God's grace we did not lose our senses.

"' How can you want me to marry you ? ' I said to her. ' I am
married.'

"' Haven't you left your Italian wife all your stock ? Let her live on it at Zara, and you stay with us. Go into partnership with my brother, or keep your own business on. You are doing well and you will still do better.'

" I must tell you, sir, I was going in for banking business at Valence, and by buying good bills on Lyons, signed by men whom Bonnard knew, I sometimes made a hundred or a hundred and twenty francs a week in this way alone. So I remained in Valence until the autumn. I did not know what to do. I was dying to marry Catherine, and I had given her a dress and a hat from Lyons. When we went out walking together, her brother, she and I, everybody had their eyes on Catherine. She was really the most beautiful girl I have seen in my life.

" ' If you will not marry me,' she would often say, ' I will be your servant. Only you must never leave me.'

" She went ahead of me to my shop, to save me the trouble of opening it. At last, sir, I was absolutely mad in love with her, and she was the same as regards me, but we were always good. At the end of autumn the allies left Valence.

" ' The inn-keepers of this town might murder me,' I said to Bonnard. ' They know I have made some money here.'

" ' Go if you will,' said Bonnard with a sigh. ' We will not force anybody. But if you will stay and marry my sister, I will give her half of my property, and if any one says anything about you, leave him to me.'

" Three times I put off the day of my departure. The last troops of the rear-guard were already at Lyons when I resolved to go. We spent the night weeping, Catherine, her brother, and myself. You see, sir, I lost my happiness by not remaining with this family. God would not permit me to be happy!

" At last I set off, the 7th of November 1814. I shall never forget that day. I could not guide my cart. I was obliged to engage a driver half-way between Valence and Vienne. The day after my departure, as I was harnessing my horse at Vienne, who should arrive at the inn?—Catherine! She at once folded me in her arms. She was known in the inn, and she pretended to have come to see an aunt of hers in the town.

" ' I want to go with you as your servant,' she repeated, the tears rolling down her face. ' If you will not take me, I will throw myself in the Rhône.'

" All the people in the inn gathered round us. Catherine, who was as a rule so reserved and never said anything, talked and wept without restraint, and kissed me before them all. I got her quickly on my cart and drove away. A quarter of a league from the town I stopped.

" ' Here we must say good-bye,' I said to her.

" She never spoke, and clutched her head in her hands with

convulsive movements. I was afraid. I saw she would throw herself in the river, if I sent her back.

" ' But I am married,' I repeated to her. ' Married before God,' I said.

" ' I know it quite well. I will be your servant.'

" Ten times I stopped my cart between Vienne and Lyons : but she would not consent to leave me.

" ' If I pass the bridge of the Rhône with her,' I said to myself, ' it will be the sign of the will of God.'

" At last, sir, without noticing it, I passed the bridge and reached Lyons. At the inn they took us for husband and wife, and gave us a single room. I started to trade in watches and diamonds, and made ten francs a day ; and, thanks to the admirable housekeeping of Catherine, we lived on less than four. I took some rooms, which we furnished very well. I then possessed thirteen thousand francs, which in the banking business brought me in about eighteen hundred francs. Never have I been so rich as in the year and a half spent with Catherine. I was so rich that I bought a little pleasure-carriage, and every Sunday we went for excursions outside the town.

" A Jew of my acquaintance came to see me one day, and got me to take him in my carriage some way from Lyons. There he said suddenly to me :

" ' Filippo, you have a wife and a son ! they are unhappy.'

" Then he gave me a letter from my wife, and disappeared. I came back alone to Lyons. The letter from my wife was filled with reproaches that touched me much less than the idea of my abandoned son. I saw from the letter that the business at Zara was going on fairly well . . . but to abandon my son ! The idea hurt me.

" All that evening I did not speak. Catherine remarked it, but she had such a good heart ! Three weeks went by without her asking me the reason of my sadness.

" ' I have a son,' I said, when she at last spoke.

" ' I guessed it,' she said to me. ' Let us go. I will be your servant at Zara.'

" ' Impossible. My wife knows everything. Look at her letter.'

" Catherine blushed very much at the insults my wife addressed to her, at the tone of scorn with which, without knowing her, my wife spoke of her. I embraced her, and did all I could to console her, but, sir, the three months I spent at Lyons after that fatal letter were hellish. I could not come to a decision.

" ' If I set off at once ! ' I said to myself one night, with Catherine sleeping by my side. As soon as the idea struck me, I felt a balm spreading through my soul. ' It must be an inspiration from God ! ' I said to myself. But then, as I looked at Catherine, I began to say : ' What madness ! I cannot do that.'

" So the grace of God abandoned me, and I fell back into my bitter sorrowful mood. Without knowing what I did, I began to dress quietly, my eyes always fixed on Catherine. All my wealth was hidden in the bed. There were five hundred francs in a desk, for a payment she had to pay for a debt in my absence. I took this money ; I went to the coach-house where my cart was kept ; I hired a horse, and set off.

" At every moment I turned my head. ' Catherine will follow me,' I said to myself. ' If I see her, I am lost.'

" To get a little peace, I took the coach two leagues from Lyons. In my trouble I arranged with a carter to take my cart to chambéry : I evidently had no need of it. I can't remember any more what determined my actions. I felt all the bitterness of my loss on reaching Chambéry. I went to a notary and made a deed of gift of all my property at Lyons to Madame Catherine Bonnard, my wife. I thought of her honour, and of the gossip of neighbours.

" After the notary was paid and I came outside with my deed, I felt I should never have the strength to write to Catherine. I returned to the notary : he wrote a letter to her in my name, and one of his clerks came to the post and sent the letter off in my presence. In a dark tavern, I also had a letter written to Bonnard in Valence. He was informed in my name of the deed of gift, that amounted at least to thirteen thousand francs. He was also told that his sister was lying very ill at Lyons, and was expecting him. I sent this letter off myself. Never since have I heard anything of them.

" I found my cart at the foot of Mont Cenis. I cannot recall why I stuck to this vehicle, which was the immediate cause of my misfortunes. The true cause was no doubt some terrible curse that Catherine launched against me. Lively and passionate as she was, young (she was then just twenty), beautiful, innocent, for she had had no weakness except for me whom she wished to serve and honour as her husband, her voice probably reached to God in a prayer for my severe punishment.

" I bought a passport and a horse. I do not know how I stopped to think at the foot of Mont Cenis that there was a frontier there. I had an idea of doing a little smuggling with my five hundred francs. I bought some watches, which I concealed. Passing proudly before the custom-house officers, I was called to stop. Having done so much smuggling in my life, I carried my head high. The custom-house men went straight to my hiding-place in the cart : probably I had been betrayed by the watchmakers. They took my watches, and fined me besides a hundred crowns. I gave them fifty francs ; they let me go.

" This misfortune shook me up. In a moment I was reduced

from five hundred francs to a hundred francs. I could sell the horse and the cart, but it was a long way from Mont Cenis to Zara. As I was tormented by these sinister thoughts, a custom-house man ran up to me crying :

"'Dog of a Jew, you must give me twenty francs! The others have tricked me, and given me five francs instead of ten, and I have had all the trouble of catching up to you.'

"It was almost dark ; the man was drunk ; and he insulted me, and seized me by the collar. Satan tempted me, and I stabbed him with my knife, and flung him into the torrent twenty feet below the road. It was the first crime of my life, and I said to myself, 'I am done for!'

"Nearing Suze, I heard a noise behind me. I put my horse at the gallop. He got his head, and I was not able to hold him back : the cart upset, and I broke my leg.

"'Catherine has cursed me,' I thought. 'Heaven is just. I shall be recognised and hanged in two months.'

"But, as you see, nothing of the sort happened."

AUGUSTIN EUGÈNE SCRIBE
1791–1861

THE PRICE OF A LIFE

JOSEPH, opening the door of the salon, came to tell us that the post-chaise was ready. My mother and my sister threw themselves into my arms. "There is yet time," said they. "It is not too late. Give up this journey and remain with us." I replied: "Mother, I am a gentleman. I am twenty years old, my country needs me, I must win fame; be it in the army, be it at court, I must be heard of, men must speak of me."

"And when you are far away, tell me, Bernard, what will become of me, your old mother?"

"You will be happy and proud to hear of your son's successes——"

"And if you are killed in some battle?"

"What matters it? What is life? Only a dream. One dreams only of glory at twenty, and when one is a gentleman; but do not fear, you will see me return to you in a few years, a colonel, a general, or, better still, with a fine position at Versailles."

"Indeed! When will that be?"

"It will come, and I shall be respected and envied by all—and then—every one will take off his hat to me—and then—I will marry my cousin Henriette, and I will find good husbands for my sisters, and we shall all live together tranquil and happy on my estates in Britanny."

"Why not do all that to-day, my son? Has not your father left you the finest fortune in the country? Where is there, for ten leagues around, a richer domain, or a more beautiful château than that of Roche-Bernard? Are you not loved and respected by your vassals? When you walk through the village, is there a single one who fails to salute you and take off his hat? Do not leave us, my son; remain here with your friends, near your sisters, near your old mother, whom perhaps you will not find here when you return. Do not waste in search of vainglory or abridge by cares and torments of all kinds the days which already go so swiftly. Life is sweet, my child, and the sun of Britanny is so bright!"

So saying she led me to the open window and pointed to the

beautiful avenues of my park; the grand old chestnut trees were in full bloom, and the air was sweet with the fragrance of the lilacs and the honeysuckles, whose leaves sparkled in the sunlight.

All the house-servants awaited me in the anteroom. They were so sad and quiet that they seemed to say to me: "Do not go, young master, do not go."

Hortense, my eldest sister, pressed me in her arms, and my little sister Amélie, who was in one corner of the room occupied in looking at some engravings in a volume of La Fontaine, came to me, and handing me the book, cried: "Read, read, my brother!" It was the fable of "The Two Pigeons."

But I repulsed them all and said: "I am twenty years old. *Je suis gentilhomme.* I *must* in honour and glory. Let me go."

And I hastened to the courtyard, and got into the post-chaise, when a woman appeared at the landing of the stairs. It was my beautiful cousin Henriette! She did not weep, she did not say a word—but, pale and trembling, she could scarcely stand. She waved me an adieu with her white handkerchief, then fell unconscious. I ran to her, raised her, put my arms around her, and swore to her eternal love; and the moment she recovered consciousness, leaving her in my mother's care, I ran to the chaise, and, without turning my head, drove away.

If I had looked at Henriette I might have wavered. A few moments afterward we were rolling along the grand route.

For a long while I thought of nothing but Henriette, my mother, and my sisters, and all the happiness I had left behind me; but these thoughts were effaced in the measure that the towers of Roche-Bernard faded from my view, and soon ambitious dreams of glory spread over my spirit. What projects! What castles in the air! What glorious deeds I performed in that chaise! Riches, honours, dignities, rewards of all kinds! I refused nothing. I merited them, and I accepted all; at last, elevating myself as I advanced on my journey, I was duke—governor of a province—and no less a personage than a marshal of France when I arrived in the evening at my destination. The voice of my valet, who addressed me modestly as Monsieur le Chevalier, forced me to abdicate for the time being, and I was obliged to return to the earth and to myself.

The following day I continued my journey and dreamed the same dreams, for the way was long. At last we arrived at Sédan, where I expected to visit the Duc de C——, an old friend of our family. He would (I thought) surely take me with him to Paris, where he was expected at the end of the month, and then he would present me at Versailles, and obtain for me, at the very least, a company of dragoons.

I arrived in Sédan in the evening—too late to present myself at the château of my friend (which was some distance from the city), so I delayed my visit until the next day, and put up at the " Armes de France," the best hotel in the place.

I supped at the table d'hôte and asked the way to take on the morrow to the château of the Duc de C——.

" Any one can show you," said a young officer who sat near me, " for it is well known the whole country round. It was in this château that died a great warrior, a very celebrated man—Maréchal Fabert ! " Then the conversation fell, as was natural between young military men, on the Maréchal Fabert. They spoke of his battles, his exploits, of his modesty, which caused him to refuse letters of nobility and the collar of his order offered him by Louis XIV. Above all, they marvelled at the good fortune which comes to some men. What inconceivable happiness for a simple soldier to rise to the rank of maréchal of France—he, a man of no family, the son of a printer ! They could cite no other case similar to his, and the masses did not hesitate to ascribe his elevation to supernatural causes. It was said that he had employed magic from his childhood, that he was a sorcerer, and that he had a compact with the devil ; and our old landlord, who had all the credulity of our Breton peasants, swore to us that in this château of the Duc de C——, where Fabert died, there had frequently been seen a black man whom no one knew ; and that the servants had seen him enter Fabert's chamber and disappear, carrying with him the soul of the maréchal, which he had bought some years before, and which, therefore, belonged to him ; and that even now, in the month of May, on the anniversary of Fabert's death, one can see at night a black man bearing a light, which is Fabert's soul.

This story amused us at dessert, and we gaily drank a bottle of champagne to the familiar demon of Fabert, praying for his patronage, and help to gain victories like those of Collioure and of La Marfée.

The next day I arose early and set out for the château, which proved to be an immense Gothic manor-house, having nothing very remarkable about it. At any other time I would not have veiwed it with any great interest ; but now I gazed at it with feelings of curiosity as I recalled the strange story told us by the landlord of the " Armes de France."

The door was opened by an old valet, and when I told him I wished to see the Duc de C——, he replied that he did not know whether his master was visible or not, or if he would receive me. I gave him my name and he went away, leaving me alone in a very large and gloomy hall, decorated with trophies of the chase and family portraits. I waited some time, but he did not return. The silence was almost oppressive ; I began to grow impatient and had already counted two or three times all the family portraits, and all the beams in the ceiling, when I heard a noise in the wainscot.

It was a door which the wind had blown open. I looked up, and perceived a very pretty boudoir lighted by two great casements and a glass door which opened on a magnificent park. I advanced a few steps into the apartment, and paused suddenly at a strange spectacle. A man (his back was turned to the door through which I had entered) was lying on a couch. He arose, and, without perceiving me, ran quickly to the window. Tears rolled down his cheeks and profound despair was imprinted on his features. He remained some time immovable, his head resting on his hands, then he commenced to walk with great strides across the room; turning, he saw me, stopped suddenly, and trembled. As for myself, I was horror-struck, and dazed in consequence of my indiscretion. I wished to retire, and murmured some incoherent apologies

"Who are you? What do you want?" said he, in a deep voice, catching me by the arm.

I was very much frightened and embarrassed, but replied: "I am the Chevalier Bernard de la Roche-Bernard, and I have just arrived from Brittany."

"I know! I know!" said he, and, throwing his arms around me, he embraced me warmly, and leading me to the couch made me sit near him, spoke to me rapidly of my father and of all my family, whom he knew so well that I concluded that it was the master of the château.

"You are Monsieur de C——, are you not?" asked I. He arose, looked at me with a strange glance, and replied: "I was, but I am no longer. I am no longer anybody." Then seeing my astonishment he said: "Not a word, young man, do not question me."

I replied, blushing: "If, Monsieur, I have witnessed, without wishing it, your chagrin and your sorrow, perhaps my devotion and my friendship can assuage your grief?"

"Yes, yes, you are right; not that you can change my condition, but you can receive, at least, my last wishes and my last vows. It is the only service that I ask of you."

He crossed the room, closed the door, then came and sat down beside me, who agitated and trembling, awaited his words. They were somewhat grave and solemn, and his physiognomy, above all, had an expression that I had never before seen. His lofty brow, which I examined attentively, seemed marked by fate. His complexion was very pale, and his eyes were black, bright, and piercing; and from time to time his features, altered by suffering, contracted under an ironical and infernal smile.

"That which I am about to relate to you," said he, will confound your reason, you will doubt, you will not believe me, perhaps; even I often doubt still. I tell myself it cannot be; but the proofs are too real; and are there not in all that surrounds us, in our organisation even, many other mysteries that we are obliged to submit to, without being able to comprehend ? "

He paused a moment, as if to gather together his thoughts, passed his hand over his brow, and continued : " I was born in this château. I had two elder brothers to whom fell the wealth and honours of our house. I had nothing to expect, nothing to look forward to but an abbé's mantle ; nevertheless, ambitious dreams of glory and power fermented in my head and made my heart throb with anticipation. Miserable in my obscurity, eager for renown, I thought only of means to acquire it at any price, and these ideas made me insensible to all the pleasures and all the sweetness of life. To me the present was nothing ; I only existed for the future, and this future presented itself to me under a most sombre aspect. I reached my thirtieth year without having accomplished anything ;—then there arose in the capital literary lights whose brilliance penetrated even to our remote province. Ah ! thought I, if I could at least make for myself a name in the world of letters, that might bring renown, and therein lies true happiness. I had for a confidant of my chagrins an old servant, an aged negro, who had served in my family many years before my birth ; he was the oldest person on the estate, or for miles around, for no one could recall his first appearance, and the country folk said that he had known the Maréchal Fabert, was present at his death, and that he was an evil spirit."

At that name, I started with surprise ; the unknown paused and asked me the cause of my embarrassment.

" Nothing," said I ; but I could not help thinking that the black man must be the one spoken of by the old landlord of the " Armes de France " the previous evening.

M. de C—— continued :

" One day in Yago's presence (that was the old negro's name) I gave way to my feelings, bemoaned my obscurity, and bewailed my useless and monotonous life, and I cried aloud in my despair : ' I would willingly give ten years of my life to be placed in the first rank of our authors ! '

" ' Ten years,' said Yago, coolly ; ' that is much, it is paying very dear for so little a thing ; no matter, I accept your ten years ; remember your promise, I will surely keep mine.'

" I cannot describe to you my great surprise on hearing him speak thus. I believed that his mind had become enfeebled by the weight of years. I shrugged my shoulders and smiled, and took no further notice of him. Some days afterward I left home for Paris. There I found myself launched into the society of men of letters ; their example encouraged and stimulated me, and I soon published several works that were very successful, which I will not now describe. All Paris rushed to see me, the journals were filled with my praises. The new name I had taken became celebrated, and even recently, young man, you have admired my works."

Here another gesture of surprise on my part interrupted this recital. " Then you are not the Duc de C——? " cried I.

" No," replied he, coldly. And I asked myself : " A celebrated man of letters ! Is this Marmontel ? is it D'Alembert ? is it Voltaire ? "

The unknown sighed, a smile of regret and contempt spread over his lips, and he continued his recital.

" This literary reputation, which had seemed to me so desirable, soon failed to satisfy a soul so ardent as mine. I aspired to still higher successes, and I said to Yago (who had followed me to Paris and who kept close watch over me) : ' This is not real glory, there is no veritable renown but that which one acquires in the career of arms. What is an author, a poet ? Nothing ! Give me a great general, or a captain in the army ! Behold the destiny that I desire, and for a great military reputation I would willingly give ten more years of my life.'

" ' I accept them,' replied Yago, quickly. ' I take them—they belong to me—do not forget it.' "

At this stage of his recital the unknown paused once more on seeing the alarm and incredulity that were depicted on my features.

" You remember, I warned you, young man," said he, " that you could not believe my story. It must seem to you a dream, a chimera—to me also ;—nevertheless the promotions, the honours that I soon obtained, were no illusions. Those brave soldiers that I led into the thickest of the fight ! Those brilliant charges ! Those captured flags ! Those victories which all France heard of ; all that was *my* work—all that glory belonged to me ! "

While he marched up and down the room with great strides, and spoke thus with warmth and with enthusiasm, astonishment and fear had almost paralysed my senses. " Who then is this person ? " thought I. " Is it Coligny ? is it Richelieu ? is it the Maréchal de Saxe ? "

From his state of exaltation my unknown had fallen again into the deepest dejection, and, approaching me, said with a sombre air : " Yago kept his promise ; and when, later on, disgusted with the vain smoke of military glory, I aspired to that which is only real and positive in this world—when at the price of five or six years of existence I desired great riches, he gladly gave them to me. Yes, young man, I have possessed vast wealth, far beyond my wildest dreams—estates, forests, and châteaux. To-day, still, all this is mine, and in my power ; if you doubt me—if you doubt the existence of Yago—wait here, he is coming, and you can see for yourself that which would confound your reason and mine were it not unfortunately too real."

The unknown approached the fireplace, looked at the timepiece, made a gesture of alarm, and said to me in a deep voice :

" This morning at daybreak I felt myself so weak and so feeble that I could scarcely rise. I rang for my *valet-de-chambre* ; it was Yago who appeared. 'What is this strange feeling ! ' asked I.

" ' Master, nothing but what is perfectly natural. The hour approaches, the moment arrives.'

" ' And what is it ? ' cried I.

" ' Can you not divine it ? Heaven has destined you sixty years to live ; you were thirty when I began to obey you.'

" ' Yago ! ' cried I in affright, ' do you speak seriously ? '

" ' Yes, master ; in five years you have spent in glory twenty-five years of life. You have sold them to me. They belong to me ; and these years that you have voluntarily given up are now added to mine.'

" ' What ! That, then, was the price of your services ? '

" ' Yes, and many others—for ages past—have paid more dearly ; for instance, Fabert, whom I protected also.'

" ' Be silent, be silent ! ' cried I ; ' this is not possible ; it cannot be true ! '

" ' As you please ; but prepare yourself ; for there only remains for you a brief half-hour of life.'

" ' You are mocking me ! '

" ' Not at all. Calculate for yourself. Thirty-five years you have had, and twenty-five years you have sold to me—total, sixty. It is your own count ; each one takes his own.' Then he wished to go away, and I felt my strength diminish. I felt my life leaving me.

" ' Yago ! Yago ! ' I cried feebly ; ' give me a few hours, a few hours more ! '

" ' No, no,' replied he, ' it would be taking away from myself, and I know better than you the value of life. There is no treasure worth two hours of existence.'

" I could scarcely speak ; my eyes were set in my head, and the chill of death congealed the blood in my veins. ' Very well ! ' said I with an effort, ' take back your gifts, for that which I have sacrificed all. Four hours more and I renounce my gold, my wealth—all this opulence that I have so much desired.'

" ' Be it so ; you have been a good master, and I am willing to do something for you. I consent.'

" I felt my strength come back, and I cried : ' Four hours—that is very little ! Yago ! Yago ! Four hours more and I renounce all my literary fame, all my works that have placed me so high in the world's esteem.'

" ' Four hours for that ! ' cried the negro with disdain ; ' it is too much. No matter. I cannot refuse your last request.'

" ' Not the last ! ' cried I clasping my hands before him. ' Yago !

Yago! I supplicate you, give me until this evening. The twelve hours, the entire day, and all my exploits, my victories, all my military renown may all be effaced from the memory of men. This day, Yago, dear Yago; this whole day, and I will be content!'

"'You abuse my kindness,' said he; 'no matter, I will give you until sunset; after that you must not ask me. This evening, then, I will come for you'—and he is gone," continued the unknown, in despairing accents—" and this day, in which I see you for the first time, is my last on earth."

Then, going to the glass door, which was open, and which led to the park, he cried: "Alas! I will no longer behold the beautiful sky, these green lawns, the sparkling fountains! I will never again breathe the balmy air of springtime. Fool that I have been! These gifts that God has given to all of us; these blessings, to which I was insensible, and of which I can only now, when it is too late, appreciate and comprehend the sweetness—and I might have enjoyed them for twenty-five years more!—and I have used up my life! I have sacrificed it for what? For a vain and sterile glory, which has not made me happy, and which dies with me! Look!" said he to me, pointing to some peasants who traversed the park, singing on their way to work. "What would I not give now to share their labours and their poverty! But I have no longer anything to give, or to hope for here below, not even misfortune!"

Just then a ray of sunlight (the sun of the month of May) shone through the casement and lit up his pale and distracted features. He seized my arm in a sort of delirium, and said to me:

"See! see there! is it not beautiful? the sun!—and I must leave all this! Ah! at least I am still alive! I will have this whole day—so pure, so bright, so radiant—this day which for me has no morrow!" He then ran down the steps of the open door, and bounded like a deer across the park, and at a detour of the path he disappeared in the shrubbery, before I hardly realised that he was gone, or could detain him. To tell the truth, I would not have had the strength. I lay back on the couch, stunned, dazed, and weak with the shock of all I had heard. I arose and walked up and down the room, to assure myself that I was awake, that I had not been under the influence of a dream. Just then the door of the boudoir opened and a servant announced: "Here is my master, the Duc de C——."

A man of sixty years and of distinguished presence advanced toward me, and, giving me his hand, apologised for having made me wait so long.

"I was not in the château. I had gone to seek my younger brother, the Comte de C——, who is ill."

"And is he in danger?" interrupted I.

" No, monsieur. Thanks to heaven," replied my host ; " but in his youth ambitious dreams of glory exalted his imagination, and a serious illness that he has had recently (and which he deemed fatal) has upset his mind, and produced a sort of delirium and mental aberration, by which he persuades himself always that he has but one day to live. It is insanity."

All was explained to me.

" Now," continued the duke, " let us come to you, young man, and see what can be done for your advancement. We will depart at the end of the month for Versailles. I will present you at court."

I blushed and replied : " I appreciate your kindness, Monsieur le Duc, and I thank you very much ; but I will not go to Versailles."

" What ! would you renounce the court and all the advantages and promotions which certainly await you there ? "

" Yes, Monsieur."

" But do you realise that with my influence you can rise rapidly, and that with a little assiduity and patience you can become distinguished in ten years ? "

" Ten years lost ! " I cried in terror.

" What ! " replied he, astonished. " Ten years is not much to pay for fortune, glory, and honours ? Come, come, my young friend. Come with me to Versailles."

" No, Monsieur le Duc. I am determined to return to Brittany, and I beg of you to receive my profound gratitude, and that of my family."

" What folly ! " cried he.

And I, remembering what I had listened to, said : " It is wisdom ! "

The next day I was en route, and with what exquisite delight did I behold my beautiful château of Roche-Bernard, the grand old trees in my park, and the bright sunshine of Brittany. I found again my vassals, my mother, my sisters, my fiancée, and my happiness, which I still retain, for one week later I married Henriette.

ALFRED DE VIGNY
1797–1863

NAPOLEON
AND POPE PIUS VII.

WE were at Fontainebleau. The Pope had just arrived. The Emperor had awaited him with great impatience as he desired the Holy Father to crown him. Napoleon received him in person, and they immediately entered the carriage—on opposite sides, at the same time, apparently with an entire neglect of etiquette, but this was only in appearance, for the movement was thoroughly calculated. It was so arranged that neither might seem to yield precedence or to exact it from the other. The ruse was characteristically Italian. They at once drove toward the palace, where all kinds of rumours were in circulation. I had left several officers in the room which preceded that of the Emperor ; and I was quite alone in his apartment.

I was standing looking at a long table, which was of Roman mosaic work, and which was absolutely loaded, covered with heaps of papers. I had often seen Napoleon enter and submit the pile of documents to a strange system of decision. He did not take the letters either by hazard or in order ; but when the number irritated him, he swept them off the table with his hand—striking right and left like a mower, until he had reduced the number to six or seven, which he opened.

Such disdainful conduct had moved me singularly. So many letters of distress and mourning cast underfoot as if by an angry wind ; so many useless prayers of widows and orphans having no chance except that of being spared by the consular hand ; so many groaning leaves, moistened by the tears of so many families trampled under his heel with as little compunction as if they were corpses on a battlefield—all these seemed to represent the fate of France. Although the hand that acted so ruthlessly was strong, it seemed always that such brutal strength was anything but admirable, and it seemed wrong that so much should be left to the caprice of such a man.

Moreover, had a little consideration been shown, Napoleon would have had so many more buttresses for his power and authority. I felt my heart rise against the man—but feebly, like the heart of one who was his slave. I thought of the letters which had been treated with such cruel contempt ; cries of anguish came from the envelopes ; and having read some of the petitions I constituted myself judge between the man and those who had sacrificed themselves so much for him, upon whose necks he was going to fasten the yoke tighter that very day. I was holding one of the papers in my hand, when the beating of the drums informed me of the arrival of Napoleon. Now you know that just as one always sees the flash from a cannon before one hears the report, one always saw him as he was heard to be approaching ; he was so active, and seemed to have so little time. When he rode into the courtyard of the palace, his attendants were scarcely able to keep up with him. The sentry had barely time to salute before the Emperor had got down from his horse and was hurrying up the staircase.

This time he had left the Pope in the carriage in order to be able to enter the palace alone, and had galloped on ahead. I heard the sound of his spurs at the same time as the drums. I had only just time enough to throw myself into an alcove where there was an old-fashioned high bedstead which was used by no one, and which was, fortunately, concealed by curtains.

The Emperor was in a state of great excitement, and strode about the room as if waiting for some one with great impatience. Having darted across the room several times, he went to the window and began to drum on the panes. A carriage rolled into the court ; he ceased beating a tattoo on the glass, and stamped with his foot as if the sight which he saw in the courtyard was anything but agreeable to him. Then he tore across the room to the door, which he opened for the Pope.

Pius VII. entered unattended. Bonaparte hastily closed the door after the old man with the care of a jailer. I will confess that I was in a state of mortal terror at being the third of the party. However, I remained motionless, listening eagerly to every word that was said.

The Pope was tall : his face was long, yellow, and had traces of great suffering, but bore the imprint of a goodness of soul and nobility of spirit which knew no bounds. He had fine, big, black eyes, and his mouth was sweetened by a smile which lent something spirituelle and vivacious to his countenance. It was a smile in which one could detect nothing of the cunning of the world, but which was full to overflowing of Christian goodness. On his head he wore a skull-cap, from under which escaped locks of his silver-streaked hair. A red velvet cloak hung negligently on his stooping shoulders, and his robe dragged at his feet. He entered slowly, with the calm and prudent step of an aged man, sank down into

one of the big Roman armchairs, which were gilded and covered
with eagles, lowered his eyes, and waited to hear what the other
Italian had to say to him.

What a scene that was ! I can see it still. It was not the genius
of the man which I noticed, but his character. Bonaparte was
not then as you knew him afterward ; he had not grown gross—
he had not the swollen face, the gouty legs, nor was he so ridiculously
stout as he afterward became. Unfortunately, in art he is almost
always represented by a sort of caricature, so that he will not be
handed down to posterity as he really was. He was not ungainly
then, but nervous and supple, lithe and active, convulsive in some
of his gestures, in some gracious ; his chest was flat and narrow—
in short, he looked just as I had seen him at Malta.

He did not stop stalking round the room when the Pope entered.
He wandered round the chair of the latter like a cautious hunter ;
then suddenly halting in front of Pius, he resumed a conversation
which had been commenced in the carriage, and which he was
evidently anxious to continue.

" I tell you again, Holy Father, I am not a free-thinker ; and I
don't agree with those who are for ever reasoning about religious
matters. I assure you that in spite of my old republicans I shall
go to mass."

The last words he threw brusquely, as it were, in the Pope's
face—incense of flattery undisguised. Then he suddenly stopped
and examined the Pope's countenance to catch the result, which
he seemed to expect to be great. The old man lowered his eyes
and rested his hands on the heads of the eagles which formed the
arms of the chair. He seemed to have assumed the attitude of a
Roman statue purposely, as if wishing to express : " I resign myself
to hearing all the profane things that he may choose to say to me ! "

Bonaparte took a turn round the room, and round the chair which
was in the middle, and it was plain to be seen that he was not satisfied
either with himself or with his adversary, and that he was reproach-
ing himself for having resumed the conversation so rashly. So
he began to talk more connectedly as he walked round the room,
all the time watching narrowly the reflection of the pontiff's face
in the mirror, and also eyeing him carefully in profile as he passed ;
but not venturing to look him full in the face for fear of appearing
too anxious about the effect of his words.

" There is one thing that hurts me very much, Holy Father,"
said he, " and that is that you consent to the coronation as you
formerly consented to the Concordat—as if you were compelled
to do so, and not as of free will. You sit there before me with the
air of a martyr, resigned to the will of heaven, and suffering for the
sake of your conscience. But that is not the fact. You are not a
prisoner. You are as free as the air."

Pius VII. smiled and looked his interlocutor in the face. He realised that the despotic nature with which he had to contend was not satisfied with obedience unless one seemed willing, even anxious, to obey.

" Yes," continued Bonaparte, " you are quite free. You may return to Rome if you like. The road is open and no one will stop you."

Without uttering a word, the Pope sighed and raised his hand and his eyes to heaven ; then very slowly he lowered his eyes and studied the cross on his bosom attentively.

Bonaparte continued to walk round the room and to talk to his captive, his voice becoming sweeter and more wheedling.

" Holy Father, were it not for the reverence I have for you I should be inclined to say that you are a little ungrateful. You seem to ignore entirely the services which France has rendered you. As far as I am able to judge, the Council of Venice, which elected you Pope, was influenced somewhat by my campaign in Italy, as well as by a word which I spoke for you. I was very much troubled at the time that Austria treated you so badly. I believe that your Holiness was obliged to return to Rome by sea for fear of passing through Austrian territory.

He stopped for the answer of his silent guest ; Pius VII. made simply the slightest inclination of the head, and remained plunged in a melancholy reverie which seemed to prevent him from hearing Napoleon.

Bonaparte then pushed a chair near to that of the Pope. I started, for in seeking the chair he had come very near my hiding-place, he even brushed the curtains which concealed me.

" It was as a Catholic really that I was so afflicted about your vexations. I have never had much time to study theology, it is true, but I maintain a great faith in the Church. She has a wonderful vitality, Holy Father, although Voltaire did you some little harm, certainly. Now if you are only willing we can do a great deal of work together in the future."

He assumed a caressing, wheedling air of innocence.

" Really, I have tried to understand your motives, but I can't for the life of me see what objection you can have to making Paris your seat. I'll leave the Tuileries to you if you like. You'll find your room waiting for you there. I scarcely ever go there myself. Don't you see, Father, it is the capital of the world. I'll do whatever you want me to ; and really, after all, I am not as bad as I am painted. If you'll leave war and politics to me you may do as you like in ecclesiastical matters. In fact, I would be your soldier. Now wouldn't that be a grand arrangement ? We could hold our councils like Constantine and Charlemagne—I would open and dissolve them ; and then I would put the keys of the world into

your hands, for, as our Lord said : ' I came with a sword,' and I
would keep the sword ; I would only bring it to you for your
blessing after each new success of our arms."

The Pope, who until then had remained as motionless as an
Egyptian statue, slowly raised his head, smiled sadly, lifted his
eyes to heaven, and said, after a gentle sigh, as if he were confiding
the thought to his invisible guardian angel :

" Commediante ! "

Napoleon leaped from his chair like a wounded tiger. He was in
one of his " yellow tempers." At first he stamped about without
uttering a word, biting his lips till the blood came. He no longer
circled round his prey cautiously, but walked from end to end of the
room with firm resounding steps, and clinking his spurs noisily.
The room shook ; the curtains trembled like trees at the approach
of a storm ; I thought that something terrible would surely happen ;
my hair began to bristle, and I put my hand to my head unwittingly.
I looked at the Pope. He did not stir, but simply pressed the heads
of the eagles with his hands.

The storm burst violently.

" Comedian ! What ? I a comedian ? Indeed, I'll play some
comedies for you that will set you all a-weeping like women and
children ! Comedian, forsooth ! You are mistaken if you think that
you may insult me with impunity. My theatre is the world ; the
rôle that I play is the double one of master and actor ; I use all of
you as comedians, popes, kings, peoples, and the string by which
I work you—*you* my puppets—is fear. You would need to be a
much heavier man than you are, Signor Chiaramonti, to dare to
applaud or hiss me. Do you know that if it be my will you will
become a simple *curé* ? As for you and your tiara, France would
mock at you if I did not seem to be serious in saluting you.

" Only four years ago nobody dared speak of Christ. Had that
state of things continued who would have cared for the Pope,
I should like to know ? Comedian ! You gentlemen are a little too
ready at getting a foothold among us. And now you are dissatisfied because I am not such a fool as to sign away the liberties
of France as did Louis XIV. But you had better not sing to me
in that tune. It is I who hold you between my thumb and finger ;
it is I who can carry you from north to south and then back again
to the north like so many marionettes ; it is I who give you some
stability because you represent an old idea which I wish to
resuscitate ; and you have not enough wit to see that, and to act
as if you were not aware of the fact. Now I'll speak to you frankly.
Trouble your head with your own affairs and don't interfere in what
you don't understand and with what doesn't in the least concern
you. You seem to think that you are necessary, you set yourselves
up as if you were of some weight, and you dress yourselves in

women's clothes. But I'll let you know that you don't impose on me with all that ; and if you don't change your tactics very soon I'll treat your robes as Charles XII. did that of the Grand Vizier—I'll tear them with my spur."

Then he ceased. I scarcely dared breathe. I advanced my head a little, not hearing his voice, to see if the poor old priest was dead with fright. The same absolutely calm attitude, the same calm expression on his face. For the second time he raised his eyes to heaven, again he sighed, and smiled bitterly as he murmured :

" Tragediante ! "

Bonaparte was at the farther end of the room, leaning against a marble chimney which was as high as he was tall. Like an arrow shot out of a bow, he rushed straight at the old man ; I thought he was going to kill him as he sat. But he suddenly stopped short, seized a Sèvres vase on which the Capitol was painted, threw it on the hearth and ground it under his heels. Then he remained terribly quiet.

I was relieved, for I felt that his reason had got the better of his temper. He became sad, and when he finally spoke in a deep voice, it was evident that in the two words uttered by the Pope he had recognised his true portrait.

" Miserable life ! " he said. Then he fell into reverie, and without speaking tore the brim of his hat. When his voice again was heard he was talking to himself :

" It's true. Tragedian or comedian, I am always playing a part— all is costume and pose. How wearying it all is, and how belittling ! Pose ! pose ! always pose ! In one case full face, in another profile— but invariably for effect. Always trying to appear what others worship, so that I may deceive the fools, keeping them between hope and fear. Dazzling them by bulletins, by prestige. Master of all of them and not knowing what to do with them. That's the simple truth after all.

" And to make myself so miserable through it all ! It really is too much. For," continued he, sitting down in an armchair and crossing his legs, " it bores me to death, the whole farce. As soon as I sit down I don't know what to do with myself. I can't even hunt for three days in succession at Fontainebleau with being weary of it. I must always be moving and making others move. I speak quite frankly. I have plans in my life which would require the lives of forty emperors to carry out, and I make new ones every morning and evening ; my imagination is always on the *qui vive* ; but before I have carried out two of them I shall be exhausted in body and mind ; for our poor lamp of life doesn't burn long enough. And I must confess that if I could carry them out I should not find that the world was one whit better than it is now ; but it *would* be better though, for it would be united. I am not a

philosopher. I don't understand many theories. Life is too
short to stop. As soon as I have an idea I put it into execution.
Others will find reasons after me for praising me if I succeed and
for abusing me if I fail. Differences of opinion are active—they
abound in France—but I keep them down while I am alive—
afterward—Well, no matter ! It is my business to succeed, and that
I intend to do. Every day I make an Iliad by my actions—every
day."

Thereupon he rose quickly. In that moment he was lively and
natural, and was not thinking of posing as he afterward did in St.
Helena ; he did not strive to make himself ideal or to pose for effect—
he was himself outside of himself. He went back to the Pope, who
had remained seated, and paced in front of him. Getting warmed
up, he spoke with a dash of irony, at an incredible rate :

" Birth is everything. Those who come into the world poor and
neglected are always desperate. That desperation turns to action
or suicide according to character. When they have courage to
attempt something as I have done, they raise the devil. But what
else is to be done ? One must live. One must find one's place and
make one's mark. I have carried everything before me like a
cannon-ball—all the worse for those who happened to be in my
way. But what else could I have done ? Each man eats
according to his appetite, and I have an insatiable one.

" Do you know, Holy Father, at Toulon I had not wherewithal to
buy myself a pair of epaulets, in place of which I had a mother and
I don't know how many brothers on my shoulders. They are all
satisfactorily settled at present. Josephine married me out of pity
in spite of her old notary, who objected that I owned nothing but
my cap and cape, and now we are going to crown her. The old
man was right, though, as to what I possessed at that time.
Imperial mantle ! Crown ! what does all that mean ? Is it mine ?
Costume ! Actor's costume ! I will put them on for an hour and
then I shall have had enough of them. Then I shall don my officer's
uniform, and ' To horse '; all my life on horseback. I couldn't
pass a single day resting, without being in danger of falling out of
the chair. I am to be envied ? Eh !

" I repeat, Holy Father ; there are only two classes of men in
the world : those who have and those who gain.

" Those who are in the first class rest, the others are restless. As
I learnt that lesson at an early age and to some purpose I shall
go a long way. There are only two men who have done anything
before they were forty years old ; Cromwell and Jean-Jacques ;
if you had given one a farm, and the other twelve hundred francs
and his servant, they would neither have commanded nor preached
nor written.

" There are workmen in buildings, in colours, in forms, and in

phrases ; I am a workman in battles. It's my business. At the
age of thirty-five I have manufactured eighteen of them, which are
called ' Victories.' I must be paid for my work. And a throne is
certainly not extravagant payment. Besides, I shall always go
on working. You will see that all dynasties will date from mine,
although I am a mere parvenu. I am elected as you are, Holy
Father—and drawn from the multitude. On this point we can
well shake hands."

And, approaching the Pope, Napoleon held out his hand. Pius
took the hand which was offered to him, but shook his head sadly,
and I saw his fine eyes cloud with tears.

Bonaparte cast a hurried glance at the tears which he had wrung
from the old Pope, and I surprised even a rapid motion in the corners
of his mouth much resembling a smile of triumph. At that moment
his intensely powerful and overbearing nature seemed to me less
admirable than that of his saintly adversary ; I blushed for all
my past admiration of Napoleon ; I felt a sadness creep over me
at the thought that the grandest policy appears little when stained
by tricks of vanity. I saw that the Emperor had gained his end
in the interview by having yielded nothing and by having drawn
a sign of weakness from the Pope. He had wished to have the last
word, and without uttering another syllable, he left the room
as abruptly as he had entered.

I could not see whether he saluted the Pope or not, but I do not
think he did.

HONORÉ DE BALZAC
1799–1850

AN EPISODE OF THE REIGN OF TERROR

ABOUT eight o'clock on the evening of January 22, 1793, an aged woman was coming down the sharp descent of the Faubourg Saint-Martin that ends in front of the church of Saint-Laurent. Snow had fallen so heavily all day long that hardly a footfall could be heard. The streets were deserted. Fears that the silence around naturally enough inspired were increased by all the terror under which France was then groaning. So the old lady had thus far met with no one else. Her sight, which had long been failing, did not enable her to distinguish far off by the light of the street lamps some passers-by, moving like scattered shadows in the huge thoroughfare of the Faubourg. She went on bravely all alone in the midst of this solitude, as if her age were a talisman that could be relied on to preserve her from any mishap.

When she had passed the Rue des Morts she thought she perceived the heavy, firm tread of a man walking behind her. It occurred to her that it was not the first time she had heard this sound. She was alarmed at the idea that she was being followed, and she tried to walk faster in order to reach a fairly well-lighted shop, in the hope that, in the light it gave, she would be able to put to the test the suspicions that had taken possession of her.

As soon as she was within the circle of light projected horizontally by the shop-front, she quickly turned her head and caught a glimpse of a human form in the foggy darkness. This vague glimpse was enough for her. She tottered for a moment under the shock of terror that overwhelmed her, for she no longer doubted that she had been followed by the stranger from the first step she had taken outside her lodging. The longing to escape from a spy gave her strength. Without being able to think of what she was doing, she began to run—as if she could possibly get away from a man who must necessarily be much more agile than herself.

After running for a few minutes she reached a confectioner's shop, entered it, and fell, rather than sat, down upon a chair that stood in front of the counter. Even while she was raising the creaking latch, a young woman, who was busy with some embroidery, raised her eyes, and through the small panes of the half-window in the shop door recognised the old-fashioned violet silk mantle in which the old lady was wrapped. She hurriedly opened a drawer as if looking for something she was to hand over to her.

It was not only by her manner and the look on her face that the young woman showed she was anxious to get rid of the stranger without delay, as if her visitor were one of those there was no pleasure in seeing ; but, besides this, she allowed an expression of impatience to escape her on finding that the drawer was empty. Then, without looking at the lady, she turned suddenly from the counter, went towards the back shop, and called her husband, who at once made his appearance.

" Wherever have you put away . . . ? " she asked of him, with an air of mystery without finishing her question, but calling his attention to the old lady with a glance of her eyes.

Although the confectioner could see nothing but the immense black silk bonnet, trimmed with bows of velvet ribbon, that formed the strange visitor's headgear, he left the shop again, after having cast at his wife a look that seemed to say, " Do you think I would leave *that* in your counter . . . ? "

Surprised at the motionless silence of the old lady, the shop-woman turned and approached her, and as she looked at her she felt herself inspired with an impulse of compassion, perhaps not unmingled with curiosity. Although the woman's complexion showed an habitual pallor, like that of one who makes a practice of secret austerities, it was easy to see that a recent emotion had brought an unusual paleness to her face. Her head-dress was so arranged as to conceal her hair. No doubt it was white with age, for there were no marks on the upper part of her dress to show that she used hair powder. The complete absence of ornament lent to her person an air of religious severity. Her features had a grave, stately look. In these old times the manners and habits of people of quality were so different from those of other classes of society, that it was easy to distinguish one of noble birth. So the young woman felt convinced that the stranger was a *ci-devant*, an ex-aristocrat, and that she had belonged to the court.

" Madame . . ." she said to her with involuntary respect, forgetting that such a title was now forbidden.

The old lady did not reply. She kept her eyes fixed on the window of the shop as if she could distinguish some fearful object in that direction.

" What is the matter, citizeness ? " asked the shopkeeper, who had returned almost immediately.

And the citizen-confectioner roused the lady from her reverie by offering her a little cardboard box wrapped in blue paper.

" Nothing, nothing, my friends," she answered in a sweet voice. She raised her eyes to the confectioner's face as if to give him a look of thanks, but seeing the red cap on his head, she uttered a cry : " Ah, you have betrayed me ! "

The young woman and her husband replied by a gesture of horror at the thought, which made the stranger blush, perhaps at having suspected them, perhaps with pleasure.

" Pardon me," she said, with childlike gentleness. Then, taking a *louis d'or* from her pocket, she offered it to the confectioner : " Here is the price we agreed on," she added.

There is a poverty that the poor readily recognise. The confectioner and his wife looked at one another, silently turning each other's attention to the old lady, while both formed one common thought. This *louis d'or* must be her last. The lady's hands trembled as she offered the piece of money, she looked at it with a sadness that had no avarice in it, but she seemed to realise the full extent of the sacrifice she made. Starvation and misery were as plainly marked on her face as the lines that told of fear and of habits of asceticism. In her dress there were traces of old magnificence. It was of worn-out silk. Her mantle was neat though threadbare, with some carefully mended lace upon it. In a word, it was a case of wealth the worse for wear. The people of the shop, hesitating between sympathy and self-interest, began by trying to satisfy their consciences with words :

" But, citizeness, you seem to be very weak——"

" Would Madame like to take something ? " said the woman, cutting her husband short.

" We have some very good soup," added the confectioner.

" It is so cold to-night. Perhaps Madame has had a chill while walking ? But you can rest here and warm yourself for a while."

" We are not as black as the devil ! " exclaimed the confectioner.

Won by the tone of kindness that found expression in the words of the charitable shopkeepers, the lady let them know she had been followed by a stranger, and that she was afraid to go back alone to her lodgings.

" Is that all ? " replied the man in the red cap, " wait a little, citizeness."

He gave the *louis d'or* to his wife. . . . Then moved by that sort of gratitude that finds its way into the heart of a dealer when he has got an exorbitant price for some merchandise of trifling value, he went and put on his National Guard's uniform, took his hat, belted on his sword, and reappeared as an armed man. But his wife had had time to reflect. In her heart, as in so many more, reflection closed the open hand of benevolence. Anxious and fearful of seeing her husband involved in some bad business, the confectioner's wife tried to pull him by the skirt of his coat and stop him. But obeying his own charitable feelings the good fellow offered at once to escort the old lady.

" It seems that the man the citizeness is afraid of is still prowling about in front of our shop," said the young woman excitedly.

" I am afraid he is," put in the lady naïvely.

" What if he were a spy ? . . . if there were some plot ? . . . Don't go, and take back that box from her. . . ."

These words, whispered in the ear of the confectioner by his wife, froze the sudden courage that had inspired him.

" Well, I'll just say a few words to him, and rid you of him soon enough," exclaimed the shopkeeper, as he opened the door and slipped hurriedly out.

The old lady, passive as a child and almost stupefied by her fear, sat down again on the chair. The good shopkeeper was soon back. His face, naturally ruddy enough and further reddened by his oven fire, had suddenly become pallid. He was a prey to such terror that his legs shook and his eyes looked like those of a drunken man.

" Do you want to get our heads cut off, you wretch of an aristocrat ? " he cried out in a fury. " Come, show us your heels, and don't let us see you again, and don't reckon on my supplying you with materials for your plots ! "

As he ended, the confectioner made an attempt to take back from the old lady the little box which she had put into one of her pockets. But hardly had his bold hands touched her dress, than the stranger, preferring to risk herself amid the perils of the street without any other protector but God, rather than to lose what she had just bought, regained all the agility of youth. She rushed to the door, opened it briskly, and vanished from the sight of wife and husband as they stood trembling and astonished.

As soon as the stranger was outside she started off at a rapid walk. But her strength soon began to desert her, and she heard the spy, who had so pitilessly followed her, making the snow crackle as he crushed it with his heavy tread. She had to stop. He stopped. She did not dare to address him, or even to look at him—it might be on account of the fear that had seized upon her, or because she could not think what to say. Then she went on again walking slowly.

The man also slackened his pace so as to remain always just at the distance that enabled him to keep her in sight. He seemed to be the very shadow of the old woman. Nine o'clock struck as the silent pair once more passed by the church of Saint-Laurent.

It is a part of the nature of all minds, even of the weakest, to find a feeling of calm succeed to any violent agitation, for if our feelings are infinite, our organism has its limits. So the stranger, finding that her supposed persecutor did her no harm, was inclined to see in him some unknown friend, who was anxious to protect her. She summed up in her mind all the circumstances that had attended the appearance of the stranger, as if seeking for some plausible motives for this consoling opinion, and was then satisfied to recognise on his part a friendly rather than an evil purpose. Forgetful of the alarm, which this man had so short a time ago caused the confectioner, she now went on with a firm step into the upper part of the Faubourg Saint-Martin.

After walking for half an hour she came to a house situated near the point where the street, which leads to the Pantin barrier, branches off from the main line of the Faubourg. Even at the present day the neighbourhood is still one of the loneliest in all Paris. A north-east wind blowing over the Buttes Chaumont and Belleville whistled between the houses, or rather the cottages, scattered about this almost uninhabited valley, in which the enclosures were formed of fences built up of earth and old bones. The desolate place seemed to be the natural refuge of misery and despair.

The man, all eagerness in the pursuit of this poor creature, who was so bold as to traverse these silent streets in the night, seemed struck by the spectacle that presented itself to his gaze. He stood still, full of thought, in a hesitating attitude, in the feeble light of a street lamp, the struggling rays of which could hardly penetrate the fog. Fear seemed to sharpen the sight of the old lady, who thought she saw something of evil omen in the looks of the stranger. She felt her terror reawakening, and took advantage of the seeming hesitation that had brought the man to a standstill to slip through a shadow to the door of a solitary house ; she pushed back a spring latch, and disappeared in an instant like a ghost upon the stage.

The unknown man, without moving from where he stood, kept his eyes fixed on the house, the appearance of which was fairly typical of that of the wretched dwelling-places of this suburb of Paris. The tumble-down hovel was built of bricks covered with a coat of yellow plaster, so full of cracks that one feared to see the whole fall down in a heap of ruins before the least effort of the wind. There were three windows to each floor, and their frames, rotten with damp and warped by the action of the sun, suggested that the cold must penetrate freely into the rooms. The lonely house looked like some old tower that time has forgotten to destroy. A feeble gleam lit up the warped and crooked window-sashes of the garret window, that showed up the roof of this poor edifice, while all the rest of the house was in complete darkness.

Not without difficulty the old woman climbed the rough and clumsy stair, in ascending which one had to lean on a rope that took the place of a hand-rail. She gave a low knock at the door of the garret room, and hurriedly took her seat on a chair, which an old man offered to her.

"Hide yourself! hide yourself!" she said to him, "though we so seldom go out, our doings are known, our steps are spied upon. . . ."

"Is there anything new then?" asked another old woman, who was seated near the fire.

"That man, who has been prowling round the house since yesterday, followed me this evening. . . ."

At these words the three inmates of the hovel looked at each other, while they showed on their faces signs of serious alarm. Of the three the old man was the least agitated, perhaps because he was the most in danger. Under the weight of a great misfortune, or under the pressure of persecution, a brave man begins, so to say, by making the complete sacrifice of himself. He counts each day as one more victory won over fate. The looks of the two women fixed upon this old man made it easy to see that he was the one object of their keen anxiety.

"Why lose our trust in God, my sisters?" he said in a voice low but full of fervour; "we sang His praises in the midst of the cries of the murderers and of the dying at the convent of the Carmelites. If He willed that I should be saved from that butchery, it was no doubt to preserve me for some destiny that I must accept without a murmur. God guards His own, and He can dispose of them according to His will. It is of yourselves, and not of me, that we must think."

"No," said one of the old women, "what are our lives compared to that of a priest?"

"Once I saw myself outside of the Abbey of Chelles, I considered myself as a dead woman," said one of the two nuns—the one who had remained in the house.

"Here are the altar breads," said the other, who had just come in, offering the little box to the priest. "But . . ." she cried out, "I hear footsteps on the stairs!"

All three listened. . . The sound ceased.

"Do not be alarmed," said the priest, "if some one tries to get to see you. A person on whose good faith we can depend must by this time have taken all necessary steps to cross the frontier, in order to come here for the letters I have written to the Duc de Langeais and the Marquis de Beauséant, asking them to see what can be done to take you away from this wretched country, and the suffering and death that await you here."

"You are not going with us then?" exclaimed the two nuns in gentle protest, and with a look of something like despair.

"My place is where there are still victims," was the priest's simple reply.

They were silent, and gazed at their protector with reverent admiration.

" Sister Martha," he said, addressing the nun who had gone to get the altar breads, " this envoy of ours should answer ' *Fiat voluntas* ' to the password ' *Hosanna.*' "

" There is some one on the stair ! " exclaimed the other nun ; and she opened a hiding-place constructed in the roof.

This time, in the deep silence, it was easy to catch the sound of the footsteps of some man, re-echoing on the stairs that were rough with lumps of hardened mud. The priest with some difficulty huddled himself into a kind of cupboard, and the nun threw some old clothes over him.

" You can shut the door," he said in a smothered voice.

The priest was hardly hidden away, when three knocks at the door made both the good women start. They were exchanging looks of inquiry without daring to utter a word. Both seemed to be about sixty years of age. Separated from the world for some forty years, they were like plants that are so used to the air of a hothouse that they die if one takes them out. Accustomed as they were to the life of the convent they had no idea of anything else. One morning their cloister had been broken open, and they had shuddered at finding themselves free. It is easy to imagine the state of nervous weakness the events of the Revolution had produced in their innocent minds. Unable to reconcile the mental habits of the cloister with the difficulties of life, and not fully understanding the circumstances in which they were placed, they were like children of whom every care had been taken till now, and who, suddenly deprived of their mother's care, pray instead of weeping. So face to face with the danger which they now saw before them, they remained silent and passive, knowing of no other defence but Christian resignation.

The man who had asked for admittance interpreted this silence in his own way. He opened the door and suddenly appeared in the room. The two nuns shuddered as they recognised the man who for some time had been prowling around their house and making inquiries about them. They remained motionless, looking at him with the anxious curiosity of untaught children who stare in silence at a stranger.

The man was tall in stature and heavily built. But there was nothing in his attitude, his general appearance, or the expression of his face to suggest that he was a bad character. Like the nuns, he kept quite still, and slowly cast his eyes round the room he had entered.

Two straw mats unrolled on the floor served for beds for the nuns. There was a table in the middle of the room, and there stood on it a brass candlestick, some plates, three knives, and a round loaf of bread.   There was a very small fire in the grate.   A few pieces of wood heaped up in a corner were a further sign of the poverty of these two recluses.   One could see that the roof was in a bad state, for the walls, covered with a coat of very old paint, were stained with brown streaks that showed where the rain had leaked through. A reliquary, rescued no doubt from the sack of the Abbey of Chelles, served as an ornament to the mantelpiece.   Three chairs, two boxes, and a shabby chest of drawers completed the furniture of the room.   A door near the fireplace suggested that there was a second room beyond.

The individual who had in such an alarming way introduced himself to this poor household had soon taken mental note of all the contents of the little room.   A feeling of pity could be traced upon his countenance, and he cast a kindly look upon the two women, and appeared to be at least as much embarrassed as they were.   The strange silence that all three had kept so far did not long continue, for at last the stranger realised the timidity and inexperience of the two poor creatures, and said to them in a voice that he tried to make as gentle as possible :

" I do not come here as an enemy, citizenesses . . ." He stopped, as if recovering himself, and went on :

" Sisters, if any misfortune comes your way, believe me I have no part in it. . . . I have a favour to ask of you."

They still kept silence.

" If I am troubling you, if . . . if I am causing you pain, say so freely . . . and I will go away ; but be assured that I am entirely devoted to you ; that if there is any kindness I can do to you, you can claim it from me without fear ; and that I am perhaps the only one who is above the law, now that there is no longer a king. . . ."

There was such an air of truth in his words, that Sister Agatha— she of the two nuns who belonged to the noble family of Langeais, and whose manners seemed to indicate that in old times she had known the splendours of festive society and had breathed the air of the court—pointed with an alert movement to one of the chairs as if asking the visitor to be seated.   The stranger showed something of pleasure mingled with sadness as he understood this gesture, but before taking the chair he waited till both the worthy ladies were seated.

" You have given a refuge here," he continued, " to a venerable priest, one of those who refused the oath, and who had a miraculous escape from the massacre at the Carmelites. . . ."

" Hosanna ! " . . . said Sister Agatha, interrupting the stranger, and looking at him with anxious curiosity.

" I don't think that is his name," he replied.

" But, sir, we have no priest here," said Sister Martha, eagerly.

" If that is so, you ought to be more careful and prudent,"

answered the stranger in a gentle tone, as he stretched out his hand to the table and took a breviary from it. " I don't suppose you know Latin, and . . ."

He said no more, for the extraordinary emotion depicted on the faces of the two poor nuns made him fear that he had gone too far. They were trembling, and their eyes filled with tears.

" Don't be alarmed," he said in a voice that seemed all sincerity, " I know the name of your guest, and your own names too, and for the last three days I have been aware of your distress and of your devoted care for the venerable Abbé de . . ."

" Hush ! " said Sister Agatha in her simplicity, putting a finger to her lips.

" You see, Sister, that if I had had in my mind the horrible idea of betraying you, I could have done so already, again and again. . . ."

Hearing these words, the priest extricated himself from his prison and came out again into the room.

" I could not possibly believe, sir," he said to the stranger, " that you were one of our persecutors, and I trust myself to you. What do you want of me ? "

The holy confidence of the priest, the nobility of mind that showed itself in his every look, would have disarmed even assassins. The mysterious man, whose coming had caused such excitement in this scene of resigned misery, gazed for a moment at the group formed by the three others ; then, taking a tone in which there was no longer any hesitation, he addressed the priest in these words :

" Father, I came to ask you to say a mass for the dead, for the repose of the soul . . . of one . . . of a sacred personage, whose body will never be laid to rest in consecrated ground. . . ."

The priest gave an involuntary shudder. The nuns, who did not yet understand to whom it was the stranger alluded, sat in an attitude of curiosity, their heads stretched forwards, their faces turned towards the two who were speaking together. The priest looked closely at the stranger, on whose face there was an unmistakable expression of anxiety, and also of earnest entreaty.

" Well," replied the priest, " come back this evening at midnight, and I shall be ready to celebrate the only rites for the dead that we may be able to offer up in expiation for the crime of which you speak. . . ."

The stranger started, but it seemed that some deep and soothing satisfaction was triumphing over his secret sorrow. After having respectfully saluted the priest and the two holy women, he took his departure, showing a kind of silent gratitude which was understood by these three generous souls.

About two hours after this scene the stranger returned, knocked softly at the door of the garret, and was admitted by Mademoiselle de Beauséant, who led him into the inner room of this poor place of refuge, where everything had been made ready for the ceremony.

Between two chimney-shafts that passed up through the room the nuns had placed the old chest of drawers, the antiquated outlines of which were hidden by a magnificent altar frontal of green watered silk. A large crucifix of ivory and ebony hung on the yellow-washed wall, contrasting so strongly with the surrounding bareness that the eye could not fail to be drawn to it. Four slender little tapers, which the sisters had succeeded in fixing on this improvised altar, by attaching them to it with sealing-wax, threw out a dim light, that was hardly reflected by the wall. This feeble illumination barely gave light to the rest of the room ; but, as it thus shone only on the sacred objects, it seemed like a light sent down from heaven on this unadorned altar. The floor was damp. The roof, which slanted down sharply on two sides, as is usual in garret rooms, had some cracks in it through which came the night wind—icy cold.

Nothing could be more devoid of all pomp, and nevertheless there was perhaps never anything more solemn than this mournful ceremony. A profound silence, in which one could have heard the least sound uttered on the highway outside, lent a kind of sombre majesty to the midnight scene. Finally, the greatness of the action itself contrasted so strongly with the poverty of its surroundings that the result was a feeling of religious awe.

On each side of the altar the two aged nuns knelt on the tiled floor without taking any notice of its deadly dampness, and united their prayers with those of the priest, who, robed in his sacerdotal vestments, placed on the altar a chalice of gold adorned with precious stones, a consecrated vessel that had been saved no doubt from the pillage of the Abbey of Chelles. Besides this chalice, a token of royal munificence, the wine and water destined for the Holy Sacrifice stood ready in two glasses, such as one would hardly have found in the poorest inn. For want of a missal the priest had placed a small prayer-book on the corner of the altar. An ordinary plate had been prepared for the washing of the hands, in this case hands all innocent and free from blood. There was the contrast of littleness with immensity ; of poverty with noble sublimity ; of what was meant for profane uses with what was consecrated to God.

The stranger knelt devoutly between the two nuns. But suddenly, as he noticed that, having no other means of marking that this was a mass offered for the dead, the priest had placed a knot of crape on the crucifix and on the base of the chalice, thus putting holy things in mourning, the stranger's mind was so mastered by some recollection that drops of sweat stood out upon his broad forehead. The four silent actors in the scene looked at each other mysteriously. Then their souls, acting and reacting on each other, inspired with one common thought, united them in devout sympathy. It seemed as if their minds had evoked the presence of the martyr whose

remains the quicklime had burned away, and that his shade was
present with them in all its kingly majesty. They were celebrating
a requiem without the presence of the body of the departed. Under
the disjointed laths and tiles of the roof four Christians were about'
to intercede with God for a King of France, and perform his obsequies
though there was no coffin before the altar. There was the purest
of devoted love, an act of wondrous loyalty performed without a
touch of self-consciousness. No doubt, in the eyes of God, it was
like the gift of the glass of water that ranks with the highest of
virtues. All the monarchy was there, finding voice in the prayers
of a priest and two poor women ; but perhaps the Revolution too
was represented by that man, whose face showed too much remorse
to leave any doubt that he was fulfilling a duty inspired by deep
repentance.

Before he pronounced the Latin words, *Introibo ad altare Dei*, the
priest, as if by an inspiration from on high, turned to the three who
were with him as the representatives of Christian France, and said
to them, as though to banish from their sight all the misery of the
garret room :

" We are about to enter into the sanctuary of God ! "

At these words, uttered with deep devotion, a holy awe took
possession of the stranger and the two nuns. Under the vast arches
of St. Peter's at Rome these Christians could not have realised the
majesty of God's Presence more plainly than in that refuge of
misery ; so true is it that between Him and man all outward things
seem useless, and His greatness comes from Himself alone. The
stranger showed a really fervent devotion. So the same feelings
united the prayers of these four servants of God and the King. The
sacred words sounded like a heavenly music in the midst of the
silence. There was a moment when the unknown man could not
restrain his tears. It was at the *Pater Noster*, when the priest added
this prayer in Latin which no doubt the stranger understood :

" *Et remitte scelus regicidis sicut Ludovicus eis remisit semetipse*
(And forgive their crime to the regicides, as Louis himself forgave
them.) "

The nuns saw two large tear-drops making lines of moisture down
the strong face of the unknown, and falling to the floor.

The Office for the Dead was recited. The *Domine salvum fac
regem*, chanted in a low voice, touched the hearts of these faithful
Royalists, who thought how the child King, for whom at that
moment they were imploring help of the Most High, was a captive
in the hands of his enemies. The stranger suddered as he
remembered that perhaps a fresh crime might be committed, in
which he would no doubt be forced to have a share.

When the Office for the Dead was ended, the priest made a sign
to the two nuns and they withdrew. As soon as he found himself

alone with the stranger, he went towards him with a sad and
gentle air, and said to him in a fatherly voice :

" My son, if you have imbrued your hands in the blood of the
martyr King, confide in me. There is no fault that is not blotted out
in God's eyes by a repentance as sincere and as touching as yours
appears to be."

At the first words uttered by the priest the stranger gave way to
an involuntary movement of alarm. But he recovered his self-
control, and looked calmly at the astonished priest.

" Father," he said to him, in a voice that showed evident signs of
emotion, " no one is more innocent than I am of the blood that has
been shed. . . ."

" It is my duty to take your word for it," said the priest.

There was a pause, during which once more he looked closely at
his penitent. Then, persisting in taking him for one of those timid
members of the National Convention who abandoned to the
executioner a sacred and inviolable head in order to save their own,
he spoke once more in a grave tone :

" Consider, my son, that in order to be guiltless of this great crime
it does not suffice merely to have had no direct co-operation in it.
Those who, although they could have defended the king, left their
swords in their scabbards, will have a very heavy account to render
to the King of Heaven. . . . Oh, yes ! " added the old priest, shaking
his head expressively from side to side. " Yes, very heavy ! . . .
for in standing idle, they have made themselves the involuntary
accomplices of this awful misdeed."

" Do you think," asked the man, as if struck with horror, " that
even an indirect participation in it will be punished ? . . . Are we
then to take it that, say, a soldier who was ordered to keep the
ground at the scaffold is guilty ? . . ."

The priest hesitated. Pleased at the dilemma in which he had
put this Puritan of Royalism, by placing him between the doctrine
of passive obedience, which, according to the partisans of the
monarchy, must be the essence of the military code, and the equally
important doctrine, which was the sanction of the respect due to the
person of the King, the stranger eagerly accepted the priest's
hesitation as indicating a favourable solution of the doubts that
seemed to harass him. Then, in order not to give the venerable
theologian further time for reflection, he said to him :

" I would be ashamed to offer you any honorarium for the funeral
service you have just celebrated for the repose of the soul of the
King, and to satisfy my own conscience. One can only pay the price
of what is inestimable by offering that which is also beyond price.
Will you therefore condescend, sir, to accept the gift I make you
of a sacred relic. . . . Perhaps the day will come when you will
understand its value."

As he ceased speaking, the stranger held out to the priest a little box that was extremely light. The latter took it in his hands automatically, so to say, for the solemnity of the words of this man, the tone in which he spoke, the reverence with which he handled the box, had plunged him into a reverie of deep astonishment. Then they returned to the room where the two nuns were waiting for them.

" You are," said the stranger to them, " in a house the proprietor of which, the plasterer, Mucius Scaevola, who lives in the first storey, is famous in the quarter for his patriotism. But all the same he is secretly attached to the Bourbons. Formerly he was a huntsman to Monseigneur the Prince de Conti, and he owes his fortune to him. By staying here you are safer than anywhere else in France. Remain here, therefore. Certain pious souls will provide for your needs, and you can wait without danger for less evil times. A year hence, on January 21st " (as he pronounced these last words, he could not conceal an involuntary start), " if this poor place is still your refuge, I shall come back to assist once more with you at a mass of expiation."

He stopped without further explanation. He saluted the silent inhabitants of the garret, took in with a last look the signs that told of their poverty, and left the room.

For the two simple nuns such an adventure had all the interest of a romance. So when the venerable abbé had told them of the mysterious present so solemnly made to him by this man, they placed the box on the table, and the feeble light of the candle, shining on the three anxious faces, showed on all of them a look of indescribable curiosity. Mademoiselle de Langeais opened the box, and found in it a handkerchief of fine cambric soiled with perspiration. As they unfolded it they saw spots on it.

" They are blood stains," said the priest.

" It is marked with the royal crown ! " exclaimed the other sister.

With a feeling of horror the two sisters dropped the precious relic. For these two simple souls the mystery that surrounded the stranger had become something inexplicable. And, as for the priest, from that day he did not even attempt to find an explanation of it in his own mind.

It was not long before the three prisoners realised that notwithstanding the Terror an invisible hand was stretched out to protect them. At first firewood and provisions were sent in for them. Then the two nuns guessed that a woman was associated with their protector, for they were sent linen and clothes that would make it possible for them to go out without attracting attention by the aristocratic fashion of the dress they had been forced to wear till then. Finally Mucius Scaevola provided them with two " civic cards," certificates of good citizenship. Often by roundabout ways they received warnings, that were necessary for the safety of the priest, and they recognised that these friendly hints came so opportunely that they could only emanate from some one who was initiated into the secrets of the state. Notwithstanding the famine from which Paris was suffering, the refugees found rations of white bread left regularly at their garret door by invisible hands. However, they thought they could identify in Mucius Scaevola the mysterious agent of this beneficence, which was always as ingenious as it was well directed.

The noble refugees in the garret could have no doubt but that their protector was the same person who had come to assist at the mass of expiation on the night of January 22nd, 1793. He thus became the object of a very special regard on the part of all three. They hoped in him only, lived only thanks to him. They had added special prayers for him to their devotions ; morning and night these pious souls offered up petitions for his welfare, for his prosperity, for his salvation. They begged God to remove all temptations from him, to deliver him from his enemies, and to give him a long and peaceful life. Their gratitude was thus, so to say, daily renewed, but was inevitably associated with a feeling of curiosity that became keener as day after day went by.

The circumstances that had attended the appearance of the stranger were the subject of their conversations. They formed a thousand conjectures with regard to him, and it was a fresh benefit to them of another kind that he thus served to distract their minds from other thoughts. They were quite determined that on the night when, according to his promise, he would come back to celebrate the mournful anniversary of the death of Louis XVI. they would not let him go without establishing more friendly relations with him.

The night to which they had looked forward so impatiently came at last. At midnight the heavy footsteps of the unknown resounded on the old wooden stair. The room had been made ready to receive him ; the altar was prepared. This time the sisters opened the door before he reached it, and both hastened to show a light on the staircase. Mademoiselle de Langeais even went down a few steps in order the sooner to see their benefactor.

" Come," she said to him in a voice trembling with affection, " come . . . you are expected."

The man raised his head, and without replying cast a gloomy look at the nun. She felt as if a mantle of ice had fallen around her, and kept silence. At the sight of him the feeling of gratitude and of curiosity died out in all their hearts. He was perhaps less cold, less taciturn, less terrible than he appeared to these souls, whom the excitement of their feelings disposed to a warm and friendly welcome. The three poor prisoners realised that the man wished to remain a stranger to them, and they accepted the situation.

The priest thought that he noticed a smile, that was at once repressed, play upon the lips of the unknown, when he remarked the preparations that had been made for his reception. He heard mass and prayed. But then he went away after having declined, with a few words of polite refusal, the invitation that Mademoiselle de Langeais offered him to share with them the little supper that had been made ready.

After the 9th Thermidor—(the fall of Robespierre)—both the nuns and the Abbé de Marolles were able to go about in Paris without incurring the least danger. The old priest's first excursion was to a perfumer's shop at the sign of the *Reine des Fleurs*, kept by Citizen Ragon and his wife, formerly perfumers to the court, who had remained faithful to the royal family. The Vendéans made use of them as their agents for corresponding with the exiled princes and the royalist committee at Paris. The Abbé, dressed as the times required, was standing on the doorstep of the shop, which was situated between the Church of Saint Roch and the Rue des Frondeurs, when a crowd, which filled all the Rue Saint-Honoré, prevented him from going out.

" What is the matter ? " he asked Madame Ragon.

" It's nothing," she replied. " It's the cart with the executioner on the way to the Place Louis XV. Ah ! we saw it often enough last year. But to-day, four days after the anniversary of January 21st, one can watch that terrible procession go by without feeling displeasure."

" Why ? " said the abbé, " it is not Christian of you to talk thus."

" But it's the execution of the accomplices of Robespierre. They did their best to save themselves, but they are going in their turn where they sent so many innocent people ! "

The crowd was pouring past like a flood. The Abbé de Marolles, yielding to an impulse of curiosity, saw, standing erect on the cart, the man who three days before had come to hear his mass.

" Who is that ? " he said, " the man who . . ."

" It's the hangman," replied Monsieur Ragon, giving the executioner the name he bore under the monarchy.

" My dear, my dear," cried out Madame Ragon, " Monsieur l'Abbé is dying ! "

And the old lady seized a bottle of smelling salts with which to revive the aged priest from a fainting fit.

" No doubt," he said, " what he gave me was the handkerchief with which the King wiped his forehead as he went to martyrdom. . . . Poor man ! . . . The steel blade had a heart when all France was heartless ! . . ."

The perfumers thought that the poor priest was raving.

A PASSION IN THE DESERT

Honoré de Balzac

" It is a terrible sight ! " she exclaimed as we left the menagerie
of Monsieur Martin.

She had just been witnessing this daring showman " performing "
in the cage of his hyena.

" By what means," she went on, " can he have so tamed these
animals as to be secure of their affection ? "

" What seems to you a problem," I responded, interrupting her,
" is in reality a fact of nature."

" Oh ! " she exclaimed, with an incredulous smile.

" You think, then, that animals are devoid of passions ? " I
asked her. " You must know that we can teach them all the
qualities of civilised existence."

She looked at me with an astonished air.

" But," I went on, " when I first saw Monsieur Martin, I confess
that, like yourself, I uttered an exclamation of surprise. I happened
to be standing by the side of an old soldier, whose right leg had been
amputated, and who had come in with me. I was struck by his
appearance. His was one of those intrepid heads, stamped with
the seal of war, upon whose brows are written the battles of
Napoleon. About this old soldier was a certain air of frankness
and of gaiety which always gains my favour. He was doubtless
one of those old troopers whom nothing can surprise ; who find
food for laughter in the dying spasms of a comrade, who gaily
bury and despoil him, who challenge bullets with indifference—
though their arguments are short enough—and who would hobnob
with the devil. After keenly looking at the showman as he was
coming from the cage, my neighbour pursed his lips with that
significant expression of contempt which superior men assume
to show their difference from the dupes. At my exclamation
of surprise at Monsieur Martin's courage he smiled, and nodding
with a knowing air, remarked, ' I understand all that.'

" ' How ? ' I answered. ' If you can explain this mystery to
me you will oblige me greatly.'

" In a few moments we had struck up an acquaintance, and went
to dine at the first restaurant at hand. At dessert a bottle of
champagne completely cleared the memory of this strange old

soldier. He told his story, and I saw he was right when he exclaimed, ' I understand all that.'

When we got home, she teased me so, and yet so prettily, that I consented to write out for her the soldier's reminiscences.

The next day she received this episode, from an epic that might be called " The French in Egypt."

During the expedition undertaken in Upper Egypt by General Desaix, a Provençal soldier, who had fallen into the hands of the Maugrabins, was taken by these Arabs into the desert beyond the cataracts of the Nile. In order to put between them and the French army a distance to assure their safety, the Maugrabins made a forced march, and did not halt till night. They then camped by the side of a well, surrounded by a clump of palm trees, where they had before buried some provisions. Never dreaming that their prisoner would think of flight, they merely bound his hands, and all of them, after eating a few dates, and giving barley to their horses, went to sleep. When the bold Provençal saw his enemies incapable of watching him, he picked up a scimitar with his teeth, and then, with the blade fixed between his knees, cut the cords that lashed his wrists, and found himself at liberty. He at once seized a carbine and a dagger ; provided himself with some dry dates and a small bag of barley, powder and balls ; girded on the scimitar, sprang on a horse, and pressed forward in the direction where he fancied the French army must be found. Impatient to regain the bivouac, he so urged the weary horse that the poor beast fell dead, its sides torn with the spurs, leaving the Frenchman alone in the midst of the desert.

After wandering for some time amidst the sand with the desperate courage of an escaping convict, the soldier was forced to stop. Night was closing in. Despite the beauty of the Eastern night he had not strength sufficient to go on. Fortunately he had reached a height on the top of which were palm trees, whose leaves, for some time visible far off, had awakened in his heart a hope of safety. He was so weary that he lay down on a granite stone, oddly shaped like a camp-bed, and went to sleep without taking the precaution to protect himself in his slumber. He had sacrificed his life, and his last thought was a regret for having left the Maugrabins, whose wandering life began to please him, now that he was far from them and from all hope of succour.

He was awakened by the sun, whose pitiless rays falling vertically upon the granite made it intolerably hot. For the Provençal had been so careless as to cast himself upon the ground in the direction opposite to that on which the green majestic palm-tops threw their shadow. He looked at these solitary trees and shuddered ! They reminded him of the graceful shafts surmounted by long foils that distinguish the Saracenic columns of the Cathedral of Arles. He counted the few palms ; and then looked about him. A terrible despair seized upon his soul. He saw a boundless ocean. The melancholy sands spread round him, glittering like a blade of steel in a bright light, as far as eye could see. He knew not whether he was gazing on an ocean or a chain of lakes as lustrous as a mirror. A fiery mist shimmered, in little ripples, above the tremulous land-scape. The sky possessed an Oriental blaze, the brilliancy which brings despair, seeing that it leaves the imagination nothing to desire. Heaven and earth alike were all aflame. The silence was terrible in its wild and awful majesty. Infinity, immensity, oppressed the soul on all sides ; not a cloud was in the sky, not a breath was in the air, not a movement on the bosom of the sand which undulated into tiny waves. Far away, the horizon was marked off, as on a summer day at sea, by a line of light as bright and narrow as a sabre's edge.

The Provençal clasped his arms about a palm tree as if it had been the body of a friend ; then, sheltered by the straight and meagre shadow, he sat down weeping on the granite, and looking with deep dread upon the lonely scene spread out before his eyes. He cried aloud as if to tempt the solitude. His voice, lost in the hollows of the height, gave forth far off a feeble sound that woke no echo ; the echo was within his heart !

The Provençal was twenty-two years old. He loaded his carbine.

"Time enough for that ! " he muttered to himself, placing the weapon of deliverance on the ground.

Looking by turns at the melancholy waste of sand and at the blue expanse of sky, the soldier dreamed of France. With delight he fancied that he smelt the Paris gutters, and recalled the towns through which he had passed, the faces of his comrades, and the slightest incidents of his life. Then his Southern imagination made him fancy, in the play of heat quivering above the plain, the pebbles of his own dear Provence. But fearing all the dangers of this cruel mirage, he went down in the direction opposite to that which he had taken when he had climbed the hill the night before. Great was his joy on discovering a kind of grotto, naturally cut out of the enormous fragments of granite that formed the bottom of the hill. The remnants of a mat showed that this retreat had once been inhabited. Then, a few steps farther, he saw palm trees with a load of dates. Again the instinct which attaches man to life awoke within his heart. He now hoped to live until the passing of some Maugrabin ; or perhaps he would soon hear the boom of cannon, for at that time Buonaparte was overrunning Egypt. Revived by this reflection, the Frenchman cut down a few bunches of ripe fruit, beneath whose weight the date trees seemed to bend, and felt sure, on tasting this unhoped-for manna, that the inhabitant of this grotto had cultivated the palm trees. The fresh and luscious substance of the date bore witness to his predecessor's care.

The Provençal passed suddenly from dark despair to well-nigh insane delight. He climbed the hill again ; and spent the remainder of the day in cutting down a barren palm tree, which the night before had served him for shelter.

A vague remembrance made him think of the wild desert beasts ; and, foreseeing that they might come to seek the spring which bubbled through the sand among the rocks, he resolved to secure himself against their visits by placing a barrier at the door of his hermitage. In spite of his exertions, in spite of the strength with which the fear of being eaten during sleep endued him, it was impossible for him to cut the palm to pieces in one day ; but he contrived to bring it down. When, towards evening, the monarch of the desert fell, the thunder of its crash resounded far, as if the mighty Solitude had given forth a moan. The soldier shuddered as if he had heard a voice that prophesied misfortune. But like an heir who does not long bewail the death of a relation, he stripped the tree of the broad, long, green leaves, and used them to repair the mat on which he was about to lie. At length, wearied by the heat and by his labours, he fell asleep beneath the red roof of his murky grotto.

In the middle of the night he was disturbed by a strange noise. He sat up ; in the profound silence he could hear a creature breathing—a savage respiration which resembled nothing human. Terror, intensified by darkness, silence, and the fancies of one suddenly awakened, froze his blood. He felt a sharp contraction of his scalp, when, as the pupils of his eyes dilated, he saw in the shadow two faint and yellow lights. At first he thought these lights were some reflection of his eyeballs, but soon, the clear brightness of the night helping him to distinguish objects in the grotto, he saw lying at two paces from him an enormous beast !

Was it a lion ?—a tiger ?—a crocodile ? The Provençal was not sufficiently educated to know the species of his enemy, but his terror was all the greater ; since his ignorance assisted his imagination. He bore the cruel torture of listening, of marking the caprices of this awful breathing, without losing a sound of it, or venturing to make the slightest movement. A smell as pungent as a fox's, but more penetrating, filled the grotto ; and when it entered his nostrils his terror passed all bounds ; he could no longer doubt the presence of the terrible companion whose royal den was serving him for bivouac. Presently the moon, now sinking, lighted up the den, and in the moon-rays gradually shone out a panther's spotted skin.

The lion of Egypt was sleeping, curled up like a great dog who is the peaceable possessor of a sumptuous kennel at a mansion door ; its eyes, which had been opened for one moment, were now closed again. Its face was turned towards the Frenchman.

A thousand troubled thoughts passed through the mind of the panther's prisoner. At first he thought of shooting it ; but there was not enough room between them to adjust his gun ; the barrel would have reached beyond the animal. And what if he awoke it ! This supposition made him motionless. Listening in the silence to the beating of his heart, he cursed the loud pulsations, fearing to disturb the sleep that gave him time to seek some means of safety. Twice he placed his hand upon his scimitar, with the intention of cutting off the head of his enemy ; but the difficulty of cutting through the short, strong fur compelled him to abandon the idea. To fail was certain death. He preferred the odds of conflict, and determined to await the daybreak. And daylight was not long in coming. The Frenchman was able to examine the panther. Its muzzle was stained with blood.

" It has eaten plenty," he reflected, without conjecturing that the feast might have been composed of human flesh ; " it will not be hungry when it wakes."

It was a female. The fur upon her breast and thighs shone with whiteness. A number of little spots like velvet looked like charming bracelets around her paws. The muscular tail was also white, but tipped with black rings. The upper part of her coat, yellow as old gold, but very soft and smooth, bore these characteristic marks, shaded into the form of roses, which serve to distinguish the panther from the other species of the genus *Felis*. This fearful visitor was snoring tranquilly in an attitude as graceful as that of a kitten lying on the cushions of an ottoman. Her sinewy blood-stained paws, with powerful claws, were spread beyond her head, which rested on them, and from which stood out the thin, straight whiskers with a gleam like silver wires.

If she had been imprisoned in a cage, the Provençal would assuredly have admired the creature's grace, and the vivid contrasts of colour that gave her garment an imperial lustre ; but at this moment he felt his sight grow dim at her sinister aspect. The presence of the panther, even sleeping, made him experience the effect which the magnetic eyes of the serpent are said to exercise upon the nightingale.

In the presence of this danger the courage of the soldier faltered, although without doubt it would have risen at the cannon's mouth. A desperate thought, however, filled his mind, and dried up at its source the chilly moisture which was rolling down his forehead. Acting as men do who, driven to extremities, at last defy their fate and nerve themselves to meet their doom, he saw a tragedy in this adventure, and resolved to play his part in it with honour to the last.

" Two days ago," he argued with himself, " the Arabs might have killed me."

Considering himself as good as dead, he waited bravely, yet with restless curiosity, for the awaking of his enemy.

When the sun shone out, the panther opened her eyes suddenly ; then she spread out her paws forcibly, as if to stretch them and get rid of cramp. Then she yawned, showing an alarming set of teeth and an indented, rasp-like tongue. " She is like a dainty lady ! " thought the Frenchman, as he saw her rolling over with a gentle and coquettish movement. She licked off the blood that stained her paws and mouth, and rubbed her head with movements full of charm. " That's it ! Just beautify yourself a little ! " the Frenchman said, his gaiety returning with his courage. " Then we must say good morning ! " And he took up the short dagger of which he had relieved the Maugrabins.

At this moment the panther turned her head towards the Frenchman, and looked at him fixedly, without advancing. The rigidity of those metallic eyes, and their insupportable brightness, made the Provençal shudder. The beast began to move towards him. He looked at her caressingly, and fixing her eyes as if to magnetise her, he let her come close up to him ; then, with a soft and gentle gesture, he passed his hand along her body, from head to tail, scratching with his nails the flexible vertebrae that divide a panther's yellow back. The beast put up her tail with pleasure ; her eyes grew softer ; and when for the third time the Frenchman accomplished this self-interested piece of flattery, she broke into a purring like a cat. But this purr proceeded from a throat so deep and powerful that it re-echoed through the grotto like the peals of a cathedral organ. The Provençal, realising the success of his caresses, redoubled them, until the imperious beauty was completely soothed and lulled.

When he felt sure that he had perfectly subdued the ferocity of his capricious companion, whose hunger had been satisfied so cruelly the night before, he got up to leave the grotto. The panther let him go ; but when he had climbed the hill, she came bounding after him with the lightness of a sparrow hopping from branch to branch, and rubbed herself against the soldier's leg, arching her back after the fashion of a cat. Then looking at her guest with eyes whose brightness had grown less inflexible, she uttered that savage cry which naturalists have compared to the sound of a saw.

" What an exacting beauty ! " cried the Frenchman, smiling. He set himself to play with her ears, to caress her body, and to scratch her head hard with his nails. Then, growing bolder with success, he tickled her skull with the point of his dagger, watching for the spot to strike her. But the hardness of the bones made him afraid of failing.

The sultana of the desert approved the action of her slave by raising her head, stretching her neck, and showing her delight by the quietness of her attitude. The Frenchman suddenly reflected that in order to assassinate this fierce princess with one blow he need only stab her in the neck. He had just raised his knife for the attempt, when the panther, with a graceful action, threw herself upon the ground before his feet, casting him from time to time a look in which, in spite of its ferocity of nature, there was a gleam of tenderness.

The poor Provençal, with his back against a palm tree, ate his dates, while he cast inquiring glances, now towards the desert for deliverers, now upon his terrible companion, to keep an eye upon her dubious clemency. Every time he threw away a date-stone, the panther fixed her eyes upon the spot with inconceivable mistrust. She scrutinised the Frenchman with a businesslike attention; but the examination seemed favourable, for when he finished his poor meal, she licked his boots, and with her rough, strong tongue removed the dust incrusted in their creases.

" But when she becomes hungry ? " thought the Provençal.

Despite the shudder this idea caused him, the soldier began examining with curiosity the proportions of the panther, certainly one of the most beautiful specimens of her kind. She was three feet high and four feet long, without the tail. This powerful weapon, as round as a club, was nearly three feet long. The head—large as that of a lioness—was distinguished by an expression of rare delicacy ; true, the cold cruelty of the tiger dominated, but there was also a resemblance to the features of a wily woman. In a word, the countenance of the solitary queen wore at this moment an expression of fierce gaiety, like that of Nero flushed with wine ; she had quenched her thirst in blood, and now desired to play.

The soldier tried to come and go, and the panther let him, content to follow him with her eyes, but less after the manner of a faithful dog than of a great Angora cat, suspicious even of the movements of its master. When he turned round he saw beside the fountain the carcase of his horse ; the panther had dragged the body all that distance. About two-thirds had been devoured. This sight reassured the Frenchman. He was thus easily able to explain the absence of the panther, and the respect which she had shown for him while he was sleeping.

This first piece of luck emboldened him about the future. He conceived the mad idea of setting up a pleasant household life, together with the panther, neglecting no means of pacifying her and of conciliating her good graces. He returned to her, and saw, to his delight, that she moved her tail with an almost imperceptible motion. Then he sat down beside her without fear, and began to play with her ; he grasped her paws, her muzzle, pulled her ears, threw her over on her back, and vigorously scratched her warm and silky sides. She let him have his way, and when the soldier tried to smooth the fur upon her paws she carefully drew in her claws,

which had the curve of a Damascus blade. The Frenchman,
who kept one hand upon his dagger, was still thinking of plunging
it into the body of the too-confiding panther; but he feared
lest she should strangle him in her last convulsions. And besides,
within his heart there was a movement of remorse that warned
him to respect an inoffensive creature. It seemed to him that he had
found a friend in this vast desert. Involuntarily he called to mind a
woman whom he once had loved, whom he sarcastically had nick-
named "Mignonne," from her jealousy, which was so fierce that
during the whole time of their acquaintance he went in fear that she
would stab him. This memory of his youth suggested the idea of
calling the young panther by this name, whose lithe agility and grace
he now admired with less terror.

Towards evening he had become so far accustomed to his perilous
position, that he almost liked the hazard of it. At last his companion had got into the habit of looking at him when he called in a
falsetto voice "Mignonne."

At sundown Mignonne uttered several times a deep and melancholy cry.

"She has been properly brought up," thought the light-hearted
soldier; "she says her prayers!" But it was, no doubt, her
peaceful attitude which brought the jest into his mind.

"All right, my little pet; I will let you get to sleep first," he said,
relying on his legs to get away as soon as she was sleeping, and to
seek some other shelter for the night.

The soldier waited with patience for the hour of flight, and when it
came, set out full speed in the direction of the Nile. But he had only
gone a quarter of a league across the sand when he heard the panther
bounding after him, uttering at intervals that saw-like cry, more
terrible even than the thudding of her leaps.

"Well!" he said to himself, "she must have taken a fancy to me.
Perhaps she has never yet met any one. It is flattering to be her
first love!" At this moment the Frenchman fell into a shifting
quicksand, so dangerous to the traveller in the desert, escape from
which is hopeless. He felt that he was sinking; he gave a cry of
terror. The panther seized him by the collar with her teeth, and
spring backwards with stupendous vigour drew him from the gulf
as if by magic.

"Ah! Mignonne!" cried the soldier, enthusiastically caressing
her, "we are friends now for life and death. But no tricks, eh?"
and he retraced his steps.

Henceforth the desert was as though it had been peopled. It
contained a being with whom he could converse, and whose ferocity
had been softened for him, without his being able to explain so
strange a friendship.

However great was his desire to keep awake and on his guard, 'he fell asleep. On awakening, Mignonne was no longer to be seen. He climbed the hill, and then perceived her afar off, coming along by leaps and bounds, according to the nature of these creatures, the extreme flexibility of whose vertebrae prevents their running.

Mignonne came up, her jaws besmeared with blood. She received the caresses of her companion with deep purrs of satisfaction. Her eyes, now full of softness, were turned, with even greater tenderness than the night before, to the Provençal, who spoke to her as to a pet.

" Ah! Beauty! you are a respectable young woman, are you not? You like petting, don't you? Are you not ashamed of yourself? You have been eating a Maugrabin! Well! they're animals, as you are. But don't you go and gobble up a Frenchman. If you do, I shall not love you ! "

She played as a young pup plays with its master, letting him roll her over, beat and pet her ; and sometimes she would coax him to caress her with a movement of entreaty.

A few days passed thus. This companionship revealed to the Provençal the sublime beauties of the desert. From the moment when he found within it hours of fear and yet of calm, a sufficiency of food, and a living creature who absorbed his thoughts, his soul was stirred by new emotions. It was a life of contrasts. Solitude revealed to him her secrets, and involved him in her charm. He discovered in the rising and the setting of the sun a splendour hidden from the world of men. His frame quivered when he heard above his head the soft whirr of a bird's wings—rare wayfarer ; or when he saw the clouds—those changeful, man-coloured voyagers— mingle in the depth of heaven. In the dead of night he studied the effects of the moon upon the sea of sand, which the simoom drove in ever-changing undulations. He lived with the Oriental day ; he marvelled at its pomp and glory ; and often, after having watched the grandeur of a tempest in the plain, in which the sands were whirled in dry red mists of deadly vapour, he beheld with ecstasy the coming on of night, for then there fell upon him the benignant coolness of the stars. He heard imaginary music in the sky. Solitude taught him all the bliss of reverie. He spent whole hours in calling trifles to remembrance, in comparing his past life with his strange present. To his panther he grew passionately attached, for he required an object of affection. Whether by a strong effort of his will he had really changed the character of his companion, or whether, thanks to the constant warfare of the desert, she found sufficient food, she showed no disposition to attack him, and at last, in her perfect tameness, he no longer felt the slightest fear.

He spent a great part of his time in sleeping, but ever, like a spider in its web, with mind alert, that he might not let deliverance escape him, should any chance to pass within the sphere described by the horizon. He had sacrificed his shirt to make a flag, which he had hoisted to the summit of a palm tree stripped of leaves. Taught by necessity, he had found the means to keep it spread by stretching it with sticks, lest the wind should fail to wave it at the moment when the hoped-for traveller might be travelling the waste of sand.

It was during the long hours when hope abandoned him that he amused himself with his companion. He had learnt to understand the different inflexions of her voice. and the expression of her glances ; he had studied the varying changes of the spots that starred her robe of gold. Mignonne no longer growled, even when he seized her by the tuft with which her terrible tail ended, to count the black and white rings which adorned it, and which glittered in the sun like precious gems. It delighted him to watch the delicate soft lines of her snowy breast and graceful head. But above all when she was gambolling in her play he watched her with delight, for the agility, the youthfulness of all her movements filled him with an ever-fresh surprise. He admired her suppleness in leaping, climbing, gliding, pressing close against him, swaying, rolling over, crouching for a bound. But however swift her spring, however slippery the block of granite, she would stop short, without motion, at the sound of the word " Mignonne ! "

One day, in the most dazzling sunshine, an enormous bird was hovering in the air. The Provençal left his panther to examine this new visitor ; but after waiting for a moment the deserted sultana uttered a hoarse growl.

" Blessed if I don't believe that she is jealous ! " he exclaimed, perceiving that her eyes were once more hard and rigid. " A woman's soul has passed into her body, that is certain ! "

The eagle disappeared in air, while he admired afresh the rounded back and graceful outlines of the panther. She was as pretty as a woman. The blonde fur blended in its delicate gradations into the dull white colour of the thighs. The brilliant sunshine made this vivid gold, with spots of brown, take on a lustre indescribable. The Provençal and the panther looked at one another understandingly ; the beauty of the desert quivered when she felt the nails of her admirer on her skull. Her eyes gave forth a flash like lightning, and then she closed them hard.

" She *has* a soul," he cried, as he beheld the desert queen in her repose, golden as the sands, white as their blinding lustre, and, like them, fiery and alone.

" Well ? " she said to me, " I have read your pleading on behalf of animals. But what was the end of these two persons so well made to understand each other ? "

" Ah ! They ended as all great passions end—through a mis-understanding. Each thinks the other guilty of a falsity, each is too proud for explanation, and obstinacy brings about a rupture."

" And sometimes in the happiest moments," she said, " a look, an exclamation, is enough ! Well, what was the end of the story ? "

" That is difficult to tell, but you will understand what the old fellow had confided to me, when, finishing his bottle of champagne, he exclaimed, ' I don't know how I hurt her, but she turned on me like mad, and with her sharp teeth seized my thigh. The action was not savage ; but fancying that she meant to kill me I plunged my dagger into her neck. She rolled over with a cry that froze my blood ; she looked at me in her last struggles without anger. I would have given everything on earth, even my cross—which then I had not won—to bring her back to life. It was as if I had slain a human being. And the soldiers who had seen my flag, and who were hastening to my succour, found me bathed in tears.

" ' Well, sir,' he went on, after a moment's silence, ' since then I have been through the wars in Germany, Spain, Russia, France ; I have dragged my carcase round the world ; but there is nothing like the desert in my eyes ! Ah ! it is beautiful—superb ! '

" ' What did you feel there ? ' I inquired of him.

" ' Oh ! that I cannot tell you. Besides, I do not always regret my panther and my clump of palm trees. I must be sad at heart for that. But mark my words. In the desert there is everything and there is nothing.'

" ' Explain yourself.'

" ' Well ! ' he continued, with a gesture of impatience, ' it is God without man.' "

THE CONSCRIPT

Honoré de Balzac

One evening in the month of November 1793 the principal people of Carentan were gathered in the salon of Madame de Dey, at whose house the assembly was held daily. Some circumstances which would not have attracted attention in a large city, but which were certain to cause a flutter in a small one, lent to this customary meeting an unusual degree of interest. Two days before, Madame de Dey had closed her door to her guests, whom she had also excused herself from receiving on the preceding day, on the pretext of an indisposition. In ordinary times, these two occurences would have produced the same effect in Carentan that the closing of all the theatres would produce in Paris. In those days existence was to a certain extent incomplete. And in 1793 the conduct of Madame de Dey might have had the most deplorable results. The slightest venturesome proceeding almost always became a question of life or death for the nobles of that period.

In order to understand the intense curiosity and the narrow-minded cunning which enlivened the Norman countenances of all those people during the evening, but especially in order that we may share the secret anxiety of Madame de Dey, it is necessary to explain the rôle that she played at Carentan. As the critical position in which she found herself at that moment was undoubtedly identical with that of many people during the Revolution, the sympathies of more than one reader will give the needed touch of colour to this narrative.

Madame de Dey, the widow of a lieutenant-general and chevalier of the Orders, had left the court at the beginning of the emigration. As she possessed considerable property in the neighbourhood of Carentan, she had taken refuge there, hoping that the influence of the Terror would not be much felt so far from Paris. This prevision, based upon exact knowledge of the province, proved to be just. The Revolution did little devastation in Lower Normandy. Although, when Madame de Dey visited her estates formerly, she used to see only the noble families of the province, she had from policy thrown her house open to the leading *bourgeois* of the town and to the new authorities, striving to make them proud of their conquest of her, without arousing either hatred or jealousy in their minds. Gracious and amiable, endowed with that indescribable gentleness of manner which attracts without resort to self-abasement or to entreaties, she had succeeded in winning general esteem by the most exquisite tact, the wise promptings of which had enabled her to maintain her stand on the narrow line where she could satisfy the demands of that mixed society, without humiliating the self-esteem of the parvenus or offending that of her former friends.

About thirty-eight years of age, she still retained, not that fresh and buxom beauty which distinguishes the young women of Lower Normandy, but a slender and aristocratic beauty. Her features were small and refined, her figure slim and willowy. When she spoke, her pale face seemed to brighten and to take on life. Her great black eyes were full of suavity, but their placid, devout expression seemed to indicate that the active principle of her existence had ceased to be. Married in the flower of her youth to an old and jealous soldier, the falseness of her position in the centre of a dissipated court contributed much, no doubt, to cast a veil of serious melancholy over a face on which the charm and vivacity of love must formerly have shone bright.

Constantly obliged to restrain the ingenuous impulses of a woman, at a time when she still feels instead of reflecting, passion had remained unsullied in the depths of her heart. So it was that her principal attraction was due to the youthful simplicity which at intervals her face betrayed, and which gave to her ideas a naïve expression of desire. Her aspect imposed respect, but there were always in her bearing and in her voice symptoms of an outreaching towards an unknown future, as in a young girl; the most unsusceptible man soon found himself falling in love with her, and nevertheless retained a sort of respectful dread, inspired by her courteous manners, which were most impressive. Her soul, naturally great, and strengthened by painful struggles, seemed to be too far removed from the common herd, and men realised their limitations.

That soul necessarily demanded an exalted passion. So that Madame de Dey's affections were concentrated in a single sentiment, the sentiment of maternity. The happiness and pleasures of which her married life had been deprived, she found in her excessive love for her son. She loved him not only with the pure and profound devotion of a mother, but with the coquetry of a mistress, the jealousy of a wife. She was unhappy when separated from him, anxious during his absence, could never see enough of him, lived only in him and for him. In order to make men understand the strength of this feeling, it will suffice to add that his son was not only Madame de Dey's only child, but her last remaining relative, the only living being to whom she could attach the fears, the hopes, and the joys of her life. The late Count de Dey was the last scion of his family, as she was the last heiress of hers.

Thus human schemes and interest were in accord with the noblest cravings of the soul to intensify in the Countess's heart a sentiment which is always strong in women. She had brought up her son only with infinite difficulty, which had made him dearer than ever to her. Twenty times the doctors prophesied his death; but, trusting in her presentiments and her hopes, she had the inexpressible joy of seeing him pass through the dangers of childhood unscathed, and of exulting in the upbuilding of his constitution in spite of the decrees of the faculty.

Thanks to constant care, her son had grown and had attained such perfect development, that at twenty years of age he was considered one of the most accomplished cavaliers at Versailles. Lastly—a piece of good fortune which does not crown the efforts of all mothers —she was adored by her son; their hearts were bound together by sympathies that were fraternal. Even if they had not been connected by the decree of nature, they would have felt instinctively for each other that affection of one being for another so rarely met with in life. Appointed sub-lieutenant of dragoons at eighteen, the young man had complied with the prevailing ideas of the requirements of honour at that period by following the princes when they emigrated.

Thus Madame de Dey, of noble birth, wealthy, and the mother of an émigré, was fully alive to the dangers of her painful situation. As she had no other aim than to preserve a great fortune for her son, she had renounced the happiness of accompanying him ; but, when she read the harsh laws by virtue of which the Republic daily confiscated the property of the émigrés at Carentan, she applauded herself for her courageous act. Was she not guarding her son's treasures at the peril of her life ?

Then, when she learned of the shocking executions ordered by the Convention, she slept undisturbed, happy to know that her only treasure was in safety, far from all perils and all scaffolds. She took pleasure in the belief that she had adopted the best course to save all his fortunes at once. Making the concessions to this secret thought which the disasters of the time demanded, without compromising her womanly dignity or her aristocratic beliefs, she enveloped her sorrows in impenetrable mystery. She had realised the difficulties which awaited her at Carentan. To go thither and assume the first place in society—was it not equivalent to defying the scaffold every day ? But, sustained by a mother's courage, she succeeded in winning the affection of the poor by relieving all sorts of misery indiscriminately, and made herself necessary to the rich by taking the lead in their pleasures.

She received the prosecuting attorney of the commune, the mayor, the president of the district, the public accuser, and even the judges of the Revolutionary Tribunal. The first four of these functionaries, being unmarried, paid court to her, in the hope of marrying her, whether by terrifying her by the injury which they had it in their power to do her, or by offering her their protection. The public accuser, formerly an attorney at Caen, where he had been employed by the Countess, tried to win her love by conduct full of devotion and generosity. A dangerous scheme ! He was the most formidable of all the suitors. He alone was thoroughly acquainted with the condition of his former client's large fortune. His passion was inevitably intensified by all the cravings of an avarice which rested upon almost unlimited power upon the right of life or death throughout the district.

This man, who was still young, displayed so much nobility in his behaviour that Madame de Dey had been unable as yet to make up her mind concerning him. But, scorning the danger that lay in a contest of wits with Normans, she employed the inventive genius and the cunning which nature has allotted to woman, to play those rivals against one another. By gaining time, she hoped to arrive safe and sound at the end of her troubles. At that time, the royalists in the interior of France flattered themselves that each day would see the close of the Revolution ; and that conviction was the ruin of a great many of them.

Despite these obstacles, the Countess had skilfully maintained her independence down to the day when, with incomprehensible imprudence, she had conceived the idea of closing her door. The interest which she inspired was so profound and so genuine that the people who came to her house that evening were greatly distressed when they learned that it was impossible for her to receive them. Then, with the outspoken curiosity which is a part of provincial manners, they inquired concerning the misfortune, the sorrow, or the disease which had afflicted Madame de Dey. To these questions, an old housekeeper called Brigitte replied that her mistress had shut herself into her room, and would not see anybody, not even her servants. The cloistral existence, so to speak, which the people of a small town lead, gives birth in them to such an unconquerable habit of analysing and commenting upon the actions of other people, that, after expressing their sympathy for Madame de Dey, without an idea whether she was really happy or unhappy, they all began to speculate upon the causes of her abrupt seclusion.

"If she were ill," said one curious individual, "she would have sent for the doctor ; but the doctor was at my house all day, playing chess. He said with a laugh that in these days there is but one disease, and that is unfortunately incurable."

This jest was put forward apologetically. Thereupon, men, women, old men, and maidens began to search the vast field of conjecture. Every one fancied that he caught a glimpse of a secret, and that secret engrossed the imaginations of them all. The next day, the suspicions became embittered. As life in a small town is open to all, the women were the first to learn that Brigitte had laid in more supplies than usual at the market. That fact could not be denied. Brigitte had been seen in the morning, in the square, and—a most extraordinary thing—she had bought the only hare that was offered for sale. Now the whole town knew that Madame de Dey did not like game. The hare became the starting-point for endless suppositions. When taking their daily walk, old men observed in the Countess's house a sort of concentrated activity which was made manifest by the very precautions which the servants took to conceal it. The valet was seen beating a rug in the garden ; on the day before, no one would have paid any heed to it ; but that rug became a link in the chain of evidence to support the romances which everybody was engaged in constructing. Every person had his own.

On the second day, when they learned that Madame de Dey

proclaimed that she was indisposed, the principal persons of
Carentan met in the evening at the house of the Mayor's brother,
an ex-merchant, a married man, of upright character and generally
esteemed, and for whom the Countess entertained a high regard.
There all the aspirants to the rich widow's hand had a more or
less probable story to tell ; and each of them hoped to turn to his
advantage the secret circumstances which forced her to compromise
herself thus. The public accuser imagined a complete drama in
which Madame de Dey's son was brought to her house by night.

The mayor favoured the idea of a priest who had not taken the
oath, arriving from La Vendée and asking her for shelter ; but the
purchase of a hare on Friday embarrassed the mayor greatly.
The president of the district was strong in his conviction that it
was a leader of Chouans or of Vendeans, hotly pursued. Others
suggested a nobleman escaped from one of the prisons of Paris.
In short, one and all suspected the Countess of being guilty of one
of those acts of generosity which the laws of that day stigmatised
as crimes, and which might lead to the scaffold. The public
accuser said in an undertone that they must hold their tongues,
and try to snatch the unfortunate woman from the abyss towards
which she was rapidly precipitating herself.

" If you talk about this business," he added, " I shall be obliged
to interfere, to search her house, and then——"

He did not finish his sentence, but they all understood his
reticence.

The Countess's sincere friends were so alarmed for her that,
during the morning of the third day, the procureur-syndic of the
commune caused his wife to write her a note to urge her to receive
as usual that evening. The old merchant, being bolder, called at
Madame de Dey's house in the morning. Trusting in the service
which he proposed to render her, he demanded to be shown to her
presence, and was thunder-struck when he saw her in the garden,
engaged in cutting the last flowers from the beds, to supply her
vases.

" Doubtless she has been sheltering her lover," said the old man
to himself, seized with compassion for the fascinating woman.

The strange expression on the Countess's face confirmed him in
his suspicions. Deeply touched by that devotion so natural to a
woman, and which always moves our admiration, because all men
are flattered by the sacrifices which a woman makes for a man,
the merchant informed the Countess of the reports which were
current in the town, and of the dangerous position in which she
stood.

" But," he said, as he concluded, " although there are some
among our officials who are not indisposed to forgive you for an
act of herosim of which a priest is the object, no one will pity you

if they discover that you are sacrificing yourself to the affections of the heart."

At these words Madame de Dey looked at the old man with an expression of desperation and terror which made him shudder, old man though he was.

"Come," said she, taking his hand and leading him to her bedroom, where, after making sure that they were alone, she took from her bosom a soiled and wrinkled letter. "Read," she cried, making a violent effort to pronounce the word.

She fell into her chair as if utterly overwhelmed. While the old gentleman was feeling for his spectacles and wiping them, she fastened her eyes upon him and scrutinised him for the first time with curiosity; then she said softly, in an altered voice:

"I trust you."

"Am I not sharing your crime?" replied the old man, simply.

She started; for the first time her heart found itself in sympathy with another heart in that little town. The old merchant suddenly understood both the distress and the joy of the Countess. Her son had taken part in the Granville expedition; he wrote to his mother from prison, imparting to her one sad but sweet hope. Having no doubt of his success in escaping, he mentioned three days in which he might appear at her house in disguise. The fatal letter contained heartrending farewells in case he should not be at Carentan on the evening of the third day; and he begged his mother to hand a considerable sum of money to the messenger, who had undertaken to carry that letter to her through innumerable perils. The paper shook in the old man's hand.

"And this is the third day!" cried Madame de Dey, as she sprang to her feet, seized the letter, and began to pace the floor.

"You have been imprudent," said the merchant; "why did you lay in provisions?"

"Why, he may arrive almost starved, worn out with fatigue, and——"

She did not finish.

"I am sure of my brother," said the old man, "and I will go and enlist him on your side."

In this emergency the old tradesman recovered the shrewdness which he had formerly displayed in his business, and gave advice instinct with prudence and sagacity. After agreeing upon all that they were both to say and to do, the old man went about, on cleverly devised pretexts, to the principal houses of Carentan, where he announced that Madame de Dey, whom he had just seen, would receive that evening in spite of her indisposition. Pitting his shrewdness against the inborn Norman cunning, in the examination to which each family subjected him in regard to the nature of the Countess's illness, he succeeded in leading astray almost everybody who was interested in that mysterious affair. His first visit produced a marvellous effect.

He stated, in the presence of a gouty old lady, that Madame de Dey had nearly died of an attack of gout in the stomach ; as the famous Tronchin had once recommended her, in such a case, to place on her chest the skin of a hare, flayed alive, and to stay in bed and not move, the Countess, who had been at death's door two days before, having followed scrupulously Tronchin's advice, found herself sufficiently recovered to see those who cared to call on her that evening.   That fable had a prodigious success, and the Carentan doctor, a royalist in secret, added to its effect by the air of authority with which he discussed the remedy.   Nevertheless, suspicion had taken too deep root in the minds of some obstinate persons, or some philosophers, to be entirely dispelled ; so that, in the evening, those who were regular habitués of Madame de Dey's salon arrived there early ; some in order to watch her face, others from friendly regard ; and the majority were impressed by the marvellous nature of her recovery.

They found the Countess seated at the corner of the huge fireplace of her salon, which was almost as modestly furnished as those of the people of Carentan ; for, in order not to offend the sensitive self-esteem of her guests, she denied herself the luxury to which she had always been accustomed, and had changed nothing in her house.   The floor of the reception-room was not even polished.   She left old-fashioned dark tapestries on the walls, she retained the native furniture, burned tallow candles, and followed the customs of the town, espousing provincial life, and recoiling neither from the most rasping pettinesses nor the most unpleasant privations.   But, realising that her guests would forgive her for any display of splendour which aimed at their personal comfort, she neglected nothing when it was a question of affording them enjoyment ; so that she always gave them excellent dinners.   She even went so far as to make a pretence at miserliness, to please those calculating minds ; and after causing certain concessions in the way of luxurious living to be extorted from her, she seemed to comply with a good grace.

About seven o'clock in the evening, therefore, the best of the uninteresting society of Carentan was assembled at her house, and formed a large circle about the fireplace.   The mistress of the house, sustained in her misery by the compassionate glances which the old tradesman bestowed upon her, submitted with extraordinary courage to the minute questionings, the trivial and stupid reasoning of her guests.   But at every blow of the knocker at her door, and whenever she heard footsteps in the street, she concealed her emotion by raising some question of interest to the welfare of the province.   She started noisy discussions concerning the quality of the season's cider, and was so well seconded by her confidant that her company almost forgot to watch her, her manner was so natural and her self-possession so imperturbable. The public accuser and one of the judges of the Revolutionary Tribunal sat silent, carefully watching every movement of her face and listening to every sound in the house, notwithstanding the uproar ; and on several occasions they asked her very embarrassing questions, which, however, the Countess answered with marvellous presence of mind. Mothers have such an inexhaustable store of courage ! When Madame de Dey had arranged the card-tables, placed everybody at a table of boston, reversis, or whist, she remained a few moments talking with some young people, with the utmost nonchalance, playing her part like a consummate actress. She suggested a game of loto—said that she alone knew where it was, and disappeared.

" I am suffocating, my poor Brigitte ! " she cried, wiping away the tears that gushed from her eyes, which gleamed with fever, anxiety, and impatience. " He does not come," she continued, looking about the chamber to which she had flown. " Here, I breathe again and I live. A few moments more, and he will be here ; for he still lives, I am certain ; my heart tells me so ! Do you hear nothing, Brigitte ? Oh ! I would give the rest of my life to know whether he is in prison or travelling through the country ! I would like not to think——"

She looked about again to make sure that everything was in order in the room. A bright fire was burning on the hearth ; the shutters were carefully closed ; the furniture glistened with cleanliness ; the way in which the bed was made proved that the Countess had assisted Brigitte in the smallest details ; and her hopes betrayed themselves in the scrupulous care which seemed to have been taken in that room, where the sweet charm of love and its most chaste caresses exhaled in the perfume of the flowers. A mother alone could have anticipated the desires of a soldier, and have arranged to fulfil them all so perfectly. A dainty meal, choice wines, clean linen, and dry shoes—in a word, all that was likely to be necessary or agreeable to a weary traveller was there set forth, so that he need lack nothing, so that the joy of home might make known to him a mother's love.

" Brigitte ? " said the Countess in a heartrending tone, as she placed a chair at the table, as if to give reality to her longings, to intensify the strength of her illusions.

" Oh ! he will come, madame ; he isn't far away. I don't doubt that he's alive and on his way here," replied Brigitte. " I put a key in the Bible and I held it on my fingers while Cottin read the Gospel of St. John ; and, madame, the key didn't turn."

" Is that a sure sign ? " asked the Countess.

"Oh! it is certain, madame; I would wager my salvation that he is still alive. God can't make a mistake."

"Despite the danger that awaits him here, I would like right well to see him."

"Poor Monsieur Auguste!" cried Brigitte; "I suppose he is somewhere on the road, on foot!"

"And there is the church clock striking eight!" cried the Countess, in dismay.

She was afraid that she had remained longer than she ought in that room, where she had faith in the life of her son because she looked upon all that meant life to him. She went downstairs; but before entering the salon, she stood a moment in the vestibule, listening to see if any sound woke the silent echoes of the town. She smiled at Brigitte's husband, who was on sentry-duty, and whose eyes seemed dazed by dint of strained attention to the murmurs in the square and in the streets. She saw her son in everything and everywhere. In a moment she returned to the salon, affecting a jovial air, and began to play loto with some young girls; but from time to time she complained of feeling ill, and returned to her chair at the fireplace.

Such was the condition of persons and things in the house of Madame de Dey, while, on the road from Paris to Cherbourg, a young man dressed in a dark carmagnole, the regulation costume at that period, strode along towards Carentan. At the beginning of the conscription, there was little or no discipline. The demands of the moment made it impossible for the Republic to equip all of its soldiers at once, and it was no rare thing to see the roads covered with conscripts still wearing their civilian dress. These young men marched in advance of their battalions to the halting-places, or loitered behind, for their progress was regulated by their ability to endure the fatigue of a long march.

The traveller with whom we have to do was some distance in advance of the column of conscripts on its way to Cherbourg, which the Mayor of Carentan was momentarily expecting, in order to distribute lodging-tickets among them. The young man walked with a heavy but still firm step, and his bearing seemed to indicate that he had long been familiar with the hardships of military life. Although the moon was shining on the pastures about Carentan, he had noticed some great white clouds which seemed on the point of discharging snow upon the country, and the fear of being surprised by a storm doubtless quickened his gait, which was more rapid than his weariness made comfortable. He had an almost empty knapsack on his back, and carried in his hand a boxwood cane, cut from one of the high, broad hedges formed by that shrub around most of the estates in Lower Normandy.

The solitary traveller entered Carentan, whose towers, of fantastic aspect in the moonlight, had appeared to him a moment before. His steps awoke the echoes of the silent streets, where he met no one ; he was obliged to ask a weaver who was still at work to point out the Mayor's abode. That magistrate lived only a short distance away, and the conscript soon found himself safe under the porch of his house, where he seated himself on a stone bench, waiting for the lodging-ticket which he had asked for. But, being summoned by the Mayor, he appeared before him, and was subjected to a careful examination. The soldier was a young man of attractive appearance, who apparently belonged to some family of distinction. His manner indicated noble birth, and the intelligence due to a good education was manifest in his features.

" What is your name ? " the Mayor asked, with a shrewd glance at him.

" Julien Jussieu," replied the conscript.

" And you come from——? " said the magistrate, with an incredulous smile.

" From Paris."

" Your comrades must be far behind ? " continued the Norman in a mocking tone.

" I am three leagues ahead of the battalion."

" Doubtless some sentimental reason brings you to Carentan, citizen conscript ? " queried the Mayor, slyly. " It is all right," he added, imposing silence, with a wave of the hand, upon the young man, who was about to speak. " We know where to send you. Here," he said, handing him the lodging-ticket ; " here, *Citizen Jussieu.*"

There was a perceptible tinge of irony in the tone in which the magistrate uttered these last two words, as he held out a ticket upon which Madame de Dey's name was written. The young man read the address with an air of curiosity.

" He knows very well that he hasn't far to go, and when he gets outside, it won't take him long to cross the square," cried the Mayor, speaking to himself, while the young man went out. " He's a bold young fellow. May God protect him ! He has an answer for everything. However, if any other than I had asked to see his papers, he would have been lost ! "

At that moment the clock of Carentan struck half-past nine ; the torches were being lighted in Madame de Dey's ante-room, and the servants were assisting their masters and mistresses to put on their cloaks, their overcoats, and their mantles ; the card-players had settled their accounts and were about to withdraw in a body, according to the usual custom in all small towns.

" It seems that the public accuser proposes to remain," said a lady, observing that that important functionary was missing when they were about to separate to seek their respective homes, after exhausting all the formulas of leave-taking.

The redoubtable magistrate was in fact alone with the Countess, who waited in fear and trembling until it should please him to go.

"Citizeness," he said at length, after a long silence in which there was something horrible, "I am here to see that the laws of the Republic are observed."

Madame de Dey shuddered.

"Have you no revelations to make to me ? " he demanded.

"None," she replied in amazement.

"Ah, madame ! " cried the accuser, sitting down beside her and changing his tone, "at this moment, for lack of a word, either you or I may bring our heads to the scaffold. I have observed your temperament, your heart, your manners, too closely to share the error into which you have led your guests to-night. You are expecting your son, I am absolutely certain."

The Countess made a gesture of denial ; but she had turned pale, the muscles of her face had contracted, by virtue of the over-powering necessity to display a deceitful calmness, and the accuser's implacable eye lost none of her movements.

"Very well ; receive him," continued the revolutionary magistrate ; "but do not let him remain under your roof later than seven o'clock in the morning. At daybreak I shall come here armed with a denunciation which I shall procure."

She gazed at him with a stupefied air, which would have aroused the pity of a tiger.

"I shall prove," he said in a gentle tone, "the falseness of the denunciation by a thorough search, and the nature of my report will place you out of the reach of any future suspicion. I shall speak of your patriotic gifts, of your true citizenship, and we shall *all* be saved."

Madame de Dey feared a trap ; she did not move, but her face was on fire and her tongue was frozen. A blow of the knocker rang through the house.

"Ah ! " cried the terrified mother, falling on her knees. "Save him ! save him ! "

"Yes, let us save him," rejoined the public accuser, with a passionate glance at her ; "let us save him though it cost *us* our lives."

"I am lost ! " she cried, while the accuser courteously raised her.

"O madame ! " he replied, with a grand oratorical gesture, "I do not choose to owe you to any one but yourself."

"Madame, here he——" cried Brigitte, who thought that her mistress was alone.

At sight of the public accuser, the older servant, whose face was flushed with joy, became rigid and deathly pale.

"What is it, Brigitte?" asked the magistrate, in a mild and meaning tone.

"A conscript that the Mayor has sent here to lodge," replied the servant, showing the ticket.

"That is true," said the accuser, after reading the paper ; "a battalion is to arrive here to-night."

And he went out.

The Countess was too anxious at that moment to believe in the sincerity of her former attorney to entertain the slightest suspicion ; she ran swiftly upstairs, having barely strength enough to stand upright ; then she opened the door of her bedroom, saw her son, and rushed into his arms, well-nigh lifeless.

"O my son, my son !" she cried, sobbing, and covering him with frenzied kisses.

"Madame——" said the stranger.

"Oh! it isn't he !" she cried, stepping back in dismay and standing before the conscript, at whom she gazed with a haggard expression.

"Blessed Lord God, what a resemblance !" said Brigitte.

There was a moment's silence, and the stranger himself shuddered at the aspect of Madame de Dey.

"Ah, monsieur !" she said, leaning upon Brigitte's husband, and feeling then in all its force the grief of which the first pang had almost killed her ; "monsieur, I cannot endure to see you any longer ; allow my servants to take my place and to attend to your wants."

She went down to her own apartments, half carried by Brigitte and her old servant.

"What, madame !" cried the maid, "is that man going to sleep in Monsieur Auguste's bed, wear Monsieur Auguste's slippers, eat the pie that I made for Monsieur Auguste ? They may guillotine me, but I——"

"Brigitte !" cried Madame de Dey.

"Hold your tongue, chatterbox !" said her husband in a low voice ; "do you want to kill madame ? "

At that moment the conscript made a noise in his room, drawing his chair to the table.

"I will not stay here," cried Madame de Dey ; "I will go to the greenhouse, where I can hear better what goes on outside during the night."

She was still wavering between fear of having lost her son and the hope of seeing him appear. The night was disquietingly silent. There was one ghastly moment for the Countess, when the battalion of conscripts marched into the town, and each man repaired to his lodging. There were disappointed hopes at every footstep and every sound ; then nature resumed its terrible tranquillity. Towards morning the Countess was obliged to return to her room. Brigitte, who watched her mistress every moment, finding that she did not come out again, went to her room and found the Countess dead.

"She probably heard the conscript dressing and walking about in Monsieur Auguste's room, singing their cursed *Marseillaise* as if he were in a stable!" cried Brigitte. "It was that which killed her!"

The Countess's death was caused by a more intense emotion, and probably by some terrible vision. At the precise moment when Madame de Dey died at Carentan, her son was shot in Le Morbihan. We might add this tragic story to the mass of other observations on that sympathy which defies the law of space—documents which some few solitary scholars are collecting with scientific curiosity, and which will one day serve as basis for a new science, a science which till now has lacked only its man of genius.

LA GRANDE BRETÈCHE

HONORÉ DE BALZAC

ABOUT one hundred yards from Vendôme, on the banks of the Loire, there stands an old dark-coloured house, surmounted by a very high roof, and so completely isolated that there is not in the neighbourhood a single evil-smelling tannery or wretched inn, such as we see in the outskirts of almost every small town. In front of the house is a small garden bordering the river, in which the boxwood borders of the paths, once neatly trimmed, now grow at their pleasure. A few willows, born in the Loire, have grown as rapidly as the hedge which encloses the garden, and half conceal the house. The plants which we call weeds adorn the slope of the bank with their luxuriant vegetation. The fruit-trees, neglected for ten years, bear no fruit; their offshoots form a dense undergrowth. The espaliers resemble hornbeam hedges. The paths, formerly gravelled, are overrun with purslane; but, to tell the truth, there are no well-marked paths. From the top of the mountain upon which hang the ruins of the old château of the Dukes of Vendôme, the only spot from which the eye can look into this enclosure, you would say to yourself that, at a period which it is difficult to determine, that little nook was the delight of some gentleman devoted to roses and tulips, to horticulture in short, but especially fond of fine fruit. You espy an arbour, or rather the ruins of an arbour, beneath which a table still stands, not yet entirely consumed by time. At sight of that garden, which is no longer a garden, one may divine the negative delights of the peaceful life which provincials lead, as one divines the existence of a worthy tradesman by reading the epitaph on his tombstone. To round out the melancholy yet soothing thoughts which fill the mind, there is on one of the walls a sun-dial, embellished with this commonplace Christian inscription : ULTIMAM COGITA. The roof of the house is terribly dilapidated, the blinds are always drawn, the balconies are covered with swallows' nests, the doors are never opened. Tall weeds mark with green lines the cracks in the steps ; the ironwork is covered with rust. Moon, sun, winter, summer, snow, have rotted the wood, warped the boards, and corroded the paint.

The deathly silence which reigns there is disturbed only by the birds, the cats, the martens, the rats and the mice, which are at liberty to run about, to fight, and to eat one another at their will. An invisible hand has written everywhere the word MYSTERY. If, impelled by curiosity, you should go to inspect the house on the street side, you would see a high gate, arched at the top, in which the children of the neighbourhood have made numberless holes. I learned later that that gate had been condemned ten years before. Through these irregular breaches you would be able to observe the perfect harmony between the garden front and the courtyard front. The same disorder reigns supreme in both. Tufts of weeds surround the pavements. Enormous cracks furrow the walls, whose blackened tops are enlaced by the countless tendrils of climbing plants. The steps are wrenched apart, the bell-rope is rotten, the gutters are broken. " What fire from heaven has passed this way ? What tribunal has ordered salt to be strewn upon this dwelling ? Has God been insulted here ? Has France been betrayed ? " Such are the questions which one asks one's self. The reptiles crawl hither and thither without answering. That empty and deserted house is an immense riddle the solution of which is known to no one.

It was formerly a small feudal estate and bore the name of La Grande Bretèche. During my stay at Vendôme, where Desplein had left me to attend a rich patient, the aspect of that strange building became one of my keenest pleasures. Was it not more than a mere ruin ? Some souvenirs of undeniable authenticity are always connected with a ruin ; but that abode, still standing, although in process of gradual demolition by an avenging hand, concealed a secret, an unknown thought ; at the very least, it betrayed a caprice. More than once, in the evening, I wandered in the direction of the hedge, now wild and uncared for, which surrounded that enclosure. I defied scratches, and made my way into that ownerless garden, that estate which was neither public nor private ; and I

remained whole hours there contemplating its disarray. Not even
to learn the story which would doubtless account for that extraordinary spectacle, would I have asked a single question of any
Vendômese gossip. Straying about there, I composed delightful
romances, I abandoned myself to little orgies of melancholy which
enchanted me.

If I had learned the cause of that perhaps most commonplace
neglect, I should have lost the unspoken poesy with which I
intoxicated myself. To me that spot represented the most diverse
images of human life darkened by its misfortunes ; now it was the air
of the cloister, minus the monks ; again, the perfect peace of the
cemetery, minus the dead speaking their epitaphic language ;
to-day, the house of the leper ; to-morrow, that of the Fates ; but
it was, above all, the image of the province; with its meditation,
with its hour-glass life. I have often wept there, but never laughed.
More than once I have felt an involuntary terror, as I heard above
my head the low rustling made by the wings of some hurrying dove.
The ground is damp ; you must beware of lizards, snakes, and toads,
which wander about there with the fearless liberty of nature ;
above all, you must not fear the cold, for, after a few seconds, you
feel an icy cloak resting upon your shoulders like the hand of the
Commendator on the neck of Don Juan. One evening I had
shuddered there ; the wind had twisted an old rusty weather-vane,
whose shrieks resembled a groan uttered by the house at the
moment that I was finishing a rather dismal melodrama, by which
I sought to explain to myself that species of monumental grief. I
returned to my inn, beset by sombre thoughts. When I had supped,
my hostess entered my room with a mysterious air, and said to me :
" Here is Monsieur Regnault, monsieur."

" Who is Monsieur Regnault ? "

" What ! monsieur doesn't know Monsieur Regnault ? That's
funny ! " she said, as she left the room.

Suddenly I saw a tall slender man, dressed in black, with his hat in
his hand, who entered the room like a ram ready to rush at his rival,
disclosing a retreating forehead, a small pointed head, and a pale
face, not unlike a glass of dirty water. You would have said that he
was the doorkeeper of some minister. He wore an old coat,
threadbare at the seams ; but he had a diamond in his shirt-frill
and gold rings in his ears.

" To whom have I the honour of speaking, monsieur ? " I asked
him.

He took a chair, seated himself in front of my fire, placed his hat
on my table, and replied, rubbing his hands :

" Ah ! it's very cold ! I am Monsieur Regnault, monsieur."

I bowed, saying to myself :

" Il Bondocani ! Look for him ! "

"I am the notary at Vendôme," he continued.

"I am delighted to hear it, monsieur," I exclaimed, "but I am not ready to make my will, for reasons best known to myself."

"Just a minute," he rejoined, raising his hand as if to impose silence upon me. "I beg pardon, monsieur, I beg pardon! I have heard that you go to walk sometimes in the garden of La Grande Bretèche."

"Yes, monsieur!"

"Just a minute," he said, repeating his gesture; "that practice constitutes a downright trespass. I have come, monsieur, in the name and as executor of the late Madame Comtesse de Merret, to beg you to discontinue your visits. Just a minute! I'm not a Turk, and I don't propose to charge you with a crime. Besides, it may well be that you are not aware of the circumstances which compel me to allow the finest mansion in Vendôme to fall to ruin. However, monsieur, you seem to be a man of education, and you must know that the law forbids entrance upon an enclosed estate under severe penalties. A hedge is as good as a wall. But the present condition of the house may serve as an excuse for your curiosity. I would ask nothing better than to allow you to go and come as you please in that house; but, as it is my duty to carry out the will of the testatrix, I have the honour, monsieur, to request you not to go into that garden again. Even I myself, monsieur, since the opening of the will, have never set foot inside that house, which, as I have had the honour to tell you, is a part of the estate of Madame de Merret. We simply reported the number of doors and windows, in order to fix the amount of the impost which I pay annually from the fund set aside for that purpose by the late countess. Ah! her will made a great deal of talk in Vendôme, monsieur."

At that, he stopped to blow his nose, the excellent man. I respected his loquacity, understanding perfectly that the administration of Madame de Merret's property was the important event of his life—his reputation, his glory, his Restoration. I must needs bid adieu to my pleasant reveries, to my romances; so that I was not inclined to scorn the pleasure of learning the truth from an official source.

"Would it be indiscreet, monsieur," I asked him, "to ask you the reason of this extraordinary state of affairs?"

At that question an expression which betrayed all the pleasure that a man feels who is accustomed to ride a hobby passed over the notary's face. He pulled up his shirt collar with a self-satisfied air, produced his snuff-box, opened it, offered it to me, and at my refusal, took a famous pinch himself. He was happy; the man who has no hobby has no idea of the satisfaction that can be derived from life. A hobby is the precise mean between passion and monomania. At that moment I understood the witty expression of Sterne in all

its extent, and I had a perfect conception of the joy with which
Uncle Toby, with Trim's assistance, bestrode his battle-horse.

" Monsieur," said Monsieur Regnault, " I was chief clerk to Master
Roguin of Paris. An excellent office, of which you may have heard ?
No ? Why, it was made famous by a disastrous failure. Not having
sufficient money to practise in Paris, at the price to which offices had
risen in 1816, I came here and bought the office of my predecessor.
I had relatives in Vendôme, among others a very rich aunt, who gave
me her daughter in marriage. Monsieur," he continued after a brief
pause, " three months after being licensed by the Keeper of the Seals
I was sent for one evening, just as I was going to bed (I was not then
married), by Madame Comtesse de Merret, to come to her Château
de Merret. Her maid, an excellent girl who works in this inn to-day,
was at my door with madame countess's carriage. But, just a
minute ! I must tell you, monsieur, that Monsieur Comte de Merret
had gone to Paris to die, two months before I came here. He died
miserably there, abandoning himself to excesses of all sorts. You
understand ?—On the day of his departure madame countess had left
La Grande Bretèche and had dismantled it. Indeed, some people
declare that she burned the furniture and hangings, and all chattels
whatsoever now contained in the estate leased by the said— What
on earth am I saying ? I beg pardon, I thought I was dictating a
lease.—That she burned them," he continued, " in the fields at
Merret. Have you been to Merret, monsieur ? No ? " he said,
answering his own question. " Ah ! that is a lovely spot ! For
about three months," he continued, after a slight shake of the head,
" monsieur count and madame countess led a strange life.

" They received no guests ; madame lived on the ground floor,
and monsieur on the first floor. When madame countess was left
alone, she never appeared except at church. Later, in her own house
at her château, she refused to see the friends who came to see her.
She was already much changed when she left La Grande Bretèche
to go to Merret. The dear woman—I say ' dear,' because this
diamond came from her ; but I actually only saw her once—the
excellent lady, then, was very ill ; she had doubtless despaired of
her health, for she died without calling a doctor ; so that many
of our ladies thought that she was not in full possession of her wits.
My curiosity was therefore strangely aroused, monsieur, when I
learned that Madame de Merret needed my services. I was not
the only one who took an interest in that story. That same
evening, although it was late, the whole town knew that I had gone
to Merret. The maid answered rather vaguely the questions that I
asked her on the road ; she told me, however, that her mistress had
received the sacrament from the curé of Merret during the day, and
that she did not seem likely to live through the night.

" I reached the château about eleven o'clock ; I mounted the main staircase. After passing through divers large rooms, high and dark, and as cold and damp as the devil, I reached the state bed-chamber where the countess was. According to the reports that were current concerning that lady—I should never end, monsieur, if I should repeat all the stories that are told about her—I had thought of her as a coquette. But, if you please, I had much difficulty in finding her in the huge bed in which she lay. To be sure, to light that enormous wainscoted chamber of the old *régime*, where every-thing was so covered with dust that it made one sneeze simply to look at it, she had only one of those old-fashioned Argand lamps. Ah! but you have never been to Merret. Well, monsieur, the bed is one of those beds of the olden time, with a high canopy of flowered material. A small night-table stood beside the bed, and I saw upon it a copy of the *Imitation of Jesus Christ*, which, by the by, I bought for my wife, as well as the lamp. There was also a large couch for the attendant, and two chairs. Not a spark of fire. That was all the furniture. It wouldn't have filled ten lines in an inventory.

" Oh! my dear monsieur, if you had seen, as I then saw it, that huge room hung with dark tapestry, you would have imagined yourself transported into a genuine scene from a novel. It was icy cold ; and, more than that, absolutely funereal," he added, raising his arm with a theatrical gesture and pausing for a moment. " By looking hard and walking close to the bed, I succeeded in discovering Madame de Merret, thanks to the lamp, the light of which shone upon the pillow. Her face was as yellow as wax, and resembled two clasped hands. She wore a lace cap, which revealed her lovely hair, as white as snow. She was sitting up, and seemed to retain that position with much difficulty. Her great black eyes, dulled by fever no doubt, and already almost lifeless, hardly moved beneath the bones which the eyebrows cover—these," he said, pointing to the arch over his eyes.—" Her brow was moist. Her fleshless hands resembled bones covered with tightly-drawn skin; her veins and muscles could be seen perfectly. She must have been very beautiful ; but at that moment I was seized with in indefinable feeling at her aspect. Never before, according to those who laid her out, had a living creature attained such thinness without dying. In short, she was horrible to look at ; disease had so wasted that woman that she was nothing more than a phantom. Her pale violet lips seemed not to move when she spoke to me. Although my profession had familiarised me with such spectacles, by taking me sometimes to the pillows of dying persons to take down their last wishes, I confess that the families in tears and despair whom I had seen were as nothing beside that solitary, silent woman in that enormous château.

" I did not hear the slightest sound, I could not detect the move-ment which the breathing of the sick woman should have imparted

to the sheets that covered her ; and I stood quite still, gazing
at her in a sort of stupor. It seems to me that I am there now.
At last her great eyes moved, she tried to raise her right hand
which fell back upon the bed, and these words came from her mouth
like a breath, for her voice had already ceased to be a voice ;
' I have been awaiting you with much impatience.'—Her cheeks
suddenly flushed. It was a great effort for her to speak, monsieur.
—' Madame,' I said. She motioned to me to be silent. At that
moment the old nurse rose and whispered in my ear : ' Don't speak ;
madame countess cannot bear to hear the slightest sound, and
what you said might excite her.'—I sat down. A few moments
later, Madame de Merret collected all her remaining strength to
move her right arm and thrust it, not without infinite difficulty,
beneath her bolster ; she paused for just a moment ; then she made
a last effort to withdraw her hand, and when she finally produced
a sealed paper, drops of sweat fell from her brow.—' I place my
will in your hands,' she said. ' Oh, *mon Dieu !* oh ! '—That was
all. She grasped a crucifix that lay on her bed, hastily put it to
her lips, and died. The expression of her staring eyes makes me
shudder even now, when I think of it. She must have suffered
terribly ! There was a gleam of joy in her last glance, a sentiment
which remained in her dead eyes.

" I carried the will away ; and when it was opened, I found that
Madame de Merret had appointed me her executor. She left all
her property to the hospital at Vendôme with the exception of a
few individual legacies. But these were her provisions with
respect to La Grande Bretèche : She directed me to leave her house,
for fifty years from the day of her death, in the same condition
as at the moment that she died ; forbidding any person whatsoever to
enter the rooms, forbidding the slightest repairs to be made, and
even setting aside a sum in order to hire keepers, if it should be
found necessary, to assure the literal execution of her purpose.
At the expiration of that period, if the desire of the testatrix has
been carried out, the house is to belong to my heirs, for monsieur
knows that notaries cannot accept legacies. If not, La Grande
Bretèche is to revert to whoever is entitled to it, but with the
obligation to comply with the conditions set forth in a codicil
attached to the will, which is not to be opened until the
expiration of the said fifty years. The will was not attacked ; and
so——"

At that, without finishing his sentence, the elongated notary
glanced at me with a triumphant air, and I made him altogether
happy by addressing a few compliments to him.

" Monsieur," I said, " you have made a profound impression
upon me, so I think I see that dying woman, paler than her sheets ;
her gleaming eyes terrify me ; and I shall dream of her to-night.

But you must have formed some conjecture concerning the provisions of that extraordinary will."

"Monsieur," he said with a comical reserve, "I never allow myself to judge the conduct of those persons who honour me by giving me a diamond."

I soon loosened the tongue of the scrupulous Vendômese notary, who communicated to me, not without long digressions, observations due to the profound politicians of both sexes whose decrees are law in Vendôme. But those observations were so contradictory and so diffuse that I almost fell asleep, despite the interest I took in that authentic narrative. The dull and monotonous tone of the notary, who was accustomed, no doubt, to listen to himself, and to force his clients and his fellow citizens to listen to him, triumphed over my curiosity.

"Aha! many people, monsieur," he said to me on the landing, "would like to live forty-five years more; but just a minute!" and with a sly expression, he placed his right forefinger on his nose, as if he would have said: "Just mark what I say."—"But to do that, to do that," he added, "a man must be less than sixty."

I closed my door, having been roused from my apathy by this last shaft, which the notary considered very clever; then I seated myself in my easy-chair, placing my feet on the andirons. I was soon absorbed in an imaginary romance à la Radcliffe, based upon the judicial observations of Monsieur Regnault, when my door, under the skilful manipulation of a woman's hand, turned upon its hinges. My hostess appeared, a stout red-faced woman, of excellent disposition, who had missed her vocation: she was a Fleming, who should have been born in a picture by Teniers.

"Well, monsieur," she said, "no doubt Monsieur Regnault has given you his story of La Grande Bretèche?"

"Yes, Mother Lepas."

"What did he tell you?"

I repeated in a few words the chilling and gloomy story of Madame de Merret. At each sentence my hostess thrust out her neck, gazing at me with the true innkeeper's perspicacity—a sort of happy medium between the instinct of the detective, the cunning of the spy, and the craft of the trader.

"My dear Madame Lepas," I added, as I concluded, "you evidently know more, eh? If not, why should you have come up here?"

"Oh! on an honest woman's word, as true as my name's Lepas——"

"Don't swear; your eyes are big with a secret. You knew Monsieur de Merret. What sort of a man was he?"

"Bless my soul! Monsieur de Merret was a fine man, whom you never could see the whole of, he was so long; an excellent gentleman, who came here from Picardy, and who had his brains very near his cap, as we say here. He paid cash for everything, in order not to have trouble with anybody. You see, he was lively. We women all found him very agreeable."

"Because he was lively?" I asked.

"That may be," she said. "You know, monsieur, that a man must have had something in front of him, as they say, to marry Madame de Merret, who, without saying anything against the others, was the loveliest and richest woman in the whole province. She had about twenty thousand francs a year. The whole town went to her wedding. The bride was dainty and attractive, a real jewel of a woman. Ah! they made a handsome couple at that time!"

"Did they live happily together?"

"Oh, dear! oh, dear! yes and no, so far as any one could tell; for, as you can imagine, we folks didn't live on intimate terms with them. Madame de Merret was a kind-hearted woman, very pleasant, who had to suffer sometimes perhaps from her husband's quick temper; but although he was a bit proud, we liked him. You see, it was his business to be like that; when a man is noble, you know——"

"However, some catastrophe must have happened, to make Monsieur and Madame de Merret separate so violently?"

"I didn't say there was any catastrophe, monsieur. I don't know anything about it."

"Good! I am sure now that you know all about it."

"Well, monsieur, I will tell you all I know. When I saw Monsieur Regnault come up to your room, I had an idea that he would talk to you about Madame de Merret in connection with La Grande Bretèche. That gave me the idea of consulting with monsieur, who seems to me a man of good judgment and incapable of playing false with a poor woman like me, who never did anybody any harm, and yet who's troubled by her conscience. Up to this time I've never dared to speak out to the people of this neighbourhood, for they're all sharp-tongued gossips. And then, monsieur, I've never had a guest stay in my inn so long as you have, and to whom I could tell the story of the fifteen thousand francs."

"My dear Madame Lepas," I said, arresting the flood of her words, "if your confidence is likely to compromise me, I wouldn't be burdened with it for a moment, for anything in the world."

"Don't be afraid," she said, interrupting me; "you shall see."

This eagerness on her part made me think that I was not the only one to whom my worthy hostess had communicated the secret of which I dreaded to be the only confidant, and I listened.

"Monsieur," she began, "when the Emperor sent Spanish or

other prisoners of war here, I had to board, at the expense of the government, a young Spaniard who was sent to Vendôme on parole. In spite of the parole, he went every day to show himself to the subprefect. He was a Spanish grandee ! Nothing less ! He had a name in *os* and *dia*, something like Bagos de Férédia. I have his name written on my register ; you can read it if you wish. He was a fine young man for a Spaniard, who they say are all ugly. He was only five feet two or three inches tall, but he was well-built ; he had little hands, which he took care of—oh ! you should have seen ; he has as many brushes for his hands as a woman has for all purposes ! He had long black hair, a flashing eye, and rather a copper-coloured skin, which I liked all the same. He wore such fine linen as I never saw before on any one, although I have entertained princesses, and among others General Bertrand, the Duke and Duchess d'Abrantès, Monsieur Decazes, and the King of Spain. He didn't eat much ; but he had polite and pleasant manners, so that I couldn't be angry with him for it. Oh ! I was very fond of him, although he didn't say four words a day, and it was impossible to have the slightest conversation with him ; if any one spoke to him, he wouldn't answer ; it was a fad, a mania that they all have, so they tell me. He read his breviary like a priest, he went to mass and to the services regularly. Where did he sit ? We noticed that later : about two steps from Madame de Merret's private chapel. As he took his seat there the first time that he came to the church, nobody imagined that there was any design in it. Besides, he never took his face off his prayer-book, the poor young man ! In the evening, monsieur, he used to walk on the mountain, among the ruins of the château. That was the poor man's only amusement ; he was reminded of his own country there. They say that there's nothing but mountains in Spain.

" Very soon after he came here he began to stay out late. I was anxious when he didn't come home till midnight ; but we all got used to his whim ; he would take the key of the door, and we wouldn't wait for him. He lived in a house that we have on Rue de Casernes. Then one of our stablemen told us that one night, when he took the horses to drink, he thought he saw the Spanish grandee swimming far out in the river, like a real fish. When he came back, I told him to be careful of the eel-grass ; he seemed vexed that he had been seen in the water. At last, monsieur, one day, or rather one morning, we didn't find him in his room ; he hadn't come home. By hunting carefully everywhere, I found a writing in his table drawer, where there were fifty of the Spanish gold-pieces which they call *portugaises*, and which were worth about five thousand francs ; and then there were ten thousand francs' worth of diamonds in a little sealed box. His writing said that in case he didn't return, he left us this money and his diamonds, on condition that we would found masses to thank God for his escape and his salvation. In those days I still had my man, who went out to look for him. And here's the funny part of the story : he brought back the Spaniard's clothes, which he found under a big stone in a sort of a shed by the river, on the château side, almost opposite La Grande Bretèche.

" My husband went there so early that no one saw him ; he burned the clothes after reading the letter, and we declared, according to Count Férédia's wish, that he had escaped. The subprefect set all the gendarmerie on his track, but, bless my soul ! they never caught him. Lepas believed that the Spaniard had drowned himself. For my part, monsieur, I don't think it ; I think rather that he was mixed up in Madame de Merret's business, seeing that Rosalie told me that the crucifix that her mistress thought so much of that she had it buried with her, was made of ebony and silver ; now, in the early part of his stay here, Monsieur Férédia had one of silver and ebony, which I didn't see afterwards. Tell me now, monsieur, isn't it true that I needn't have any remorse about the Spaniard's fifteen thousand francs, and that they are fairly mine ? "

" Certainly. But did you never try to question Rosalie ? " I asked her.

" Oh ! yes, indeed, monsieur. But would you believe it ? That girl is like a wall. She knows something, but it's impossible to make her talk."

After conversing a moment more with me, my hostess left me beset by undefined and dismal thoughts, by a romantic sort of curiosity, a religious terror not unlike the intense emotion that seizes us when we enter a dark church at night and see a dim light in the distance under the lofty arches ; a vague figure gliding along, or the rustling of a dress or a surplice ; it makes us shudder. La Grande Bretèche and its tall weeds, its condemned windows, its rusty ironwork, its closed doors, its deserted rooms, suddenly appeared before me in fantastic guise. I tried to penetrate that mysterious abode, seeking there the kernel of that sombre story, of that drama which had caused the death of three persons. In my eyes Rosalie was the most interesting person in Vendôme. As I scrutinised her, I detected traces of some inmost thought, despite the robust health that shone upon her plump cheeks. There was in her some seed of remorse or of hope ; her manner announced a secret, as does that of the devotee who prays with excessive fervour, or that of the infanticide, who constantly hears her child's last cry. However, her attitude was artless and natural, her stupid smile had no trace of criminality, and you would have voted her innocent simply by glancing at the large handkerchief with red and blue squares which covered her vigorous bust, confined by a gown with white and violet stripes.

"No," I thought, "I won't leave Vendôme without learning the whole story of La Grande Bretèche. To obtain my end, I will become Rosalie's friend, if it is absolutely necessary."

"Rosalie?" I said one evening.

"What is it, monsieur?"

"You are not married?"

She started slightly.

"Oh! I sha'n't lack men when I take a fancy to be unhappy!" she said, with a laugh.

She speedily overcame her inward emotion; for all women, from the great lady down to the servant at an inn, have a self-possession which is peculiar to them.

"You are fresh and appetising enough not to lack suitors. But tell me, Rosalie, why did you go to work in an inn when you left Madame de Merret's? Didn't she leave you some money?"

"Oh, yes! but my place is the best in Vendôme, monsieur."

This reply was one of those which judges and lawyers call dilatory. Rosalie seemed to me to occupy in that romantic story the position of the square in the middle of the chessboard; she was at the very centre of interest and of truth; she seemed to me to be tied up in the clue; there was in that girl the last chapter of a romance; and so, from that moment, Rosalie became the object of my attentions. By dint of studying the girl, I observed in her, as in all women to whom we devote all our thoughts, a multitude of good qualities: she was neat and clean, and she was fine-looking—that goes without saying; she had also all the attractions which our desire imparts to women, in whatever station of life they may be. A fortnight after the notary's visit, I said to Rosalie one evening, or rather one morning, for it was very early:

"Tell me all that you know about Madame de Merret."

"Oh, don't ask me that, Monsieur Horace!" she replied in alarm.

Her pretty face darkened, her bright colour vanished, and her eyes lost their humid, innocent light. But I insisted.

"Well," she rejoined, "as you insist upon it, I will tell you; but keep my secret."

"Of course, of course, my dear girl; I will keep all your secrets with the probity of a thief, and that is the most loyal probity that exists."

"If it's all the same to you," she said, "I prefer that it should be with your own."

Thereupon she arranged her neckerchief, and assumed the attitude of a story-teller; for there certainly is an attitude of trust and security essential to the telling of a story. The best

stories are told at a certain hour, and at the table, as we all are now.
No one ever told a story well while standing, or fasting. But if it
were necessary to reproduce faithfully Rosalie's diffuse eloquence,
a whole volume would hardly suffice. Now, as the event of which
she gave me a confused account occupied, between the loquacity
of the notary and that of Madame Lepas, the exact position of the
mean terms of an arithmetical proportion between the two extremes,
it is only necessary for me to repeat it to you in a few words.
Therefore I abridge.

The room which Madame de Merret occupied at La Grande
Bretèche was on the ground floor. A small closet, about four feet
deep, in the wall, served as her wardrobe. Three months before
the evening, the incidents of which I am about to narrate, Madame
de Merret had been so seriously indisposed that her husband left
her alone in her room and slept in a room on the first floor. By
one of those chances which it is impossible to foresee, he returned
home, on the evening in question, two hours later than usual,
from the club to which he was accustomed to go to read the newspapers and to talk politics with the people of the neighbourhood.
His wife supposed that he had come home, and had gone to bed and
to sleep. But the invasion of France had given rise to a lively
discussion ; the game of billiards had been very close, and he had
lost forty francs, an enormous sum at Vendôme, where everybody
hoards money, and where manners are confined within the limits of
a modesty worthy of all praise, which perhaps is the source of a
true happiness of which no Parisian has a suspicion.

For some time past Monsieur de Merret had contented himself with
asking Rosalie if his wife were in bed ; at the girl's reply, always in
the affirmative, he went immediately to his own room with the
readiness born of habit and confidence. But on returning home
that evening, he took it into his head to go to Madame de Meret's
room, to tell her of his misadventure and perhaps also to console
himself for it. During dinner he had remarked that Madame de
Merret was very coquettishly dressed ; he said to himself as he
walked home from the club, that his wife was no longer ill, that
her convalescence had improved her ; but he perceived it, as
husbands notice everything, a little late. Instead of calling Rosalie,
who at that moment was busy in the kitchen, watching the cook
and the coachman play a difficult hand of *brisque*, Monsieur de
Merret went to his wife's room, lighted by his lantern, which he had
placed on the top step of the stairs. His footstep, easily recognised,
resounded under the arches of the corridor. At that instant that
he turned the knob of his wife's door, he fancied that he heard
the door of the closet that I have mentioned close ; but when
he entered, Madame de Merret was alone, standing in front of the
hearth. The husband naïvely concluded that Rosalie was in the

closet ; however, a suspicion, that rang in his ears like the striking of a lock, made him distrustful ; he looked at his wife and detected in her eyes something indefinable of confusion and dismay.

" You come home very late," she said.

That voice, usually so pure and so gracious, seemed to him slightly changed. He made no reply, but at that moment Rosalie entered the room. That was a thunderclap to him. He walked about the room, from one window to another, with a uniform step and with folded arms.

" Have you learned anything distressing, or are you ill ? " his wife timidly asked him, while Rosalie undressed her.

He made no reply.

" You may go," said Madame de Merret to her maid ; " I will put on my curl-papers myself."

She divined some catastrophe simply from the expression of her husband's face, and she preferred to be alone with him. When Rosalie was gone, or was supposed to be gone, for she stayed for some moments in the corridor, Monsieur de Merret took his stand in front of his wife, and said to her coldly :

" Madame, there is some one in your closet ? "

She looked at her husband calmly, and replied simply :

" No, monsieur."

That " no " tore Monsieur de Merret's heart, for he did not believe it ; and yet his wife had never seemed to him purer and more holy than she seemed at that moment. He rose to open the closet door ; Madame de Merret took his hand, stopped him, looked at him with a melancholy expression, and said in a voice strangely moved :

" If you find no one, reflect that all is at an end between us ! "

The indescribable dignity of his wife's attitude reawoke the gentleman's profound esteem for her, and inspired in him one of those resolutions which require only a vaster theatre in order to become immortal.

" No," he said, " I will not do it, Josephine. In either case, we should be separated for ever. Listen ; I know all the purity of your soul, and I know that you lead the life of a saint, and that you would not commit a mortal sin to save your life."

At these words, Madame de Merret looked at her husband with a haggard eye.

" See, here is your crucifix ; swear to me before God that there is no one there, and I will believe you, I will never open that door."

Madame de Merret took the crucifix and said :

" I swear it."

" Louder," said the husband, " and repeat after me : ' I swear before God that there is no one in that closet.' "

She repeated the words without confusion.

"It is well," said Monsieur de Merret coldly. After a moment's silence: "This is a very beautiful thing that I did not know you possessed," he said, as he examined the crucifix of ebony encrusted with silver and beautifully carved.

"I found it at Duvivier's; when that party of prisoners passed through Vendôme last year, he bought it of a Spanish monk."

"Ah!" said Monsieur de Merret, replacing the crucifix on the nail. And he rang. Rosalie did not keep him waiting. Monsieur de Merret walked hastily to meet her, led her into the embrasure of the window looking over the garden, and said to her in a low voice:

"I know that Gorenflot wants to marry you, that poverty alone prevents you from coming together, and that you have told him that you would not be his wife until he found some way to become a master mason. Well, go to him, and tell him to come here with his trowel and his tools. Manage so as not to wake anybody in his house but him; his fortune will exceed your desires. Above all, go out of this house without chattering, or——"

He frowned. Rosalie started, and he called her back.

"Here, take my pass-key," he said.

"Jean!" shouted Monsieur de Merret in the corridor, in a voice of thunder.

Jean, who was both his coachman and his confidential man, left his game of *brisque* and answered the summons.

"Go to bed, all of you," said his master, motioning to him to come near. And he added, but in an undertone: "When they are all asleep, *asleep*, do you understand, you will come down and let me know."

Monsieur de Merret, who had not lost sight of his wife while giving his orders, calmly returned to her side in front of the fire, and began to tell her about the game of billiards and the discussion at the club. When Rosalie returned she found monsieur and madame talking most amicably. The gentleman had recently had plastered all the rooms which composed his reception-apartment on the ground floor. Plaster is very scarce in Vendôme, and the cost of transportation increases the price materially; so he had purchased quite a large quantity, knowing that he would readily find customers for any that he might have left. That circumstance suggested the design which he proceeded to carry out.

"Gorenflot is here, monsieur," said Rosalie in an undertone.

"Let him come in," replied the Picard gentleman aloud.

Madame de Merret turned pale when she saw the mason.

"Gorenflot," said her husband, "go out to the carriage-house and get some bricks, and bring in enough to wall up the door of this closet; you can use the plaster that I had left over to plaster the wall." Then beckoning Rosalie and the workman to him, he said in a low tone: "Look you, Gorenflot, you will sleep here to-night.

But to-morrow morning you shall have a passport to go abroad, to a city which I will name to you. I will give you six thousand francs for your journey. You will remain ten years in that city; if you are not satisfied there, you can settle in another city, provided that it is in the same country. You will go by way of Paris, where you will wait for me. There I will give you a guarantee to pay you six thousand francs more on your return, in case you have abided by the conditions of our bargain. At that price you should be willing to keep silent concerning what you have done here to-night. As for you, Rosalie, I will give you ten thousand francs, which will be paid to you on the day of your wedding, provided that you marry Gorenflot; but, in order to be married, you will have to be silent; if not, no dower."

"Rosalie," said Madame de Merret, "come here and arrange my hair."

The husband walked tranquilly back and forth, watching the door, the mason, and his wife, but without any outward sign of injurious suspicion. Gorenflot was obliged to make a noise; Madame de Merret seized an opportunity, when the workman was dropping some bricks, and when her husband was at the other end of the room, to say to Rosalie:

"A thousand francs a year to you, my dear child, if you can tell Gorenflot to leave a crack at the bottom.—Go and help him," she said coolly, aloud.

Monsieur and Madame de Merret said not a word while Gorenflot was walling up the door. That silence was the result of design on the husband's part, for he did not choose to allow his wife a pretext for uttering words of double meaning; and on Madame de Merret's part, it was either prudence or pride. When the wall was half built, the crafty mason seized a moment when the gentleman's back was turned, to strike his pickaxe through one of the panes of the glass door.

At four o'clock, about daybreak, for it was September, the work was finished. The mason remained in the house under the eye of Jean, and Monsieur de Merret slept in his wife's chamber. In the morning, on rising, he said carelessly:

"Ah! by the way, I must go to the mayor's office, for the passport."

He put his hat on his head, walked towards the door, turned back and took the crucifix. His wife fairly trembled with joy.

"He will go to Duvivier's," she thought.

As soon as the gentleman had left the room, Madame de Merret rang for Rosalie; then, in a terrible voice, she cried:

"The pickaxe; the pickaxe! and to work! I saw how Gorenflot understood last night; we shall have time to make a hole, and stop it up."

In a twinkling Rosalie brought her mistress a sort of small axe, and she, with an ardour which no words can describe, began to demolish the wall. She had already loosened several bricks, when, as she stepped back to deal a blow even harder than the preceding ones, she saw Monsieur de Merret behind her ; she fainted.

" Put madame on her bed," said the gentleman coldly.

Anticipating what was likely to happen during his absence, he had laid a trap for his wife ; he had simply written to the mayor, and had sent a messenger to Duvivier. The jeweller arrived just as the disorder in the room had been repaired.

" Duvivier," asked Monsieur de Merret, " didn't you buy some crucifixes from the Spaniards who passed through here ? "

" No, monsieur."

" Very well, I thank you," he said, exchanging with his wife a tiger-like glance.—" Jean," he added, turning towards his confidential valet, " you will have my meals served in Madame de Merret's room ; she is ill, and I shall not leave her until she is well again."

The cruel man remained with his wife twenty days. During the first days, when there was a noise in the walled-up closet and Josephine attempted to implore him in behalf of the dying unknown, he replied, not allowing her to utter a word :

" You have sworn on the cross that there was no one there."

THE ATHEIST'S MASS

HONORÉ DE BALZAC

DOCTOR BIANCHON—a physician to whom science owes a beautiful physiological theory, and who, though still a young man, has won himself a place among the celebrities of the Paris School, a centre of light to which all the doctors of Europe pay homage—practised surgery before devoting himself to medicine. His early studies were directed by one of the greatest surgeons in France, the celebrated Desplein, who was regarded as a luminary of science. Even his enemies admitted that with him was buried a technical skill he could not bequeath to any successor. Like all men of genius he left no heirs. All that was peculiarly his own he carried to the grave with him.

The glory of great surgeons is like that of actors whose work exists only so long as they live, and of whose talent no adequate idea can be formed when they are gone. Actors and surgeons, and also great singers like those artists who increase tenfold the power of music by the way in which they perform it—all these are the heroes of a moment. Desplein is a striking instance of the similarity of the destinies of such transitory geniuses. His name, yesterday so famous, to-day almost forgotten, will live among the specialists of his own branch of science without being known beyond it.

But is not an unheard-of combination of circumstances required for the name of a learned man to pass from the domain of science into the general history of mankind? Had Desplein that universality of acquirements that makes of a man the expression, the type of a century? He was gifted with a magnificent power of diagnosis. He could see into the patient and his malady by an acquired or natural intuition, that enabled him to grasp the peculiar characteristics of the individual, and determined the precise moment, the hour, the minute, when he should operate, taking into account both atmospheric conditions and the special temperament of his patient. In order thus to be able to work hand in hand with Nature, had he studied the ceaseless union of organised and elementary substances contained in the atmosphere, or supplied by the earth to man, who absorbs and modifies them so as to derive from them an individual result? Or did he proceed by that power of deduction and analogy to which the genius of Cuvier owed so much?

However that may be, this man had made himself master of all the secrets of the body. He knew it in its past as in its future, taking the present for his point of departure. But did he embody in his own person all the science of his time, as was the case with Hippocrates, Galen and Aristotle? Did he lead a whole school towards new worlds of knowledge? No. And while it is impossible to deny to this indefatigable observer of the chemistry of the human body the possession of something like the ancient science of Magism—that is to say, the knowledge of principles in combination, of the causes of life, of life as the antecedent of life, and what it will be through the action of causes preceding its existence—it must be acknowledged that all this was entirely personal to him. Isolated during his life by egotism, this egotism was the suicide of his fame. His tomb is not surmounted by a pretentious statue proclaiming to the future the mysteries that genius has unveiled for it.

But perhaps the talents of Desplein were linked with his beliefs, and therefore mortal. For him the earth's atmosphere was a kind of envelope generating all things. He regarded the earth as an egg in its shell, and unable to solve the old riddle as to whether the egg or the hen came first, he admitted neither the hen nor the egg.

He believed neither in a mere animal nature giving origin to the race of man, nor in a spirit surviving him. Desplein was not in doubt. He asserted his theories. His plain open atheism was like that of many men, some of the best fellows in the world, but invincibly atheistic—atheists of a type of which religious people do not admit the existence. This opinion could harldy be otherwise with a man accustomed from his youth to dissect the highest of beings, before, during, and after life, without finding therein that one soul that is so necessary to religious theories. He recognised there a cerebral centre, a nervous centre, and a centre for the respiratory and circulatory system, and the two former so completely supplemented each other, that during the last part of his life he had the conviction that the sense of hearing was not absolutely necessary for one to hear, nor the sense of vision absolutely necessary for sight, and that the solar plexus could replace them without one being aware of the fact. Desplein, recognising these two souls in man, made it an argument for his atheism, without however assuming anything as to the belief in God. This man was said to have died in final impenitence, as many great geniuses have unfortunately died, whom may God forgive.

Great as the man was, his life had in it many " littlenesses " (to adopt the expression used by his enemies, who were eager to diminish his fame), though it would perhaps be more fitting to call them apparent contradictions. Failing to understand the motives on which high minds act, envious and stupid people at once seize hold of any surface discrepancies to base upon them an indictment, on which they straightway ask for judgment. If, after all, success crowns the methods they have attacked, and shows the coordination of preparation and result, all the same something will remain of these charges flung out in advance. Thus in our time Napoleon was condemned by his contemporaries for having spread the wings of the eagle towards England. They had to wait till 1822 for the explanation of 1804, and of the flat-bottomed boats of Boulogne.

In the case of Desplein, his fame and his scientific knowledge not being open to attack, his enemies found fault with his strange whims, his singular character. For he possessed in no small degree that quality which the English call " eccentricity." Now he would be attired with a splendour that suggested Crébillon's stately tragedy ; and then he would suddenly affect a strange indifference in the matter of dress. One saw him now in a carriage, now on foot. By turns sharp-spoken and kindly ; assuming an air of closeness and stinginess, but at the same time ready to put his fortune at the disposal of exiled professors of his science, who would do him the honour of accepting his help for a few days—no one ever gave occasion for more contradictory judgments. Although

for the sake of obtaining a decoration that doctors were not allowed
to canvass for, he was quite capable of letting a prayer-book slip
out of his pocket when at court, you may take it that in his own
mind he made a mockery of everything.

He had a deep disdain for men, after having caught glimpses of
their true character in the midst of the most solemn and the most
trivial acts of their existence. In a great man all his characteristics
are generally in keeping with each other. If one of these giants
has more talent than wit, it is all the same true that his wit is something deeper than that of one of whom all that can be said is that
" He is a witty fellow." Genius always implies a certain insight
into the moral side of things. This insight may be applied to one
special line of thought, but one cannot see the flower without at
the same time seeing the sun that produces it. The man who,
hearing a diplomatist whom he was saving from death ask, " How
is the Emperor ? " remarked, " The courtier is recovering, and the
man will recover with him ! " was not merely a doctor or a surgeon,
but was also not without a considerable amount of wit. Thus
the patient, unwearying observation of mankind might do something
to justify the exorbitant pretensions of Desplein, and make one
admit that, as he himself believed, he was capable of winning as
much distinction as a Minister of State as he had gained as a surgeon.

Amongst the problems that the life of Desplein presented to the
minds of his contemporaries, we have chosen one of the most interesting, because the key to it will be found in the ending of the
story, and will serve to clear him of many stupid accusations made
against him.

Among all Desplein's pupils at the hospital, Horace Bianchon
was one of those to whom he was most strongly attached. Before
becoming a resident student at the Hôtel Dieu, Horace Bianchon
was a medical student, living in the Quartier Latin in a wretched
lodging-house, known by the name of the Maison Vauquer. There
the poor young fellow experienced the pressure of that acute poverty,
which is a kind of crucible, whence men of great talent are expected
to come forth pure and incorruptible, like a diamond that can be
subjected to blows of all kinds without breaking. Though the
fierce fire of passion has been aroused, they acquire a probity that
it cannot alter, and they become used to struggles that are the lot
of genius, in the midst of the ceaseless toil, in which they curb
desires that are not to be satisfied. Horace was an upright young
man, incapable of taking any crooked course in matters where
honour was involved ; going straight to the point ; ready to pawn
his overcoat for his friends, as he was to give them his time and his
long vigils. In a word, Horace was one of those friends who do not
trouble themselves as to what they are to receive in return for what
they bestow, taking it for granted that, when it comes to their

turn, they will get more than they give. Most of his friends had
for him that heart-felt respect which is inspired by unostentatious
worth, and many of them would have been afraid to provoke his
censure. But Horace manifested these good qualities without any
pedantic display. Neither a puritan nor a preacher, he would in
his simplicity enforce a word of good advice with any oath, and was
ready for a bit of good cheer when the occasion offered. A pleasant
comrade, with no more shyness than a trooper, frank and outspoken—not as a sailor, for the sailor of to-day is a wily diplomatist—but as a fine young fellow, who has nothing in his life to
be ashamed of, he went his way with head erect and with a cheerful
mind. To sum it all up in one word, Horace was the Pylades
of more than one Orestes, creditors nowadays playing most real-
istically the part of the Furies. He bore his poverty with that
gaiety which is perhaps one of the chief elements of courage, and,
like all those who have nothing, he contracted very few debts. As
enduring as a camel, as alert as a wild deer, he was steadfast in his
ideas and in his conduct.

The happiness of Bianchon's life began on the day when the
famous surgeon became acquainted with the good qualities and the
defects, which, each as well as the other, make Dr. Horace Bianchon
doubly dear to his friends. When the teacher of a hospital class
receives a young man into his inner circle, that young man has,
as the saying goes, his foot in the stirrup. Desplein did not fail
to take Bianchon with him as his assistant to wealthy houses, where
nearly always a gratuity slipped into the purse of the student, and
where, all unconsciously, the young provincial had revealed to him
some of the mysteries of Parisian life. Desplein would have him
in his study during consultations, and found work for him there.
Sometimes he would send him to a watering-place as companion
to a rich invalid,—in a word, he was preparing a professional
connection for him.   The result of all this was that after a certain
time the tyrant of the operating theatre had his right-hand man.
These two—one of them at the summit of professional honours
and science, and in the enjoyment of an immense fortune and an
equal renown, the other a modest cipher without fortune or fame—
became intimate friends. The great Desplein told everything to
his pupil. Bianchon came to know the mysteries of this temperament, half lion, half bull, that in the end caused an abnormal
expansion of the great man's chest and killed him by enlargement
of the heart. He studied the odd whims of this busy life, the schemes
of its sordid avarice, the projects of this politician disguised as a
man of science. He was able to forecast the disappointments that
awaited the one touch of sentiment that was buried in a heart not
of stone though made to seem like stone.

One day Bianchon told Desplein that a poor water-carrier in the

Quartier Saint-Jacques was suffering from a horrible illness caused by overwork and poverty. This poor native of Auvergne had only potatoes to eat during the hard winter of 1821. Desplein left all his patients. At the risk of breaking down his horse, he drove at full speed, accompanied by Bianchon, to the poor man's lodging, and himself superintended his removal to a private nursing home established by the celebrated Dubois in the Faubourg Saint-Denis. He went to attend to the man himself, and gave him, when he had recovered, money enough to buy a horse and a water-cart. The Auvergnat distinguished himself by an unconventional proceeding. One of his friends fell sick, and he at once brought him to Desplein, and said to his benefactor :

" I would not think of allowing him to go to any one else."

Overwhelmed with work as he was, Desplein grasped the water-carrier's hand and said to him :

" Bring them all to me."

He had this poor fellow from the Cantal admitted to the Hôtel Dieu, where he took the greatest care of him. Bianchon had on many occasions remarked that his chief had a particular liking for people from Auvergne, and especially for the water-carriers ; but as Desplein took a kind of pride in his treatment of his poor patients at the Hôtel Dieu, his pupil did not see anything very strange in this.

One day when Bianchon was crossing the Place Saint-Sulpice he caught sight of his teacher going into the church about nine o'clock in the morning. Desplein, who at this period would not go a step without calling for his carriage, was on foot, and slipped in quietly by the side door in the Rue du Petit Lion, as if he was going into some doubtful place. The student was naturally seized by a great curiosity, for he knew the opinions of his master ; so Bianchon too slipped into Saint-Sulpice and was not a little surprised to see the famous Desplein, this atheist, who thought very little of angels as beings who give no scope for surgery, this scoffer, humbly kneeling, and where ? . . . in the Lady Chapel, where he heard a mass, gave an alms for the church expenses and for the poor, and remained throughout as serious as if he were engaged in an operation.

Bianchon's astonishment knew no bounds. " If," he said to himself, " I had seen him holding one of the cords of the canopy at a public procession on Corpus Christi I might just laugh at him ; but at this time of day, all alone, without any one to see him, this is certainly something to set one thinking ! "

Bianchon had no wish to appear to be playing the spy on the chief surgeon of the Hôtel Dieu, so he went away. It so happened that Desplein asked him to dine with him that day, not at his house but at a restaurant. Between the cheese and the dessert Bianchon, by cleverly leading up to it, managed to say something about the mass, and spoke of it as a mummery and a farce.

" A farce," said Desplein, " that has cost Christendom more bloodshed than all the battles of Napoleon, all the leeches of Broussais. It is a papal invention, that only dates from the sixth century. What torrents of blood were not shed to establish the feast of Corpus Christi, by which the Court of Rome sought to mark its victory in the question of the real presence, and the schism that has troubled the Church for three centuries ! The wars of the Count of Toulouse and the Albigenses were the sequel of that affair. The Vaudois and the Albigenses refused to recognise the innovation."

In a word Desplein took a pleasure in giving vent to all his atheistic ardour, and there was a torrent of Voltairian witticisms, or, to describe it more accurately, a detestable imitation of the style of the modern anti-clerical journalists.

" Hum ! " said Bianchon to himself, " what has become of my devotee of this morning ? "

He kept silent. He began to doubt if it was really his chief that he had seen at Saint-Sulpice. Desplein would not have taken the trouble to lie to Bianchon. They knew each other too well. They had already exchanged ideas on points quite as serious, and discussed systems of the nature of things, exploring and dissecting them with the knives and scapels of incredulity.

Three months went by. Bianchon took no further step in connection with the incident, though it remained graven in his memory. One day that year one of the doctors of the Hôtel Dieu took Desplein by the arm in Bianchon's presence, as if he had a question to put to him.

" Whatever do you go to Saint-Sulpice for, my dear master ? " he said to him.

" To see one of the priests there, who has caries in the knee, and whom Madame the Duchess of Angoulême did me the honour to recommend to my care," said Desplein.

The doctor was satisfied with this evasion, but not so Bianchon.

" Ah, he goes to see diseased knees in the church ! Why, he went to hear mass ! " said the student to himself.

Bianchon made up his mind to keep a watch on Desplein. He remembered the day, the hour, when he had caught him going into Saint-Sulpice, and he promised himself that he would be there next year on the same day and at the same hour, to see if he would catch him again. In this case the recurring date of his devotions would give ground for a scientific investigation, for one ought not to expect to find in such a man a direct contradiction between thought and action.

Next year, on the day and at the hour, Bianchon, who by this time was no longer one of Desplein's resident students, saw the surgeon's carriage stop at the corner of the Rue de Tournon and the Rue du Petit Lion. His friend got out, passed stealthily along by the wall of Saint-Sulpice, and once more heard his mass at the Lady altar. It was indeed Desplein, the chief surgeon of the hospital, the atheist at heart, the devotee at haphazard. The problem was getting to be a puzzle. The persistence of the illustrious man of science made it all very complicated. When Desplein had gone out Bianchon went up to the sacristan, who came to do his work in the chapel, and asked him if that gentleman was a regular attendant there.

" Well, I have been here twenty years," said the sacristan " and all that time M. Desplein has come four times a year to be present at this mass. He founded it."

" A foundation made by him ! " said Bianchon, as he went away. " Well, it is more wonderful than all the mysteries."

Some time passed by before Dr. Bianchon, although the friend of Desplein, found an opportunity to talk to him of this singular incident in his life. Though they met in consultation or in society, it was difficult to get that moment of confidential chat alone together, when two men sit with their feet on the fender, and their heads resting on the backs of their arm-chairs, and tell each other their secrets. At last, after a lapse of seven years, and after the Revolution of 1830, when the people had stormed the Archbishop's house, when Republican zeal led them to destroy the gilded crosses that shone like rays of light above the immense sea of house-tops, when unbelief side by side with revolt paraded the streets, Bianchon again came upon Desplein as he entered the church of Saint-Sulpice. The doctor followed him in, and took his place beside him, without his friend taking any notice of him, or showing the least surprise. Together they heard the mass he had founded.

" Will you tell me, my dear friend," said Bianchon to Desplein, when they left the church, " the reason for this monkish proceeding of yours ? I have already caught you going to mass three times, you of all men ! You must tell me the meaning of this mystery, and explain to me this flagrant contradiction between your opinions and your conduct. You don't believe in God and you go to mass ! My dear master, you are bound to give me an answer."

" I am like a good many devotees, men deeply religious to all appearance, but quite as much atheists as we can be, you and I."

And then there was a torrent of epigrams referring to certain political personages, the best known of whom presents us in our own time with a new edition of the *Tartuffe* of Molière.

" I am not asking you about all that," said Bianchon. " But I do want to know the reason for what you have just been doing here. Why have you founded this mass ? "

" My word ! my dear friend," said Desplein, " I am on the brink

of the grave, and I may just as well talk to you about the early days
of my life."

Just then Bianchon and the great man were in the Rue des
Quatre Vents, one of the most horrible streets in Paris. Desplein
pointed to the sixth storey of one of those high, narrow-fronted
houses that stand like obelisks. The outer door opens on a passage,
at the end of which is a crooked stair, lighted by small inner windows.
It was a house with a greenish-coloured front, with a furniture
dealer installed on the ground floor, and apparently a different type
of wretchedness lodging in every storey. As he raised his arm with a
gesture that was full of energy, Desplein said to Bianchon :

" I lived up there for two years ! "

" I know that. D'Arthez used to live there. I came there nearly
every day when I was quite a young fellow, and in those days we
used to call it ' the store bottle of great men ! ' Well, what comes
next ? "

" The mass that I have just heard is connected with events that
occurred when I was living in that garret in which you tell me
D'Arthez once lived, the room from the window of which there is a
line hanging with clothes drying on it, just above the flower-pot.
I had such a rough start in life, my dear Bianchon, that I could
dispute with any one you like the palm for suffering endured here in
Paris. I bore it all, hunger, thirst, want of money, lack of clothes,
boots, linen—all that is hardest in poverty. I have tried to warm
my frozen fingers with my breath in that ' store bottle of great men,'
which I should like to revisit with you. As I worked in the winter
a vapour would rise from my head and I could see the steam of
perspiration as we see it about the horses on a frosty day. I don't
know where one finds the foothold to stand up against such a life.
I was all alone, without help, without a penny to buy books or to
pay the expenses of my medical education : without a friend, for
my irritable, gloomy, nervous character did me harm.

" No one would recognise in my fits of irritation the distress, the
struggles of a man who is striving to rise to the surface from his place
in the very depths of the social system. But I can say to you, in
whose presence I have no need to cloak myself in any way, that
I had that basis of sound ideas and impressionable feelings, which
will always be part of the endowment of men strong enough to climb
up to some summit, after having long plodded through the morass
of misery. I could not look for any help from my family or my native
place beyond the insufficient allowance that was made to me. To
sum it all up, at that time my breakfast in the morning was a roll
that a baker in the Rue du Petit Lion sold cheaply to me because it
was from the baking of yesterday or the day before, and which
I broke up into some milk ; thus my morning meal did not cost me
more than a penny. I dined only every second day, in a boarding-.

house where one could get a dinner for eightpence. Thus I spent only fourpence-halfpenny a day.

" You know as well as I do what care I would take of such things as clothes and boots ! I am not sure that in later life we feel more trouble at the treachery of a colleague than we have felt, you and I, at discovering the mocking grimace of a boot-sole that is coming away from the sewing, or at hearing the rending noise of a torn coat-cuff. I drank only water. I looked at the cafés with the greatest respect. The Café Zoppi seemed to mè like a promised land, where the Luculluses of the Quartier Latin had the exclusive right of entry. ' Shall I ever,' I used sometimes to ask myself, ' shall I ever be able to go in there to take a cup of coffee and hot milk, or to play a game of dominoes ? '

" Well, I brought to my work the furious energy that my poverty inspired. I tried rapidly to get a grasp of exact knowledge so as to acquire an immense personal worth in order to deserve the position I hoped to reach in the days when I would have come forth from my nothingness. I consumed more oil than bread. The lamp that lighted me during these nights of persistent toil cost me more than my food. The struggle was long, obstinate, without encouragement. I had won no sympathy from those around me. To have friends must one not associate with other young fellows, and have a few pence to take a drink with them, and go with them wherever students are to be found ? I had nothing. And no one in Paris quite realises that *nothing* is really *nothing*. If I ever had any occasion to reveal my misery I felt in my throat that nervous contraction that makes our patients sometimes imagine there is a round mass coming up the gullet into the larynx. Later on I have come across people who, having been born in wealth and never wanted for anything, knew nothing of that problem of the Rule of Three : A young man is to a crime as a five franc piece is to the unknown quantity X. These gilded fools would say to me :

" ' But why do you get into debt ? Why ever do you contract serious obligations ? '

" They remind me of that princess who, on hearing that the people were in want of bread, said : ' Why don't they buy sponge cakes ? ' I should like very much to see one of those rich men, who complains that I ask him for too high a fee when there has to be an operation—yes, I should like to see him all alone in Paris, without a penny, without luggage, without a friend, without credit, and forced to work his five fingers to the bone to get a living. What would he do ? Where would he go to satisfy his hunger ? Bianchon, if you have sometimes seen me bitter and hard, it was because I was then thinking at once of my early troubles and of the heartlessness, the selfishness of which I have seen a thousand instances in the highest circles ; or else I was thinking of the obstacles that hatred, envy, jealousy, calumny have raised up between me and success. In Paris, when certain people see you ready to put your foot in the stirrup, some of them pull at the skirt of your coat, others loosen the saddle-girth ; this one knocks a shoe off your horse, that one steals your whip ; the least treacherous of the lot is the one you see coming to fire a pistol at you point blank.

" You have talent enough, my dear fellow, to know soon enough the horrible, the unceasing warfare that mediocrity carries on against the man that is its superior. If one evening you lose twenty-five *louis*, next morning you will be accused of being a gambler, and your best friends will say that you lost twenty-five thousand francs last night. If you have a headache, you will be set down as a lunatic. If you are not lively, you will be set down as unsociable. If to oppose this battalion of pygmies you call up your own superior powers, your best friends will cry out that you wish to devour everything, that you claim to lord it and play the tyrant. In a word, your good qualities will be turned into defects, your defects will be turned into vices, and your virtues will be crimes. If you have saved some one, it will be said that you have killed him. If your patient reappears, it will be agreed that you have made sure of the present at the expense of his future ; though he is not dead, he will die. If you stumble, it will be a fall ! Invent anything whatever, and assert your rights, and you will be a difficult man to deal with, a sharp fellow, who does not like to see young men succeed. So, my dear friend, if I do not believe in God, I believe even less in man. Do you not recognise in me a Desplein that is quite different from the Desplein about whom every one speaks ill ? But we need not dig into that heap of mud.

" Well, I was living in that house, I had to work to be ready to pass my first examination, and I had not a farthing. You know what it is ! I had come to one of those crises of utter extremity when one says to oneself : ' I will enlist ! ' I had one hope. I was expecting from my native place a trunk full of linen, a present from some old aunts, who, knowing nothing of Paris, think about providing one with dress shirts, because they imagine that with thirty francs a month their nephew dines on ortolans. The trunk arrived while I was away at the Medical School. It had cost forty francs, carriage to be paid. The concierge of the house, a German cobbler, who lived in a loft, had paid the money and held the trunk. I took a walk in the Rue des Fosse-Saint-Germain-des-Prés and in the Rue de l'École de Médicine without being able to invent a stratagem which would put the trunk in my possession, without my being obliged to pay down the forty francs, which of course I meant to pay after selling the linen. My stupidity seemed a very fair sign to me that I was fit for no vocation but surgery. My dear friend, delicately organised natures, whose powers are exercised in some higher sphere, are wanting in that spirit of intrigue which is fertile in resources and shifts. Genius such as theirs depends on chance. They do not seek out things, they come upon them.

" At last, after dark, I went back to the house, just at the moment when my next-room neighbour was coming in, a water-carrier named Bourgeat, a man from Saint-Flour in Auvergne. We knew each other in the way in which two lodgers come to know each other, when both have their rooms on the same landing, and they can hear each other going to bed, coughing, getting up, and end by becoming quite used to each other. My neighbour informed me that the landlord, to whom I owed three months' rent, had sent me notice to quit. I must clear out next day. He himself was to be evicted on account of his business. I passed the most sorrowful night of my life.

" Where was I to find a porter to remove my poor belongings, my books ? How was I to pay the porter and the concierge ? Where could I go ? With tears in my eyes I repeated these insoluble questions, as lunatics repeat their catchwords. I fell asleep. For the wretched there is a divine sleep full of beautiful dreams. Next morning, while I was eating my porringer full of bread crumbled into milk, Bourgeat came in, and said to me in bad French :

" ' Mister Student, I'm a poor man, a foundling of the hospice of Saint-Flour, without father or mother, and not rich enough to marry. You are not much better off for relations, or better provided with what counts ? Now, see here, I have down below a hand-cart that I have hired at a penny an hour. All our things can be packed on it. If you agree, we will look for a place where we can lodge together, since we are turned out of this. And after all, it's not the earthly paradise.'

" ' I know it well, my good Bourgeat,' said I to him, ' but I am in a great difficulty. There's a trunk for me downstairs that contains linen worth a hundred crowns, with which I could pay the landlord and what I owe to the concierge, and I have not got as much as a hundred sous.'

" ' Bah ! I have found some bits of coin,' Bourgeat answered me joyfully, showing me an old purse of greasy leather. ' Keep your linen.'

" Bourgeat paid my three months, and his own rent, and settled with the concierge. Then he put our furniture and my box of linen on his hand-cart and drew it through the streets, stopping at every house that showed a ' Lodgings to Let ' card. As for me I would go upstairs to see if the place to let would suit us. At noon we were still wandering about the Quartier Latin without having found anything. The rent was the great obstacle. Bourgeat proposed to me to have lunch at a wine-shop, at the door of which we left the hand-cart. Towards evening, in the Cour de Rohan off the Passage du Commerce, I found, under the roof at the top of a house, two rooms, one on each side of the staircase. We got them for a rent of sixty francs a year each. So there we were housed, myself and my humble friend.

" We dined together. Bourgeat, who earned some fifty sous a day, had saved about a hundred crowns. . . . He would soon be in a position to realise his ambition and buy a water-cart and a horse. When he found out how I was situated—and he wormed out my secrets with a depth of cunning and at the same time with a kindly good nature that still moves my heart to-day when I think of it—he renounced for some time to come the ambition of his life. Bourgeat had been a street seller for twenty-two years. He sacrificed his hundred crowns for my future."

At this point Desplein took a firm grip of Bianchon's arm.

" He gave me the money required for my examinations ! This man understood, my friend, that I had a mission, that the needs of my intelligence came before his. He busied himself with me, he called me his ' little one,' he lent me the money I wanted to buy books ; he came in sometimes quite quietly to watch me at my work ; finally he took quite a motherly care to see that I substituted a wholesome and abundant diet for the bad and insufficient fare to which I had been condemned. Bourgeat, a man of about forty, had the features of a burgess of the middle ages, a full rounded forehead, a head that a painter might have posed as the model for a Lycurgus. The poor man felt his heart big with affection seeking for some object. He had never been loved by anything but a poodle, that had died a short time before, and about which he was always talking to me, asking if by any possibility the Church would consent to have prayers for its soul. His dog, he said, had been really like a Christian, and for twelve years it had gone to church with him, without ever barking, listening to the organ without so much as opening its mouth, and remaining crouched beside him with a look that made one think it was praying with him.

" This man transferred all his affection to me. He took me up as a lonely, suffering creature. He became for me like a most watchful mother, the most delicately thoughtful of benefactors, in a word the ideal of that virtue that rejoices in its own good work. When I met him in the street he gave me an intelligent look, full of a nobility that you cannot imagine ; he would then assume a gait like that of a man who was carrying no burden ; he seemed delighted at seeing me in good health and well dressed. It was such devoted affection as one finds among the common people, the love of the little shop-girl raised to a higher level. Bourgeat ran my errands. He woke me up in the night at the appointed hour. He trimmed my lamp, scrubbed our landing. He was a good servant as well as a good father to me, and as cleanly in his work as an English maid. He looked after our housekeeping. Like Philopoemen he sawed up our firewood, and he set about all his actions with a simplicity in performing them that at the same time preserved his dignity, for he seemed to realise that the end in view ennobled it all.

" When I left this fine fellow to enter the Hôtel Dieu as a resident student, he felt a kind of sorrowful gloom come over him at the thought that he could no longer live with me. But he consoled himself by looking forward to getting together the money that would be necessary for the expenses of my final examination, and he made me promise to come to see him on all my holidays. Bourgeat was proud of me. He loved me for my own sake and for his own. If you look up my essay for the doctorate you will see that it was dedicated to him. In the last year of my indoor course I had made enough money to be able to repay all I owed to this worthy Auvergnat, by buying him a horse and a water-cart. He was exceedingly angry at finding that I was thus depriving myself of my money, and nevertheless he was delighted at seeing his desires realised. He laughed and he scolded me. He looked at his water-barrel and his horse, and he wiped away a tear as he said to me :

" ' It's a pity ! Oh, what a fine water-cart ! You have done wrong ! . . . The horse is as strong as if he came from Auvergne ! '

" He absolutely insisted on buying for me that pocket-case of instruments mounted with silver that you have seen in my study, and which is for me the most valued of my possessions. Although he was enraptured with my first successes he never let slip a word or a gesture that could be taken to mean, ' It is to me that this man's success is due ! ' And nevertheless, but for him, I should have been killed by my misery. The poor man broke himself down for my sake. He had eaten nothing but bread seasoned with garlic, in order that I might have coffee while I sat up at my work. He fell sick. You may imagine how I passed whole nights at his bedside. I pulled him through it the first time, but two years after there was a relapse, and notwithstanding the most assiduous care, notwithstanding the greatest efforts of science, he had to succumb. No king was ever cared for as he was. Yes, Bianchon, to snatch this life from death I tried unheard-of things. I wanted to make him live long enough to allow him to see the results of his work, to realise all his wishes, to satisfy the one gratitude that had filled my heart, to extinguish a fire that burns in me even now !

" Bourgeat," continued Desplein, after a pause, with evident emotion, " Bourgeat, my second father, died in my arms, leaving me all he possessed by a will which he had made at a public notary's, and which bore the date of the year when we went to lodge in the Cour de Rohan. He had the faith of a simple workman. He loved

the Blessed Virgin as he would have loved his mother. Zealous
Catholic as he was, he had never said a word to me about my own
lack of religion. When he was in danger of death he begged me
to spare nothing to obtain the help of the Church for him. I had
mass said for him every day. Often in the night he expressed to
me his fears for his future ; he was afraid that he had not lived a
holy enough life. Poor man ! he used to work from morning to
night. Who is heaven for, then, if there is a heaven ? He received
the last sacraments like the saint that he was, and his death was
worthy of his life.

" I was the only one who followed his funeral. When I had laid
my one benefactor in the earth, I tried to find out how I could
discharge my debt of gratitude to him. I knew that he had neither
family nor friends, neither wife nor children. But he believed !
He had religious convictions, and had I any right to dispute them ?
He had spoken to me timidly of masses said for the repose of the
dead ; he did not seek to impose this duty on me, thinking that
it would be like asking to be paid for his services to me. As soon
as I could arrange for the endowment, I gave the Saint-Sulpice
the sum necessary to have four masses said there each year. As
the only thing that I could offer to Bourgeat was the fulfilment
of his pious wishes, I go there in his name on the day the mass is
said at the beginning of each quarter of the year, and say the
prayers for him that he wished for. I say them in the good faith
of one who doubts : ' My God, if there is a sphere where after
their death you place those who have been perfect, think of good
Bourgeat ; and if he has still anything to suffer, lay these sufferings
on me, so that he may enter the sooner into what they call Paradise ! " This, my dear friend, is all that a man who holds my
opinions can allow himself. God must be good-hearted, and He
will not take it ill on my part. But I swear to you, I would give
my fortune for the sake of finding the faith of Bourgeat coming
into my brain."

Bianchon, who attended Desplein in his last illness, does not
venture to affirm, even now, that the famous surgeon died an
atheist. Will not those who believe take pleasure in the thought
that perhaps the poor Auvergnat came to open for him the gate
of Heaven, as he had already opened for him the portals of that
temple on earth, on the façade of which one reads : *To great men
from their grateful motherland* ?

THE CHRIST IN FLANDERS

HONORÉ DE BALZAC

AT a dimly remote period in the history of Brabant, communication between the Island of Cadzand and the Flemish coast was kept up by a boat which carried passengers from one shore to the other. Middelburg, the chief town in the island, destined to become so famous in the annals of Protestantism, at that time only numbered some two or three hundred hearths ; and the prosperous town of Ostend was an obscure haven, a straggling village where pirates dwelt in security among the fishermen and the few poor merchants who lived in the place.

But though the town of Ostend consisted altogether of some score of houses and three hundred cottages, huts, or hovels built of the driftwood of wrecked vessels, it nevertheless rejoiced in the possession of a governor, a garrison, a forked gibbet, a convent, and a burgomaster, in short, in all the institutions of an advanced civilisation.

Who reigned over Brabant and Flanders in those days ? On this point tradition is mute. Let us confess at once that this tale savours strongly of the marvellous, the mysterious, and the vague ; elements which Flemish narrators have infused into a story retailed so often to gatherings of workers on winter evenings, that the versions vary widely in poetic merit and incongruity of detail. It has been told by every generation, handed down by grandames at the fireside, narrated night and day, and the chronicle has changed its complexion somewhat in every age. Like some great building that has suffered many modifications of successive generations of architects, some sombre weather-beaten pile, the delight of a poet, the story would drive the commentator and the industrious winnower of words, facts, and dates to despair. The narrator believes in it, as all superstitious minds in Flanders likewise believe ; and is not a whit wiser nor more credulous than his audience. But as it would be impossible to make a harmony of all the different renderings, here are the outlines of the story ; stripped, it may be, of its picturesque quaintness, but with all its bold disregard of historical truth, and its moral teaching approved by religion—a myth, the blossom of imaginative fancy ; an allegory that the wise may interpret to suit themselves. To each his own pasturage, and the task of separating the tares from the wheat.

The boat that served to carry passengers from the Island of
Cadzand to Ostend was upon the point of departure ; but before
the skipper loosed the chain that secured the shallop to the little
jetty where people embarked, he blew a horn several times to warn
late lingerers, this being his last journey that day. Night was
falling. It was scarcely possible to see the coast of Flanders by
the dying fires of the sunset, or to make out upon the hither shore
any forms of belated passengers hurrying along the wall of the
dykes that surrounded the open country, or among the tall reeds
of the marshes. The boat was full.

"What are you waiting for ? Let us put off ! " they cried.

Just at that moment a man appeared a few paces from the jetty,
to the surprise of the skipper, who had heard no sound of footsteps.
The traveller seemed to have sprung up from the earth, like a
peasant who had laid himself down on the ground to wait till the
boat should start, and had slept till the sound of the horn awakened
him. Was he a thief ? or some one belonging to the custom-
house or the police ?

As soon as the man appeared on the jetty to which the boat was
moored, seven persons who were standing in the stern of the
shallop hastened to sit down on the benches, so as to leave no
room for the new-comer. It was the swift and instinctive working
of the aristocratic spirit, an impulse of exclusiveness that comes
from the rich man's heart. Four of the seven personages belonged
to the most aristocratic families in Flanders. First among them
was a young knight with two beautiful greyhounds ; his long hair
flowed from beneath a jewelled cap ; he clanked his gilded spurs,
curled the ends of his moustache from time to time with a swag-
gering grace, and looked round disdainfully on the rest of the crew.

A high-born damsel, with a falcon on her wrist, only spoke with
her mother or with a churchman of high rank, who was evidently
a relation. All these persons made a great deal of noise, and talked
among themselves as though there were no one else in the boat ;
yet close beside them sat a man of great importance in the district,
a stout burgher of Bruges, wrapped about with a vast cloak. His
servant, armed to the teeth, had set down a couple of bags filled
with gold at his side. Next to the burgher came a man of learning,
a doctor of the University of Louvain, who was travelling with his
clerk. This little group of folk, who looked contemptuously at
each other, was separated from the passengers in the forward part
of the boat by the bench of rowers.

The belated traveller glanced about him as he stepped on board,
saw that there was no room for him in the stern, and went to the
bows in quest of a seat. They were all poor people there. At first
sight of the bareheaded man in the brown camlet coat and trunk-hose
and plain stiff linen collar, they noticed that he wore no ornaments,

carried no cap nor bonnet in his hand, and had neither sword nor purse at his girdle, and one and all took him for a burgomaster sure of his authority, a worthy and kindly burgomaster like so many a Fleming of old times, whose homely features and characters have been immortalised by Flemish painters. The poorer passengers, therefore, received him with demonstrations of respect that provoked scornful tittering at the other end of the boat. An old soldier, inured to toil and hardship, gave up his place on the bench to the new-comer, and seated himself on the edge of the vessel, keeping his balance by planting his feet against one of those transverse beams, like the backbone of a fish, that hold the planks of a boat together. A young mother, who bore her baby in her arms, and seemed to belong to the working-class in Ostend, moved aside to make room for the stranger.

There was neither servility nor scorn in her manner of doing this ; it was a simple sign of the goodwill by which the poor, who know by long experience the value of a service and the warmth that fellowship brings, give expression to the openheartedness and the natural impulses of their souls ; so artlessly do they reveal their good qualities and their defects. The stranger thanked her by a gesture full of gracious dignity, and took his place between the young mother and the old soldier. Immediately behind him sat a peasant and his son, a boy ten years of age. A beggar woman, old, wrinkled, and clad in rags, was crouching, with her almost empty wallet, on a great coil of rope that lay in the prow. One of the rowers, an old sailor, who had known her in the days of her beauty and prosperity, had let her come in " for the love of God," in the beautiful phrase that the common people use.

" Thank you kindly, Thomas," the old woman had said. " I will say two *Paters* and two *Aves* for you in my prayers to-night."

The skipper blew his horn for the last time, looked along the silent shore, flung off the chain, ran along the side of the boat, and took up his position at the helm. He looked at the sky, and as soon as they were out in the open sea he shouted to the men : " Pull away, pull with all your might ! The sea is smiling at a squall, the witch ! I can feel the swell by the way the rudder works, and the storm in my wounds."

The nautical phrases, unintelligible to ears unused to the sound of the sea, seemed to put fresh energy into the oars ; they kept time together, the rhythm of the movement was still even and steady, but quite unlike the previous manner of rowing ; it was as if a cantering horse had broken into a gallop. The gay company seated in the stern amused themselves by watching the brawny arms, the tanned faces, and sparkling eyes of the rowers, the play of the tense muscles, the physical and mental forces that were being exerted to bring them for a trifling toll across the channel. So far from pitying the rowers'

distress, they pointed out the men's faces to each other, and laughed
at the grotesque expressions on the faces of the crew who were
straining every muscle ; but in the fore part of the boat the soldier,
the peasant, and the old beggar woman watched the sailors with the
sympathy naturally felt by toilers who live by the sweat of their
brow and know the rough struggle, the strenuous excitement of
effort. These folk, moreover, whose lives were spent in the open air,
had all seen the warnings of danger in the sky, and their faces were
grave. The young mother rocked her child, singing an old hymn of
the Church for a lullaby.

" If we ever get there at all," the soldier remarked to the peasant,
" it will be because the Almighty is bent on keeping us alive."

" Ah ! He is the Master," said the old woman, " but I think it
will be His good pleasure to take us to Himself. Just look at that
light down there . . ." and she nodded her head as she spoke
towards the sunset.

Streaks of fiery red glared from behind the masses of crimson-
flushed brown cloud that seemed about to unloose a furious gale.
There was a smothered murmur of the sea, a moaning sound that
seemed to come from the depths, a low warning growl, such as a dog
gives when he only means mischief as yet. After all, Ostend was
not far away. Perhaps painting, like poetry, could not prolong the
existence of the picture presented by sea and sky at that moment
beyond the time of its actual duration. Art demands vehement
contrasts, wherefore artists usually seek out Nature's most striking
effects, doubtless because they despair of rendering the great and
glorious charm of her daily moods ; yet the human soul is often
stirred as deeply by her calm as by her emotion, and by silence as
by storm.

For a moment no one spoke on board the boat. Every one
watched that sea and sky, either with some presentiment of danger,
or because they felt the influence of the religious melancholy that
takes possession of nearly all of us at the close of the day, the hour of
prayer, when all nature is hushed save for the voices of the bells.
The sea gleamed pale and wan, but its hues changed, and the surface
took all the colours of steel. The sky was almost overspread with
livid grey, but down in the west there were long narrow bars like
streaks of blood ; while lines of bright light in the eastern sky,
sharp and clean as if drawn by the tip of a brush, were separated by
folds of cloud, like the wrinkles on an old man's brow. The whole
scene made a background of ashen greys and half-tints, in strong
contrast to the bale-fires of the sunset. If written language might
borrow of spoken language some of the bold figures of speech
invented by the people, it might be said with the soldier that " the
weather had been routed," or, as the peasant would say, " the sky
glowered like an executioner." Suddenly a wind arose from the

quarter of the sunset, and the skipper, who never took his eyes off the sea, saw the swell on the horizon line, and cried :

" Stop rowing ! "

The sailors stopped immediately, and let their oars lie on the water.

" The skipper is right," said Thomas coolly. A great wave caught up the boat, carried it high on its crest, only to plunge it, as it were, into the trough of the sea that seemed to yawn for them. At this mighty upheaval, this sudden outbreak of the wrath of the sea, the company in the stern turned pale, and sent up a terrible cry.

" We are lost ! "

" Oh, not yet ! " said the skipper calmly.

As he spoke, the clouds immediately above their heads were torn asunder by the vehemence of the wind. The grey mass was rent and scattered east and west with ominous speed, a dim uncertain light from the rift in the sky fell full upon the boat, and the travellers beheld each other's faces. All of them, the noble and the wealthy, the sailors and the poor passengers alike, were amazed for a moment by the appearance of the last comer. His golden hair, parted upon his calm serene forehead, fell in thick curls about his shoulders ; and his face, sublime in its sweetness and radiant with divine love, stood out against the surrounding gloom. He had no contempt for death ; he knew that he should not die. But if at the first the company in the stern forgot for a moment the implacable fury of the storm that threatened their lives, selfishness and their habits of life soon prevailed again.

" How lucky that stupid burgomaster is, not to see the risks we are all running ! He is just like a dog, he will die without a struggle," said the doctor.

He had scarcely pronounced this highly judicious dictum when the storm unloosed all its forces. The wind blew from every quarter of the heavens, the boat span round like a top, and the sea broke in.

" Oh ! my poor child ! My poor child ! . . . Who will save my baby ? " the mother cried in a heartrending voice.

" You yourself will save it," the stranger said.

The thrilling tones of that voice went to the young mother's heart and brought hope with them ; she heard the gracious words through all the whistling of the wind and the shrieks of the passengers.

" Holy Virgin of Good Help, who art at Antwerp, I promise thee a thousand pounds of wax and a statue, if thou wilt rescue me from this ! " cried the burgher, kneeling upon his bags of gold.

" The Virgin is no more at Antwerp than she is here," was the doctor's comment on this appeal.

" She is in heaven," said a voice that seemed to come from the sea.

" Who said that ? "

" 'Tis the devil ! " exclaimed the servant. " He is scoffing at the Virgin of Antwerp."

" Let us have no more of your Holy Virgin at present," the skipper cried to the passengers. " Put your hands to the scoops and bale the water out of the boat. And the rest of you," he went on, addressing the sailors, " pull with all your might ! Now is the time ; in the name of the devil who is leaving you in this world, be your own Providence ! Every one knows that the channel is fearfully dangerous ; I have been to and fro across it these thirty years. Am I facing a storm for the first time to-night ? "

He stood at the helm, and looked, as before, at his boat and at the sea and sky in turn.

" The skipper always laughs at everything," muttered Thomas.

" Will God leave us to perish along with those wretched creatures ? " asked the haughty damsel of the handsome cavalier.

" No, no, noble maiden. . . . Listen ! " and he caught her by the waist and said in her ear, " I can swim ; say nothing about it ! I will hold you by your fair hair and bring you safely to the shore ; but I can only save you."

The girl looked at her aged mother. The lady was on her knees entreating absolution of the Bishop, who did not heed her. In the beautiful eyes the knight read a vague feeling of filial piety, and spoke in a smothered voice.

" Submit yourself to the will of God. If it is His pleasure to take your mother to Himself, it will doubtless be for her happiness—in the other world," he added, and his voice dropped still lower. " And for ours in this," he thought within himself.

The Dame of Rupelmonde was lady of seven fiefs beside the barony of Gâvres.

The girl felt the longing for life in her heart, and for love that spoke through the handsome adventurer, a young miscreant who haunted churches in search of a prize, an heiress to marry, or ready money. The Bishop bestowed his benison on the waves, and bade them be calm ; it was all that he could do. He thought of his mistress, and of the delicate feast with which she would welcome him ; perhaps at that very moment she was bathing, perfuming herself, robing herself in velvet, fastening her necklace and her jewelled clasps, and the perverse Bishop so far from thinking of the power of Holy Church, of his duty to comfort Christians and exhort them to trust in God, that worldly regrets and lover's sighs mingled with the holy words of the breviary. By the dim light that shone on the pale faces of the company, it was possible to see their differing expressions as the boat was lifted high in air by a wave, to be cast back into the dark depths ; the shallop quivered like a fragile leaf, the plaything of the north wind in the autumn ; the hull creaked, it seemed ready to go to pieces. Fearful shrieks went up, followed by an awful silence

There was a strange difference between the behaviour of the folk
in the bows and that of the rich or great people at the other end of
the boat. The young mother clasped her infant tightly to her breast
every time that a great wave threatened to engulf the fragile vessel ;
but she clung to the hope that the stranger's words had set in her
heart. Each time that her eyes turned to his face she drew fresh
faith at the sight, the strong faith of a helpless woman, a mother's
faith. She lived by that divine promise, the loving words from his
lips ; the simple creature waited trustingly for them to be fulfilled,
and scarcely feared the danger any longer.

The soldier, holding fast to the vessel's side, never took his eyes
off the strange visitor. He copied on his own rough and swarthy
features the imperturbability of the other's face, applying to this
task the whole strength of a will and intelligence but little corrupted
in the course of a life of mechanical and passive obedience. So
emulous was he of a calm and tranquil courage greater than his own,
that at last, perhaps unconsciously, something of that mysterious
nature passed into his own soul. His admiration became an instinctive zeal for this man, a boundless love for and belief in him,
such a love as soldiers feel for their leader when he has the power of
swaying other men, when the halo of victories surrounds him, and
the magical fascination of genius is felt in all that he does. The poor
outcast was murmuring to herself :

" Ah ! miserable wretch that I am ! Have I not suffered enough
to expiate the sins of my youth ? Ah ! wretched woman, why did
you lead the gay life of a frivolous Frenchwoman ? Why did you
devour the goods of God with churchmen, the substance of the poor
with extortioners and fleecers of the poor ? Oh ! I have sinned
indeed !—Oh my God ! my God ! let me finish my time in hell here
in this world of misery."

And again she cried, " Holy Virgin, Mother of God, have pity
upon me ! "

" Be comforted, mother. God is not a Lombard usurer. I may
have killed people good and bad at random in my time, but I am not
afraid of the resurrection."

" Ah ! master lancepesade, how happy those fair ladies are, to be
so near to a bishop, a holy man ! They will get absolution for their
sins," said the old woman. " Oh ! if I could only hear a priest say
to me, ' Thy sins are forgiven ! ' I should believe it then."

The stranger turned towards her, and the goodness in his face
made her tremble.

" Have faith," he said, " and you will be saved."

" May God reward you, good sir," she answered. " If what you
say is true, I will go on pilgrimage barefooted to Our Lady of
Loretto to pray to her for you and for me."

The two peasants, father and son, were silent, patient, and submissive to the will of God, like folk whose wont it is to fall in instinctively with the ways of Nature like cattle. At the one end of the boat stood riches, pride, learning, debauchery, and crime—human society, such as art and thought and education and worldly interests and laws have made it ; and at this end there were terror and wailing, innumerable different impulses all repressed by hideous doubts—at this end, and at this only, the agony of fear.

Above all these human lives stood a strong man, the skipper ; no doubts assailed him, the chief, the king, the fatalist among them. He was trusting in himself rather than in Providence, crying, " Bale away ! " instead of " Holy Virgin ! " defying the storm, in fact, and struggling with the sea like a wrestler.

But the helpless poor at the other end of the wherry ! The mother rocking on her bosom the little one who smiled at the storm, the woman once so frivolous and gay, and now tormented with bitter remorse ; the old soldier covered with scars, a mutilated life the sole reward of his unflagging loyalty and faithfulness. This veteran could scarcely count on the morsel of bread soaked in tears to keep the life in him, yet he was always ready to laugh, and went his way merrily, happy when he could drown his glory in the depths of a pot of beer, or could tell tales of the wars to the children who admired him, leaving his future with a light heart in the hands of God. Lastly, there were the two peasants, used to hardships and toil, labour incarnate, the labour by which the world lives. These simple folk were indifferent to thought and its treasures, ready to sink them all in a belief ; and their faith was but so much the more vigorous because they had never disputed about it nor analysed it. Such a nature is a virgin soil, conscience has not been tampered with, feeling is deep and strong ; repentance, trouble, love, and work have developed, purified, concentrated, and increased their force of will a hundred times, the will—the one thing in man that resembles what learned doctors call the Soul.

The boat, guided by the well-nigh miraculous skill of the steersman, came almost within sight of Ostend, when, not fifty paces from the shore, she was suddenly struck by a heavy sea and capsized. The stranger with the light about his head spoke to this little world of drowning creatures :

" Those who have faith shall be saved ; let them follow me ! "

He stood upright, and walked with a firm step upon the waves. The young mother at once took her child in her arms, and followed at his side across the sea. The soldier too sprang up, saying in his homely fashion, " Ah ! *nom d'un pipe !* I would follow *you* to the devil " ; and without seeming astonished by it, he walked on the water. The old worn-out sinner, believing in the omnipotence of God, also followed the stranger.

The two peasants said to each other, " If they are walking on the sea, why should we not do as they do ? " and they also arose and hastened after the others. Thomas tried to follow, but his faith tottered ; he sank in the sea more than once, and rose again, but the third time he also walked on the sea. The bold steersman clung like a remora to the wreck of his boat. The miser had had faith, and had risen to go, but he tried to take his gold with him, and it was his gold that dragged him down to the bottom. The learned man had scoffed at the charlatan and at the fools who listened to him ; and when he heard the mysterious stranger propose to the passengers that they should walk on the waves, he began to laugh, and the ocean swallowed him. The girl was dragged down into the depths by her lover. The Bishop and the older lady went to the bottom, heavily laden with sins, it may be, but still more heavily laden with incredulity and confidence in idols, weighted down by devotion, into which alms-deeds and true religion entered but little.

The faithful flock, who walked with a firm step high and dry above the surge, heard all about them the dreadful whistling of the blast ; great billows broke across their path, but an irresistible force cleft a way for them through the sea. These believing ones saw through the spray a dim speck of light flickering in the window of a fisherman's hut on the shore, and each one, as he pushed on bravely towards the light, seemed to hear the voice of his fellow crying, " Courage ! " through all the roaring of the surf ; yet no one had spoken a word—so absorbed was each by his own peril. In this way they reached the shore.

When they were all seated near the fisherman's fire, they looked round in vain for their guide with the light about him. The sea washed up the steersman at the base of the cliff on which the cottage stood ; he was clinging with might and main to the plank as a sailor can cling when death stares him in the face ; the MAN went down and rescued the almost exhausted seaman ; then he said, as he held out a succouring hand above the man's head :

" Good, for this once ; but do not try it again ; the example would be too bad."

He took the skipper on his shoulders, and carried him to the fisherman's door, knocked for admittance for the exhausted man ; then, when the door of the humble refuge opened, the Saviour disappeared.

The Convent of Mercy was built for sailors on this spot, where for long afterwards (so it was said) the footprints of Jesus Christ could be seen in the sand ; but in 1793, at the time of the French invasion, the monks carried away this precious relic, that bore witness to the Saviour's last visit to earth.

There at the convent I found myself shortly after the Revolution of 1830. I was weary of life. If you had asked me the reason of my despair, I should have found it almost impossible to give it, so languid had grown the soul that was melted within me. The west wind had slackened the springs of my intelligence. A cold, grey light poured down from the heavens, and the murky clouds that passed overhead gave a boding look to the land ; all these things, together with the immensity of the sea, said to me, " Die to-day or die to-morrow, still must we not die ? " And then——. I wandered on, musing on the doubtful future, on my blighted hopes. Gnawed by these gloomy thoughts, I turned mechanically into the convent church, with the grey towers that loomed like ghosts through the sea mists. I looked round with no kindling of the imagination at the forest of columns, at the slender arches set aloft upon the leafy capitals, a delicate labyrinth of sculpture. I walked with careless eyes along the side aisles that opened out before me like vast portals, ever turning upon their hinges. It was scarcely possible to see, by the dim light of the autumn day, the sculptured groinings of the roof, the delicate and clean-cut lines of the mouldings of the graceful pointed arches. The organ pipes were mute.

There was no sound save the noise of my own footsteps to awaken the mournful echoes lurking in the dark chapels. I sat down at the base of one of the four pillars that supported the tower, near the choir. Thence I could see the whole of the building. I gazed, and no ideas connected with it arose in my mind. I saw without seeing the mighty maze of pillars, the great rose-windows that hung like a network suspended as by a miracle in air above the vast doorways. I saw the doors at the end of the side aisles, the aerial galleries, the stained-glass windows framed in archways, divided by slender columns, fretted into flower forms and trefoil by fine filigree work of carved stone. A dome of glass at the end of the choir sparkled as if it had been built of precious stones set cunningly. In contrast to the roof with its alternating spaces of whiteness and colour, the two aisles lay to right and left in shadow so deep that the faint grey outlines of their hundred shafts were scarcely visible in the gloom. I gazed at the marvellous arcades, the scroll-work, the garlands, the curving lines, the arabesques interwoven and interlaced, and strangely lighted, until by sheer dint of gazing my perceptions became confused, and I stood upon the border-land between illusion and reality, taken in the snare set for the eyes, and almost light-headed by reason of the multitudinous changes of the shapes about me.

Imperceptibly a mist gathered about the carven stonework, and I only beheld it through a haze of fine golden dust, like the motes that hover in the bars of sunlight slanting through the air of a chamber. Suddenly the stone lacework of the rose-windows gleamed through this vapour that had made all forms so shadowy.

Every moulding, the edges of every carving, the least detail of the sculpture was dipped in silver. The sunlight kindled fires in the stained windows, their rich colours sent out glowing sparks of light. The shafts began to tremble, the capitals were gently shaken. A light shudder as of delight ran through the building, the stones were loosened in their setting, the wall-spaces swayed with graceful caution. Here and there a ponderous pier moved as solemnly as a dowager when she condescends to complete a quadrille at the close of a ball. A few slender and graceful columns, their heads adorned with wreaths of trefoil, began to laugh and dance here and there. Some of the pointed arches dashed at the tall lancet windows, who, like ladies of the Middle Ages, wore the armorial bearings of their houses emblazoned on their golden robes. The dance of the mitred arcades with the slender windows became like a fray at a tourney.

In another moment every stone in the church vibrated, without leaving its place ; for the organ-pipes spoke, and I heard divine music mingling with the songs of angels, an unearthly harmony, accompanied by the deep notes of the bells, that boomed as the giant towers rocked and swayed in their square bases. This strange Sabbath seemed to me the most natural thing in the world ; and I, who had seen Charles X. hurled from his throne, was no longer amazed by anything. Nay, I myself was gently swaying with a see-saw movement that influenced my nerves pleasurably in a manner of which it is impossible to give any idea. Yet in the midst of this heated riot, the cathedral choir felt cold as if it were a winter day, and I became aware of a multitude of women, robed in white, silent and impassive, sitting there. The sweet incense smoke that arose from the censers was grateful to my soul. The tall wax candles flickered. The lectern, gay as a chanter undone by the treachery of wine, was skipping about like a peal of Chinese bells.

Then I knew that the whole cathedral was whirling round so fast that everything appeared to be undisturbed. The colossal Figure on the crucifix above the altar smiled upon me with a mingled malice and benevolence that frightened me ; I turned my eyes away, and marvelled at the bluish vapour that slid across the pillars, lending to them an indescribable charm. Then some graceful women's forms began to stir on the friezes. The cherubs who up-held the heavy columns shook out their wings. I felt myself uplifted by some divine power that steeped me in infinite joy, in a sweet and languid rapture. I would have given my life, I think, to have prolonged these phantasmagoria for a little, but suddenly a shrill voice clamoured in my ears :

" Awake and follow me ! "

A withered woman took my hand in hers ; its icy coldness crept through every nerve. The bones of her face showed plainly through the sallow, almost olive-tinted wrinkles of the skin. The shrunken, ice-cold, old woman wore a black robe, which she trailed in the dust, and at her throat there was something white, which I dared not examine. I could scarcely see her wan and colourless eyes, for they were fixed in a stare upon the heavens. She drew me after her along the aisles, leaving a trace of her presence in the ashes that she shook from her dress. Her bones rattled as she walked, like the bones of a skeleton ; and as we went I heard behind me the tinkling of a little bell, a thin, sharp sound that rang through my head like the notes of a harmonica.

"Suffer ! " she cried, "suffer ! So it must be ! "

We came out of the church ; we went through the dirtiest streets of the town, till we came at last to a dingy dwelling, and she bade me enter in. She dragged me with her, calling to me in a harsh, tuneless voice like a cracked bell :

"Defend me ! defend me ! "

Together we went up a winding staircase. She knocked at a door in the darkness, and a mute, like some familiar of the Inquisition, opened to her. In another moment we stood in a room hung with ancient, ragged tapestry, amid piles of old linen, crumpled muslin, and gilded brass.

"Behold the wealth that shall endure for ever ! " said she.

I shuddered with horror ; for just then, by the light of a tall torch and two altar candles, I saw distinctly that this woman was fresh from the graveyard. She had no hair. I turned to fly. She raised her fleshless arm and encircled me with a band of iron set with spikes, and as she raised it a cry went up all about us, the cry of millions of voices—the shouting of the dead !

"It is my purpose to make thee happy for ever," she said. "Thou art my son."

We were sitting before the hearth, the ashes lay cold upon it ; the old shrunken woman grasped my hand so tightly in hers that I could not choose but stay. I looked fixedly at her, striving to read the story of her life from the things among which she was crouching. Had she indeed any life in her ? It was a mystery. Yet I saw plainly that once she must have been young and beauti-ful ; fair, with all the charm of simplicity, perfect as some Greek statute, with the brow of a vestal.

"Ah ! ah ! " I cried, "now I know thee ! Miserable woman, why hast thou prostituted thyself ? In the age of thy passions, in the time of they prosperity, the grace and purity of thy youth were forgotten. Forgetful of thy heroic devotion, thy pure life, thy abundant faith, thou didst resign thy primitive power and thy spiritual supremacy for fleshly power. Thy linen vestments, thy couch of moss, the cell in the rock, bright with rays of the Light Divine, were forsaken ; thou hast sparkled with diamonds, and shone with the glitter of luxury and pride. Then, grown bold and insolent, seizing and overturning all things in thy course like a courtesan eager for pleasure in her days of splendour, thou hast steeped thyself in blood like some queen stupefied by empery. Dost thou not remember to have been dull and heavy at times, and the sudden marvellous lucidity of other moments ; as when Art emerges from an orgy ?   Oh ! poet, painter, and singer, lover of splendid ceremonies and protector of the arts, was thy friendship for art perchance a caprice, that so thou shouldst sleep beneath magnificent canopies ?

"Was there not a day when, in thy fantastic pride, though chastity and humility were prescribed to thee, thou hadst brought all things beneath thy feet, and set thy foot on the necks of princes ; when earthly dominion, and wealth, and the mind of man bore thy yoke ?   Exulting in the abasement of humanity, joying to witness the uttermost lengths to which man's folly would go, thou hast bidden thy lovers walk on all fours, and required of them their lands and wealth, nay, even their wives if they were worth aught to thee. Thou hast devoured millions of men without a cause ; thou hast flung away lives like sand blown by the wind from West to East. Thou hast come down from the heights of thought to sit among the kings of men. Woman ! instead of comforting men, thou hast tormented and afflicted them ! Knowing that thou couldst ask and have, thou hast demanded—blood ! A little flour surely should have contented thee, accustomed as thou hadst been to live on bread and to mingle water with thy wine. Unlike all others in all things, formerly thou wouldst bid thy lovers fast, and they obeyed. Why should thy fancies have led thee to require things impossible ?   Why, like a courtesan spoiled by her lovers, hast thou doted on follies, and left those undeceived who sought to explain and justify all thy errors ? Then came the days of thy later passions, terrible like the love of a woman of forty years, with a fierce cry thou hast sought to clasp the whole universe in one last embrace—and thy universe recoiled from thee !

"Then old men succeeded to thy young lovers ; decrepitude came to thy feet and made thee hideous. Yet, even then, men with the eagle power of vision said to thee in a glance, ' Thou shalt perish ingloriously, because thou hast fallen away, because thou hast broken the vows of thy maidenhood. The angel with peace written on her forehead, who should have shed light and joy along her path, has been a Messalina, delighting in the circus, in debauchery, and abuse of power. The days of thy virginity cannot return ; henceforward thou shalt be subject to a master. Thy hour has come ; the hand of death is upon thee. Thy heirs believe that thou art rich ; they will kill thee and find nothing. Yet try at least to fling away this raiment no longer in fashion ; be once more as in the days of old !—Nay, thou art dead, and by thy own deed ! '

"Is not this thy story?" so I ended. "Decrepit, toothless, shivering crone, now forgotten, going thy ways without so much as a glance from passers-by ! Why art thou still alive ? What doest thou in that beggar's garb, uncomely and desired of none ? Where are thy riches ?—for what were they spent ? Where are thy treasures ?—what great deeds hast thou done ? "

At this demand, the shrivelled woman raised her bony form, flung off her rags, and grew tall and radiant, smiling as she broke forth from the dark chrysalid sheath. Then like a butterfly, this diaphanous creature emerged, fair and youthful, clothed in white linen, an Indian from creation issuing her palms. Her golden hair rippled over her shoulders, her eyes glowed, a bright mist clung about her, a ring of gold hovered above her head, she shook the flaming blade of a sword towards the spaces of heaven.

"See and believe ! " she cried.

And suddenly I saw, afar off, many thousands of cathedrals like the one that I had just quitted ; but these were covered with pictures and with frescoes, and I heard them echo with entrancing music. Myriads of human creatures flocked to these great buildings, swarming about them like ants on an ant-heap. Some were eager to rescue books from oblivion or to copy manuscripts, others were helping the poor, but nearly all were studying. Up above this countless multitude rose giant statues that they had erected in their midst, and by the gleams of a strange light from some luminary as powerful as the sun, I read the inscriptions on the bases of the statues—Science, History, Literature.

The light died out. Again I faced the young girl. Gradually she slipped into the dreary sheath, into the ragged cere-cloths, and became an aged woman again. Her familiar brought her a little dust, and she stirred it into the ashes of her chafing-dish, for the weather was cold and stormy ; and then he lighted for her, whose palaces had been lit with thousands of wax-tapers, a little cresset, that she might see to read her prayers through the hours of night.

"There is no faith left in the earth ! . . ." she said.

In such a perilous plight did I behold the fairest and the greatest, the truest and most life-giving of all Powers.

"Wake up, sir, the doors are just about to be shut," said a hoarse voice. I turned and beheld the beadle's ugly countenance ; the man was shaking me by the arm, and the cathedral lay wrapped in shadows as a man is wrapped in his cloak.

"Belief," I said to myself, "is Life ! I have just witnessed the funeral of a monarchy, now we must defend the Church."

EL VERDUGO

Honoré de Balzac

MIDNIGHT had just sounded from the belfry tower of the little town of Menda. A young French officer, leaning over the parapet of the long terrace at the farther end of the castle gardens, seemed to be unusually absorbed in deep thought for one who led the reckless life of a soldier ; but it must be admitted that never were the hour, the scene, and the night more favourable to meditation.

The blue dome of the cloudless sky of Spain was overhead ; he was looking out over the coy windings of a lovely valley lit by the uncertain starlight and the soft radiance of the moon. The officer, leaning against an orange tree in blossom, could also see, a hundred feet below him, the town of Menda, which seemed to nestle for shelter from the north wind at the foot of the crags on which the castle itself was built. He turned his head and caught sight of the sea ; the moonlit waves made a broad frame of silver for the landscape.

There were lights in the castle windows. The mirth and movement of a ball, the sounds of the violins, the laughter of the officers and their partners in the dance were borne towards him, and blended with the far-off murmur of the waves. The cool night had a certain bracing effect upon his frame, wearied as he had been by the heat of the day. He seemed to bathe in the air, made fragrant by the strong, sweet scent of flowers and of aromatic trees in the gardens.

The castle of Menda belonged to a Spanish grandee, who was living in it at that time with his family. All through the evening the elder daughter of the house had watched the officer with such a wistful interest that the Spanish lady's compassionate eyes might well have set the young Frenchman dreaming. Clara was beautiful ; and although she had three brothers and a sister, the broad lands of the Marqués de Légañès appeared to be sufficient warrant for Victor Marchand's belief that the young lady would have a splendid dowry. But how could he dare to imagine that the most fanatical believer in blue blood in all Spain would give his daughter to the son of a grocer in Paris ? Moreover, the French were hated. It was because the Marquis had been suspected of an attempt to raise the country in favour of Ferdinand VII. that General G——, who governed the province, had stationed Victor Marchand's battalion in the little town of Menda to overawe the neighbouring districts, which received

the Marqués de Légañès' word as law. A recent despatch from
Marshal Ney had given ground for fear that the English might ere
long effect a landing on the coast, and had indicated the Marquis as
being in correspondence with the Cabinet in London.

In spite, therefore, of the welcome with which the Spaniards had
received Victor Marchand and his soldiers, that officer was always on
his guard. As he went towards the terrace, where he had just
surveyed the town and the districts confided to his charge, he had
been asking himself what construction he ought to put upon the
friendliness which the Marquis had invariably shown him, and how
to reconcile the apparent tranquillity of the country with his
General's uneasiness. But a moment later these thoughts were
driven from his mind by the instinct of caution and very legitimate
curiosity. It had just struck him that there was a very fair number
of lights in the town below. Although it was the Feast of Saint
James, he himself had issued orders that very morning that all
lights must be put out in the town at the hour prescribed by military
regulations. The castle alone had been excepted in this order.
Plainly here and there he saw the gleam of bayonets, where his own
men were at their accustomed posts ; but in the town there was a
solemn silence, and not a sign that the Spaniards had given themselves up to the intoxication of a festival. He tried vainly for a
while to explain this breach of the regulations on the part of the
inhabitants ; the mystery seemed but so much the more obscure
because he had left instructions with some of his officers to do
police duty that night, and make the rounds of the town.

With the impetuosity of youth, he was about to spring through a
gap in the wall preparatory to a rapid scramble down the rocks,
thinking to reach a small guard-house at the nearest entrance into
the town more quickly than by the beaten track, when a faint sound
stopped him. He fancied that he could hear the light footstep of a
woman along the gravelled garden walk. He turned his head and
saw no one ; for one moment his eyes were dazzled by the wonderful
brightness of the sea, the next he saw a sight so ominous that he
stood stock-still with amazement, thinking that his senses must be
deceiving him. The white moonbeams lighted the horizon, so that
he could distinguish the sails of ships still a considerable distance out
at sea. A shudder ran through him ; he tried to persuade himself
that this was some optical delusion brought about by chance effects
of moonlight on the waves ; and even as he made the attempt, a
hoarse voice called to him by name. The officer glanced at the gap
in the wall ; saw a soldier's head slowly emerge from it, and knew
the grenadier whom he had ordered to accompany him to the castle.

" Is that you, Commandant ? "

" Yes. What is it ? " returned the young officer in a low voice.
A kind of presentiment warned him to act cautiously.

" Those beggars down there are creeping about like worms ; and, by your leave, I came as quickly as I could to report my little reconnoitring expedition."

" Go on," answered Victor Marchand.

" I have just been following a man from the castle who came round this way with a lantern in his hand. A lantern is a suspicious matter with a vengeance ! I don't imagine that there was any need for that good Christian to be lighting tapers at this time of night. Says I to myself, ' They mean to gobble us up ! ' and I set myself to dogging his heels ; and that is how I found out that there is a pile of faggots, sir, two or three steps away from here."

Suddenly a dreadful shriek rang through the town below, and cut the man short. A light flashed in the Commandant's face, and the poor grenadier dropped down with a bullet through his head. Ten paces away a bonfire flared up like a conflagration. The sounds of music and laughter ceased all at once in the ballroom ; the silence of death, broken only by groans, succeeded to the rhythmical murmur of the festival. Then the roar of cannon sounded from across the white plain of the sea.

A cold sweat broke out on the young officer's forehead. He had left his sword behind. He knew that his men had been murdered, and that the English were about to land. He knew that if he lived he would be dishonoured ; he saw himself summoned before a court-martial. For a moment his eyes measured the depth of the valley ; the next, just as he was about to spring down, Clara's hand caught his.

" Fly ! " she cried. " My brothers are coming after me to kill you. Down yonder at the foot of the cliff you will find Juanito's Andalusian. Go ! "

She thrust him away. The young man gazed at her in dull bewilderment ; but obeying the instinct of self-preservation, which never deserts even the bravest, he rushed across the park in the direction pointed out to him, springing from rock to rock in places unknown to any save the goats. He heard Clara calling to her brothers to pursue him ; he heard the footsteps of the murderers ; again and again he heard their balls whistling about his ears ; but he reached the foot of the cliff, found the horse, mounted, and fled with lightning speed.

A few hours later the young officer reached General G——'s quarters, and found him at dinner with the staff.

" I put my life in your hands ! " cried the haggard and exhausted Commandant of Menda.

He sank into a seat, and told his horrible story. It was received with an appalling silence.

" It seems to me that you are more to be pitied than to blame," the terrible General said at last. " You are not answerable for the

Spaniard's crimes, and unless the Marshal decides otherwise, I acquit you."

These words brought but cold comfort to the unfortunate officer. " When the Emperor comes to hear about it ! " he cried.

" Oh, he will be for having you shot," said the General, " but we shall see. Now we will say no more about this," he added severely, " except to plan a revenge that shall strike a salutary terror into this country, where they carry on war like savages."

An hour later a whole regiment, a detachment of cavalry, and a convoy of artillery were upon the road. The General and Victor marched at the head of the column. The soldiers had been told of the fate of their comrades, and their rage knew no bounds. The distance between headquarters and the town of Menda was crossed at a well-nigh miraculous speed. Whole villages by the way were found to be under arms ; every one of the wretched hamlets was surrounded, and their inhabitants decimated.

It so chanced that the English vessels still lay out at sea, and were no nearer the shore, a fact inexplicable until it was known afterwards that they were artillery transports which had outsailed the rest of the fleet. So the townsmen of Menda, left without the assistance on which they had reckoned when the sails of the English appeared, were surrounded by French troops almost before they had had time to strike a blow. This struck such terror into them that they offered to surrender at discretion. An impulse of devotion, no isolated instance in the history of the Peninsula, led the actual slayers of the French to offer to give themselves up ; seeking in this way to save the town, for from the General's reputation for cruelty it was feared that he would give Menda over to the flames, and put the whole population to the sword. General G—— took their offer, stipulating that every soul in the castle from the lowest servant to the Marquis should likewise be given up to him. These terms being accepted, the General promised to spare the lives of the rest of the townsmen, and to prohibit his soldiers from pillaging or setting fire to the town. A heavy contribution was levied, and the wealthiest inhabitants were taken as hostages to guarantee payment within twenty-four hours.

The General took every necessary precaution for the safety of his troops, provided for the defence of the place, and refused to billet his men in the houses of the town. After they had bivouacked, he went up to the castle and entered it as a conqueror. The whole family of Légañès and their household were gagged, shut up in the great ballroom, and closely watched. From the windows it was easy to see the whole length of the terrace above the town.

The staff was established in an adjoining gallery, where the General forthwith held a council as to the best means of preventing the landing of the English. An aide-de camp was despatched to

Marshal Ney, orders were issued to plant batteries along the coast, and then the General and his staff turned their attention to their prisoners. The two hundred Spaniards given up by the towns-folk were shot down then and there upon the terrace. And after this military execution, the General gave orders to erect gibbets to the number of the prisoners in the ballroom in the same place, and to send for the hangman out of the town. Victor took advantage of the interval before dinner to pay a visit to the prisoners. He soon came back to the General.

" I am come in haste," he faltered out, " to ask a favour."

" *You* ! " exclaimed the General, with bitter irony in his tones.

" Alas ! " answered Victor, " it is a sorry favour. The Marquis has seen them erecting the gallows, and hopes that you will com-mute the punishment for his family ; he entreats you to have the nobles beheaded."

" Granted," said the General.

" He further asks that they may be allowed the consolation of religion, and that they may be unbound ; they give you their word that they will not attempt to escape."

" That I permit," said the General, " but you are answerable for them."

" The old noble offers you all that he has if you will pardon his youngest son."

" Really ! " cried the Commander. " His property is forfeit already to King Joseph." He paused ; a contemptuous thought set wrinkles in his forehead, as he added, " I will do better than they ask. I understand what he means by that last request of his. Very good. Let him hand down his name to posterity ; but when-ever it is mentioned, all Spain shall remember his treason and its punishment ! I will give the fortune and his life to any one of the sons who will do the executioner's office. . . There, don't talk any more about them to me."

Dinner was ready. The officers sat down to satisfy an appetite whetted by hunger. Only one among them was absent from the table—that one was Victor Marchand. After long hesitation he went to the ballroom, and heard the last sighs of the proud house of Légañês. He looked sadly at the scene before him. Only last night, in this very room, he had seen their faces whirled past him in the waltz, and he shuddered to think that those girlish heads, with those of the three young brothers, must fall in a brief space by the executioner's sword. There sat the father and mother, their three sons and two daughters, perfectly motionless, bound to their gilded chairs. Eight serving men stood with their hands tied behind them. These fifteen prisoners, under sentence of death, exchanged grave glances ; it was difficult to read the thoughts that filled them from their eyes, but profound resignation and regret that their enterprise should have failed so completely was written on more than one brow.

The impassive soldiers who guarded them respected the grief of their bitter enemies. A gleam of curiosity lighted up all faces when Victor came in. He gave orders that the condemned prisoners should be unbound, and himself unfastened the cords that held Clara a prisoner. She smiled mournfully at him. The officer could not refrain from lightly touching the young girl's arm ; he could not help admiring her dark hair, her slender waist. She was a true daughter of Spain, with a Spanish complexion, a Spaniard's eyes, blacker than the raven's wing beneath their long curving lashes.

" Did you succeed ? " she asked, with a mournful smile, in which a certain girlish charm still lingered.

Victor could not repress a groan. He looked from the faces of the three brothers to Clara, and again at the three young Spaniards. The first, the oldest of the family, was a man of thirty. He was short, and somewhat ill made ; he looked haughty and proud, but a certain distinction was not lacking in his bearing, and he was apparently no stranger to the delicacy of feeling for which in olden times the chivalry of Spain was famous. His name was Juanito. The second son, Felipe, was about twenty years of age ; he was like his sister Clara ; and the youngest was a child of eight. In the features of the little Manuel a painter would have discerned something of that Roman steadfastness which David has given to the children's faces in his Republican *genre* pictures. The old Marquis, with his white hair, might have come down from some canvas of Murillo's. Victor threw back his head in despair after this survey ; how should one of these accept the General's offer ! nevertheless he ventured to intrust it to Clara. A shudder ran through the Spanish girl, but she recovered herself almost instantly, and knelt before her father.

" Father," she said, " bid Juanito swear to obey the commands that you shall give him, and we shall be content."

The Marquesa trembled with hope, but as she lent towards her husband and learned Clara's hideous secret, the mother fainted away. Juanito understood it all, and leapt up like a caged lion. Victor took it upon himself to dismiss the soldiers, after receiving an assurance of entire submission from the Marquis. The servants were led away and given over to the hangman and their fate. When only Victor remained on guard in the room, the old Marqués de Légañès rose to his feet.

" Juanito," he said. For all answer Juanito bowed his head in a way that meant refusal ; he sank down into his chair, and fixed tearless eyes upon his father and mother in an intolerable gaze. Clara went over to him and sat on his knee ; she put her arms about him, and pressed kisses on his eyelids, saying gaily :

" Dear Juanito, if you but knew how sweet death at your hands will be to me ! I shall not be compelled to submit to the hateful touch of the hangman's fingers. You will snatch me away from the evils to come and . . Dear, kind Juanito, you could not bear the thought of my belonging to any one—well, then ? "

The velvet eyes gave Victor a burning glance ; she seemed to try to awaken in Juanito's heart his hatred for the French.

" Take courage," said his brother Felipe, " or our well-nigh royal line will be extinct."

Suddenly Clara sprang to her feet. The group round Juanito fell back, and the son who had rebelled with such good reason was confronted with his aged father.

" Juanito, I command you ! " said the Marquis solemnly.

The young Count gave no sign, and his father fell on his knees ; Clara, Manuel, and Felipe unconsciously followed his example, stretching out suppliant hands to him who must save their family from oblivion, and seeming to echo their father's words.

" Can it be that you lack the fortitude of a Spaniard and true sensibility, my son ? Do you mean to keep me on my knees ? What right have you to think of your own life and of your own sufferings ?—Is this my son, madam ? " the old Marquis added, turning to his wife.

" He will consent to it," cried the mother in agony of soul. She had seen a slight contraction of Juanito's brows which she, his mother, alone understood.

Mariquita, the second daughter, knelt, with her slender clinging arms about her mother ; the hot tears fell from her eyes, and her little brother Manuel upbraided her for weeping. Just at that moment the castle chaplain came in ; the whole family surrounded him and led him up to Juanito. Victor felt that he could endure the sight no longer, and with a sign to Clara he hurried from the room to make one last effort for them. He found the General in boisterous spirits ; the officers were still sitting over their dinner and drinking together ; the wine had loosened their tongues.

An hour later, a hundred of the principal citizens of Menda were summoned to the terrace by the General's orders to witness the execution of the family of Légañès. A detachment had been told off to keep order among the Spanish townsfolk, who were marshalled beneath the gallows whereon the Marquis's servants hung ; the feet of those martyrs of their cause all but touched the citizen's heads. Thirty paces away stood the block ; the blade of a scimitar glittered upon it, and the executioner stood by in case Juanito should refuse at the last.

The deepest silence prevailed, but before long it was broken by the sound of many footsteps, the measured tramp of a picket of soldiers, and the jingling of their weapons. Mingled with these came other noises—loud talk and laughter from the dinner-table where the officers were sitting ; just as the music and the sound of the dancer's feet had drowned the preparations for last night's treacherous butchery.

All eyes turned to the castle, and beheld the family of nobles coming forth with incredible composure to their death. Every brow was serene and calm. One alone among them, haggard and overcome, leant on the arm of the priest, who poured forth all the consolations of religion for the one man who was condemned to live. Then the executioner, like the spectators, knew that Juanito had consented to perform his office for a day. The old Marquis and his wife, Clara and Mariquita, and their two brothers knelt a few paces from the fatal spot. Juanito reached it, guided by the priest. As he stood at the block the executioner plucked him by the sleeve, and took him aside, probably to give him certain instructions. The confessor so placed the victims that they could not witness the executions, but one and all stood upright and fearless, like Spaniards, as they were.

Clara sprang to her brother's side before the others.

" Juanito," she said to him, " be merciful to my lack of courage. Take me first ! "

As she spoke, the footsteps of a man running at full speed echoed from the walls, and Victor appeared upon the scene. Clara was kneeling before the block ; her white neck seemed to appeal to the blade to fall. The officer turned faint, but he found strength to rush to her side. " The General grants you your life if you will consent to marry me," he murmured.

The Spanish girl gave the officer a glance full of proud disdain.

" Now, Juanito ! " she said in her deep-toned voice.

Her head fell at Victor's feet. A shudder ran through the Marquesa de Légañès, a convulsive tremor that she could not control, but she gave no other sign of her anguish.

" Is this where I ought to be, dear Juanito ? Is it all right ? " little Manuel asked his brother.

" Oh, Mariquita, you are weeping ! " Juanito said when his sister came.

" Yes," said the girl ; " I am thinking of you, poor Juanito ; how unhappy you will be when we are gone."

Then the Marquis's tall figure approached. He looked at the block where his children's blood had been shed, turned to the mute and motionless crowd, and said in a loud voice as he stretched out his hands to Juanito :

" Spaniards ! I give my son a father's blessing. Now, Marquis, strike ' without fear ' ; thou art ' without reproach.' "

But when his mother came near, leaning on the confessor's

arm—" She fed me from her breast ! " Juanito cried, in tones that drew a cry of horror from the crowd. The uproarious mirth of the officers over their wine died away before that terrible cry. The Marquesa knew that Juanito's courage was exhausted ; at one bound she sprang to the balustrade, leapt forth, and was dashed to pieces on the rocks below. A cry of admiration broke from the spectators. Juanito swooned.

" General," said an officer, half drunk by this time, " Marchand has just been telling me something about this execution ; I will wager that it was not by your orders—— "

" Are you forgetting, gentlemen, that in a month's time five hundred families in France will be in mourning, and that we are still in Spain ? " cried General G——. " Do you want us to leave our bones here ? "

But not a man at the table, not even a subaltern, dared to empty his glass after that speech.

In spite of the respect in which all men hold the Marqués de Légañès, in spite of the title of *El Verdugo* (the executioner) conferred upon him as a patent of nobility by the King of Spain, the great noble is consumed by a gnawing grief. He lives a retired life, and seldom appears in public. The burden of his heroic crime weighs heavily upon him, and he seems to wait impatiently till the birth of a second son shall release him, and he may go to join the Shades that never cease to haunt him.

A SEASHORE DRAMA

Honoré de Balzac

Young men almost always have a pair of compasses with which they delight to measure the future ; when their will is in accord with the size of the angle which they make, the world is theirs. But this phenomenon of moral life takes place only at a certain age. That age, which in the case of all men comes between the years of twenty-two and twenty-eight, is the age of noble thoughts, the age of first conceptions, because it is the age of unbounded desires, the age at which one doubts nothing ; he who talks of doubt speaks of impotence. After that age, which passes as quickly as the season for sowing, comes the age of execution. There are in a certain sense

two youths : one during which one thinks, the other during which
one acts ; often they are blended, in men whom nature has favoured,
and who, like Caesar, Newton, and Bonaparte, are the greatest
among great men.

I was reckoning how much time a thought needs to develop
itself ; and, compasses in hand, standing on a cliff a hundred
fathoms above the ocean, whose waves played among the reefs,
I laid out my future, furnishing it with works, as an engineer draws
fortresses and palaces upon vacant land. The sea was lovely ;
I had just dressed after bathing ; I was waiting for Pauline, my
guardian angel, who was bathing in a granite bowl full of white
sand, the daintiest bath-tub that Nature ever designed for any of
her sea-fairies. We were at the extreme point of Le Croisic, a tiny
peninsula of Britanny ; we were far from the harbour, in a spot
which the authorities considered so inaccessible that the customs
officers almost never visited it. To swim in the air after swimming in
the sea ! Ah ! who would not have swum into the future ? Why
did I think ? Why does evil happen ? Who knows ? Ideas come
to your heart, or your brain, without consulting you. No courtesan
was ever more whimsical or more imperious than is conception in an
artist ; it must be caught, like fortune, by the hair, when it comes.
Clinging to my thought, as Astolpho clung to his hippogriff,
I galloped through the world, arranging everything therein to suit
my pleasure.

When I looked about me in search of some omen favourable to the
audacious schemes which my wild imagination advised me to undertake, a sweet cry, the cry of a woman calling in the silence of the
desert, the cry of a woman coming from the bath, refreshed and
joyous, drowned the murmur of the fringe of foam tossed constantly
back and forth by the rising and falling of the waves in the inden-
tations of the shore. When I heard that note, uttered by the soul,
I fancied that I had seen on the cliff the foot of an angel, who, as
she unfolded her wings, had called to me : " Thou shalt have
success ! " I descended, radiant with joy and light as air ; I went
bounding down, like a stone down a steep slope. When she saw
me, she said to me : " What is the matter ? " I did not answer,
but my eyes became moist. The day before, Pauline had understood my pain, as she understood at that moment my joy, with the
magical sensitiveness of a harp which follows the variations of the
atmosphere. The life of man has some glorious moments ! We
walked silently along the shore. The sky was cloudless, the sea
without a ripple ; others would have seen only two blue plains,
one above the other ; but we who understood each other without
need of speech, we who could discover between those two swaddling-
cloths of infinity the illusions with which youth is nourished, we
pressed each other's hand at the slightest change which took place

either in the sheet of water or in the expanse of air ; for we took those trivial phenomena for material interpretations of our twofold thought.

Who has not enjoyed that unbounded bliss in pleasures, when the soul seems to be released from the bonds of the flesh, and to be restored as it were to the world whence it came ?   Pleasure is not our only guide in those regions.   Are there not times when the sentiments embrace each other as of their own motion, and fly thither, like two children who take each other's hands and begin to run without knowing why or whither ?   We walked along thus.

At the moment that the roofs of the town appeared on the horizon, forming a greyish line, we met a poor fisherman who was returning to Le Croisic.   His feet were bare, his canvas trousers were ragged on the edges, with many holes imperfectly mended ;   he wore a shirt of sail-cloth, wretched list suspenders, and his jacket was a mere rag.   The sight of that misery distressed us—a discord, as it were, in the midst of our harmony.   We looked at each other, to lament that we had not at that moment the power to draw upon the treasury of Abu-l-Kásim.   We saw a magnificent lobster and a crab hanging by a cord which the fisherman carried in his right hand, while in the other he had his nets and his fishing apparatus. We accosted him, with the purpose of buying his fish, an idea which occurred to both of us, and which expressed itself in a smile, to which I replied by slightly pressing the arm which I held and drawing it closer to my heart.   It was one of those nothings which the memory afterward transforms into a poem, when, sitting by the fire, we recall the time when that nothing moved us, the place where it happened, and that mirage, the effects of which have never been defined, but which often exerts an influence upon the objects which surround us, when life is pleasant and our hearts are full.

The loveliest places are simply what we make them.   Who is the man, however little of a poet he may be, who has not in his memory a boulder that occupies more space than the most famous landscape visited at great expense ?   Beside that boulder what tempestuous thoughts !   there, a whole life mapped out ;   here, fears banished ; there, rays of hope entered the heart.   At that moment, the sun, sympathising with these thoughts of love and of the future, cast upon the yellowish sides of that cliff an ardent beam ;   some mountain wild-flowers attracted the attention ;   the tranquillity and silence magnified that uneven surface, in reality dark of hue, but made brilliant by the dreamer ;   then it was beautiful, with its meagre vegetation, its warm-hued camomile, its Venus's hair, with the velvety leaves.   A prolonged festivity, superb decorations, placid exaltation of human strength !   Once before, the Lake of Bienne, seen from Île St.-Pierre, had spoken to me thus ;   perhaps the cliff of Le Croisic would be the last of those delights. But, in that case, what would become of Pauline ?

" You have had fine luck this morning, my good man," I said to the fisherman.

" Yes, monsieur," he replied, stopping to turn towards us the tanned face of those who remain for hours at a time exposed to the reflection of the sun on the water.

That face indicated endless resignation ; the patience of the fisherman, and his gentle manners. That man had a voice without trace of harshness, kindly lips, no ambition ; an indefinably frail and sickly appearance. Any other type of face would have displeased us.

" Where are you going to sell your fish ? "

" At the town."

" How much will you get for the lobster ? "

" Fifteen sous."

" And for the crab ? "

" Twenty sous."

" Why so much difference between the lobster and the crab ? "

" The crab is much more delicate, monsieur ; · and then it's as cunning as a monkey, and don't often allow itself to be caught."

" Will you let us have both for a hundred sous ? " said Pauline. The man was thunderstruck.

" You shan't have them ! " I said laughingly ; " I will give ten francs. We must pay for emotions all that they are worth."

" Very well," she replied, " I propose to have them ; I will give ten francs two sous."

" Ten sous."

" Twelve francs."

" Fifteen francs."

" Fifteen francs fifty," she said.

" One hundred francs."

" One hundred and fifty."

I bowed. At that moment we were not rich enough to carry the bidding any farther. The poor fisherman did not know whether he ought to be angry as at a practical joke, or to exult ; we relieved him from his dilemma by giving him the name of our landlady and telling him to take the lobster and the crab to her house.

" Do you earn a living ? " I asked him, in order to ascertain to what cause his destitution should be attributed.

" With much difficulty and many hardships," he replied. " Fishing on the seashore, when you have neither boat nor nets, and can fish only with a line, is a risky trade. You see, you have to wait for the fish or the shell-fish to come, while the fishermen with boats can go out to sea after them. It is so hard to earn a living this way, that I am the only man who fishes on the shore. I pass whole days without catching anything. The only way I get anything is when a crab forgets himself and goes to sleep, as this one did, or a lobster is fool enough to stay on the rocks. Sometimes, after a high sea, the wolf-fish come in, and then I grab them."

" Well, take one day with another, what do you earn ? "

" Eleven or twelve sous. I could get along with that if I were alone ; but I have my father to support, and the poor man can't help me, for he's blind."

At that sentence, uttered with perfect simplicity, Pauline and I looked at each other without a word.

" You have a wife or a sweetheart ? "

He cast at us one of the most pitiful glances that I ever saw, as he replied :

" If I had a wife, then I should have to let my father go : I couldn't support him, and a wife and children too."

" Well, my poor fellow, how is it that you don't try to earn more by carrying salt to the harbour, or by working in the salt marshes ? "

" Oh ? I couldn't do that for three months, monsieur. I am not strong enough ; and if I should die, my father would have to beg. What I must have is a trade that requires very little skill and a great deal of patience."

" But how can two people live on twelve sous a day ? "

" Oh, monsieur, we eat buckwheat cakes, and barnacles that I take off the rocks."

" How old are you ? "

" Thirty-seven."

" Have you ever been away from here ? "

" I went to Guérande once, to draw my lot in the draft, and I went to Savenay, to show myself to some gentlemen who measured me. If I had been an inch taller I should have been drafted. I should have died on the first long march, and my poor father would have been asking alms to-day."

I had thought out many dramas ; Pauline was accustomed to intense emotions, living with a man in my condition of health ; but neither of us had ever listened to more touching words than those of that fisherman. We walked some distance in silence, both of us measuring the silent depths of that unknown life, admiring the nobility of that self-sacrifice which was unconscious of itself ; the strength of his weakness surprised us ; that unconscious generosity made us small in our own eyes. I saw that poor creature, all instinct, chained to that rock as a galley-slave is chained to his ball, watching for twenty years for shell-fish to support himself, and sustained in his patience by a single sentiment. How many hours passed on the edge of that beach ! how many hopes crushed by a squall, by a change of weather ! He hung over the edge of a granite

shelf, his arms stretched out like those of an Indian fakir, while his
father, sitting on a stool, waited in silence and darkness for him to
bring him the coarsest of shell-fish and of bread, if the sea were
willing.

" Do you ever drink wine ? " I asked him.

" Three or four times a year."

" Well, you shall drink some to-day, you and your father, and we
will send you a white loaf."

" You are very kind, monsieur."

" We will give you your dinner if you will guide us along the shore
as far as Batz, where we are going, to see the tower which overlooks
the basin and the coast between Batz and Le Croisic."

" With pleasure," he said.   " Go straight ahead, follow the road
you are now on ; I will overtake you after I have got rid of my fish
and my tackle."

We nodded simultaneously, and he hurried off towards the town,
light at heart.   That meeting held us in the same mental situation
in which we were previously, but it had lowered our spirits.

" Poor man ! " said Pauline, with that accent which takes away
from a woman's compassion whatever there may be offensive in
pity ; " does it not make one feel ashamed to be happy when one
sees such misery ? "

" Nothing is more cruel than to have impotent desires," I replied.

" Those two poor creatures, father and son, will no more know how
keen our sympathy is than the world knows how noble their lives
are ; for they are laying up treasures in heaven."

" What a wretched country ! " she said, as she pointed out to me,
along a field surrounded by a loose stone wall, lumps of cow-dung
arranged symmetrically.   " I asked some one what those were.
A peasant woman, who was putting them in place, answered that she
was *making wood*.   Just fancy, my dear, that when these blocks of
dung are dried, these poor people gather them, pile them up, and
warm themselves with them.   During the winter they are sold, like
lumps of peat.   And what do you suppose the best paid dressmaker
earns ? Five sous a day," she said, after a pause ; " but she gets
her board."

" See," I said to her, " the winds from the ocean wither or uproot
everything ; there are no trees ; the wrecks of vessels that are
beyond use are sold to the rich, for the cost of transportation
prevents them from using the firewood in which Britanny abounds.
This province is beautiful only to great souls ; people without courage
could not live here ; it is no place for anybody except poets or
barnacles.   The storehouse for salt had to be built on the cliff, to
induce anybody to live in it.   On one side, the sea ; on the other,
the sands ; above, space."

We had already passed the town and were within the species of desert which separates Le Croisic from the village of Batz. Imagine, my dear uncle, a plain two leagues in length, covered by the gleaming sand that we see on the seashore. Here and there a few rocks raised their heads, and you would have said that they were gigantic beasts lying among the dunes. Along the shore there is an occasional reef, about which the waves play, giving them the aspect of great white roses floating on the liquid expanse and coming to rest on the shore. When I saw that plain bounded by the ocean on the right, and on the left by the great lake that flows in between Le Croisic and the sandy heights of Guérande, at the foot of which there are salt marshes absolutely without vegetation, I glanced at Pauline and asked her if she had the courage to defy the heat of the sun, and the strength to walk through the sand.

" I have on high boots ; let us go thither," she said, pointing to the tower of Batz, which circumscribed the view by its enormous mass, placed there like a pyramid, but a slender, indented pyramid, so poetically adorned that it allowed the imagination to see in it the first ruins of a great Asiatic city. We walked a few yards and sat down under a rock which was still in the shadow ; but it was eleven o'clock in the morning, and that shadow, which ceased at our feet, rapidly disappeared.

" How beautiful the silence is," she said to me ; " and how its intensity is increased by the regular plashing of the sea on the beach ! "

" If you choose to abandon your understanding to the three immensities that surround us, the air, the water, and the sand, listening solely to the repeated sound of the flow and the outflow," I replied, " you will not be able to endure its language ; you will fancy that you discover therein a thought which will overwhelm you. Yesterday, at sunset, I had that sensation ; it prostrated me "

" Oh, yes, let us talk," she said, after a long pause. " No orator can be more terrible than this silence. I fancy that I have discovered the causes of the harmony which surrounds us," she continued. " This landscape, which has only three sharp colours, the brilliant yellow of the sand, the blue of the sky, and the smooth green of the sea, is grand without being wild, it is immense without being a desert, it is changeless without being monotonous ; it has only three elements, but it is diversified."

" Women alone can express their impressions thus," I replied ; " you would drive a poet to despair, dear heart, whom I divined so perfectly."

" The excessive noonday heat imparts a gorgeous colour to those three expressions of infinity," replied Pauline, laughing. " I can imagine here the poesy and the passion of the Orient."

" And I can imagine its despair."

"Yes," she said ; "that dune is a sublime cloister."

We heard the hurried step of our guide ; he had dressed himself in his best clothes. We said a few formal words to him ; he evidently saw that our frame of mind had changed, and, with the reserve that misfortune imparts, he kept silent. Although we pressed each other's hands from time to time, to advise each other of the unity of our impressions, we walked for half an hour in silence, whether because we were overwhelmed by the heat, which rose in shimmering waves from the sand, or because the difficulty of walking absorbed our attention. We walked on, hand in hand, like two children ; we should not have taken a dozen steps if we had been arm in arm. The road leading to Batz was not marked out ; a gust of wind was enough to efface the footprints of horses or the wheel-ruts ; but our guide's practised eye recognised the road by the droppings of cattle or of horses. Sometimes it went down towards the sea, sometimes rose towards the upland, at the caprice of the slopes, or to skirt a rock. At noon we were only half-way.

"We will rest there," said I, pointing to a promontory formed of rocks high enough to lead one to suppose that we should find a grotto there.

When I spoke, the fisherman, who had followed the direction of my finger, shook his head and said :

"There's some one there ! People who go from Batz to Le Croisic, or from Le Croisic to Batz, always make a détour in order not to pass that rock."

The man said this in a low voice, and we divined a mystery.

"Is he a thief and assassin ? "

Our guide replied only by a long-drawn breath which increased our curiosity.

"But will anything happen to us if we pass by there ? "

"Oh no ! "

"Will you go with us ? "

"No, monsieur."

"We will go then, if you assure us that we shall be in no danger."

"I don't say that," replied the fisherman hastily ; "I say simply that the man who is there won't say anything to you, or do any harm to you. Oh, bless my soul ! he won't so much as move from his place ! "

"Who is he pray ? "

"A man ! "

Never were two syllables uttered in such a tragic tone. At that moment we were twenty yards from that reef, about which the sea was playing ; our guide took the road which skirted the rocks ; we went straight ahead, but Pauline took my arm. Our guide quickened his pace in order to reach the spot where the two roads

met again at the same time that we did. He evidently supposed
that, after seeing the man, we would quicken our pace. That
circumstance kindled our curiosity, which then became so intense
that out hearts throbbed as if they had felt a thrill of fear. Despite
the heat of the day and the fatigue caused by walking through
the sand, our hearts were still abandoned to the indescribable
langour of a blissful harmony of sensations ; they were filled with
that pure pleasure which can only be described by comparing it
to the pleasure which one feels in listening to some lovely music,
like Mozart's *Andiano mio ben*. Do not two pure sentiments, which
blend, resemble two beautiful voices singing ? In order fully to
appreciate the emotion which seized us, you must share the semi-
voluptuous condition in which the events of that morning had
enveloped us. Gaze for a long while at a turtle-dove perched on a
slender twig, near a spring, and you will utter a cry of pain when
you see a hawk pounce upon it, bury its steel claws in its heart,
and bear it away with the murderous rapidity that powder communicates to the bullet.

When we had walked a yard or two across the open space that
lay in front of the grotto, a sort of platform a hundred feet above
the ocean, and sheltered from its rage by a succession of steep
rocks, we were conscious of an electric shock not unlike that caused
by a sudden noise in the midst of the night. We had spied a man
seated on a boulder of granite, and he had looked at us. His
glance, like the flash of a cannon, came from two bloodshot eyes,
and his stoical immobility could be compared only to the un-
changing posture of the masses of granite which surrounded him.
His eyes moved slowly ; his body, as if it were petrified, did not
move at all. After flashing at us that glance which gave us such
a rude shock, he turned his eyes to the vast expanse of the ocean,
and gazed at it, despite the dazzling light which rose therefrom,
as the eagles are said to gaze at the sun, without lowering the lids,
which he did not raise again. Try to recall, my dear uncle, one of
those old druidical oaks, whose gnarled trunk, newly stripped of
its branches, rises fantastically above a deserted road, and you
will have an accurate image of that man. He had one of those
shattered herculean frames, and the face of Olympian Jove, but
ravaged by age, by the hard toil of the seafaring man, by grief,
by coarse food, and blackened as if struck by lightning. As I
glanced at his calloused, hairy hands, I saw chords which resembled
veins of iron. However, everything about him indicated a robust
constitution. I noticed a large quantity of moss in a corner of
the grotto, and upon a rough table, hewn out by chance in the
midst of the granite, a broken loaf covering an earthen jug. Never
had my imagination, when it carried me back to the deserts where
the first hermits of Christianity lived, conceived a face more grandly

religious or more appallingly penitent than was the face of that
man.

Even you, who have listened to confessions, my dear uncle, have
perhaps never met with such sublime remorse ; but that remorse
was drowned in the waves of prayer, the incessant prayer of silent
despair. That fisherman, that sailor, that rude Breton, was sublime by virtue of some unknown sentiment. But had those eyes
wept ? Had that statuelike hand struck its fellow-man ? Was that
stern forehead, instinct with pitiless uprightness, on which, however, strength had left those marks of gentleness which are the
accompaniment of all true strength—was that forehead, furrowed
by wrinkles, in harmony with a noble heart ? Why was that man
among the granite ? Why the granite in that man ? Where was
the man ? Where was the granite ? A whole world of thoughts
rushed through our minds. As our guide had anticipated, we had
passed in silence, rapidly ; and when he met us, we were tremulous
with terror, or overwhelmed with amazement. But he did not use
the fulfilment of his prediction as a weapon against us.

" Did you see him ? " he asked.

" Who is that man ? " said I.

" They call him *The Man of the Vow*."

You can imagine how quickly our two faces turned toward our
fisherman at those words ! He was a simple-minded man ; he
understood our silent question ; and this is what he said, in his
own language, the popular tone of which I shall try to retain :

" Madame, the people of Le Croisic, like the people of Batz,
believe that that man is guilty of something, and that he is doing
a penance ordered by a famous priest to whom he went to confess,
a long way beyond Nantes. Other people think that Cambremer—
that's his name—has an evil spell that he communicates to everybody who passes through the air he breathes. So a good many
people, before they pass that rock, look to see what way the wind
is. If it's from *galerne*," he said, pointing towards the west, " they
wouldn't go on, even if it was a matter of searching for a piece of
the true Cross ; they turn back, because they're frightened. Other
people, the rich people of Le Croisic, say that he's made a vow,
and that's why he's called *The Man of the Vow*. He is always there,
night and day ; never comes out.

" These reports about him have some appearance of sense. You
see," he added, turning to point out a thing which we had not
noticed, " he has stuck up there, on the left, a wooden cross, to
show that he has put himself under the protection of God, the
Blessed Virgin, and the saints. Even if he hadn't consecrated
himself like that, the fear everybody has of him would make him
as safe there as if he were guarded by soldiers. He hasn't said a
word since he shut himself up there in the open air ; he lives on

bread and water that his brother's daughter brings him every
morning—a little maid of twelve years, that he's left his property
to ; and she's a pretty thing, as gentle as a lamb, a nice little girl
and very clever.　She has blue eyes as long as that," he said, holding up his thumb, " and a cherub's head of hair.

" When any one says to her : ' I say, Pérotte ' (that means
Pierrette amongst us," he said, interrupting himself : " she is
consecrated to St. Pierre ; Cambremer's name is Pierre, and he
was her godfather), ' I say, Pérotte, what does your uncle say to
you ? ' ' He don't say anything,' she'll answer, ' not anything at
all, nothing ! ' ' Well, then, what does he do to you ? ' ' He
kisses me on the forehead Sundays ! ' ' Aren't you afraid of him ? '
' Why no, he's my godfather.' He won't let any one else bring him
anything to eat.　Pérotte says that he smiles when she comes ;
but that's like a sunbeam in a fog, for they say he's as gloomy as
a fog."

" But," I said, " you arouse our curiosity without gratifying
it.　Do you know what brought him here ?　Was it grief, was it
repentance, was it insanity, was it crime, was it—— ? "

" Oh ! only my father and I know the truth of the thing, Monsieur.
My dead mother worked for a judge to whom Cambremer told the
whole story, by the priest's order ; for he wouldn't give him
absolution on any other condition, according to what the people
at the harbour said.　My poor mother overheard what Cambremer
said, without meaning to, because the judge's kitchen was right
next to his study, and she listened.　She's dead, and the judge
who heard him is dead.　My mother made father and me promise
never to tell anything to the people about here ; but I can tell
you that the night my mother told it to us, the hair on my head
turned grey."

" Well, tell us, my fine fellow ; we will not mention it to anybody."
The fisherman looked at us, and continued thus :

" Pierre Cambremer, whom you saw yonder, is the oldest of the
Cambremers, who have always been sailors, from father to son ;
that's what their name says—the sea has always bent under them.
The man you saw was a boat fisherman.　So he had boats and went
sardine-fishing ; he went deep-sea fishing too, for the dealers.
He'd have fitted out a vessel and gone after cod, if he hadn't been
so fond of his wife ; a fine woman she was, a Brouin from Guérande ;
a magnificent girl, and she had a big heart.　She was so fond of
Cambremer that she'd never let her man leave her any longer than
he had to, to go after sardines.　They used to live over there—
look ! " said the fisherman, ascending a hillock to point to an islet
in the little inland sea between the dunes, across which we were
walking, and the salt marshes of Guérande.　" Do you see that
house ?　That was his.

" Jacquette Brouin and Cambremer never had but one child, a
boy ; and they loved him like—like what shall I say ?—indeed,
like people love their only child ; they were mad over him. If their
little Jacques had put dirt in the saucepan, saving your presence,
they'd have thought it was sugar. How many times we've seen
'em at the fair, buying the prettiest fallals for him ! It was all
nonsense—everybody told 'em so. Little Cambremer, seeing that
he was allowed to do whatever he wanted to, became as big a rogue
as a red ass.

" When any one went to the elder Cambremer and told him :
' Your boy nearly killed little So-and-so,' he'd laugh and say :
' Bah ! he'll make a fine sailor ! he'll command the king's fleet.'
And when somebody else said : ' Pierre Cambremer, do you know
that your boy put out the little Pougaud girl's eye ? ' Pierre said :
' He'll be fond of the girls ! ' He thought everything was all right.
So my little scamp, when he was ten years old, used to be at every-
body, and amuse himself cutting off hens' heads, cutting pigs open ;
in short, he rolled in blood like a polecat. ' He'll make a famous
soldier ! ' Cambremer would say ; ' he's got a taste for blood.'
I remember all that, you see," said the fisherman.

" And so did Cambremer too," he continued after a pause.
" When he got to be fifteen or sixteen years old, Jacques Cambremer
was—what shall I say ?—a shark. He used to go to Guérande to
enjoy himself, or to Savenay to make love to the girls. Then he
began to steal from his mother, who didn't dare to say anything
to her husband. Cambremer was so honest that he'd travel twenty
leagues to pay back two sous, if he had been overpaid in settling an
account. At last the day came when his mother was stripped clean.
While his father was away fishing, the boy carried off the sideboard,
the dishes, the sheets, the linen, and left just the four walls ; he'd
sold everything to get money to go to Nantes and raise the devil.
The poor woman cried for whole days and nights. She couldn't help
telling the father about that, when he came home ; and she was
afraid of the father—not for herself, oh no ? When Pierre
Cambremer came home and found his house furnished with things
people had lent his wife, he said :

" ' What does all this mean ? '

" The poor woman was nearer dead than alive.

" ' We've been robbed,' said she.

" ' Where's Jacques ? '

" ' Jacques is on a spree.'

" No one knew where the villain had gone.

" ' He goes on too many sprees ! ' said Pierre.

" Six months later, the poor man learned that his son was in
danger of falling into the hands of justice at Nantes. He went there
on foot ; made the journey faster than he could have gone by sea,

got hold of his son, and brought him back here. He didn't ask him :
' What have you been doing ? ' He just said to him :

" ' If you don't behave yourself here with your mother and me
for two years, going fishing and acting like an honest man, you'll
have an account to settle with me ! '

" The idiot, counting on his father's and mother's stupidity, made
a face at him. At that Pierre fetched him a crack that laid Master
Jacques up in bed for six months. The poor mother almost died of
grief. One night, when she was sleeping peacefully by her husband's
side, she heard a noise, got out of bed, and got a knife-cut on her arm.
She shrieked and some one brought a light. Pierre Cambremer
found his wife wounded ; he thought that a robber did it—as if
there was any such thing in our province, where you can carry ten
thousand francs in gold from Le Croisic to St.-Nazaire, without fear,
and without once being asked what you've got under your arm !
Pierre looked for Jacques, but couldn't find him.

" In the morning, the little monster had the face to come home
and say that he'd been to Batz. I must tell you that his mother
didn't know where to hide her money. Cambremer always left his
with Monsieur Dupotet at Le Croisic. Their son's wild ways had
eaten up crowns by the hundred, francs by the hundred, and louis
d'or ; they were almost ruined, and that was pretty hard for folks
who used to have about twelve thousand francs, including their
island. No one knew what Cambremer paid out at Nantes to clear
his son. Bad luck raised the deuce with the family. Cambremer's
brother was in a bad way and needed help. To encourage him,
Pierre told him that Jacques and Pérotte (the younger Cambremer's
daughter) should marry.

" Then he employed him in the fishing, so that he could earn his
living ; for Joseph Cambremer was reduced to living by his work.
His wife had died of a fever, and he had had to pay for a wet-nurse
for Pérotte. Pierre Cambremer's wife owed a hundred francs to
different people on the little girl's account, for linen and clothes, and
for two or three months' wages for that big Frelu girl, who had a
child by Simon Gaudry, and who nursed Pérotte. Mère Cambremer
had sewed a Spanish coin into the cover of her mattress, and marked
it : ' For Pérotte.' She had had a good education ; she could
write like a clerk, and she'd taught her son to read ; that was the
ruin of him. No one knew how it happened, but that scamp of a
Jacques scented the gold, stole it and went off to Le Croisic on a
spree.

" As luck would have it, Goodman Cambremer came in with his
boat. As he approached the beach, he saw a piece of paper floating ;
he picked it up and took it to his wife, who fell flat when she recognised her own written words. Cambremer didn't say anything, but
he went to Le Croisic, and found out that his son was playing

billiards ; then he sent for the good woman who keeps the café, and said :

" ' I told Jacques not to spend a gold-piece that he'll pay you with ; I'll wait outside ; you bring it to me, and I'll give you silver for it.'

" The good woman brought him the money. Cambremer took it, said : ' All right ! ' and went home. The whole town heard about that. But here's something that I know, and that other people only suspect in a general way. He told his wife to clean up their room, which was on the ground floor ; he made a fire on the hearth, lighted two candles, placed two chairs on one side of the fireplace and a stool on the other. Then he told his wife to put out his wedding clothes and to get into her own. When he was dressed, he went to his brother and told him to watch in front of the house and tell him if he heard any noise on either of the beaches, this one or the one in front of the Guérande salt marshes. When he thought that his wife was dressed, he went home again, loaded a gun, and put it out of sight in the corner of the fireplace. Jacques came at last ; it was late ; he had been drinking and playing billiards till ten o'clock ; he had come home by the point of Carnouf. His uncle heard him hailing, crossed to the beach in front of the marsh to fetch him, and rowed him to the island without a word. When he went into the house, his father said to him :

" ' Sit down there,' pointing to the stool. ' You are before your father and mother, whom you have outraged, and who have got to try you.'

" Jacques began to bellow, because Cambremer's face was working in a strange way. The mother sat as stiff as an oar.

" ' If you call out, if you move, if you don't sit on your stool as straight as a mast, I'll shoot you like a dog,' said Pierre, pointing his gun at him.

" The son was dumb as a fish ; the mother didn't say anything.

" ' Here,' said Pierre to his son, ' is a paper that was wrapped round a Spanish gold-piece ; the gold-piece was in your mother's bed ; nobody else knew where she had put it ; I found the paper on the water as I was coming ashore ; you gave this Spanish gold-piece to Mother Fleurant to-night, and your mother can't find hers in her bed. Explain yourself ! '

" Jacques said that he didn't take the money from his mother, and that he had had the coin ever since he went to Nantes.

" ' So much the better,' said Pierre. ' How can you prove it ? '

" ' I had it before.'

" ' You didn't take your mother's ? '

" ' No.'

" ' Will you swear it by your everlasting life ? '

" He was going to swear ; his mother looked up at him and said :

" ' Jacques, my child, be careful ; don't swear, if it isn't true. You may mend your ways and repent ; there's time enough still.'

" And she began to cry.

" ' You're neither one thing nor the other,' he said, ' and you've always wanted to ruin me.'

" Cambremer turned pale, and said :

" ' What you just said to your mother will lengthen your account. Come to the point ! Will you swear ? '

" ' Yes.'

" ' See,' said Pierre, ' did your piece have this cross which the sardine-dealer who paid it to me had made on ours ? '

" Jacques sobered off, and began to cry.

" ' Enough talk,' said Pierre. ' I don't say anything about what you've done before this. I don't propose that a Cambremer shall be put to death on the public square at Le Croisic. Say your prayers, and make haste ! A priest is coming to confess you.'

" The mother went out, so that she needn't hear her son's sentence. When she had left the room, Cambremer the uncle arrived with the rector of Piriac ; but Jacques wouldn't say anything to him. He was sly ; he knew his father well enough to be sure that he wouldn't kill him without confession.

" ' Thank you, monsieur ; excuse us,' said Cambremer to the priest, when he saw that Jacques was obstinate. ' I meant to give my son a lesson, and I ask you not to say anything about it.—If you don't mend your ways,' he said to Jacques, ' the next time will be the last, and I'll put an end to it without confession.'

" He sent him off to bed. The boy believed what he had heard, and imagined that he could arrange matters with his father. He went to sleep. The father sat up. When he saw that his son was sound asleep, he stuffed his mouth with hemp and tied a strip of canvas over it very tight ; then he bound his hands and feet. Jacques stormed and wept blood, so Cambremer told the judge. What could you expect ! The mother threw herself at the father's feet.

" ' He has been tried,' he said ; ' you must help me put him in the boat.'

" She refused. Cambremer took him to the boat all alone, laid him in the bottom, tied a stone round his neck, and rowed abreast of the rock where he is now. Then the poor mother, who had got her brother-in-law to bring her over here, cried : ' Mercy ! ' All in vain ; it had the effect of a stone thrown at a wolf. The moon was shining ; she saw the father throw their son into the water, the son to whom her heart still clung ; and as there wasn't any wind, she heard a splash, then nothing more, not a sound or a bubble ; the sea's a famous keeper, I tell you ! When he came ashore here to quiet his wife, who was groaning, Cambremer found her about the same as dead. The two brothers couldn't carry her, so they had to put her in the boat that had just held the son, and they took her home, going round through Le Croisic passage. Ah ! *La Belle Brouin*, as they called her, didn't last a week. She died asking her husband to burn the accursed boat. He did it, too. As for him, he was like a crazy man ; he didn't know what he wanted, and he staggered when he walked, like a man who can't carry his wine. Then he went off for ten days, and when he came back he planted himself where you saw him, and since he's been there he hasn't said a word."

The fisherman took only a moment or two in telling us this story, and he told it even more simply than I have written it. The common people make few comments when they tell a story ; they select the point that has made an impression on them, and interpret it as they feel it. That narrative was as sharp and incisive as a blow with an axe.

" I shall not go to Batz," said Pauline, as we reached the upper end of the lake.

We returned to Le Croisic by way of the salt marshes, guided through their labyrinth by a fisherman who had become as silent as we. The current of our thoughts had changed. We were both absorbed by depressing reflections, saddened by that drama which explained the swift presentiment that we had felt at the sight of Cambremer. We both had sufficient knowledge of the world to divine all that our guide had not told us of that triple life. The misfortunes of those three people were reproduced before us as if we had seen them in the successive scenes of a drama, to which that father, by thus expiating his necessary crime, had added the dénouement. We dared not look back at that fatal man who terrified a whole province.

A few clouds darkened the sky ; vapours were rising along the horizon. We were walking through the most distressingly desolate tract of land that I have even seen ; the very soil beneath our feet seemed sickly and suffering—salt marshes, which may justly be termed the scrofula of the earth. There the ground is divided into parcels of unequal size, all enclosed by enormous heaps of grey earth, and filled with brackish water, to the surface of which the salt rises. These ravines, made by the hand of man, are subdivided by causeways along which workmen walk, armed with long rakes, with which they skim off the brine, and carry the salt to round platforms built here and there, when it is in condition to pile. For two hours we skirted that dismal chess-board, where the salt is so abundant that it chokes the vegetation, and where we saw no other living beings than an occasional *paludier*—the name given to the men who gather the salt.

These men, or rather this tribe of Bretons, wear a special costume : a white jacket not unlike that worn by brewers.   They intermarry, and there has never been an instance of a girl of that tribe marrying anybody except a *paludier*.   The ghastly aspect of those swamps, where the surface of the mire is neatly raked, and of that greyish soil, which the Breton flora hold in horror, harmonised with the mourning of our hearts.   When we reached the place where we were to cross the arm of the sea which is formed by the eruption of the water into that basin, and which serves doubtless to supply the salt marshes with their staple, we rejoiced to see the meagre vegetation scattered along the sandy shore.   As we crossed, we saw, in the centre of the lake, the islet where the Cambremers lived ; we looked the other way.

When we reached our hotel, we noticed a billiard-table in a room on the ground floor ; and, when we learned that it was the only public billiard-table in Le Croisic, we prepared for our departure that night.   The next day we were at Guérande.   Pauline was still depressed, and I could already feel the coming of the flame that is consuming my brain.   I was so cruelly tormented by my visions of those three lives that she said to me :

" Write the story, Louis ; in that way you will change the nature of this fever."

So I have written it down for you, my dear uncle ; but it has already destroyed the tranquillity that I owed to the sea-baths and to our visit here.

FACINO CANE

HONORÉ DE BALZAC

I WAS living in a small street of which doubtless you do not even know the name, the Rue des Lesdiguières.   It begins at the Rue St. Antoine opposite the fountain near the Place de la Bastille, and runs into the Rue de la Cerisaie.   The love of learning had flung me into a garret where I worked during the night, and I passed the day in a neighbouring library, the *Bibliothèque de Monsieur*.   I lived frugally.   I had accepted all those conditions of a monastic life that are so necessary to workers.   When it was fine I barely allowed myself a walk on the Boulevard Bourdon.   One passion

only drew me away from my studious habits, but was not even
that a sort of study ? I would go out to observe the manners of the
Faubourg, its inhabitants and their characters.

As badly dressed as the workmen themselves and careless about
keeping up an appearance, I did not make them in any way
suspicious of me. I could mingle freely with them, and watch
them making their bargains and quarrelling amongst themselves
as they left their work. With me the power of observation had
already become intuitive. It penetrated to the soul, without
leaving the body out of account : or rather, it grasped so well the
outer details, that it went at once beyond them ; it gave me the
power of living the life of the individual on whom I brought it
to bear, thus permitting me in fancy to substitute myself for him
as the dervish in the *Arabian Nights* took the body and soul of
the persons over whom he pronounced certain words.

When between eleven o'clock and midnight I met a workman and
his wife returning together from the Ambigu Comique, I amused
myself by following them from the Boulevard du Pont-aux-Choux
as far as the Boulevard Beaumarchais. These good people would
talk at first of the piece they had just seen. From one thing to
another they would get on to their own affairs. The mother
would be dragging her child by the hand without heeding either its
complaints or its questions. The pair would reckon up the money
that would be paid them next day, and spend it in twenty different
ways. Then came household details ; complaints as to the excessive price of potatoes, or about the length of the winter and the
dearness of peat fuel ; strong representations as to the amount
owing to the baker ; and at last disputes that became a bit angry,
and in which the character of each came out in picturesque
expressions.

While listening to these people I could enter into their life ; I felt
myself with their rags on my back ; I walked with my feet in their
broken shoes ; their desires, their needs all came into my soul, or
my soul passed into theirs. It was the dream of one who was still
wide awake. With them I grew angry against the foremen of the
workshops who tyrannised over them, or against the bad custom
that forced them to come again and again to ask in vain for their
pay. To get away from my ordinary occupations, to become some
one else by this over excitation of my mental faculties, and to
play this game at my will—this was my recreation. To what do
I owe this gift ? Is it a kind of second sight ? or is it one of those
powers the abuse of which would lead to insanity ? I have never
investigated the sources of this faculty of mine ; I possess it and
I make use of it, that is all.

I need only tell you that in those days I had analysed the elements
of that heterogeneous mass called " the people," so that I could

estimate their good and bad qualities. Already I knew all that was to be learned from that famous Faubourg, that nursery of Revolutions, which gives shelter at once to heroes, inventors, and practical scientists, and knaves and scoundrels,—to virtues and vices, all huddled together by misery, stifled by poverty, drowned in wine, wasted by strong drink. You would never imagine how many unknown adventures, how many forgotten dramas belong to that city of sorrow. How many horrible and beautiful things ! For imagination would never go so far as the reality that is hidden there, and that no one can go there and discover. One has to go down to too great a depth if one is to find out those wonderful scenes of living tragedy or comedy, masterpieces that chance has brought into being.

I know not why I have so long kept untold the story that I am going to relate to you ; it is one of those strange tales that are laid by in the bag from which memory draws them out at haphazard like the numbers of a lottery. I have plenty of others quite as singular as this one, buried away in the same fashion ; but they will have their turn, believe me.

One day my housekeeper, a working-man's wife, came and asked me to honour with my presence the wedding of one of her sisters. In order to enable you to understand what sort of a wedding it would be I must tell you that I used to pay forty sous a month to this poor creature, who came in every morning to make my bed, polish my shoes, brush my clothes, sweep the room, and get my breakfast ready. For the rest of her time she went to turn the handle of a mangle, and by this hard work earned ten sous a day. Her husband, a cabinet-maker, earned four francs.

But, as their household included three children, they could barely pay for the bread they ate. I have never come across more real respectability than that of this man and wife. Five years after I had left the neighbourhood Dame Vaillant came to wish me a happy name day, and brought me a bunch of flowers and some oranges as presents—she who had never been in a position to save ten sous. Poverty had drawn us together. I was never able to pay her more then ten francs, often borrowed for the occasion. This will explain my promise to go to the wedding ; I counted on taking an unobtrusive part in the rejoicings of these poor people.

The feast and the dance were both held at a wine shop in the Rue de Charenton, in a large room on the first storey. It was lighted with lamps with tin reflectors ; the paper showed grease spots at the level of the tables, and along the walls there were wooden benches. In this room some eighty people, dressed in their Sunday clothes, decked out with flowers and ribbons, all full of the holiday spirit, danced with flushed faces as if the world was coming to an end. The happy pair kissed each other amid a general outbreak of satisfaction, and one heard " Eh ! eh ! " and " Ah ! ah ! "

pronounced in a tone of amusement, that all the same was more respectable than the timid ogling of young women of a better class. Every one manifested a rough and ready pleasure that had in it something infectious.

But neither the general aspect of the gathering, nor the wedding, nor anything of the kind, has really to do with our story. Only I want you to keep in mind the quaint setting of it all. Imagine to yourself the shabby shop, with its decorations of red paint, smell the odour of the wine, listen to the shouts of delight, keep to the Faubourg, in the midst of these workers, these old men, these poor women abandoning themselves to one night of pleasure.

The orchestra was made up of three blind men from the Hospice des Quinze-Vingts ; the first was the violin, the second the clarionet, and the third the flageolet. All three were paid one lump sum of seven francs for the night. At this price, of course, they gave us neither Rossini nor Beethoven ; they played what they liked and what they could, and with a charming delicacy of feeling no one found fault with them for it ! Their music was such a rough trial to my ears, that, after a glance at the audience, I looked at the trio of blind men, and recognising the uniform of the hospice, I felt from the first disposed to be indulgent. These artists were seated in the deep bay of a window, and thus in order to be able to distinguish their features one had to be near them.

I did not at once come close to them ; but when I approached them I cannot say how it was, but all was over with me, I forgot the marriage and the music ; my curiosity was excited to the highest pitch, for my soul passed into the body of the clarionet player. The violin and the flageolet had both commonplace features, the well-known face of the blind, with its strained look, all attention and seriousness ; but that of the clarionet player was one of those phenomenal faces that make the artist or the philosopher stop at once to look at them.

Imagine a plaster mask of Dante, lighted up with the red glare of an Argand-lamp, and crowned with a forest of silver-white hair. His blindness added to the bitter sorrowful expression of this splendid face, for one could imagine the dead eyes were alive again ; a burning light seemed to shine out from them, the expression of a single ceaseless desire that had set its deep marks on the rounded forehead, which was scored by wrinkles like the lines of an old wall. The old man was blowing away at haphazard, without paying the least attention to time or tune, his fingers rising and falling, and moving the old keys through mere mechanical habit. He did not trouble about making what is called in the slang of the orchestra " quacks," and the dancers took no more notice of this than the two comrades of my Italian did—for I made up my mind that he must be an Italian, and an Italian he was. There was something noble and commanding to be seen in this aged Homer, who kept all to himself some Odyssey destined to forgetfulnes. It was a nobility so real that it still triumphed over his obscurity; an air of command so striking that it rose superior to his poverty.

None of the strong feelings that lead a man to good as well as to evil, that make of him a convict or a hero, were wanting to this splendidly outlined face, with its sallow Italian complexion, and the shadows of the iron-grey eyebrows that threw their shade over the deep cavities in which one would tremble at seeing the light of thought appear once more, as one fears to see brigands armed with torch and dagger show themselves at the mouth of a cavern. There was a lion in that cage of flesh, a lion of which the fury had uselessly spent itself on the iron of its bars. The fire of despair had burned out among its ashes, the lava had cooled; but rifts, fallen rocks, and a little smoke told of the violence of the eruption, the ravages of the fire. These ideas called up by the aspect of the man were as warmly pictured in my mind, as they were coldly marked upon his face.

In the interval between each dance the violin and the flageolet, becoming seriously occupied with a bottle and glasses, hung their instruments to a button of their reddish tunics, and stretched out a hand to a little table standing in the bay of the window, on which were their refreshments. They always offered the Italian a full glass, which he could not have got unaided, for the table was behind his chair. Each time the clarionet thanked them with a friendly nod of his head. Their movements were carried out with that precision which always seems so astonishing in the case of the blind folk from the Quinze-Vingts, and which seems to make one think they can see. I drew near to the three blind men to listen to them, but when I stood near them they somehow scrutinised me, and doubtless failing to recognise the workman type in me, they said not a word.

" From what country are you, you who play the clarionet ? "

" From Venice," answered the blind man, with a slight Italian accent.

" Were you born blind, or were you blinded by . . ."

" By a mishap," he replied sharply; " a cursed amaurosis in my eyes."

" Venice is a beautiful city. I have always had an idea of going there."

The face of the old man became animated, its furrows rose and fell, he was strongly moved.

" If I went there with you, you would not lose your time," said he to me.

" Don't talk of Venice to him," said the violin to me, " or our Doge will start his story. Besides that he has already two bottles under his belt, the old prince ! "

" Come, let us be getting on, Père Canard," said the flageolet.

All three began to play ; but all the time that they were going through the four parts of the quadrille the Venetian was sizing me up ; he guessed the extraordinary interest I took in him. His face lost its cold expression of sadness. Some hope or other brightened all his features—played like a blue flame in the wrinkles of his face. He smiled as he wiped his forehead—that forehead with its bold and terrible look ; finally he became quite gay, like a man who is getting up on his hobby.

" What is your age ? " I asked him.

" Eighty-two years."

" How long have you been blind ? "

" It will soon be fifty years," he replied, in a tone which suggested that his regret was not only for the loss of his sight, but also for some great power of which he had been deprived.

" But why do they call you the Doge ? " I asked him.

" Ah ! that's a joke," he said ; " I am a patrician of Venice, and I could have been a Doge as well as any one else."

" What is your name then ? "

" Here," he said, " I am old Canet. My name has never appeared otherwise on the local registers. But in Italian it is Marco Facino Cane, Prince of Varese."

" What ! Are you descended from the famous condottiere, Facino Cane, whose conquests passed into the possession of the Dukes of Milan ? "

" É vero (that's true)," said he. " In those times the son of Cane, to escape being killed by the Visconti, took refuge in Venice, and had his name inscribed in the Golden Book of nobility. But now neither the Book nor any of the House of Cane is left ! "

And he made a startling gesture to signify his feeling that patriotism was dead, and his disgust for human affairs.

" But if you were a Senator of Venice, you must have been rich. How did you come to lose your fortune ? "

At this question he raised his head, turning to me as if regarding me with a movement full of truest tragedy, and replied to me :

" In the midst of misfortunes ! "

He no longer thought of drinking ; with a wave of his hand he refused the glass of wine which the old flageolet player offered him at this moment, then he bowed down his head.

These details were not of a kind to put an end to my curiosity. During the quadrille that the three instruments played in mechanical style, I watched the old Venetian noble with the feelings that devour a man of only twenty. I saw Venice and the Adriatic, and I saw its ruin in this ruined face. I was moving about in that city so beloved of its inhabitants. I went from the Rialto to the Grand Canal, from the Riva degli Schiavoni to the Lido ; I came back to its cathedral so sublime in its originality ; I looked up at the windows of the Casa d'Oro, each of which has different ornaments ; I contemplated its old palaces, so rich in marbles—in a word, all those wonders that move the student's feelings all the more when he can colour them with his fancy, and does not spoil the poetry of his dreams by the sight of the reality.

I traced backward the course of the life of this scion of the greatest of the condottieri, seeking out in it the traces of his misfortunes and the causes of the deep physical and moral degradation that made the sparks of greatness and nobility that shone again at that moment seem all the finer. Our thoughts were no doubt in mutual accord, for I believe that blindness makes mental communication much more rapid, by preventing the attention from dispersing itself on external things. I had not long to wait for a proof of our bond of feeling. Facino Cane stopped playing, rose, came to me and said, " Come out," in a way that produced on me the effect of an electric shock. I gave him my arm and we went away.

When we were in the street, he said to me :

" Will you take me to Venice, guide me there ? Will you have confidence in me ? You will be richer than the ten richest firms of Amsterdam or London ; richer than the Rothschilds ; in a word, rich as the *Arabian Nights*."

I thought the man was mad. But there was in his voice a power that I obeyed. I let him lead me, and he took me in the direction of the ditches of the Bastille, as if he still had the use of his eyes. He sat down on a stone in a very lonely place, where, since then, the bridge has been built under which the Canal Saint Martin passes to the Seine. I took my place on another stone facing the old man whose white hairs glittered like threads of silver in the moonlight. The silence, hardly disturbed by such stormy sounds as reached us from the Boulevards, the brightness of the night, all helped to make the scene something fantastic.,

" You talk of millions to a young man, and you think that he would hesitate to endure a thousand ills to secure them ! Are you not making a jest of me ? "

" May I die without confession," said he fiercely, " if what I am about to tell you is not true ! I was once a young man of twenty as you are now. I was rich. I was handsome. I was a noble. I began with the first of all follies—love. I loved as men no longer love, going so far as to hide in a chest at the risk of being stabbed, without

having received anything else but the promise of a kiss. To die for
her seemed to me worth a whole life. In 1760 I fell in love with one
of the Vendramini, a girl of eighteen, married to a certain Sagredo,
one of the richest of the Senators, a man of thirty years, madly
devoted to his wife. My love and I, we were as innocent as two
little cherubs when the husband surprised us talking love together.
I was unarmed ; he was armed, but he missed me. I sprang on him,
I strangled him with my two hands, twisting his neck like a chicken's.
I wanted to go away with Bianca, but she would not go with me.
That's what women are like ! I went away alone. I was condemned
in my absence, my property was confiscated for the benefit of my
heirs ; but I had carried off with me my diamonds, five pictures by
Titian rolled up, and all my gold. I went to Milan, where I was not
molested, for my affair did not interest the State.

"One little remark before going on," he said, after a pause.
"Whether it is true or not that a woman's fancies influence her
child before its birth, it is certain that my mother had a passion for
gold while she was expecting mine. I have a monomania for gold,
the satisfaction of which is so necessary for my very life, that in
whatever circumstances I have been, I have never been without some
gold in my possession. I am always handling gold. When I was
young I always wore jewels, and I always carried about with me
two or three hundred ducats."

As he said these words he took two ducats out of his pocket and
showed them to me.

"I can smell gold. Although I am blind, I stop in front of the
jewellers' shops. This passion was my ruin. I became a gambler,
to have the enjoyment of gold. I was not a swindler ; I was
swindled. I ruined myself. When I had no longer any of my fortune
left I was seized with a wild longing to see Bianca again. I returned
secretly to Venice. I found her once more ; I was happy for six
months, hidden with her, supported by her. I had a delightful
thought of thus living my life to the end. Her hand was sought by
the Proveditore of the Republic. He guessed he had a rival ; in
Italy they can almost smell them ; he spied on us, and surprised us
together, the coward ! You can imagine what a sharp fight tnere was.
I did not kill him, but I wounded him seriously. That adventure
broke off my happiness. Since that day I never found any one like
Bianca. I have had many pleasures. I lived at the court of
Louis XV. in the midst of the most famous women, but nowhere
did I find the characteristics, the graces, the love of my fair
Venetian.

"The Proveditore had his followers. He called them. The palace
was surrounded. I defended myself, hoping to die before the eyes of
my dear Bianca, who helped me to kill the Proveditore. Formerly
this woman had refused to share my flight ; now, after six months of

happiness, she was ready to die my death, and received several blows. Entangled in a big cloak that they threw over me, I was rolled in it, carried to a gondola and conveyed to the dungeons of the Pozzi. I was only twenty-two years old then, and I held so fast to the fragment of my broken sword, that to get it from me they would have had to cut off my wrist. By a strange chance, or rather inspired by a thought for the future, I hid this bit of steel in a corner, in case it might be of use to me. I was given medical care. None of my wounds was mortal. At twenty-two one can recover from anything. I was doomed to die by decapitation, but I pretended to be ill in order to gain time. I believed that I was in a dungeon next to the canal. My plan was to escape by making a hole through the wall and swimming across the canal at the risk of drowning myself.

" Here are some of the reasons on which I based my hopes :

" Whenever the jailer brought me my food I read, by the light he carried, inscriptions scrawled upon the walls, such as, ' Towards the palace,' ' Towards the canal,' ' Towards the underground passage,' and at last succeeded in making out a general plan of the place. There were some small difficulties about it, but they could be explained by the actual state of the Palace of the Doges, which is not completed. With the cleverness that the desire to regain one's liberty gives one, by feeling with my fingers the surface of a stone, I succeeded in deciphering an Arabic inscription, by which the writer of the words intimated to his successors that he had loosened two stones in the lowest course of masonry, and dug beyond them eleven feet of a tunnel. In order to continue his task it was necessary to spread over the floor of the dungeon itself the little bits of stone and mortar produced by the work of excavation.

" Even if my keepers or the inquisitors had not felt quite easy in their minds on account of the very structure of the building, which made only an external surveillance necessary, the arrangement of the Pozzi dungeons, into which one descends by a few steps, made it possible gradually to raise the level of the floor without its being noticed by the jailers. The immense amount of work he had done had proved to be superfluous, at least for the man who had undertaken it, for the fact that it had been left unfinished told of the death of the unknown prisoner. In order that his zeal might not be useless for ever, it was necessary that some future prisoner should know Arabic ; but I had studied Eastern languages at the Armenian convent of Venice. A sentence written on the back of one of the stones told the fate of this unfortunate man, who had died the victim of his immense riches, which Venice had coveted, and of which she had taken possession. It took me a month to arrive at any result. Whilst I was at work, and during the intervals when I was overwhelmed with fatigue, I heard the sound of gold, I thought I could see gold before me, I was dazzled by diamonds ! . . . Oh ! just wait.

" One night, my piece of steel, now blunted, came upon wood. I sharpened my broken fragment of a sword and made a hole in the wood. In order to work I used to drag myself along like a serpent on my stomach, and I stripped so as to dig like a mole, with my hands out in front of me, stretched on the stones I had already burrowed through. In two days I was to appear before my judges, so during this night I meant to make a last effort. I cut through the wood, and my blade struck against nothing beyond it.

" Imagine my surprise when I put my eye to the hole ! I had penetrated the wainscot of an underground room, in which a dim light allowed me to see a great heap of gold. The Doge and one of the Council of Ten were in this cellar. I heard their voices. From their talk I gathered that here was the secret hoard of the Republic, the gifts of the Doges, and the reserves of booty known as the ' share of Venice,' and levied on the produce of over-sea expeditions.

" I was saved !

" When next the jailer came, I proposed to him to assist me to escape, and to go away with me, taking off with us all that we could carry. There was no reason to hesitate, and he agreed. A ship was about to sail for the Levant. Every precaution was taken. Bianca lent her aid to the plans I dictated to my accomplice. In order not to arouse suspicion Bianca was to rejoin us only at Smyrna. In a single night the hole was enlarged, and we climbed down into the secret treasury of Venice. What a night ! I saw four huge casks full of gold. In the room before that, silver was in the same profusion, piled up in two heaps, leaving a path in the middle by which to pass through the room, with the coins sloping up in piles on each side till they reached a height of five feet at the walls. I thought the jailer would go mad.

" He sang, he danced, he laughed, he cut capers among the gold. I threatened to strangle him if he wasted our time or made a noise. In his joy he did not at first notice a table on which were the diamonds. I threw myself upon it so cleverly that I was able, unseen by him, to fill with them my sailor's jacket and the pockets of my trousers. Mon Dieu ! but I did not take one-third of them. Under this table there were ingots of gold. I persuaded my comrade to fill as many sacks as we could carry with gold, pointing out to him that this was the only way in which our plunder would not lead to our being discovered abroad.

" ' Pearls, jewels, and diamonds would only lead to our being recognised,' I said to him.

" Whatever might be our eagerness for it, we could not take away more than two thousand pounds of gold, and this required six journeys through the prison to get it to the gondola. The sentinel at the water gate had been won over at the price of a sack of ten pounds of gold. As for the two gondoliers, they were under the impression that they were serving the Republic. We made our start at daybreak. When we were in the open sea, and when I remembered that night, when I recalled all the sensations I had felt, and when I saw again in imagination that vast treasure house, where, according to my estimate, I was leaving thirty millions in silver, twenty millions in gold, and many millions in diamonds, pearls, and rubies, there came upon me something like a fit of madness—I had the gold fever.

" We arranged to be put ashore at Smyrna, and there we at once embarked for France. When we were getting on board of the French ship Heaven did me the favour of ridding me of my accomplice. At the moment I did not realise the full result of this ill-natured stroke of chance, at which I rejoiced exceedingly. We were so utterly unnerved, that we had remained in a half-dazed condition without saying a word to each other, waiting till we were in safety to enjoy ourselves as we wished. It is not surprising that this rogue had his head a bit turned. You will see later on how God punished me !

" I did not feel I was safe till I had sold two-thirds of my diamonds in London and Amsterdam, and exchanged my gold dust for notes that could be cashed. For five years I hid myself in Madrid. Then, in 1770, I came to Paris under a Spanish name, and had a most brilliant career there. Bianca had died. But in the midst of my enjoyments, and when I had a fortune of six million francs at my command, I was struck with blindness. I have no doubt that this infirmity was the result of my stay in the dungeon, and of my toils when I burrowed through the stone, though perhaps my mania for seeing gold implied an abuse of the power of sight that predestined me to the loss of my eyes.

" At this time I was in love with a woman to whom I intended to unite my lot. I had told her the secret of my name. She belonged to a powerful family, and I hoped for everything from the favour shown me by Louis XV. I had put my trust in this woman, who was the friend of Madame du Barry. She advised me to consult a famous oculist in London. But after we had stayed some months in that city, the woman gave me the slip one day in Hyde Park, after having robbed me of all my fortune, and left me without any resource. For being obliged to conceal my real name, which would hand me over to the vengeance of Venice, I could not appeal to any one for help. I was afraid of Venice.

" My infirmity was taken advantage of by spies with whom this woman had surrounded me. I spare you the story of adventures worthy of Gil Blas. Then came your Revolution. I was forced to become an inmate of the Quinze-Vingts Hospice, where this creature arranged for my admission, after having kept me for two years at the Bicêtre Asylum as a lunatic. I have never been able to kill her, for I could not see to do it, and I was too poor to hire another hand. If before I lost Benedetto Capri, my jailer, I had questioned him as to the position of my dungeon, I might have ascertained exactly where the treasure lay, and returned to Venice when the Republic was annihilated by Napoleon. . . .

" However, notwithstanding my blindness, let us go back to Venice ! I will rediscover the door of the prison, I shall see the gold through its walls, I shall smell it even under waters beneath which it is buried. For the events that overthrew the power of Venice were of such a kind that the secret of this treasure must have died with Vendramino, the brother of Bianca, a Doge who I hoped would have made my peace with the Council of Ten. I wrote letters to the First Consul, I proposed an arrangement with the Emperor of Austria, but every one turned me away as a madman ! Come, let us start for Venice, let us start even if we have to beg our way ! We shall come back millionaires. We will repurchase my property and you shall be my heir. You will be Prince of Varese ! "

In my astonishment at these revelations, which in my imagination assumed all the aspect of a poem, and looking at this grey head, and the dark waters of the ditches of the Bastille, stagnant water like that of the Venetian canals, I made no reply. Facino Cane concluded doubtless that I judged him as all the rest had done with a scornful pity, and he made a gesture that expressed all the philosophy of despair.

The narration had perhaps carried him back to his days of happiness at Venice. He seized his clarionet and played in a melancholy tone a Venetian air, a barcarolle, and, as he played, he regained the skill of his first years, the talent of a patrician lover. It was something like the lament by the rivers of Babylon. But gold soon reasserted its mastery.

" That treasure ! " he said to me, " I always see it, as in a waking dream. I walk about in the midst of it. The diamonds sparkle, and I am not as blind as you think. The gold and the diamonds illuminate my darkness, the night of the last Facino Cane, for my title goes to the Memmi. Mon Dieu ! the murderer's punishment has begun soon enough ! Ave Maria. . . ."

He recited some prayers which I could not hear.

" We shall go to Venice ! " I said to him, when he rose.

" I have found a man, then ! " he exclaimed, and his face lighted up.

I gave him my arm and took him home. At the door of the Quinze-Vingts he grasped my hand, while some of the guests

from the wedding party passed on their way home with deafening
shouts.

" Shall we start to-morrow ? " said the old man.

" As soon as we have a little money."

" But we can go on foot. I will beg alms. I am strong, and
one feels young when one sees gold in front of one."

Facino Cane died that winter after two months of lingering
illness. The poor fellow had a catarrh.

VICTOR HUGO
1802–1885

CLAUDE GUEUX

CLAUDE GUEUX was a poor workman, living in Paris about eight years ago, with his mistress and child. Although his education had been neglected, and he could not even read, the man was naturally clever and intelligent, and thought deeply over matters. Winter came with its attendant miseries—want of work, want of food, want of fuel. The man, the woman, and the child were frozen and famished. The man turned thief. I know not what he stole. What signifies, as the result was the same? To the woman and child it gave three days' bread and warmth; to the man, five years' imprisonment. He was taken to Clairvaux—the abbey now converted into a prison, its cells into dungeons, and the altar itself into a pillory. This is called progress.

Claude Gueux, the honest workman, who turned thief from force of circumstances, had a countenance which impressed you—a high forehead somewhat lined with care, dark hair already streaked with grey, deep-set eyes beaming with kindness, while the lower part clearly indicated firmness mingled with self-respect. He rarely spoke, yet there was a certain dignity in the man which commanded respect and obedience. A fine character, and we shall see what society made of it.

Over the prison workshop was an inspector, who rarely forgot that he was the gaoler also to his subordinates, handing them the tools with one hand, and casting chains upon them with the other. A tyrant, never using even self-reasoning; with ideas against which there was no appeal; hard rather than firm, at times he could even be jocular—doubtless a good father, a good husband, really not vicious, but *bad*. He was one of those men who never can grasp a fresh idea, who apparently fail to be moved by any emotion; yet with hatred and rage in their hearts look like blocks of wood, heated on the one side but frozen on the other. This man's chief characteristic was obstinacy; and so proud was he of this very stubbornness that he compared himself with Napoleon—an optical delusion, like taking the mere flicker of a candle for a star. When he had made up his mind to a thing, however absurd, he would carry out that absurd idea. How often it happens, that, when a catastrophe occurs, if we inquire into the cause we find it originated through the obstinacy of one with little ability but having full faith in his own powers.

Such was the inspector of the prison workshop at Clairvaux—a man of flint placed by society over others, who hoped to strike sparks out of such material ; but a spark from a like source is apt to end in a conflagration.

The inspector soon singled out Claude Gueux, who had been numbered and placed in the workshop, and, finding him clever, treated him well. Seeing Claude looking sad (for he was ever thinking of her he termed his wife), and being in a good humour, by way of pastime to console the prisoner he told him the woman had become one of the unfortunate sisterhood, and had been reduced to infamy ; of the child nothing was known.

After a time Claude had accustomed himself to prison rule, and by his calmness of manner and a certain amount of resolution clearly marked in his face, he had acquired a great ascendency over his companions, who so much admired him that they asked his advice, and tried in all ways to imitate him. The very expression in his eyes clearly indicated the man's character ; besides, is not the eye the window of the soul, and what other result could be anticipated than that the intelligent spirit should lead men with few ideas, who yield to the attraction as the metal does to the lodestone ? In less than three months Claude was the virtual head of the workshop, and at times he almost doubted whether he was king or prisoner, being treated something like a captive Pope, surrounded by his Cardinals.

Such popularity ever has its attendant hatred ; and though beloved by the prisoners, Claude was detested by the gaolers. To him two men's rations would have been scarcely sufficient. The inspector laughed at this, as his own appetite was large ; but what would be mirth to a duke, to a prisoner would be a great misfortune. When a free man, Claude Gueux could earn his daily four-pound loaf and enjoy it ; but as a prisoner he daily worked, and for his labour received one pound and a half of bread and four ounces of meat : it naturally followed that he was always hungry.

He had just finished his meagre fare, and was about to resume his labours, hoping in work to forget famine, when a weakly-looking young man came toward him, holding a knife and his untasted rations in his hand, but seemingly afraid to address him.

" What do you want ? " said Claude, roughly.

" A favour at your hands," timidly replied the young man.

" What is it ? " said Claude.

" Help me with my rations ; I have more than I can eat."

For a moment Claude was taken aback, but without further ceremony he divided the food in two and at once partook of one-half.

"Thank you," said the young man; "allow me to share my rations with you every day."

"What is your name?" said Claude.

"Albin."

"Why are you here?" added Claude.

"I robbed."

"So did I," said Claude.

The same scene took place daily between this man old before his time (he was only thirty-six) and the boy of twenty, who looked at the most seventeen. The feeling was more like that of father and son than one brother to another; everything created a bond of union between them—the very toil they endured together, the fact of sleeping in the same quarters and taking exercise in the same courtyard. They were happy, for were they not all the world to each other? The inspector of the workshop was so hated by the prisoners that he often had recourse to Claude Gueux to enforce his authority; and when a tumult was on the point of breaking out, a few words from Claude had more effect than the authority of ten warders. Although the inspector was glad to avail himself of this influence, he was jealous all the same, and hated the superior prisoner with an envious and implacable feeling—an example of might over right, all the more fearful as it was secretly nourished. But Claude cared so much for Albin that he thought little about the inspector.

One morning as the warders were going their rounds one of them summoned Albin, who was working with Claude, to go before the inspector.

"What are you wanted for?" said Claude.

"I do not know," replied Albin, following the warder.

All day Claude looked in vain for his companion, and at night, finding him still absent, he broke through his ordinary reserve and addressed the turnkey. "Is Albin ill?" said he.

"No," replied the man.

"How is it that he has never put in an appearance to-day?"

"His quarters have been changed," was the reply.

For a moment Claude trembled, then calmly continued, "Who gave the order?"

"Monsieur D——." This was the inspector's name.

On the following night the inspector, Monsieur D——, went his rounds as usual. Claude, who had perceived him from the distance, rose, and hastened to raise his woollen cap and button his grey woollen vest to the throat—considered a mark of respect to superiors in prison discipline.

" Sir," said Claude, as the inspector was about to pass him,
" has Albin really been quartered elsewhere ? "

" Yes," replied the inspector.

" Sir, I cannot live without him. You know the rations are
insufficient for me, and Albin divided his portion with me. Could
you not manage to let him resume his old place near me ? "

" Impossible ; the order cannot be revoked."

" By whom was it given ? "

" By me."

" Monsieur D——," replied Claude, " on you my life
depends."

" I never cancel an order once given."

" Sir, what have I ever done to you ? "

" Nothing."

" Why, then," cried Claude, " separate me from Albin ? "

" Because I do," replied the inspector, and with that he passed on.

Claude's head sank down, like the poor caged lion deprived of
his dog ; but the grief, though so deeply felt, in no way changed
his appetite—he was famished. Many offered to share their rations
with him, but he steadily refused, and continued his usual routine
in silence—breaking it only to ask the inspector daily, in tones of
anguish mingled with rage, something between a prayer and a
threat, these two words : " And Albin ? "

The inspector simply passed on, shrugging his shoulders ; but
had he only observed Claude he would have seen the evident
change, noticeable to all present, and he would have heard these
words, spoken respectfully but firmly :

" Sir, listen to me ; send my companion to me. It would be
wise to do so, I can assure you. Remember my words ! "

On Sunday he had sat for hours in the courtyard, with his head
bowed in his hands, and when a prisoner called Faillette came up
laughing, Claude said : " I am judging some one."

On October 25, 1831, as the inspector went his rounds, Claude,
to draw his attention, smashed a watch-glass he had found in the
passage. This had the desired effect.

" It was I," said Claude. " Sir, restore my comrade to me."

" Impossible," was the answer.

Looking the inspector full in the face, Claude firmly added :
" Now, reflect ! To-day is the 25th of October ; I give you till
the 4th of November."

A warder remarked that Claude was threatening Monsieur D——,
and ought at once to be locked up.

" No, it is not a case of blackhole," replied the inspector, smiling
disdainfully ; " we must be considerate with people of this stamp."

The following day Claude was again accosted by one of the
prisoners named Pernot, as he was brooding in the courtyard.

" Well, Claude, you are sad indeed ; what are you pondering
over ? "

" I fear some evil threatens that good Monsieur D——," answered
Claude.

Claude daily impressed the fact on the inspector how much
Albin's absence affected him, but with no result save four-and-
twenty hours' solitary confinement.

On the 4th of November he looked round his cell for the little
that remained to remind him of his former life. A pair of scissors,
and an old volume of the *Émile*, belonging to the woman he had
loved so well, the mother of his child—how useless to a man who
could neither work nor read !

As Claude walked down the old cloisters, so dishonoured by its
new inmates and its fresh whitewashed walls, he noticed how
earnestly the convict Ferrari was looking at the heavy iron bars
that crossed the window, and he said to him : " To-night I will
cut through these bars with these scissors," pointing to the pair
he still held in his hand.

Ferrari laughed incredulously, and Claude joined in the mirth.
During the day he worked with more than ordinary ardour, wishing
to finish a straw hat, which he had been paid for in advance by
a tradesman at Troyes—M. Bressier.

Shortly before noon he made some excuse to go down into the
carpenters' quarters, a storey below his own, at the time the warders
were absent.   Claude received a hearty welcome, as he was equally
popular here as elsewhere.

" Can any one lend me an axe ? " he said.

" What for ? "

Without exacting any promises of secrecy he at once replied :
" To kill the inspector with to-night."

Claude was at once offered several ; choosing the smallest, he hid
it beneath his waistcoat and left. Now, there were twenty-seven
prisoners present, and not one of those men betrayed him ; they
even refrained from talking upon the subject among themselves,
waiting for the terrible event which must follow.

As Claude passed on, seeing a young convict of sixteen yawning
idly there, he strongly advised him to learn how to read. Just
then Faillette asked what he was hiding.

Claude answered unhesitatingly : " An axe to kill Monsieur
D—— to-night ; but can you see it ? "

" A little," said Faillette.

At seven o'clock the prisoners were locked in their several workshops.   It was then the custom for the warders to leave them,
until the inspector had been his rounds.

In Claude's workshop a most extraordinary scene took place, the
only one of the kind on record.   Claude rose and addressed his

companions, eighty-four in number, in the following words :

" You all know Albin and I were like brothers. I liked him at first for sharing his rations with me, afterwards because he cared for me. Now I never have sufficient, though I spend the pittance I earn in bread. It could make no possible difference to the inspector, Monsieur D——, that we should be together ; but he chose to separate us simply from a love of tormenting, for he is a bad man. I asked again and again for Albin to be sent back, without success ; and when I gave him a stated time, the 4th November, I was thrust into a dungeon. During that time I became his judge, and sentenced him to death on November the 4th. In two hours he will be here, and I warn you I intend to kill him. But have you anything to say ? "

There was a dead silence. Claude then continued telling his comrades, the eighty-four thieves, his ideas on the subject—that he was reduced to a fearful extremity, and compelled by that very necessity to take the law into his own hands ; that he knew full well he could not take the inspector's life without sacrificing his own, but that as the cause was a just one he would bear the consequences, having come to this conclusion after two months' calm reflection ; that if they considered resentment alone hurried him on to such a step they were at once to say so, and to state their objections to the sentence being carried out.

One voice alone broke the silence which followed, saying, " Before killing the inspector, Claude ought to give him a chance of relenting."

" That is but just," said Claude, " and he shall have the benefit of the doubt."

Claude then sorted the few things a poor prisoner is allowed, and gave them to the comrades he mostly cared for after Albin, keeping only the pair of scissors. He then embraced them all—some not being able to withhold their tears at such a moment. Claude continued calmly to converse during this last hour, and even gave way to a trick he had as a boy, of extinguishing the candle with a breath from his nose. Seeing him thus, his companions afterward owned that they hoped he had abandoned his sinister idea. One young convict looked at him fixedly, trembling for the coming event.

" Take courage, young fellow," said Claude, gently ; " it will be but the work of a minute."

The workship was a long room with a door at both ends, and with windows each side overlooking the benches, thus leaving a pathway up the centre for the inspector to review the work on both sides of him. Claude had now resumed his work—something like Jacques Clement, who did not fail to repeat his prayers.

As the clock sounded the last quarter to nine, Claude rose and placed himself near the entrance, apparently calm. Amid the most profound silence the clocks struck nine ; the door was thrown open, and the inspector came in as usual alone, looking quite jovial and self-satisfied, passing rapidly along, tossing his head at one ; grinding words out to another, little heeding the eyes fixed so fiercely upon him. Just then he heard Claude's step, and turning quickly around said ;

 "What are you doing here ? Why are you not in your place ? " just as he would have spoken to a dog.

Claude answered respectfully, " I wish to speak to you, sir."

" On what subject ? "

" Albin."

" Again ! "

" Always the same," said Claude.

" So then," replied the inspector, walking along, " you have not had enough with twenty-four hours in the blackhole."

Claude, following him closely, replied : " Sir, return my companion to me ! "

" Impossible ? "

" Sir," continued Claude, in a voice which would have moved Satan, " I implore you to send Albin back to me ; you will then see how I will work. You are free, and it would matter but little to you ; you do not know the feeling of having only one friend. To me it is everything, encircled by the prison walls. You can come and go at your pleasure ; I have but Albin. Pray let him come back to me ! You know well he shared his food with me. What can it matter to you that a man named Claude Gueux should be in this hall, having another by his side called Albin ? You have but to say ' Yes,' nothing more. Sir, my good sir, I implore you in the name of Heaven to grant my prayer ! "

Claude, overcome with emotion, waited for the answer.

" Impossible ! " replied the inspector, impatiently ; " I will not recall my words. Now go, you annoyance ! " And with that he hurried on toward the outer door, amid the breathless silence maintained by the eighty-four thieves.

Claude, following and touching the inspector, gently asked :

" Let me at least know why I am condemned to death. Why did you separate us ? "

" I have already answered you : because I chose," replied the inspector.

With that he was about to lift the latch, when Claude raised the axe, and without one cry the inspector fell to the ground, with his skull completely cloven from three heavy blows dealt with the rapidity of lightning. A fourth completely disfigured his face, and Claude, in his mad fury, gave another and a useless blow ; for the inspector was dead.

Claude, throwing the axe aside, cried out, " Now for the other ! "

The other was himself ; and taking the scissors, *his wife's*, he plunged them into his breast. But the blade was short, and the chest was deep, and vainly he strove to give the fatal blow. At last, covered with blood, he fell fainting across the dead. Which of the two would be considered the victim ?

When Claude recovered consciousness he was in bed, surrounded by every care and covered with bandages. Near him were Sisters of Charity, and a recorder, ready to take down his deposition, who with much interest inquired how he was. Claude had lost a great deal of blood ; but the scissors had done him a bad turn, inflicting wounds not one of which was dangerous : the only mortal blows he had struck were on the body of Monsieur D——. Then the interrogator commenced.

" Did you kill the inspector of the prison workshops at Clairvaux ? "

" Yes," was the reply.

" Why did you do so ? "

" Because I did."

Claude's wounds assumed a more serious aspect, and he was prostrated with a fever which threatened his life. November, December, January, February passed, in nursing and preparations, and Claude in turn was visited by doctor and judge—the one to restore him to health, the other to glean the evidence needful to send him to the scaffold.

On the 16th of March, 1832, perfectly cured, Claude appeared in court at Troyes, to answer the charge brought against him. His appearance impressed the court favourably ; he had been shaved and stood bareheaded, but still clad in prison garb. The court was well guarded by a strong military guard, to keep the witnesses within bounds, as they were all convicts.

But an unexpected difficulty occurred : not one of these men would give evidence ; neither questions nor threats availed to make them break their silence, until Claude requested them to do so. Then they in turn gave a faithful account of the terrible event ; and if one, from forgetfulness or affection for the accused, failed to relate the whole facts, Claude supplied the deficiency. At one time the women's tears fell fast.

The usher now called the convict Albin. He came in trembling with emotion and sobbing painfully, and threw himself into Claude's arms. Turning to the Public Prosecutor, Claude said :

" Here is a convict who gives his food to the hungry," and stooping, he kissed Albin's hand.

All the witnesses having been examined, the counsel for the prosecution then rose to address the court. " Gentlemen of the jury, society would be utterly put to confusion if a public prosecution did not condemn great culprits like him, who," etc.

After the long address by the prosecution, Claude's counsel rose. Then followed the usual pleading for and against, which ever takes place at the criminal court.

Claude in his turn gave evidence, and every one was astonished at his intelligence; there appeared far more of the orator about this poor workman than the assassin. In a clear and straightforward way he detailed the facts as they were—standing proudly there, resolved to tell the whole truth. At times the crowd was carried away by his eloquence. This man, who could not read, would grasp the most difficult points of argument, yet treat the judges with all due deference. Once Claude lost his temper, when the counsel for the prosecution stated that he had assassinated the inspector without provocation.

" What ! " cried Claude, " I had no provocation ? Indeed ! A drunkard strikes me—I kill him ; then you would allow there was provocation, and the penalty of death would be changed for that of the galleys. But a man who wounds me in every way during four years, humiliates me for four years, taunts me daily, hourly, for four years, and heaps every insult on my head—what follows ? You consider I had no provocation ! I had a wife for whom I robbed—he tortured me about her. I had a child for whom I robbed—he taunted me about this child. I was hungry, a friend shared his bread with me—he took away my friend. I begged him to return my friend to me—he cast me into a dungeon. I told him how much I suffered—he said it wearied him to listen. What then would you have me do ? I took his life ; and you look upon me as a monster for killing this man, and you decapitate me ; then do so."

Provocation such as this the law fails to acknowledge, because the blows leave no marks to show.

The judge then summed up the case in a clear and impartial manner, dwelling on the life Claude had led, living openly with an improper character ; then he had robbed, and ended by being a murderer. All this was true. Before the jury retired, the judge asked Claude if he had any questions to ask, or anything to say.

"Very little," said Claude. " I am a murderer, I am a thief ; but I ask you, gentlemen of this jury, why did I kill ? Why did I steal ? "

The jury retired for a quarter of an hour, and according to the judgment of these twelve countrymen—*gentlemen of the jury*, as they are styled—Claude Gueux was condemned to death. At the very outset several of them were much impressed with the name of Gueux (vagabond), and that influenced their decision.

When the verdict was pronounced, Claude simply said : " Very well ; but there are two questions these gentlemen have not answered. Why did this man steal ? What made him a murderer ? "

He made a good supper that night, exclaiming, " Thirty-six years have now passed me." He refused to make any appeal until the last minute, but at the instance of one of the sisters who nursed him he consented to do so. She in her fulness of heart gave him a five-franc piece.

His fellow-prisoners, as we have already noticed, were devoted to him, and placed all the means at their disposal to help him to escape. They threw into his dungeon, through the air-hole, a nail, some wire, the handle of a pail : any one of these would have been enough for a man like Claude to free himself from his chains. He gave them all up to the warder.

On the 8th of June, 1832, seven months and four days after the murder, the recorder of the court came, and Claude was told that he had but one hour more to live, for his appeal had been rejected.

" Indeed," said Claude, coldly ; " I slept well last night, and doubtless I shall pass my next even better."

First came the priest, then the executioner. He was humble to the priest, and listened to him with great attention, regretting much that he had not had the benefit of religious training, at the same time blaming himself for much in the past. He was courteous in his manner to the executioner ; in fact he gave up all—his soul to the priest, his body to the executioner.

While his hair was being cut, some one mentioned how the cholera was spreading, and Troyes at any moment might become a prey to this fearful scourge. Claude joined in the conversation, saying, with a smile, " There is one thing to be said—I have no fear of the cholera ! " He had broken half of the scissors—what remained he asked the jailor to give to Albin ; the other half lay buried in his chest. He also wished the day's rations to be taken to his friend. The only trifle he retained was the five franc piece that the sister had given him, which he kept in his right hand after he was bound.

At a quarter to eight the dismal procession usual in such cases left the prison. Pale, but with a firm tread, Claude Gueux slowly mounted the scaffold, keeping his eyes fixed on the crucifix the priest carried—an emblem of the Saviour's suffering. He wished to embrace the priest and the executioner, thanking the one and pardoning the other ; the executioner simply repulsed him. Just before he was bound to the infernal machine he gave the five-franc piece to the priest, saying, " For the poor."

The hour had scarcely struck its eight chimes when this man, so noble, so intelligent, received the fatal blow which severed his head from his body.

A market-day had been chosen for the time of execution, as there would be more people about ; for there are still in France small towns that glory in having an execution. The guillotine that day remained, inflaming the imagination of the mob to such an extent that one of the tax-gatherers was nearly murdered. Such is the admirable effect of public executions !

We have given the history of Claude Gueux's life, more to solve a difficult problem than for aught else. In his life there are two questions to be considered—before his fall and after his fall. What was his training and what was the penalty ? This must interest society generally ; for this man was well gifted, his instincts were good. Then what was wanting ? On this revolves the grand problem which would place society on a firm basis.

What Nature has begun in the individual, let society carry out. Look at Claude Gueux. An intelligent and most noble-hearted man, placed in the midst of evil surroundings, he turned thief. Society placed him in a prison where the evil was yet greater, and he ended with becoming a murderer. Can we really blame him, or ourselves ?—questions which require deep thought, or the result will be that we shall be compelled to shirk this most important subject. The facts are now before us, and if the government gives no thought to the matter, what are the rulers about ? . . .

JENNY

VICTOR HUGO

I

IT was night. The cabin, poor, but warm and cosy, was full of a half-twilight, through which the objects of the interior were but dimly visible by the glimmer of the embers which flickered on the hearth and reddened the dark rafters overhead. The fisherman's nets were hanging on the wall. Some homely pots and pans twinkled on a rough shelf in the corner. Beside a great bed with long, falling curtains, a mattress was extended on a couple of old benches, on which five little children were asleep like cherubs in a nest. By the bedside, with her forehead pressed against the counterpane, knelt the children's mother. She was alone. Outside the cabin the black ocean, dashed with stormy foam-flakes, moaned and murmured, and her husband was at sea.

From his boyhood he had been a fisherman. His life, as one may say, had been a daily fight with the great waters ; for every day the children must be fed, and every day, rain, wind, or tempest, out went his boat to fish. And while, in his four-sailed boat, he plied his solitary task at sea, his wife at home patched the old sails, mended the nets, looked to the hooks, or watched the little fire, where the fish-soup was boiling. As soon as the five children were asleep, she fell upon her knees and prayed to Heaven for her husband in his struggle with the waves and darkness. And truly such a life as his was hard. The likeliest place for fish was a mere speck among the breakers, not more than twice as large as his own cabin—a spot obscure, capricious, changing on the moving desert, and yet which had to be discovered in the fog and tempest of a winter night, by sheer skill and knowledge of the tides and winds. And there—while the gliding waves ran past like emerald serpents, and the gulf of darkness rolled and tossed, and the straining rigging groaned as if in terror—there, amidst the icy seas, he thought of his own Jenny; and Jenny, in her cottage, thought of him with tears.

She was thinking of him then and praying. The sea-gull's harsh and mocking cry distressed her, and the roaring of the billows on the reef alarmed her soul. But she was wrapped in thoughts—thoughts of their poverty. Their little children went bare-footed winter and summer. Wheatbread they never ate ; only bread of barley. Heavens ! the wind roared like the bellows of a forge, and the sea-coast echoed like an anvil. She wept and trembled. Poor wives whose husbands are at sea ! How terrible to say, " My dear ones—father, lover, brothers, sons—are in the tempest." But Jenny was still more unhappy. Her husband was alone—alone without assistance on this bitter night. Her children were too little to assist him. Poor mother ! Now she says, " I wish they were grown up to help their father." Foolish dream ! In years to come, when they are with their father in the tempest, she will say with tears, " I wish they were but children still."

II

Jenny took her lantern and her cloak. " It is time," she said to herself, " to see whether he is coming back, whether the sea is calmer, and whether the light is burning on the signal-mast." She went out. There was nothing to be seen—barely a streak of white on the horizon. It was raining, the dark, cold rain of early morning. No cabin window showed a gleam of light.

All at once, while peering round her, her eyes perceived a tumble-down old cabin which showed no sign of light or fire. The door was swinging in the wind ; the worm-eaten walls seemed scarcely able to support the crazy roof, on which the wind shook the yellow, filthy tufts of rotten thatch.

" Stay," she cried, " I am forgetting the poor widow whom my husband found the other day alone and ill. I must see how she is getting on."

She knocked at the door and listened. No one answered. Jenny shivered in the cold sea-wind.

" She is ill. And her poor children ! She has only two of them ; but she is very poor, and has no husband."

She knocked again, and called out, " Hey, neighbour ! " But the cabin was still silent.

" Heaven ! " she said, " how sound she sleeps, that it requires so much to wake her."

At that instant the door opened of itself. She entered. Her lantern illumined the interior of the dark and silent cabin, and showed her the water falling from the ceiling as through the openings of a sieve. At the end of the room an awful form was lying : a woman stretched out motionless, with bare feet and sightless eyes. Her cold white arm hung down among the straw of the pallet. She was dead. Once a strong and happy mother, she was now only the spectre which remains of poor humanity, after a long struggle with the world.

Near the bed on which the mother lay, two little children—a boy and a girl—slept together in their cradle, and were smiling in their dreams. Their mother, when she felt that she was dying, had laid her cloak across their feet and wrapt them in her dress, to keep them warm when she herself was cold.

How sound they slept in their old, tottering cradle, with their calm breath and quiet little faces ! It seemed as if nothing could awake these sleeping orphans. Outside, the rain beat down in floods, and the sea gave forth a sound like an alarm bell. From the old creviced roof, through which blew the gale, a drop of water fell on the dead face, and ran down it like a tear.

III

What had Jenny been about in the dead woman's house ? What was she carrying off beneath her cloak ? Why was her heart beating ? Why did she hasten with such trembling steps to her own cabin, without daring to look back. What did she hide in her own bed, behind the curtain ? What had she been stealing ?

When she entered the cabin, the cliffs were growing white. She sank upon the chair beside the bed. She was very pale ; it seemed as if she felt repentance. Her forehead fell upon the pillow, and at intervals, with broken words, she murmured to herself, while outside the cabin moaned the savage sea.

" My poor man ! O Heavens, what will he say ? He has already so much trouble. What have I done now ? Five children on our hands already ! Their father toils and toils, and yet as if he had not care enough already, I must give him this care more. Is that he ? No, nothing. I have done wrong—he would do quite right to beat me. Is that he ? No ! So much the better. The door moves as if someone were coming in ; but no. To think that I should feel afraid to see him enter ! "

Then she remained absorbed in thought, and shivering with the cold, unconscious of all outward sounds, of the black cormorants, which passed shrieking, and of the rage of wind and sea.

All at once the door flew open, a streak of the white light of morning entered, and the fisherman, dragging his dripping net, appeared upon the threshold, and cried, with a gay laugh, " Here comes the Navy."

" You ! " cried Jenny ; and she clasped her husband like a lover, and pressed her mouth against his rough jacket.

" Here I am, wife," he said, showing in the firelight the good-natured and contented face which Jenny loved so well.

" I have been unlucky," he continued.

" What kind of weather have you had ? "

" Dreadful."

" And the fishing ? "

" Bad. But never mind. I have you in my arms again, and I am satisfied. I have caught nothing at all, I have only torn my net. The deuce was in the wind to-night. At one moment of the tempest I thought the boat was foundering, and the cable broke. But what have you been doing all this time ? "

Jenny felt a shiver in the darkness.

" I ? " she said, in trouble. " Oh, nothing ; just as usual. I have been sewing. I have been listening to the thunder of the sea, and I was frightened."

" Yes ; the winter is a hard time. But never mind it now."

Then, trembling as if she were going to commit a crime :

" Husband ! " she said, " our neighbour is dead. She must have died last night, soon after you went out. She has left two little children, one called William and the other Madeline. The boy can hardly toddle, and the girl can only lisp. The poor, good woman was in dreadful want."

The man looked grave. Throwing into a corner his fur cap sodden by the tempest : " The deuce," he said, scratching his head. " We already have five children ; this makes seven. And already in bad weather we have to go without our supper. What shall we do now ? Bah, it is not my fault ; it's God's doing. These are things too deep for me. Why has He taken away their mother from these mites ? These matters are too difficult to understand. One has to be a scholar to see through them. Such tiny scraps of children ! Wife, go and fetch them. If they are awake, they must be frightened to be alone with their dead mother. We will bring them up with ours. They will be brother and sister to our five. When God sees that we have to feed this little girl and boy besides our own, He will let us take more fish. As for me, I will drink water. I will work twice as hard. Enough. Be off and bring them ! But what is the matter ? Does it vex you ? You are generally quicker than this."

His wife drew back the curtain.

" Look ! " she said.

PROSPER MÉRIMÉE
1803–1870

THE TAKING OF THE REDOUBT

A FRIEND of mine, a soldier, who died in Greece of fever some years since, described to me one day his first engagement. His story so impressed me that I wrote it down from memory. It was as follows :—

I joined my regiment on September 4. It was evening. I found the colonel in the camp. He received me rather brusquely, but having read the general's introductory letter he changed his manner, and addressed me courteously.

By him I was presented to my captain, who had just come in from reconnoitring. This captain, whose acquaintance I had scarcely time to make, was a tall, dark man, of harsh, repelling aspect. He had been a private soldier, and had won his cross and epaulettes upon the field of battle. His voice, which was hoarse and feeble, contrasted strangely with his gigantic stature. This voice of his he owed, as I was told, to a bullet which had passed completely through his body at the battle of Jena.

On learning that I had just come from college at Fontainebleau, he remarked, with a wry face, " My lieutenant died last night."

I understood what he implied—" It is for you to take his place, and you are good for nothing."

A sharp retort was on my tongue, but I restrained it.

The moon was rising behind the redoubt of Cheverino, which stood two cannon-shots from our encampment. The moon was large and red, as is common at her rising ; but that night she seemed to me of extraordinary size. For an instant the redoubt stood out coal-black against the glittering disk. It resembled the cone of a volcano at the moment of eruption.

An old soldier, at whose side I found myself, observed the colour of the moon.

" She is very red," he said. " It is a sign that it will cost us dear to win this wonderful redoubt."

I was always superstitious, and this piece of augury, coming at that moment, troubled me. I sought my couch, but could not sleep. I rose, and walked about awhile, watching the long line of fires upon the heights beyond the village of Cheverino.

When the sharp night air had thoroughly refreshed my blood I went back to the fire. I rolled my mantle round me, and I shut my eyes, trusting not to open them till daybreak. But sleep refused to visit me. Insensibly my thoughts grew doleful. I told myself that I had not a friend among the hundred thousand men who filled that plain. If I were wounded, I should be placed in hospital, in the hands of ignorant and careless surgeons. I called to mind what I had heard of operations. My heart beat violently, and I mechanically arranged, as a kind of rude cuirass, my handkerchief and pocket-book upon my breast. Then, over-powered with weariness, my eyes closed drowsily, only to open the next instant with a start at some new thought of horror.

Fatigue, however, at last gained the day. When the drums beat at daybreak I was fast asleep. We were drawn up in rank. The roll was called, then we stacked our arms, and everything announced that we should pass another uneventful day.

But about three o'clock an aide-de-camp arrived with orders. We were commanded to take arms.

Our sharp-shooters marched into the plain. We followed slowly, and in twenty minutes we saw the outposts of the Russians falling back and entering the redoubt. We had a battery of artillery on our right, another on our left, but both some distance in advance of us. They opened a sharp fire upon the enemy, who returned it briskly, and the redoubt of Cheverino was soon concealed by volumes of thick smoke. Our regiment was almost covered from the Russians' fire by a piece of rising ground. Their bullets (which besides were rarely aimed at us, for they preferred to fire upon our cannoneers) whistled over us, or at worst knocked up a shower of earth and stones.

Just as the order to advance was given, the captain looked at me intently. I stroked my sprouting moustache with an air of unconcern ; in truth, I was not frightened, and only dreaded lest I might be thought so. These passing bullets aided my heroic coolness, while my self-respect assured me that the danger was a real one, since I was veritably under fire. I was delighted at my self-possession, and already looked forward to the pleasure of describing in Parisian drawing-rooms the capture of the redoubt of Cheverino.

The colonel passed before our company. "Well," he said to me, "you are going to see warm work in your first action."

I gave a martial smile, and brushed my cuff, on which a bullet, which had struck the earth at thirty paces distant, had cast a little dust.

It appeared that the Russians had discovered that their bullets did no harm, for they replaced them by a fire of shells, which began to reach us in the hollows where we lay. One of these, in its explosion, knocked off my shako and killed a man beside me.

" I congratulate you," said the captain, as I picked up my shako. " You are safe now for the day."

I knew the military superstition which believes that the axiom *non bis in idem* is as applicable to the battlefield as to the courts of justice. I replaced my shako with a swagger.

" That's a rude way to make one raise one's hat," I said, as lightly as I could. And this wretched piece of wit was, in the circumstances, received as excellent.

" I compliment you," said the captain. " You will command a company to-night ; for I shall not survive the day. Every time I have been wounded the officer below me has been touched by some spent ball ; and," he added, in a lower tone, " all their names began with P."

I laughed sceptically ; most people would have done the same ; but most would also have been struck, as I was, by these prophetic words. But, conscript though I was, I felt that I could trust my thoughts to no one, and that it was my duty to seem always calm and bold.

At the end of half an hour the Russian fire had sensibly diminished. We left our cover to advance on the redoubt.

Our regiment was composed of three battalions. The second had to take the enemy in flank ; the two others formed the storming party. I was in the third.

On issuing from behind the cover, we were received by several volleys, which did but little harm. The whistling of the balls amazed me. " But after all," I thought, " a battle is less terrible than I expected."

We advanced at a smart run, our musketeers in front. All at once the Russians uttered three hurrahs—three distinct hurrahs—and then stood silent, without firing.

" I don't like that silence," said the captain. " It bodes no good."

I began to think our people were too eager. I could not help comparing, mentally, their shouts and clamour with the striking silence of the enemy.

We quickly reached the foot of the redoubt. The palisades were broken and the earthworks shattered by our balls. With a roar of " Vive l'Empereur ! " our soldiers rushed across the ruins.

I raised my eyes. Never shall I forget the sight which met my view. The smoke had mostly lifted, and remained suspended, like a canopy, at twenty feet above the redoubt. Through a bluish mist could be perceived, behind their shattered parapet, the Russian Grenadiers, with rifles lifted, as motionless as statues. I can see them still—the left eye of every soldier glaring at us, the right hidden by his lifted gun. In an embrasure, at a few feet distant, a man with a fusee stood by a cannon.

I shuddered. I believed that my last hour had come.

"Now for the dance to open!" cried the captain. These were the last words I heard him speak.

There came from the redoubt a roll of drums. I saw the muzzles lowered. I shut my eyes; I heard a most appalling crash of sound, to which succeeded groans and cries. Then I looked up, amazed to find myself still living. The redoubt was once more wrapped in smoke. I was surrounded by the dead and wounded. The captain was extended at my feet; a ball had carried off his head, and I was covered with his blood. Of all the company, only six men, except myself, remained erect.

This carnage was succeeded by a kind of stupor. The next instant the colonel, with his hat on his sword's point, had scaled the parapet with a cry of " Vive l'Empereur ! " The survivors followed him. All that succeeded is to me a kind of dream. We rushed into the redoubt, I know not how; we fought hand to hand in the midst of smoke so thick that no man could perceive his enemy. I found my sabre dripping blood; I heard a shout of " Victory "; and, in the clearing smoke, I saw the earthworks piled with dead and dying. The cannons were covered with a heap of corpses. About two hundred men in the French uniform were standing, without order, loading their muskets or wiping their bayonets. Eleven Russian prisoners were with them.

The colonel was lying, bathed in blood, upon a broken cannon. A group of soldiers crowded round him. I approached them.

"Who is the oldest captain ? " he was asking of a sergeant.

The sergeant shrugged his shoulders most expressively.

"Who is the oldest lieutenant ? "

"This gentleman, who came last night," replied the sergeant, calmly.

The colonel smiled bitterly.

"Come, sir," he said to me, " you are now in chief command. Fortify the gorge of the redoubt at once with waggons, for the enemy is out in force. But General C—— is coming to support you."

"Colonel," I asked him, " are you badly wounded ? "

"Pish, my dear fellow ! The redoubt is taken ! "

MATEO FALCONE

Prosper Mérimée

Going out of Porto-Vecchio and turning north-west, towards the interior of the island, you see the land rise pretty sharply, and, after a three hours' walk along winding paths, obstructed by great

lumps of rock, and sometimes cut by ravines, you reach the edge
of a most extensive bush country—the *mâquis*. The *mâquis* is the
home of the Corsican shepherds and of whoever is in trouble with
the police. You must know that the Corsican peasant, to save himself the trouble of manuring, sets fire to a stretch of wood ; if the
flames spread further than is necessary, so much the worse ; but
whatever happens, he is sure of a good harvest from sowing on this
ground, fertilised by the ashes of the trees it bore. When the corn has
been gathered (they leave the straw, which would be a trouble to
collect), the tree roots, which have stayed in the ground without
wasting away, put forth very heavy shoots in the following spring,
which in a few years reach a height of seven or eight feet. It is this
species of close thicket that they call the *mâquis*. It is made up of
different kinds of trees and shrubs mixed and entangled as God wills.
Only with a hatchet in his hand can a man open himself a way
through, and there are *mâquis* so thick and bushy that the wild
rams themselves are unable to penetrate them.

If you have killed a man, go into the *mâquis* of Porto-Vecchio, and
you will live there in safety, with a good gun, powder and shot ; you
must not forget a brown cloak with a hood to it, that will serve as
covering and mattress. The shepherds give you milk, cheese, and
chestnuts, and you will have nothing to fear from the law, or the
dead man's relations, except when you have to go down into the
town to renew your stock of ammunition.

Mateo Falcone, when I was in Corsica, had his house half a
league's distance from the *mâquis*. He was a fairly rich man in the
countryside ; living as a gentleman, that is to say, without doing
anything, on the produce of his flocks, that shepherds, a kind of
nomads, pastured here and there over the mountains. When I saw
him, two years after the incident I am about to relate to you, he
seemed to me fifty years old at most. Imagine a man small but
sturdy, with crisp hair, black as jet, large quick eyes, and a complexion the colour of boot-leather. His skill with the gun passed
for extraordinary, even in his country, where there are so many
good shots. For example, Mateo would never fire at a wild ram with
buck-shot ; at a hundred and twenty paces, he would bring it down
with a bullet in the head or the shoulder as he chose. He used his
weapon as easily at night as in the day-time, and I heard this proof
of his skill, that will perhaps seem incredible to those who have not
travelled in Corsica. At eighty paces, a lighted candle was placed
behind a piece of transparent paper as big as a plate. He aimed.
The candle was blown out, and, after a minute in the most absolute
darkness, he fired and pierced the paper three times out of four.

With such transcendent merit, Mateo Falcone had won a great
reputation. Men said he was as good a friend as he was a dangerous
enemy : obliging too, and charitable, he lived at peace with every-

body in the neighbourhood of Porto-Vecchio. But it was said of him that, at Corte, whence he had taken his wife, he had disembarrassed himself in the most vigorous manner of a rival accounted as redoubtable in war as in love ; at least, to Mateo was attributed a certain shot that had surprised his rival shaving before a little mirror hung in his window. The affair was hushed up, and Mateo married. His wife Giuseppa had given him first three girls (at which he was enraged) and finally a boy, whom he called Fortunato, the hope of his family, heir to the name. The daughters were well married : their father could count at need on the poniards and carbines of his sons-in-law. The son was only ten years old, but already promised well.

One autumn day, Mateo went out early with his wife to visit one of his flocks in a clearing in the *mâquis*. Little Fortunato wanted to accompany him, but the clearing was too far away ; besides, it was very necessary that some one should stay to guard the house ; the father refused ; we shall see if he had not good reason to regret it.

He had been away some hours, and little Fortunato was tranquilly stretched in the sun, looking at the blue mountains, and thinking that next Sunday he would be going to dinner in the town, at the house of his uncle the Corporal, when he was suddenly interrupted in his meditations by the sound of a gun. He stood up and turned to the side of the plain whence the sound came. Other gunshots followed, fired at irregular intervals, and always nearer and nearer ; at last, a man appeared in the path leading from the plain to Mateo's house, a pointed cap on his head, like those worn by the mountaineers, bearded, in tatters, dragging himself with difficulty, leaning on his gun. He had just received a bullet in the thigh.

The man was an outlaw, who, having set off by night to get powder in the town, had fallen on the way into an ambuscade of Corsican light infantry. After a vigorous defence, he had succeeded in making good his retreat, hotly pursued, and firing from rock to rock. But he had not much start of the soldiers, and his wound made it impossible for him to reach the *mâquis* before being caught up.

He came up to Fortunato, and said :

" You are Mateo Falcone's son ? "

" Yes."

" I am Gianetto Sanpiero. The yellow collars are after me. Hide me, for I can go no further."

" And what will my father say, if I hide you without his leave ? "

" He will say you have done right."

" Who knows ? "

" Hide me quickly ; they are coming."

" Wait till my father comes back."

" Wait ! Confound it ! They will be here in five minutes. Come, hide me, or I'll kill you."

Fortunato answered him with the utmost calm :

" Your gun is not loaded, and there are no cartridges in your bandolier."

" I have my dagger."

" But will you run as quick as I ? "

He made a bound and put himself out of reach.

" You are not the son of Mateo Falcone. Will you let me be arrested in front of your house ?

The child seemed touched.

" What will you give me if I hide you ? " he said, coming nearer.

The bandit rummaged in a leather pouch that hung at his belt, and took out a five-franc piece that he had no doubt kept to buy powder. Fortunato smiled at the sight of the piece of silver ; he seized it and said to Gianetto :

" Fear nothing."

Instantly he made a great hole in a hayrick placed near the house. Gianetto squatted down in it, and the child covered him up so as to leave him a little air to breathe, and yet so that it was impossible to suspect that a man was concealed in the hay. He bethought himself too of an ingenious piece of savage cunning. He fetched a cat and her little ones, and established them on the hayrick, to make believe that it had not been stirred for some time. Then, noticing traces of blood on the path close to the house, he covered them carefully with dust, and, that done, lay down again in the sun with the utmost tranquillity.

Some minutes later, six men in brown uniform with yellow collars, commanded by an adjutant, were before Mateo's door. The adjutant was distantly connected with Falcone. (It is well known that in Corsica degrees of relationship are counted farther than elsewhere.) His name was Tiodoro Gamba : he was a man of energy, much feared by the bandits, many of whom he had already run down.

" Good-day, little cousin," said he, accosting Fortunato. " How you have grown ! Did you see a man pass by just now ? "

" Oh, I am not yet as big as you, cousin," the child answered with a simple air.

" That will come. But tell me, haven't you seen a man go by ? "

" Have I seen a man go by ? "

" Yes ; a man with a pointed cap, and a waistcoat worked in red and yellow ? "

" A man with a pointed cap, and a waistcoat worked in red and yellow ? "

" Yes ; answer quickly, and do not repeat my questions."

" This morning, Monsieur the Curé went past our door on his horse Piero. He asked me how papa was, and I told him. . . ."

" Ah, you young scamp, you are playing the fool ! Tell me at

once which way Gianetto went ; he is the man we are after, and
I am sure he took this path."

" Who knows ! "

" Who knows ?   I know you have seen him."

" Does one then see passers-by when one is asleep ? "

" Rogue, you were not asleep ; the gunshots woke you up."

" So you think, cousin, that your carbines make so much noise ?
My father's rifle makes much more."

" May the devil take you, cursed scamp that you are ! I am very
sure you have seen Gianetto. Perhaps you have even hidden him.
Come, mates, into the house with you, and see if our man is not
there. He was only going on one foot, and he has too much sense,
the rascal, to try and reach the *mâquis* limping. Besides, the traces
of blood stop here."

" And what will papa say ? " asked Fortunato, chuckling ; " what
will he say when he hears that his house was entered while he was
out ? "

" Rogue ! " said Adjutant Gamba, taking him by the ear, " do
you know that, if I like, I can make you change your tune ? Perhaps
if I give you a score of blows with the flat of the sword, you will
speak at last."

And Fortunato went on chuckling.

" My father is Mateo Falcone," he said with emphasis.

" Do you know, little scamp, that I can take you off to Corte or to
Bastia ? I will put you to sleep in a cell, on straw, with irons on your
feet, and I will have your head cut off unless you say where is
Gianetto Sanpiero."

The child broke into a laugh at this ridiculous threat. He said
again :

" My father is Mateo Falcone."

" Adjutant," said one of the troopers under his breath, " do not
let us get into trouble with Mateo."

It was clear that Gamba was embarrassed. He spoke in a low
voice to his men, who had already gone through the house. It
was not a long business, for a Corsican's cottage is made up of a
single square room. The furniture consists of a table, benches,
chests, household utensils, and the weapons of the chase. Meanwhile,
little Fortunato stroked his cat, and seemed to find a malicious
enjoyment in the discomfiture of the troopers and his cousin.

A soldier came up to the hayrick. He saw the cat, and carelessly
stuck a bayonet in the hay, shrugging his shoulders, as if he felt he
were taking a ridiculous precaution. Nothing stirred ; and the
child's face did not betray the slightest emotion.

The adjutant and his men cursed their luck ; they were already
looking seriously towards the plain, as if ready to go back whence
they had come, when their leader, convinced that threats would

make no impression on Falcone's son, wished to make a final attempt, and try the effect of caresses and gifts.

"Little cousin," said he, " you seem to be a wide-awake young rogue ! You will go far. But you are playing a risky game with me ; and, if it were not for fear of troubling my cousin Mateo, devil take it, if I would not carry you off with me."

" Bah ! "

" But, when my cousin returns, I shall tell him the whole story, and he will give you the whip till the blood comes, for telling lies."

" How do you know ? "

" You will see. . . . But look here. . . . Be a good boy, and I will give you something."

" As for me, cousin, I will give you a piece of advice ; and that is, that if you dawdle any longer, Gianetto will be in the *mâquis*, and it will take a smarter fellow than you to go and look for him there."

The adjutant pulled a silver watch out of his pocket, worth a good ten crowns ; and, noticing that little Fortunato's eyes glittered as they looked at it, dangled the watch at the end of its steel chain, and said :

" Scamp ! you would be glad enough to have a watch like this hanging from your neck ; you would walk in the streets of Porto-Vecchio, proud as a peacock ; and people would ask you, ' What time is it ? ' and you would say to them, ' Look at my watch.' "

" When I am big, my uncle the Corporal will give me a watch."

" Yes ; but your uncle's son has one already . . . not as fine as this it is true . . . and yet he is younger than you."

The child sighed.

" Well, would you like the watch, little cousin ? "

Fortunato, ogling the watch out of the corners of his eyes, was like a cat to whom one offers a whole chicken. The cat dares not put a claw on it, feeling that one is laughing at him, and turns away his eyes from time to time, so as not to succumb to the temptation ; but he licks his lips continually ; and seems to say to his master, " What a cruel joke this is ! "

And yet, Adjutant Gamba seemed to be making a real offer of the watch. Fortunato did not put out his hand, but said, with a bitter smile :

" Why are you laughing at me ? "

" By God ! I am not laughing. Only tell me where is Gianetto, and the watch is yours."

Fortunato allowed an incredulous smile to escape him ; and, fixing his black eyes on those of the adjutant, tried to read in them the good faith he sought for in the words.

" May I lose my epaulettes," cried the adjutant, " if I do not

give you the watch on that condition! My fellows are witnesses,
and I cannot unsay it."

As he spoke, he brought the watch nearer and nearer till it
almost touched the pale cheek of the child, whose face showed
clearly how covetousness and the respect due to hospitality were
contending in his soul. His bare breast heaved convulsively, and
he seemed almost choking. Meanwhile the watch swung, and
twisted, and sometimes touched the tip of his nose. At last,
little by little, his right hand rose towards the watch; he touched
it with the tip of his fingers; its whole weight was in his hand,
without the adjutant, however, letting go the end of the chain . . .
the face was blue . . . the case newly burnished . . . it seemed
all on fire in the sun. . . . The temptation was too strong.

Fortunato lifted his left hand also, and indicated with his thumb,
over his shoulder, the hayrick on which he leant. The adjutant
instantly understood. He dropped the end of the chain. Fortunato felt himself sole possessor of the watch. He leapt with the
agility of a deer, and put ten paces between himself and the hayrick, that the troopers immediately set to work to bring down.

It was not long before they saw the hay stir; a bleeding man
came out of it, with a dagger in his hand; but, when he tried
to get on his feet, his congealed wound prevented him from standing
upright. He fell. The adjutant flung himself upon him and wrested
away his poniard. Immediately he was strongly bound, in spite
of his resistance.

Gianetto, laid on the ground, and tied up like a bundle of sticks,
turned his head towards Fortunato, who had come up again.

"Son of . . . !" he said, with more scorn than anger.

The child threw him the piece of silver he had had from him,
feeling that he no longer deserved it; but the proscribed man did
not seem to notice the action. He said very tranquilly to the
adjutant:

"My dear Gamba, I cannot walk; you will have to carry me
to the town."

"You were running just now, quicker than a young goat,"
retorted the cruel victor; "but be easy: I am so glad to have got
you, I would carry you a league on my back without feeling the
weight. Anyhow, comrade, we will make you a litter with branches
and your cloak, and we shall find horses at the farm of Crespoli."

"Good," said the prisoner; "you will put a little straw on the
litter, won't you, to make me more comfortable."

While the troopers were busy, some in making a sort of stretcher
with branches of a chestnut-tree, others in dressing Gianetto's
wound, Mateo Falcone and his wife appeared suddenly at the bend
of a path that led to the *mâquis*. The woman was in front, bending
heavily under the weight of a huge sack of chestnuts, while her

husband strutted along, carrying nothing but a gun in his hand, and another slung on his back.   It is beneath the dignity of a man to carry any other burden than his weapons.

Mateo's first thought on seeing the soldiers was that they had come to arrest him.   But why this idea ?   Had Mateo then some quarrel with the law ?   Not at all.   He enjoyed a good reputation. He was " well spoken of " as the saying is ; but he was a Corsican and a mountaineer, and there are few Corsican mountaineers who, if they look well into their memories, do not find there some peccadillo, a gunshot or a dagger-blow, or other bagatelle.   Mateo had a clearer conscience than most ; for it was ten years since he had aimed his gun at a man ; but he was prudent nevertheless, and got ready to make a good defence, if need be.

" Wife," said he, to Giuseppa, " put down your sack, and be ready."

She instantly obeyed.   He gave her the gun from his bandolier, which might have inconvenienced him.   He cocked the one he had in his hand, and advanced slowly towards his house, keeping along the trees by the side of the path, and ready, at the slightest sign of hostility, to throw himself behind the biggest trunk, whence he would be able to fire from cover.   His wife walked at his heels, holding his spare gun and his cartridge-box.   It is the business of a good wife, in case of battle, to load her husband's weapons.

The adjutant, on the other side, was considerably troubled at seeing Mateo advance in this manner, with measured steps, his gun ready, and his finger at the trigger.

" If by chance," he thought, " Mateo should be a relation of Gianetto, or a friend, and should wish to defend him, the bullets of his two guns will reach two of us, as sure as a letter by post, and, if he should aim at me in spite of our relationship . . . ! "

In the difficulty he made a very courageous resolve, and that was to go forward to meet Mateo by himself and tell him about the matter, accosting him as an old acquaintance ; but the short distance that separated him from Mateo seemed terribly long.

" Hola there, old comrade," he cried, " how are you, old man ? It is I, Gamba, your cousin."

Mateo, without answering a word, had stopped, and, as the other spoke, slowly raised the barrel of his gun, so that at the moment when the adjutant came up to him it was pointed to the sky.

" Good-day, brother," [1] said the adjutant, holding out his hand. " It is a very long time since I last saw you."

" Good-day, brother."

" 'I had come to give good-day to you in passing, and to my cousin Pepa.   We have made a long march to-day ; but we must not complain of being tired, for we have made a famous capture.

[1] *Buon giorno, fratello*, is the ordinary Corsican greeting.

We have just got hold of Gianetto Sanpiero."

" God be praised," cried Giuseppa ; " he robbed us of a milch-goat last week."

These words rejoiced Gamba.

" Poor devil," said Mateo, " he was hungry."

" The rogue defended himself like a lion," pursued the adjutant, a little taken aback ; " he killed one of my troopers, and, not content with that, broke Corporal Chardon's arm ; but that is no great harm, he was only a Frenchman. . . . Then he had hidden himself so well that the devil could not have discovered him. Without my little cousin Fortunato, I should never have been able to find him."

" Fortunato ! " cried Mateo.

" Fortunato ! " repeated Giuseppa.

" Yes, Gianetto had hidden himself under that hayrick over there ; but my little cousin showed me the trick. I shall tell his uncle the Corporal, and he will send him a fine present for his pains. And his name and yours shall be in the report that I send to the Public Prosecutor."

" Curse it ! " said Mateo, very low.

They had come up to the soldiers. Gianetto was already laid on his litter, ready to start. When he saw Mateo with Gamba he smiled an odd smile ; then, turning towards the door of the house, he spat on the threshold, and said :

" The house of a traitor."

Only a man ready to die would have dared to apply the name of traitor to Falcone. A good dagger thrust, that would leave no need of a second, would have instantly avenged the insult. But Mateo's only movement was to put his hand to his forehead like a stunned man.

Fortunato had gone into the house on seeing the arrival of his father. He soon reappeared with a bowl of milk, which he presented with downcast eyes to Gianetto.

" Keep off ! " shouted the bandit with a voice of thunder.

Then, turning to one of the troopers :

" Let's have a drink, comrade," he said.

The soldier put his flask in his hands, and the bandit drank the water given him by a man with whom he had just been exchanging gunshots. Then he asked that his hands should be fastened crossed on his breast, instead of tied behind his back.

" I like," said he, " to lie at my ease."

They did their best to satisfy him ; then the adjutant gave the signal for the start, said " Good-bye " to Mateo, who did not answer, and went down at a smart pace towards the plain.

Ten minutes passed before Mateo opened his mouth. The child looked uneasily, now at his mother, and now at his father, who, leaning on his gun, considered him with an expression of concentrated rage.

"You begin well," said Mateo at last, in a voice calm, but terrifying to those who knew the man.

"Father!" cried the child, coming nearer, with tears in his eyes as if to throw himself at his knees.

But Mateo shouted at him:

"Out of my presence!"

And the child stopped short, and sobbed, motionless, a few steps from his father.

Giuseppa came up. She had just noticed the watch-chain, one end of which hung out of Fortunato's shirt.

"Who gave you that watch?" she asked sternly.

"My cousin, the adjutant."

Falcone seized the watch, and, flinging it violently against a stone, broke it in a thousand pieces.

"Woman," said he, "is this child mine?"

The brown cheeks of Giuseppa became brick red.

"What are you saying, Mateo? Do you know to whom you are speaking?"

"Well, this child is the first of his race to be a traitor."

The sobs and chokes of Fortunato redoubled, and Falcone kept his lynx eyes always fixed upon him. At last he struck the ground with the butt of his gun, then threw it across his shoulder, and took once more the path to the *mâquis*, shouting to Fortunato to follow him. The child obeyed.

Giuseppa ran after Mateo and caught him by the arm.

"He is your son," she said in a trembling voice, fixing her black eyes on her husband's as if to read what was passing in his soul.

"Leave me," answered Mateo; "I am his father."

Giuseppa kissed her son and went weeping back into the cottage. She threw herself on her knees before an image of the Virgin, and prayed fervently. Meanwhile Falcone walked some two hundred paces along the path, and did not stop until he went down into a small ravine. He felt the earth with the butt of his gun, and found it soft and easy to dig. The place seemed suitable to his purpose.

"Fortunato, go up to that big rock."

The child did as he was told, and then knelt.

"Say your prayers."

"Father, my father, do not kill me."

"Say your prayers!" repeated Mateo in a terrible voice.

The child, stammering and sobbing, recited the *Pater* and the *Credo*. The father responded *Amen* in a loud voice at the end of each prayer.

"Are those all the prayers you know?"

"Father, I know the *Ave Maria*, too, and the litany my aunt taught me."

" It is very long, but never mind."

The child finished the litany in a stifled voice.

" Have you done ? "

" O father, have mercy ! forgive me ! I will not do it again !
I will beg my cousin the Corporal ever so hard that Gianetto may
be pardoned ! "

He was still speaking ; Mateo had cocked his gun, and took aim,
saying :

" May God forgive you ! "

The child made a desperate effort to get up and embrace his
father's knees ; but he had not the time. Mateo fired, and
Fortunato fell stone-dead.

Without throwing a glance at the corpse, Mateo took the path
to his house, to get a spade for the digging of his son's grave. He
had only gone a few yards when he met Giuseppa, running, alarmed
by the gunshot.

" What have you done ? " she cried.

" Justice."

" Where is he ? "

" In the ravine. I am going to bury him. He died a Christian ;
I will have a mass sung for him. Let them tell my son-in-law,
Tiodoro Bianchi, to come and live with us."

TAMANGO

PROSPER MÉRIMÉE

CAPTAIN LEDOUX was a good sailor. He had begun by being
a simple seaman, and then assistant helmsman. At the battle
of Trafalgar he had his left hand smashed by a splinter of wood ;
he lost his hand, and was discharged with good certificates.
Repose hardly suited him, and, when an opportunity of re-em-
barkation presented itself, he served as second lieutenant on board
a privateer. The money he got from some prizes made it possible
for him to buy books and study the theory of navigation, of whose
practice he had already a perfect understanding. In time he
became captain of a private lugger, with three guns and a crew of
sixty men, and the coasting sailors of Jersey have not yet forgotten his exploits.

The peace made him miserable : he had amassed a small fortune
during the war, and had hoped to increase it at the expense of the

English. He was obliged to offer his services to peaceable merchants; and, since he had the reputation of a resolute and experienced man, he was readily entrusted with a ship. When the slave-trade was forbidden, and it was necessary, in order to carry it on, not only to elude the vigilance of the French customs-officers, which was not very difficult, but also, a more risky affair, to escape the English cruisers, Captain Ledoux became a valuable man to the merchants in ebony.

Very different from most sailors who have languished, as he had, a long time in subordinate positions, he had not that profound horror of innovation, and that spirit of routine, that they too often carry into the higher ranks. On the contrary, Captain Ledoux had been the first to advise his owner to use iron tanks to hold water and keep it sweet. On his boat, the handcuffs and chains with which slave-ships are provided were made after a new system, and carefully varnished to protect them from rust. But what brought him most credit among the slave merchants was the building, that he personally superintended, of a brig designed for the trade, a clean sailer, narrow, long like a ship of war, and able none the less to accommodate a very large number of blacks. He called her the *Esperance*. It was his idea that the 'tween decks, narrow and shut in as they were, should be only three feet four inches in height. He maintained that this size allowed slaves of a reasonable height to be comfortably seated; and what need have they of getting up?

"When they get to the colonies," said Ledoux, "they will be only too long on their feet."

The negroes, arranged in two parallel lines, with their backs against the sides of the vessel, left an empty space between their feet, used, in all other slave-ships, for moving about. Ledoux thought of placing other negroes in this space, lying at right angles to the rest. In this way his ship held ten more blacks than any other of the same tonnage. It would have been strictly possible to place yet more, but one must have some humanity, and leave a nigger at least a space five feet long and two broad in which to disport himself during a voyage of six weeks and more. "For, after all," said Ledoux to his owner, to justify this liberal allowance, "the niggers are men like the whites."

The *Esperance* left Nantes on a Friday, as superstitious people have since remarked. The inspectors, who made a scrupulous examination of the brig, did not discover six big cases full of chains, handcuffs, and those irons that are called, for some reason or other, "bars of Justice." Nor were they at all astonished at the enormous provision of water that the *Esperance* was to carry, although, according to her papers, she was only going as far as Senegal, to trade there in wood and ivory. The voyage is not a long one, it is true, but there is no harm in taking precautions. If one should be surprised by a calm, what would become of one without water?

The *Esperance*, then, sailed on a Friday, well fitted and equipped throughout. Ledoux would, perhaps, have liked masts a little more solid; however, he could not complain, since the building has been under his own direction. His voyage to the African coast was fortunate in every way. He cast anchor in the river of Joale (I believe) at a time when the English cruisers were not watching that part of the coast. The native merchants came immediately on board. The moment could not have been more favourable. Tamango, a famous warrior and man-seller, had just brought a great quantity of slaves to the coast, and was getting rid of them cheaply, as a man who knew that it was in his power to re-stock the market as soon as his goods should become scarce.

Captain Ledoux went ashore and paid his call on Tamango. He found him with two of his wives, some lesser merchants and overseers, in a straw hut that had been hastily built for him. Tamango had dressed himself out to receive the white captain. He was clad in an old blue military tunic, still bearing the corporal's stripes; but on each shoulder hung two epaulettes fastened to the same button, flapping, one before and one behind. Since he had no shirt, and the tunic was a little short for a man of his height, a considerable strip of black skin, which looked like a large belt, appeared between the white facings of the tunic and his drawers of Guinea cloth. A big cavalry sabre was hung from a cord at his side, and he held in his hands a fine double-barrelled gun of English make. Thus equipped, the African warrior believed that he surpassed in elegance the most accomplished dandy in Paris or London.

Captain Ledoux observed him silently for some time, while Tamango, throwing a chest like a grenadier on parade before a strange general, enjoyed the impression he thought he was making on the white man. Ledoux, after examining him like a connoisseur, turned to his second in command, and said:

"There's a rascal I should sell for a thousand crowns, if I could get him safe and sound to Martinique."

They sat down, and a sailor who knew a little of the negro language served as interpreter. After the first polite compliments had been exchanged, a boy brought a basket of bottles of brandy. They drank, and the captain, to put Tamango in a good humour, made him a present of a pretty copper powder-flask decorated with a portrait of Napoleon in relief. When the present had been accepted with suitable gratitude, they left the hut and sat down in the shade before the brandy bottles. Tamango made a sign for the slaves he had to sell to be brought before them.

They appeared in a long string, their bodies bent with weariness

and terror, each one with his neck in a six-foot fork, whose points
were fastened with a wooden bar close behind his head.   When they
are to get on the move, one of the overseers takes the handle of the
first slave's fork on his shoulder ; this slave looks after the fork of
the man immediately behind him ; the second carries the fork of the
third slave ; and so on.   When they are to halt, the leader of the file
sticks the pointed handle of his fork in the ground, and the whole
column comes to a stand.   There is obviously no use in thinking of
escape by flight, when one carries a great stick six feet long fastened
to one's neck.

The captain shrugged his shoulders as each slave, male or female,
passed before him ; he found the men weakly, the women too young
or too old, and complained of the decay of the black race.

" It is degenerating in every way," he would say ; " once things
were very different.   The women were five feet six inches tall, and
four of the men could have turned the capstan of a frigate by
themselves to lift the main anchor."

However, in the midst of his criticism, he made a first choice of
the sturdiest and most handsome blacks.   He was willing to pay for
these at the ordinary rates, but he demanded a great reduction on
the others.   Tamango, on his side, was looking after his interests,
praising his merchandise, and speaking of the scarcity of men, and
the perils of the trade.   He finished by setting a price, I do not know
what, on the slaves that the white captain wished to take on board.

As soon as the interpreter had put Tamango's proposition into
French, Ledoux almost fell backwards with surprise and indignation : then, muttering some terrible oaths, he got up, as if to
break off all treaty with so unreasonable a man.   Then Tamango
begged him to stay, and succeeded with difficulty in getting him to
sit down again.   Another bottle was opened, and the discussion
recommenced.   It was now the black's turn to find the white man's
offers unreasonable and absurd.   For a long time they shouted, and
argued, and drank prodigious quantities of brandy, but the brandy
had very different effects on the two contracting parties.   The more
the Frenchman drank, the lower the prices he offered ; the more the
African drank, the more he lessened his demands.

In this way, at the end of the basket, they came to an agreement.
Some cheap cotton, some powder, some flints, three casks of brandy,
and fifty guns in bad repair, were given in exchange for one hundred
and sixty slaves.   The captain, in order to confirm the bargain,
clapped his hand in that of the more than half-drunken black, and
the slaves were instantly handed over to the French sailors, who
hurried to remove their wooden forks, and to substitute collars
and handcuffs of iron ; a good example of the superiority of
European civilisation.

There still remained a score and a half of slaves ; they were children, old men, and sick women. The ship was full.

Tamango, who did not know what to do with this trash, offered
to sell them to the captain at a bottle of brandy apiece. The offer
was tempting. Ledoux remembered that at the representation of
" The Sicilian Vespers," at Nantes, he had seen a good number of
big fat men enter a pit that was already full, and yet succeed in
finding sitting room, by virtue of the compressibility of the human
body. He took the twenty slenderest slaves of the thirty.

Then Tamango asked only a glass of brandy apiece for the ten
who were left. Ledoux remembered that in public conveyances
children only pay for and only occupy half places. He accordingly
took three children, but declared that he had no mind to burden
himself with a single other black. Tamango, seeing that he had still
seven slaves on his hands, took his gun, and aimed at the woman
who came first : she was the mother of the three children.

" Buy, or I kill her," he said to the white ; " a little glass of
brandy, or I fire."

" And what the devil do you want me to do with her ? " asked
Ledoux.

Tamango fired, and the slave fell dead on the ground.

" Another ! " cried Tamango, aiming at a broken-down old man ;
" a glass of brandy, or else . . ."

One of his wives pulled his arm aside, and the shot went at
random. She had just recognised, in the old man her husband was
about to kill, a *guru*, or magician, who had foretold that she was to
be Queen.

Tamango, infuriated with the brandy, was beside himself when
he saw his wishes opposed. He struck his wife roughly with the butt
of his gun ; then, turning to Ledoux :

" See here," he said, " I give you this woman."

She was pretty. Ledoux looked at her smiling, and took her by
the hand.

" I shall find a place to put her," said he.

The interpreter was a humane man. He gave Tamango a cardboard snuff-box, and asked for the six slaves who were left. He
freed them from their forks, and let them go where they thought
fit. They immediately made off, some this way, some that, not
knowing in the least how they were to get back to their country,
two hundred leagues from the coast.

Meanwhile the captain said good-bye to Tamango, and busied
himself in getting his cargo as quickly as possible on board. It was
imprudent to stay long up river ; the cruisers might reappear, and
he meant to set sail the next day. As for Tamango, he lay down on
the grass in the shade, to sleep off the effects of the brandy.

When he awoke, the vessel was already under sail, and going
down the river. Tamango, whose head was still muddled by the

debauch of the day before, asked for his wife, Ayché. They told him she had had the misfortune to displease him, and that he had given her as a present to the white captain, who had taken her on board. Tamango, stupefied at this news, smote his head, then took his gun, and, since the river made several turns before emptying itself in the sea, ran by the shortest road to a little bay half a league from the mouth. There he hoped to find a canoe in which he could overtake the brig, whose voyage would be retarded by the twistings of the river. He was not mistaken ; he had just time to throw himself into a canoe and join the slave-ship.

Ledoux was surprised to see him, and still more so to hear him ask for the return of his wife.

" A thing once given is not to be taken back," he replied.

And he turned his back on him.

The black insisted, offering to give back some of the things he had had in exchange for the slaves. The captain broke into a laugh, and said that Ayché was a very good woman, and that he meant to keep her. At this poor Tamango wept floods of tears, and uttered cries of misery as piercing as those of a poor wretch under a surgical operation. One minute he was running about the deck calling for his beloved Ayché, and the next he was beating his head on the planks as if to kill himself. Unmoved throughout, the captain, pointing to the land, made signs that it was time for him to leave. Tamango persisted. He offered even his golden epaulettes, his gun, and his sabre. All was in vain.

During this discussion, the lieutenant of the *Espérance* said to the captain :

" We lost three slaves last night, so we have some room. Why not take this sturdy rogue, who is worth in himself alone more than the three who are dead ? " Ledoux reflected that Tamango would sell for a good thousand crowns ; that this voyage, which seemed likely to be very profitable, would probably be his last ; and that, finally, since his fortune was made and he was giving up the slave-trade, it did not much matter to him whether he left a good or evil reputation on the coast of Guinea. Besides, there was absolutely no one on the shore, and the African warrior was entirely at his mercy. All that had to be done was to remove his weapons ; for it would have been dangerous to lay a hand on him while they were still in his possession. Ledoux accordingly asked for his gun, as if to examine it, and make sure it was worth as much as the beautiful Ayché. In testing the triggers, he was careful to let the powder fall from the priming. The lieutenant, for his part, got possession of the sabre ; and, when Tamango had been thus disarmed, two strong sailors flung themselves upon him, knocked him down, and proceeded to bind him. The black's resistance was heroic.

Recovering from his first surprise, he made a long struggle with the two sailors, in spite of the disadvantages of his position. Thanks to his prodigious strength, he succeeded in getting to his feet. With a blow of the fist he grounded the man who was holding him by the neck ; he left a bit of his coat in the hand of the other sailor, and rushed like a madman at the lieutenant to snatch away his sabre. The lieutenant struck him on the head with it, and gave him a large wound, though not very deep. Tamango fell a second time. They instantly bound him securely, hand and foot. While he was struggling, he uttered cries of rage, and flung himself about like a wild boar taken in the nets ; but, when he saw that all resistance was useless, he shut his eyes, and did not make another movement. His powerful, rapid breathing was the only sign that he was still alive.

" My word ! " cried Captain Ledoux, " the blacks he sold will have a good laugh when they see him a slave in his turn. They will see by this there is a Providence above."

Meanwhile poor Tamango was bleeding to death. The charitable interpreter, who had saved the lives of six slaves the day before, came up to him, bound his wound, and gave him a few words of consolation. I do not know what he could say to him. The black remained motionless as a corpse. Two sailors had to carry him below like a package, to the place that was to be his. For two days he would neither eat nor drink ; he was scarcely seen to open his eyes. His comrades in captivity, lately his prisoners, saw his appearance in their midst with dull astonishment. Such was the fear with which he still inspired them, that not one of them dared to jeer at the misery of him who had caused their own.

Favoured with a good wind from the land, the vessel speedily slipped away from the African coast. Free already from anxiety about the English cruisers, the captain no longer thought of anything but the enormous profits awaiting him in the colonies towards which he was making his way. His ebony wood was keeping sound. No contagious diseases. Only twelve niggers, and they of the feeblest, had died from heat ; a mere bagatelle. He took the precaution of making all his slaves come on deck every day, so that his human cargo should suffer as little as possible from the fatigues of the voyage. Turn by turn, a third of the poor wretches had an hour in which to take in their provision of air for the whole day. A part of the crew, armed to the teeth, mounted guard over them for fear of a revolt ; care was taken besides never entirely to remove their irons. Sometimes a sailor, who knew how to play the fiddle, regaled them with a concert. It was odd then to see all those black figures turn towards the musician, lose by degrees their expression of dull despair, burst into laughter, and (when their chains allowed them) clap their hands. Exercise is necessary for health ; and so another of the salutary practices of Captain Ledoux was to set his slaves frequently dancing, as one makes horses prance, when they are on board ship for a long voyage.

"Now then, my children, dance, be happy," thundered the captain, cracking an enormous coach-whip.

And immediately the poor blacks leapt and danced.

Tamango's wound kept him below hatches for some time. He appeared at last on deck ; and first, proudly lifting his head in the midst of the timorous crowd of slaves, he threw a glance, sad but calm, over the immense stretch of water surrounding the boat ; then he lay down, or rather let himself fall on the deck, without even caring to arrange his irons so as to be as little uncomfortable as possible. Ledoux was seated on the quarter-deck, tranquilly smoking his pipe. Ayché, without irons, dressed in an elegant robe of blue cotton, her feet in pretty morocco-leather slippers, was carrying a tray of liqueurs in her hand, ready to pour him out a drink. It was clear that she held a high position in the captain's service. A black, who detested Tamango, signed to him to look in that direction. Tamango turned, saw her, uttered a cry, and, leaping up, ran towards the quarter-deck before the sailors on guard could prevent so enormous a breach of naval discipline.

"Ayché !" he thundered, and Ayché screamed with terror. "Do you believe there is no MAMA-JUMBO in the country of the white men ? "

The sailors were already running up with lifted clubs ; but Tamango folded his arms, and, as if indifferent, went quietly back to his place, while Ayché, bursting into tears, seemed petrified by the mysterious words.

The interpreter explained what was this terrible Mama-Jumbo, whose mere name produced such terror.

"It is the nigger's Bogey Man," he said. "When a husband is afraid lest his wife should do what plenty of wives do in France as well as in Africa, he threatens her with Mama-Jumbo. I have seen Mama-Jumbo myself, and fathomed the trick ; but the blacks . . . the blacks are such fools they understand nothing. Imagine that one evening, while the women are amusing themselves with a dance, a *folgar*, as they call it in their gibberish, suddenly a strange music is heard, coming from a little wood, very thick and very dark. They see no one to make it ; all the musicians are hidden in the wood. There are reed flutes, and wooden tabours, *balafos*, and guitars made from the halves of gourds. They are all playing a tune to bring the devil on earth. The women no sooner hear that tune than they start trembling ; they would make off, but their husbands hold them back : they know well what is coming next. All at once there comes out of the wood a great white figure as high as our topmast, with a head as big as a bushel measure, eyes as large as hawse-holes, and a mouth like the devil's, with fire inside. The thing walks slowly,

slowly ; and it never goes more than half a cable's length from the
wood. The women cry :

" ' Behold Mama-Jumbo ! '

" They bawl like oyster-women. Then their husbands say :

" ' Now then, you jades, tell us if you have behaved yourselves ;
if you lie, there is Mama-Jumbo to eat you all raw."

" There are some who are foolish enough to confess, and then
their husbands beat them to a jelly."

" And so what was this white figure, this Mama-Jumbo ? " the
captain asked.

" Oh, it was a wag muffled up in a big white sheet, carrying,
instead of a head, a hollowed pumpkin furnished with a lighted
candle, on the end of a long pole. It was nothing more cunning
than that, but it needs no great expense of cleverness to deceive the
blacks. With all that, the Mama-Jumbo is a good invention, and
I wish my wife believed in it."

" As for mine," said Ledoux, " if she is not frightened of Mama-
Jumbo, she is afraid of Martin-Rod ; and she knows, too, how I
would give it her if she played me some trick. We are not long-
suffering in the family of Ledoux, and although I have only one
hand left, it still makes pretty good play with a rope's end. As
for your joker down there, who talks of Mama-Jumbo, tell him to
behave himself, and not frighten this little woman here, or I will
have his back so flayed that his hide will no longer be black, but
as red as a raw beefsteak."

With these words the captain went down to his cabin, summoned
Ayché, and tried to console her : but neither caresses, nor even
blows, for one loses patience at last, could bring the beautiful
negress to reason ; she wept floods of tears. The captain went on
deck again in a bad temper, and scolded the officer of the watch
over the manœuvre he was ordering at the time.

That night, when almost all the crew were fast asleep, the men
of the watch heard first a low song, solemn, lugubrious, coming
from the 'tween decks, and then a woman's scream, horribly
piercing. Immediately afterwards the coarse voice of Captain
Ledoux, swearing and threatening, and the noise of his terrible
whip resounded throughout the ship. An instant later, all was
silent again. The next day Tamango appeared on deck with a
scarred face, but an air as proud, as resolute as before.

Ayché had no sooner seen him than, leaving the quarter-deck,
where she was sitting beside the captain, she ran swiftly to Tamango,
knelt before him, and said in accents of utter despair :

" Forgive me, Tamango, forgive me ! "

Tamango watched her fixedly for a minute ; then, noticing that
the interpreter was some way off :

" A file ! " he said.

And he lay down on the deck, turning his back on Ayché. The captain scolded her sharply, even gave her a blow or two, and forbade her to speak to her ex-husband; but he was far from suspecting the meaning of the short words they had exchanged, and asked no questions on the subject.

Meanwhile Tamango, shut up with the other slaves, exhorted them night and day to make a generous attempt to regain their liberty. He spoke to them of the small numbers of the white men, and pointed out the continually increasing carelessness of their guards; then, without explaining himself exactly, he said that he would know how to take them back to their country, boasted his knowledge in the occult sciences, with which the blacks are much taken up, and threatened with the vengeance of the devil those who should refuse to help him in his scheme. In his harangues he used only the Berber dialect, known to the greater part of the slaves, but not understood by the interpreter. The reputation of the orator, the habit the slaves were in of fearing and obeying him, came marvellously to the aid of his eloquence, and the blacks begged him to fix a day for their deliverance long before he himself believed he was in a position to effect it.

He replied vaguely to the conspirators that the time was not come, and that the devil, who was appearing to him in his dreams, had not yet warned him, but that they should hold themselves in readiness for the first signal. However, he lost no opportunity of experimenting on the watchfulness of his guards. On one occasion, a sailor, leaving his gun leaning on the parapet, was amusing himself by watching a troop of flying-fish that were following the vessel; Tamango took the gun and began to handle it, copying with grotesque gesture the movements he had seen made by soldiers at drill. The gun was taken from him after an instant; but he had learnt that he could touch a weapon without awaking immediate suspicion; and, when the time should come for making use of one, he would be a bold man who should try to wrest it from his hands.

One day Ayché threw him a biscuit, making him a signal that he alone understood. The biscuit contained a little file; on this instrument depended the success of the conspiracy. Tamango was very careful at first not to show the file to his companions; but, when night was come, he began to murmur unintelligible words that he accompanied with bizarre gestures. He grew by degrees so excited as to cry aloud. To hear the varied intonations of his voice, one would have said he was engaged in a lively conversation with an invisible person. The slaves all trembled, not doubting but that the devil was at that very moment in the midst of them. Tamango put an end to the scene with a cry of joy.

"Comrades," said he, "the spirit I have conjured up has at last given me what he had promised, and I have in my hand the instrument of our deliverance. Now you need nothing but a little courage to set yourselves at liberty."

He made those who were near him touch the file, and the imposture, stupid as it was, found credence among men still stupider.

After long expectation the great day of vengeance and liberty arrived. The conspirators, bound to each other by a solemn oath, had settled their plan after mature deliberation. The most determined, with Tamango at their head, when it was their turn to go on deck, were to possess themselves of the weapons of the guards ; others were to go to the captain's cabin and get hold of the guns that were stored there. Those who had succeeded in filing their irons were to commence the attack ; but, in spite of the stubborn work of many nights, the greater number of slaves were still unable to take an active part in the engagement. Accordingly, three sturdy blacks had been entrusted with the killing of the man who carried the manacle-key in his pocket, after which they were to go instantly and free their chained companions.

On that day Captain Ledoux was in a delightful temper ; contrary to his usual practice, he pardoned a ship's boy who had deserved a thrashing. He complimented the officer of the watch on his navigation, told the crew he was pleased with them, and announced that at Martinique, where they would shortly arrive, each man was to receive a bonus. All the sailors, full of agreeable ideas, were mentally planning the spending of this gratuity. They were thinking of brandy and the coloured women of Martinique, when Tamango and the other conspirators were made to come on deck.

They had been careful so to file their irons that they should not seem severed, and yet that the slightest effort should suffice to break them. Besides, they made such a jingling with them that any one who heard them would have said they were carrying a double weight. After taking breaths of air for some time, they joined hands and danced, while Tamango chanted the war-song of his family, that he sang in other times before going into battle. When the dance had gone on for some time Tamango, as if overcome by fatigue, lay down full length at the feet of a sailor who was carelessly leaning on the parapet of the ship ; all the conspirators did the same. In this way each sailor was surrounded by several blacks.

All at once, as soon as he had noiselessly broken his irons, Tamango loosed a great shout that was to serve as a signal, seized the sailor who was close to him violently by the legs, upset him, and putting a foot on his stomach, wrested his gun from him, and made use of it to kill the officer of the watch. Simultaneously each sailor of the watch was assailed, disarmed, and instantly slaughtered. A war-cry rose throughout the ship. The boat-swain, who had the key of the irons, was one of the first to fall. Then a crowd of blacks poured out on the decks. Those who could not find weapons seized the capstan bars, or the oars of the sloop. From that moment the crew of Europeans was lost. However, a few sailors rallied on the quarter-deck ; but they lacked arms and resolution.

Ledoux was still alive and had lost none of his courage. Observing that Tamango was the soul of the conspiracy, he thought that if he could kill him he could make quick work of his accomplices. He accordingly ran to meet him, sabre in hand, calling him with loud shouts. Tamango instantly rushed upon him. He held a gun by the end of the barrel, and was using it like a club. The two leaders met on one of the gangways, a narrow passage communicating between the forecastle and the after-deck. Tamango struck the first blow. The white avoided it by a nimble movement of the body. The butt struck the deck, and broke, and the shock was so violent that the gun escaped from Tamango's hands. He was defenceless, and Ledoux, with a smile of diabolic joy, prepared to run him through ; but Tamango was as agile as his country's panthers. He threw himself into his adversary's arms, and gripped the hand with which he was holding the sabre. The one struggled to retain the weapon, the other to wrest it away. In this furious wrestle both fell ; but the African was underneath. Undismayed, he squeezed his adversary with his full strength, and bit him in the throat with such violence that the blood spurted out as if under the teeth of a lion. The sabre slipped from the captain's weakening grip. Tamango seized it ; then, getting up, his mouth all bloody, he drove it again and again through his already half-dead enemy.

The victory was no longer in suspense. The few sailors who were left tried to beg pity from the rebels ; but all, even the interpreter, who had never done them any harm, were pitilessly massacred. The lieutenant died with honour. He had gone aft to one of those little cannon that turn on a pivot and are charged with grapeshot. He managed the gun with his left hand, and defended himself so well with a sword in his right that he brought round him a crowd of blacks. Then, pressing the trigger of the gun, he made a broad road paved with dead and dying, through the midst of the dense mass. An instant later he was cut to pieces.

When the corpse of the last white had been slashed and cut to pieces, and flung into the sea, the blacks, satiated with vengeance, looked up at the sails of the vessel, which, steadily filled by a fresh breeze, seemed to be still in the service of their oppressors, and taking the conquerors, in spite of their triumph, towards the land of slavery.

" Then nothing has been done," they thought bitterly. " Will that great fetish of the white men be willing to take us back to our country, we who have spilled the blood of his masters ? "

Some said that Tamango would know how to make him obey. Tamango was instantly summoned with loud shouts.

He did not hurry to make his appearance. He was found standing in the poop cabin, resting one hand on the captain's bloody sabre, and absently offering the other to his wife Ayché, who was kissing it, kneeling before him. The joy of victory did not lessen a dark anxiety that was betrayed in his whole manner. Less clownish than the others, he better understood the difficulties of his position.

He appeared at last on deck, affecting a calm that he did not feel. Urged by a hundred confused voices to direct the course of the vessel, he went up to the helm with slow steps, as if to postpone for a little the moment that, for himself and for the others, was to decide the extent of his power.

In the whole vessel there was not one black, however stupid, who had not noticed the influence that a certain wheel and the box placed in front of it exercised on the movements of the ship ; but there was always a great mystery for them in this mechanism. Tamango examined the compass for a long time, moving his lips, as though he were reading the characters he saw traced there ; then he put his hand to his forehead and took the thoughtful attitude of a man making a mental calculation. All the blacks crowded round him, mouths gaping, eyes wide open, following his slightest gesture. At last, with the mixture of fear and hardihood that is given by ignorance, he gave a violent jerk to the steering wheel.

Like a generous courser rearing under the spur of an imprudent horseman, the good ship *Esperance* bounded over the waves at this unheard-of manœuvre. One would have said that in her indignation she wished to engulf herself and her ignorant pilot. The proper connection between the positions of the sails and the rudder being rudely broken, the vessel heeled over so violently that she seemed on the point of sinking. Her long yards were plunged in the sea. Many men were knocked down ; some fell overboard. Presently the ship rose proudly from the surge, as if to make one more fight with destruction. The wind redoubled its force, and, all at once, with a horrible noise, the two masts fell, broken a few feet above the deck, covering the ship with wreckage and a heavy network of ropes.

The horrified negroes fled below the hatches, shrieking with terror ; but, since the wind no longer found purchase, the vessel righted and abandoned herself to the gentle tossing of the waves. Then the more courageous of the blacks came again on the decks and cleared them of the wreckage that encumbered them. Tamango remained motionless, resting his elbow on the binnacle, hiding his face in his folded arms. Ayché was with him, but dared not say a word to him. Little by little the blacks came up to them ; a murmur rose, which presently changed into a storm of reproaches and insults.

" Traitor ! impostor ! " they cried, " you are the cause of all our misfortunes ; it was you who sold us to the white men, it was you who urged us to revolt against them. You had boasted to us of your knowledge, you had promised to take us back to our country. We believed you, fools that we were, and behold, we have all had a narrow escape from death because you offended the white man's fetish."

Tamango proudly lifted his head, and the negroes about him shrank back afraid. He picked up two guns, signed to his wife to follow him, and walked towards the forepart of the vessel. There he made himself a rampart with empty casks and planks ; he settled himself in this species of entrenchment, from which protruded the menacing bayonets of his two guns. They left him in peace. Among the rebels, some were weeping ; others, raising their hands to heaven, invoked their fetishes and those of the white men ; some, on their knees before the compass, whose perpetual motion was a marvel to them, prayed to it to take them to their country ; some lay in gloomy dejection on the deck. In the midst of these despairing men should be pictured women and children howling with fright, and a score of wounded begging the help that no one thought of giving them.

Suddenly a nigger appeared on the deck, his face radiant. He announced that he had just found the place where the white men kept their brandy ; his joy and his manner were a sufficient proof that he had that moment tried it. This news suspended for the moment the poor wretches' cries. They ran to the storeroom and glutted themselves with liquor. An hour later they were to be seen leaping and laughing on the deck, abandoning themselves to all the extravagances of the most brutal drunkenness. Their dances and songs were accompanied by the groans and sobs of the wounded. In this way passed the rest of the day and all the night.

In the morning, on waking up, fresh despair. A great number of wounded had died during the night. The ship was surrounded by floating corpses. The sea was rough and the sky clouded. A council was held. Some novices in the magic art, who had not dared to speak of their knowledge before Tamango, offered their services one after another. Each vain attempt added to their discouragement. At last they spoke again of Tamango, who had not yet left his barricade. After all he was the wisest amongst them, and he alone could take them from the horrible situation in which he had placed them. An old man approached him with offers of peace. He begged him to come and give his advice ; but Tamango, stern as Coriolanus, was deaf to his prayers. At night, in the midst of the disorder, he had provided himself with biscuits and salt meat. He seemed determined to live alone in his retreat.

There was still the brandy. That at least gives forgetfulness of the sea, slavery, and approaching death. One sleeps, and dreams of Africa, and sees the gum-tree forests, the straw-covered huts, and the baobabs, whose shade covers a whole village. The orgy of the day before began again. In this way many days went by. Their life was made up of shrieking and groaning and tearing their hair, and then getting drunk and sleeping. Many died of drink ; some flung themselves in the sea, or stabbed themselves to death.

One morning Tamango left his stronghold, and came as far as the stump of the mainmast.

"Slaves," said he, "the Spirit has appeared unto me in a dream, and revealed the means of taking you hence and bringing you back to your country. Your ingratitude should make me abandon you ; but I have pity on the cries of these women and children. I forgive you : listen to me."

All the blacks bent their heads respectfully, and gathered round him.

"The whites," Tamango went on, "alone know the words of power that move these big houses of wood ; but we can guide as we will these light boats that are not unlike those of our own country."

He pointed to the sloop and the other boats of the brig.

"Let us fill them with food, embark, and row with the wind ; my Master and yours will make it blow towards our country."

They believed him. Never was project more insane. Ignorant of the use of the compass, under an unfamiliar sky, he could do nothing but wander at random. According to his notions, he imagined that if he rowed straight ahead, he would reach at least some land inhabited by black men, for the black men possess the earth, and the white men live in their ships. He had heard his mother say that.

Soon all was ready for the embarkation ; but the sloop and one small boat were all that were fit for use. There was not enough room for the eighty negroes still alive. They had to abandon all the wounded and sick. The greater number of these asked them to kill them before leaving.

The two boats, launched with infinite difficulty, and laden beyond measure, left the ship in a choppy sea that threatened to swamp them every moment. The little boat got away first. Tamango and Ayché had taken their places in the sloop, which, heavier built and laden, lagged considerably behind. They could still hear the plaintive cries of some poor wretches left on board the brig, when a fair-sized wave took the sloop broadside on, and filled her with water. The little boat saw their disaster, and her rowers redoubled their efforts, for fear of having to pick up some of the wrecked. Almost all in the sloop were drowned. A dozen only were able to regain the vessel. Of this number were Tamango and Ayché. When the sun set, they saw the small boat disappear below the horizon ; but no one knows what became of it.

Why should I weary the reader with a disgusting description of the tortures of hunger ? About twenty persons in a small space, now tossed by a stormy sea, now roasted by a burning sun, quarrel day by day over the scanty remains of their provisions. Each scrap of biscuit costs a battle, and the weak die, not because the strong kill them, but because they leave them to their death. At the end of a few days there was no longer a living thing on the brig *Esperance* but Tamango and his wife Ayché.

. . . .

One night the sea was rough, the wind blew, and the darkness was such that one could not see the prow of the vessel from the poop. Ayché was lying on a mattress in the captain's cabin, and Tamango was sitting at her feet. For a long time there had been silence between them.

" Tamango," said Ayché at last, " all that you suffer, you suffer because of me."

" I do not suffer," he answered bluntly, and threw on the mattress, besides his wife, the half biscuit that remained to him.

" Keep it for yourself," she said, gently refusing the biscuit ; " I am not hungry any more. Besides, why eat ? Is not my hour come ? "

Tamango got up without reply, went tottering on deck, and sat down at the foot of a broken mast. With his head bowed on his breast, he whistled the song of his family. Suddenly a great shout sounded through the noise of wind and sea. A light appeared. He heard other shouts and a big black vessel slipped swiftly by his own ; so near that the yards passed over his head. He saw only two faces lit by a lantern hung from a mast. These men shouted once again before their ship, carried along by the wind, disappeared into the darkness. Undoubtedly the look-out men had seen the wrecked vessel ; but the storm prevented them from tacking about. The next day there was not a sail on the horizon. Tamango lay down on his mattress and closed his eyes. His wife Ayché had died that night.

. . . .

I do not know how long afterwards an English frigate, the *Bellona*, sighted a ship, dismasted and apparently deserted by her crew. When a sloop was sent alongside, there was found a dead negress and a nigger so fleshless and emaciated that he was like a mummy. He was unconscious, but had still a breath of life. The surgeon took him in hand and nursed him, and when the *Bellona* reached Kingstown, Tamango was in perfect health. They asked him for his story. He told them what he knew of it. The planters of the island wanted him hanged as a rebel negro ; but the governor, who was a humane man, interested himself in him, and found his actions justifiable, since after all he had only exerted the legitimate right of self-defence ; and since those he had killed were only Frenchmen. They gave him his liberty, that is to say, set him to work for the Government ; but he had six sous a day and his food. He was a very fine-looking man. The colonel of the 75th saw him, and took him to make a cymbal-player of him in the regimental band. He learnt a little English ; but he scarcely spoke. Instead he drank rum and grog in inordinate quantities. He died in hospital of inflammation of the lungs.

THE BLUE ROOM

Prosper Mérimée

A young man was walking with an agitated air about the railway station. He had blue glasses, and although he had not a cold in his head, he kept putting his handkerchief to his nose. In his left hand he held a little black bag, containing, as I learnt later, a silk dressing-gown and some Turkish trousers.

From time to time he went to the entrance and looked up and down the street ; then he drew out his watch and studied the time-table. It was an hour before the train went ; but there are some folk who are always afraid of being late. The train was not one of those that busy people take—few first class carriages. And the hour it went was not that which allows business men to leave as soon as their work is done, and arrive in time for dinner at their country-houses. When the passengers began to show themselves, a Parisian would have seen by their air that they were farmers or little traders of the suburbs.

Still, each time any one entered the station, each time a cab stopped at the gate, the heart of the young man in blue glasses swelled out like a balloon ; his knees trembled ; his bag almost fell from his hand ; and his glasses nearly tumbled from his nose, on which, it might be said in passing, they were placed wrong side round.

It was still worse when, after a long wait, there appeared through a side door, coming precisely from the only point that was not subjected to continual observation, a woman clad in black, with a thick veil over her face, holding in her hand a bag of brown morocco, containing, as I afterwards discovered, a wonderful dressing-gown and a pair of blue satin slippers. The woman and the young man came towards each other, looking to the right and the left, but never before them. They came together, touched hands, and stayed for some minutes without saying a word panting, trembling, overcome by one of those poignant emotions, for which I would give a hundred years of philosophic meditations.

" Léon," said the young woman—I have forgotten to say she was young and pretty—" Léon, what happinesss ! Never should I have known you in those blue glasses ! "

" What joy ! " said Léon. " I should have never recognised you under that black veil ! "

" What joy ! " she continued. " Let us get our seats quick. If the train started without us ! . . . (And she squeezed his arm.) Nobody guesses what is happening. At this moment I am with Clara and her husband, going to their country-house, where I ought to-morrow to say good-bye ! . . . And," she added laughing and lowering her head, " it is just an hour since I went away with Clara, and to-morrow, . . . after having passed the last evening with her . . . (again she squeezed his arm), to-morrow, in the morning, she will leave me at the station, where I shall find Ursule, whom I have sent on ahead at my aunt's. . . . Oh ! I have thought out everything ! Let us get our tickets. . . . It is impossible we should be found out ! Oh ! If they want to know our names at the end ? I have already forgotten. . . ."

" Monsieur and Madame Duru."

" No ! not Duru. There was a shoemaker at the boarding-school with that name."

" Then, Dumont ? . . ."

" Daumont ! "

" Very well ! But they will not question us ! "

A bell rang, the door of the waiting-room opened, and the young woman, always carefully veiled, darted into a carriage with her young companion. For the second time the bell rang, a porter shut the door of their compartment.

" We are alone ! " they cried joyfully.

But at that very moment a man of about fifty, dressed all in black, with a broad serious face, entered the carriage and settled down in a corner. The engine whistled and the train set off. The young couple, withdrawing as far as they could from their inconvenient neighbour, began to talk in whispers, and, as an extra precaution, in English.

" Sir," said the other passenger, in the same language and with a much purer English accent, " if you want to talk secrets, you had better not use English before me. I am an Englishman. Sorry to trouble you ; but in the other compartment there was only one man, and as a matter of principle I never travel with a single man. He looked to me like a Judas. And this might have tempted him."

He pointed to his travelling-bag that he had thrown on a cushion before him.

" If I can't sleep, I will read."

And he did loyally try to sleep. Opening his bag, he took out a travelling-cap, put it on his head, and kept his eyes shut for some minutes. Then opening them with a movement of impatience, he groped in his bag for spectacles, then for a Greek book. At last he began to read very attentively. In getting the book out of the bag he had overturned many things, all thrown in anyhow. Among other articles he drew out was a pretty thick bundle of Bank of England notes, placed them on the seat in front of him, and before putting them back in the bag he showed them to the young man and asked him if he could change bank-notes at a certain town.

" Probably. It is on the way to England," said Léon.

It was to this town that the young couple were going. There is a little hotel there, fairly clean, where travellers usually stay only on Saturday evening. It is pretended that the rooms are good ; but the landlord and his servants are not far enough removed from Paris to keep a really good inn. Léon had come across the place some time before, when he was not wearing blue glasses, and after the account he gave of it, his sweetheart felt she would like to see it.

Besides, on this day, she was in such a frame of mind that the walls of a prison would have seemed to her full of charm if she had been shut in there with Léon. However, the train went on, the Englishman read his Greek without turning to look at his companions, who chatted in such whispers that only lovers could have understood. Perhaps I shall not surprise my readers by admitting that they were eloping lovers. And what was really deplorable was that they were not married, and there were great difficulties in the way of their marriage.

They reached their stopping-place. The Englishman was the first to alight. While Léon was helping his sweetheart to get out of the carriage without showing her ankles, a man darted from a neighbouring compartment on to the platform. He was pale, even yellow, with sunken, bloodshot eyes and a straggling beard— quite a criminal in appearance. His suit was clean but thread-worn. His frock-coat once black, now grey at the elbows and at the back, was buttoned to the chin, probably to hide a waistcoat still shabbier. He came up to the Englishman, and in a very humble voice :

" Uncle ! " he said to him.

" Leave me alone, you wretch," cried the Englishman, his grey
eye lighting up with anger, as he began to walk out of the station.

" Don't drive me to despair," said the other man, in a tone at
once sorrowful and threatening.

" Will you be good enough to look after my bag a moment ? "
said the old Englishman, throwing his bag at the feet of Léon.

Seizing the arm of the man who had accosted him, he pushed
him in a corner, where he hoped he would not be overheard, and
there he spoke to him for a moment in a very harsh voice. Then,
taking from his pocket some papers, he put them in the hand of
the man who had called him uncle. The man took the papers
without any thanks, and almost at once went away and disappeared.

There is only one hotel in the town, so you must not be astonished
that, at the end of a few minutes, all the characters in this truthful
tale met again there. In France every traveller who has the luck
to have a well-dressed woman on his arm is sure of obtaining the
best room in all the hotel : thus is it established that we are the
most polished nation in Europe.

If the room given to Léon was the best, it would be rash to
conclude that it was excellent. There was a great wooden bed,
with curtains of chintz, on which was printed in violet the magical
story of Pyramus and Thisbe. The walls were covered with a
painted paper representing a view of Naples, and crowded with
figures. Unhappily, idle and indiscreet travellers had added
moustaches and pipes to all the figures, male and female ; and
many foolish remarks in prose and verse were written in pencil on
the sky and on the sea. Against this background hung several
engravings : *Louis Philippe swearing to the Charta of* 1830 ; *The
First Meeting of Julie and Saint Preux ;* the *Regrets* and the *Hope
of Happiness* after Dubuffe. This room was called the Blue Room,
because the two arm-chairs to the right and left of the fire-place
were in Dutch velvet of this colour. But for many years past
they had been hidden under coverings of grey, glazed cloth with
amaranth frills.

While the maids of the hotel gathered round the young lady and
offered her their services, Léon, who was not wanting in good sense,
even when in love, went to the kitchen to order dinner. He had
to use all his eloquence and resort to bribery to get the promise of
a private dinner ; but greatly was he disconcerted when he learnt
that in the big dining-room adjoining the Blue Room the officers
of the 3rd Hussars, who were about to relieve the officers of the
3rd Light Infantry, were joining the latter that very day in a
farewell dinner that would take place with much cordiality.

The landlord swore by all his gods that, apart from the gaiety
natural to all French soldiers, the Hussars and the Light Infantry

were noted in the town for their gentleness and their good conduct, and that their presence would not inconvenience Madame in the least, the custom of the officers being to end the dinner before midnight.

As Léon went back to the Blue Room, worried over this affair, he saw that the old Englishman had taken the room next to his. The door was open. The Englishman, sitting before a table on which were placed a glass and a bottle, looked at the ceiling with deep attention, as though he were counting the flies that were walking there.

"What does it matter who our neighbours are?" said Léon to himself. "The Englishman will soon be drunk, and the soldiers will have gone away before midnight."

In entering the Blue Room his first care was to make sure that the communicating doors were properly closed and locked. On the side of the Englishman there was a double door; the wall was thick. On the side of the Hussars the partition was thinner; but the door had a lock and key. After all, it was a more effectual barrier against curiosity than the curtains of a cab are; and how many people think they are isolated from the world in a cab!

Certainly the richest imagination cannot picture a more complete happiness than that of two young lovers who, after long waiting, find themselves alone, far from the eyes of jealous and curious people, so that they can relate at leisure their bygone troubles and relish the delights of a perfect meeting. But the devil always finds some means of pouring his drop of bitterness into the cup of felicity. While eating a pretty poor dinner in the Blue Room, composed of some dishes stolen from the banquet of the officers, Léon and his lady had to suffer a good deal from the conversation that those gentlemen held in the neighbouring room. Their talk turned on matters that had nothing to do with strategy and tactics, and I cannot possibly report it.

It was a long string of coarse stories, accompanied by outbursts of laughter in which it was sometimes difficult for our lovers not to take part. Léon's sweetheart was not a prude, but there are some things a woman does not like to hear, even in company with the man she loves. The situation became more and more embarrassing; and when the officers were beginning their dessert, Léon went down to the kitchen to beg the landlord to tell the gentlemen there was a sick lady in the next room, and to ask them to have the politeness to make a little less noise.

The landlord, as always happens in army dinners, was quite flurried, and did not know what to say. For at the moment when Léon gave him the message for the officers, a waiter asked him for champagne for the Hussars, and a maid for a bottle of port for the Englishman.

" I told him we had no port," she added.

" You are a fool. I keep every kind of wine. I will find him his bottle of port ! Bring me a bottle of ratafia, a bottle of fifteen, and a decanter of brandy."

After having manufactured the port in a turn of the hand, the landlord entered the dining-room and gave the message from Léon. It first excited a furious storm. Then a bass voice, that dominated all the others, demanded what kind of woman they had for a neighbour.

" My faith, messieurs," said the landlord, " she is very pretty and she is very shy. Marie Jeanne says she has a wedding ring. So it may be a bride who has come here for her honeymoon, as they sometimes do."

" A bride ! " shouted forty voices. " She must come and drink with us. We will toast her health, and teach her husband his duties ! "

At these words there was a great clanking of spurs, and our couple trembled, thinking that their room was going to be taken by storm. But suddenly a voice stayed the movement. Evidently it was one of the chiefs that spoke. He reproached the officers with their impoliteness, and told them to sit down, and speak decently without shouting. Then he added some words in too low a voice to be heard in the Blue Room. They were received with deference, but not without exciting a certain restrained hilarity.

From this moment there was a comparative silence in the officers' room, and our loving pair blessed the salutary effects of discipline, and began to talk together with more ease. But after so much upset, it took some time to recover those tender emotions which anxieties, the fatigues of travelling, and above all the coarse merriment of their neighbours, had greatly troubled. At their age, however, the thing is not very difficult, and they soon forgot all the unpleasantness of their adventurous expedition, and began to think only of its pleasures.

They fancied they had made peace with the Hussars. Alas ! it was only a truce. The moment when they were least expecting it, when they were thousands of leagues away from this sublunary world, behold ! twenty-four bugles, sustained by several trombones, poured out the air known to French soldiers, " Ours is the victory ! " How could any one resist such a tempest ? The poor lovers were much to be pitied.

No, not very much. For in the end the officers came out of the dining-room, defiling before the door of the Blue Room with much clank of sabres and spurs, and shouting one after the other, " Good-night, madame, the bride."

Then all sound ceased. No, I am mistaken. The Englishman came out into the corridor and cried :

" Waiter, bring me another bottle of that same port ! "

Calmness settled at last on the little inn. The night was sweet, the moon at full. From time immemorial lovers have delighted to look at our satellite. Léon and his lady opened their window, that looked on a little garden, and breathed with joy the cool air, fragrant with the scent of clematis. They did not remain at the window very long. A man was walking in the garden, his head bowed, his arms crossed, a cigar in his mouth. Léon thought he recognised the nephew of the Englishman who loved the good wine of Portugal.

I hate useless details, and besides I am not obliged to tell the reader all that took place, hour by hour, in the inn. So I will only say that the candle, burning on the mantelpiece in the Blue Room, was more than half consumed, when, in the bedroom of the Englishman, hitherto silent, a strange noise was heard, such as a heavy body might produce in its fall. And with this noise there mingled a sort of cracking, not less strange, followed by a stifled cry and several indistinct words, resembling a curse. The young couple in the Blue Room were startled. Perhaps they had been aroused by the fall ; for on both of them the mysterious noise produced an almost sinister impression.

" It is our Englishman dreaming," said Léon, trying to smile. He wished to reassure his companion, but he shivered involuntarily. Two or three minutes afterwards, a door was opened in the corridor, very carefully it seemed, then it was shut very quietly. Some one could be heard walking slowly and uneasily, who, to all appearance, was trying to pass without being heard.

" What a cursed place ! " cried Léon.

" Ah, it is like heaven ! . . ." said the young lady, letting her head fall on Léon's shoulder. " I am so sleepy. . . ."

She sighed and fell asleep again almost at once. But Léon was worried, and his imagination began to dwell on several things that, in another frame of mind, he would have passed over. The sinister figure of the Englishman's nephew was recalled to his memory. There was hatred in the glance he gave his uncle, whilst speaking to him with humility, no doubt because he was asking for money. What could be easier than for a man, still young and vigorous, and desperate besides, to climb from the garden to the window of the next room ? . . . Moreover, he was staying in the inn, since he was walking in the garden at night. Perhaps . . . even probably . . . indubitably, he knew that there was a thick bundle of bank-notes in his uncle's bag. . . . And that heavy blow, like a club falling on a bald head ! . . . that stifled cry ! . . . that frightful oath, and then the creeping steps afterwards ! The nephew had the air of a murderer. . . . But a hotel full of officers is not a good place for a murderer. No doubt this Englishman, like a prudent man, had locked his door, especially knowing what sort of fellow was hanging about. He mistrusted him, since he did not want to go up to him with his bag in his hand. . . . But why think of such hideous things when you are so happy ?

That was what Léon said to himself. In the middle of his thoughts, which I refrain from analysing at length, and which came to him almost as confused as the visions of a dream, he had his eyes fixed mechanically on the communicating door between the Blue Room and the Englishman's room.

In France the doors do not shut well. Between this one and the floor there was an opening of nearly half an inch. Suddenly, through this opening, scarcely lighted by the reflection from the waxed floor, there appeared something blackish, flat, resembling the blade of a knife, for the edge, touched by the light from the candle, showed a thin brilliant line. This moved slowly in the direction of a little slipper of blue satin, thrown indiscreetly a little way from the door. Was it some insect like a centipede ? . . . No ; it was not an insect, it had no fixed shape. . . . Two or three brown trails, each with its line of light at the edge, penetrate into the Blue Room. Their movement quickens, owing to the slope of the floor ; they advance rapidly, and begin to touch the little slipper. No more doubt ! It is a liquid, and its colour can now be seen distinctly by the light of the candle—it is blood ! And while Léon, motionless, stared with horror at the frightful thing, the young lady slept on peacefully, and her regular breath warmed the neck and shoulder of the terrified man.

The care that Léon had taken to order dinner as soon as he arrived at the inn is sufficient to prove that he had a good head on his shoulders and was able to look ahead. He did not belie his character on this occasion. He made no movement, and all the force of his mind bent in an effort to come to some decision in the presence of the frightful misfortune that threatened him.

I imagine that most of my readers, and especially my lady readers, full themselves with the spirit of heroism, will blame Léon for his inactivity and his lack of courage. He ought, I shall be told, to have run to the Englishman's room and arrested the murderer. At the very least, he should have pulled his bell and aroused the people of the inn. To this I must answer, first, that in French inns the bell-rope is only an ornament in the bedrooms : there is no apparatus in metal attached to the other end of the cord. I will also add, respectfully but firmly, that, if it is wrong to let an Englishman die in the next room, it is not at all praise-worthy to sacrifice to an old foreigner the young and pretty woman who is sleeping with her head on your shoulder. What would have happened if Léon had shouted out and awakened everybody in the inn ? Gendarmes, a magistrate and his clerk would soon have arrived. Before asking him what he had seen or heard, these gentlemen are so inquisitive by profession that they would have started by asking Léon :

" What is your name ?   Where are your papers ?   And madame ? Why are you staying together in this Blue Room ?   You will both have to appear before the court of assize and give evidence that, on such a date, at such an hour at night, you have been witnesses to such and such things."

Now, it was precisely this idea of the magistrate and the police that first presented itself to the mind of Léon.   There are some problems in life that are difficult to solve.   Is it better to let an unknown foreigner be murdered, or lose and bring dishonour upon a beloved woman ?   Léon did what most men would have done in his place.   He did not stir.   With his eyes fixed on the blue slipper, and the little red stream that touched it, he remained for some time as though he was fascinated, while a cold sweat came on his forehead, and his heart beat in his breast enough to break it open. A crowd of horrible thoughts and odd images beset him, and an inner voice said to him every minute, " In an hour everything will be known, and it is your fault ! "   However, through continually asking himself, " Whatever shall I do in this affair ? " a man often ends by finding some rays of hope.

" If we leave this accursed hotel," said Léon to himself, " before they discover what has happened in the next room, perhaps we shall be able to cover up our traces.   Nobody knows us here.   They have only seen me in blue glasses, and they have never seen her without her veil.   We are only two steps from the station, and in an hour we shall be far away from this town."

Then, as he had well studied the time-table in arranging his elopement, he remembered that a train to Paris passed at eight o'clock.   Soon after that, he and his lady would be lost in the immensity of that city, that hides so many criminals.   Who could there discover two innocent persons ?   But if any one entered the Englishman's room before eight o'clock?   All the problem was there.

Well convinced there was nothing else he could do, he made a desperate effort to shake off the drowsiness that had long been gaining on him.   But at his first movement his companion awoke and kissed him.   At the touch of his icy cheek she gave a little cry.

" What is the matter ? " she said anxiously.   " Your forehead is like marble."

" It is nothing," he replied in a shaky voice.   " I heard a noise in the next room."

Getting out of bed, he took the blue slipper away, and placed an armchair before the communicating door, so as to hide from his sweetheart the frightful stream which, having now ceased to spread, formed a large pool on the floor.   Then he opened the door and listened in the corridor. He even dared to try the door of the Englishman's room. It was locked. There was already some stir in the inn. The day was dawning. Some stablemen were grooming the horses in the yard, and, on the second floor, an officer was coming downstairs with clanking spurs. He was going to see that the horses were properly looked after.

Léon returned to the Blue Room, and, with circumlocutions and euphemisms, and all the precautions that love could suggest, he told his lady in what situation they were.

It was dangerous to remain, and dangerous to go too soon, and still more dangerous to wait in the inn until the discovery was made in the next room. It is useless to describe the fright caused by this information ; the tears that followed it ; the wild proposals that were made ; how many times the two unhappy creatures threw themselves in each others arms, saying, " Pardon me ! " " Pardon me ! " Each blamed themselves. They promised to die together ; for the young lady was sure they would be found guilty of the murder of the Englishman ; and as they were not certain they would be permitted to kiss on the scaffold, they stifled each other with embraces, and watered each other with their tears.

At last, having said many absurdities and many loving things, they recognised, in the midst of a thousand kisses, that Léon's plan of departing by the eight o'clock train was the only practical one. But there were still two mortal hours to pass. At each step in the corridor they trembled in all their limbs. Each squeak of a boot announced to them the arrival of the police. Their little luggage was packed in the twinkling of an eye. The young lady wished to burn the blue slipper in the fire-place, but Léon took it and after wiping it on the under bedclothes, he kissed it, and put it in his pocket. He was surprised to find it had a vanilla fragrance : his lady liked the same perfume as the Empress Eugénie.

Already everybody was awake in the inn. They could hear the waiters laughing, the maids singing, the soldiers brushing the officers' clothes. Seven o'clock chimed. Léon wished to get his love to take a cup of coffee but she declared her throat was so tight that she would die if she tried to drink anything. Léon, putting on his blue glasses, went down to pay his bill. The landlord begged his pardon for the noise that had been made. He still could not understand it, for the officers were always so quiet. Léon assured him he had heard nothing, and had slept excellently.

" Now your neighbour in the other room," continued the landlord, " cannot have inconvenienced you, for he has not made much noise. I wager he is still sleeping like the dead."

Léon leant heavily against the desk to prevent himself from falling, and his lady, who had resolved to come with him, clutched his arm, pressing her veil over her eyes.

" It is an English lord," went on the landlord pitilessly. " He always wants the best of everything. Ah, he is a gentleman ! But all the English are not like him. There is another here who is a mean rascal. He finds everything too dear—the room and the dinner. He wanted me to give him a hundred and fifty francs for a Bank of England note of five pounds. But is it good ? Here, sir, you ought to know that, for I heard you speaking English with Madame. Is it a good one ? "

He held out a five pound bank-note. On one of the corners was a little red stain that Léon understood.

" I think it is quite good," he said in a strangled voice.

" Oh, you have plenty of time," continued the landlord. " The train is not due till eight o'clock, and it is always late. Won't you sit down, madame ? you seem tired."

At this moment a plump maid entered.

" Some warm water, quick," she said, " for the tea of milord ! Get a sponge also ! He has broken his bottle of port and all his room is flooded."

Léon let himself fall into a chair ; his companion did the same. A strong desire to laugh took them both, and they had some trouble not to give way. The young lady shook him joyfully by the hand.

" Decidedly," said Léon to the landlord, " we will not go till the afternoon. Prepare a really good lunch for us at twelve."

THE
GAME OF BACKGAMMON

Prosper Mérimée

The motionless sails hung glued against the masts ; the sea was smooth as a mirror ; the heat was stifling, the calm hopeless. On a sea-voyage the means of entertainment at command of a vessel's guests are soon exhausted. People know each other too well after passing four months together in a wooden house of a hundred and twenty feet in length. When you see the first lieutenant approaching, you know at once that he will talk to you of Rio de Janeiro, where he has just been ; then of the famous Essling Bridge that he saw built by the Marine Guards, of whom he was one. At the end of a fortnight you know even the expressions he affects, the punctuations of his phrases, the different intonations of his voice. When has he ever neglected a melancholy pause after the first occurrence in his tale of the words " The Emperor " . . . ? " If you had see him then ! ! ! " (three points of exclamation) he invariably adds. And the episode of the trumpeter's horse, and the cannon-ball that ricochetted and carried away a cartridge-case with seven thousand five hundred francs' worth of gold and jewels, etc. etc. !—The second lieutenant is a great politician ; he comments every day on the last number of the *Constitutionnel* that he brought away with him from Brest ; or, if he leave the sublimities of politics for a descent to literature, will regale you with the plot of the last vaudeville he saw played. Good heavens ! . . .

The Marine Commissioner had a very interesting story. How he delighted you the first time he described his escape from the hulks of Cadiz ! But, at the twentieth repetition, upon my honour, it was unbearable. And the ensigns, and the midshipmen ! The memory of their conversations makes the hair rise on my head. The captain is usually the least tiresome person on board. In his quality of autocrat he is in a state of secret hostility against his whole staff ; he annoys, and sometimes is oppressive ; but there is a certain pleasure in cursing at him. If he has a passion for scolding his subordinates, they have the pleasure of seeing their superior look ridiculous, and that is a consolation.

On the vessel in which I had embarked the officers were the best men in the world, all good fellows, friendly as brothers, but each one more tedious than the last. The captain was the mildest of men, and (an exception) no busybody. It was always with regret that he exerted his absolute authority. None the less the voyage seemed long to me, and especially this calm which overtook us when only a few days from sight of land . . . !

One day after dinner, that our enforced idleness had made us protract as long as was humanly possible, we were all assembled on the deck watching the monotonous but always majestic spectacle of a sunset over the sea. Some were smoking, others reading, for the twentieth time, one of the thirty volumes of our dreary library ; all were yawning till the tears came. An ensign, seated beside me, was amusing himself with all the gravity befitting a serious business, by dropping point downwards on the deck the dirk usually carried by marine officers in undress uniform.

It was an amusement of sorts, and it needed some skill to make the point stick quite perpendicularly in the wood. Wishing to imitate the ensign, and having no dirk of my own, I wanted to borrow the captain's, but he refused me. He was oddly fond of the weapon, and it would have annoyed him to see it serve for so futile an amusement. The dirk had once belonged to a brave officer who had unfortunately died in the last war. . . . I guessed that a story was to follow, and was not mistaken. The captain began without waiting to be pressed ; as for the officers about us, since each one of them knew Lieutenant Roger's misfortunes by heart, they made an immediate and prudent retreat. Here is something like the captain's tale :—

Roger, when I met him, was my senior by three years ; he was a lieutenant, I an ensign. I assure you he was one of the best officers in our corps ; good-hearted too, witty, well educated, talented—in a word, a delightful young man. He was, unfortunately, a little proud and sensitive ; this was due, I think, to the fact that he was illegitmate, and that he feared lest his birth should lose him respect in society ; but, to tell the truth, of all his faults, the greatest was a violent and continual desire of standing first wherever he happened to be. His father, whom he had never seen, made him an allowance that would have been more than sufficient for his needs, if Roger had not been generosity itself. Everything he had was at the disposal of his friends. When he had just touched his quarter's money, he would say to any one who went to see him with a sad and careworn face, " Well, comrade, and what is the matter with you ? You don't seem able to make much of a noise when you slap your pockets ; come now, here is my purse, take what you want, and come and have dinner with me."

There came to Brest a young and very pretty actress called Gabrielle, who was not long in making her conquests among the naval and military officers. She was not a regular beauty, but she had a figure, fine eyes, a little foot, and a fairly saucy way with her ; and all that is very pleasing when one is in the latitude of twenty to twenty-five. It was said too that she was the most capricious creature of her sex, and her manner of playing did not give the lie to her reputation. One day she would play entrancingly, and one would have called her a *comédienne* of the first order ; the next, in the same piece, she would be cold, insensible, repeating her words like a child saying its catechism. What especially interested us young men was an anecdote current about her. It appeared that she had been kept in great magnificence in Paris by a senator, who, as they say, was mad on her. One day this man put his hat on in her presence ; she asked him to take it off, and even complained that he was lacking in respect for her. The senator laughed, shrugged his shoulders, and said, settling himself in a chair, " At least I can be at ease in the house of a woman I pay." A heavy blow, delivered by the white hand of Gabrielle, instantly paid him for his reply, and sent his hat to the other side of the room. Thenceforward complete rupture. Bankers and generals had made considerable offers to the lady ; but she had refused them all, and become an actress, in order, as she put it, to live in independence.

When Roger saw her and heard the story he decided that she was made for him, and, with the rather brutal frankness of which we sailors are accused, he took these means of showing her how deeply

he was smitten by her charms. He bought the most beautiful and
rarest flowers that he could find at Brest, made a bouquet of them
that he tied with a fine pink ribbon, and very carefully arranged in
the knot a roll of twenty-five napoleons ; it was all he possessed at
the moment. I remember I went in the wings with him during an
interval. He made Gabrielle a very short compliment on the grace
with which she wore her dress, offered her the bouquet, and asked
if he might come and see her at her house. All this was said in three
words.

So long as Gabrielle only saw the flowers, and the handsome young
man who presented them, she smiled on him, accompanying her smile
with one of the most gracious of bows ; but when she had the
bouquet in her hands, and felt the weight of the gold, her face
changed more swiftly than the sea lifted by a tropical hurricane ;
and certainly she was scarcely less malicious, for she threw the
bouquet and the napoleons with all her strength at the head of
my poor friend, who carried the marks on his face for over a week.
The manager's bell sounded, and Gabrielle went on and played at
random.

Roger picked up his bouquet and his roll of money with a very
abashed air, went to a café to offer the bouquet (without the money)
to the girl behind the bar, and tried, in drinking punch, to forget
his cruel lady. He did not succeed ; and, in spite of the annoyance
he felt at being unable to show himself with his black eye, he became
madly amorous of the choleric Gabrielle. He wrote her twenty
letters a day, and what letters ! submissive, tender, respectful—
letters one could have sent to a princess. The first were sent back
to him unopened ; the rest received no reply. Roger, however,
kept up some hope, until we found that the orange-seller of the
theatre was wrapping up his oranges in Roger's love-letters, given
him, with refined malice, by Gabrielle. This was a terrible blow
to our friend's pride. However, his passion did not weaken.
He spoke of demanding the actress in marriage, and when told that
the Minister of Marine would never give his consent, he declared
he would blow out his brains.

While things were so, it happened that the officers of a line
regiment, in garrison at Brest, wanted Gabrielle to repeat a vaudeville couplet, which she refused from pure caprice. The officers
and the actress were both so obstinate that the former hissed till
the curtain was lowered, and the latter left the place. You know
what the pit is like in a garrison town. It was agreed between the
officers that the next day and the days following the culprit should
be hissed without mercy, and that she should not be allowed to
play a single part until she had apologised with sufficient humility
to expiate her crime. Roger had not been present at this performance ; but he learnt the same evening of the scandal that had

set the whole theatre in an uproar, and so of the projects of vengeance plotted for the morrow. His decision was instantly made.

The next day, when Gabrielle appeared, hoots and hisses enough to split the ears came from the officers' benches. Roger, who had placed himself purposely quite close to the brawlers, stood up and addressed the noisiest in terms so outrageous that all their anger was instantly turned upon himself. Then, with great sang-froid, he took his note-book from his pocket, and wrote down the names that were shouted to him from all sides; he would have made appointments to do battle with the whole regiment, if a great number of naval officers had not interfered from *esprit de corps* and drawn challenges from the greater part of his adversaries. The tumult was truly terrific.

The whole garrison was confined for several days; but, when we were again at liberty, there was a terrible account to settle. There were threescore of us on the field. Roger alone fought with three officers successively; he killed one of them, and grievously wounded the other two, without receiving a scratch. I was less fortunate: a cursed lieutenant, who had been a fencing-master, gave me a great sword-thrust in the chest, from which I nearly died. That duel, or rather battle, was a fine spectacle, I assure you. The navy had the advantage throughout, and the regiment was obliged to leave Brest.

You may well think that our superior officers did not forget the author of the quarrel. For fiteen days there was a sentinel at his door.

When he was no longer under arrest, I left the hospital and went to see him. What was my surprise, on entering his quarters, to see him seated at lunch with Gabrielle. They looked as if they had had for some time a perfect understanding. Already they were calling each other " thou," and drinking out of the same glass. Roger presented me to his lady-love as his best friend, and told her how I had been wounded in the species of skirmish whose first cause had been herself. That brought me a kiss from the fair lady. This girl had altogether martial inclinations.

They spent three months together, perfectly happy, not separated for a moment. Gabrielle seemed madly in love with him, and Roger avowed that he had not known what love was before knowing Gabrielle.

A Dutch frigate came into the harbour. The officers gave us a dinner. We drank freely of all sorts of wine; and, when the table had been cleared, not knowing what to do, for these gentlemen spoke very bad French, we began to play. The Dutchmen seemed to have plenty of money; and their first lieutenant especially wished to play for stakes so high that not one of us cared to have a game with him. Roger, who did not usually play, thought it his business, this being so, to sustain the honour of his country. He played accordingly, and agreed to whatever the Dutch lieutenant proposed. He won at first, then lost. After some alternations of winning and losing, they separated without advantage on either side. We dined the Dutch officers in return. We played again. Roger and the lieutenant took up their battle. In short, during several days, they made appointments at the café or on board, trying all sorts of games, mostly backgammon, and always increasing their stakes, so that they came to be playing for twenty-five napoleons a game. It was a huge sum for poor officers like us : more than two months' pay ! At the end of a week Roger had lost all the money he possessed, and three or four thousand francs borrowed right and left.

You are right in suspecting that Roger and Gabrielle had ended by setting up a common household and a common purse ; that is to say, Roger, who had just touched a big share of prize-money, had contributed ten or twenty times as much as the actress. However, he always considered that this sum belonged principally to his lady, and he had kept only fifty napoleons for his personal expenses. He had had, none the less, to use this reserve in order to go on playing. Gabrielle did not make the slightest protest.

The household wealth went the same way as his pocket-money. Soon Roger was reduced to playing for his last twenty-five napoleons. He applied himself horribly ; and the game was long and well fought. There came a moment when Roger, holding the dice-box, had but one chance to win ; I think he needed the six four. The night was advanced. An officer who had watched their play for a long time had ended by falling asleep in a chair. The Dutchman was tired and sleepy ; besides he had drunk a great deal of punch. Roger alone was well awake, and a prey to the most violent despair. He trembled as he threw the dice. He threw them so roughly on the board that the shock brought a candle to the floor. The Dutchman turned first towards the candle, that had just covered his new trousers with wax, and then looked at the dice. They showed six and four. Roger, pale as death, took the twenty-five napoleons. They went on playing. The luck became favourable to my unfortunate friend, who, however, made mistake after mistake, and played as if he wished to lose. The Dutch lieutenant grew wild, doubled, and tenfold increased the stakes ; always he lost. I think I see him still ; a big, phlegmatic blonde, with a face that seemed made of wax. He rose at last, after losing forty thousand francs, that he paid without his face betraying the slightest emotion.

Roger said :

" What we have done this evening does not count, you were half asleep ; I do not want your money."

" You are joking," replied the stolid Dutchman ; " I played very well, but the dice have been against me. I am sure of being able to beat you always, and give you four holes (48 points). Goodnight ! "

And he left him.

We learnt the next day that, made desperate by his losses, he had blown out his brains in his cabin, after drinking a bowl of punch.

The forty thousand francs won by Roger were spread on a table, and Gabrielle contemplated them with a smile of satisfaction.

" Behold us quite rich," said she ; "what shall we do with all this money ? "

Roger said nothing in reply ; he seemed stupefied since the Dutchman's death.

" We must do a thousand mad things," Gabrielle continued ; " money so easily gained must be spent in the same fashion. Let us buy a carriage and look down on the Maritime Prefect and his wife. I would like to have diamonds and Cashmeres. Ask for leave of absence, and let us go to Paris ; here we shall never come to the end of such a lot of money."

She stopped to look at Roger, who with his eyes fixed on the floor, resting his head in his hands, had not heard her, and seemed to be turning over in his mind the most sinister ideas.

" What the devil is the matter with you, Roger ? " she cried, putting a hand on his shoulder. " I believe you are sulky with me ; I cannot get a word from you."

" I am very unhappy," he said at last with a stifled sigh.

" Unhappy ! God forgive me, you are not feeling remorseful over plucking that fat *mynheer* ? "

He lifted his head and looked at her with haggard eyes.

" What does it matter ? " she pursued, " what does it matter that he took the thing tragically and blew out what few brains he had ? I do not pity players who lose ; and his money is certainly better in our hands than in his own ; he would have spent it in drinking and smoking, while we, we are going to commit a thousand extravagances, each one more elegant than the one before."

Roger walked up and down the room, his head bowed on his breast, his eyes half shut and filled with tears. You would have pitied him if you had seen him.

" Do you know," said Gabrielle, " that any one who did not know your romantic sensibilities might well believe you had cheated ? "

" And if that were the truth ? " he cried in a hollow voice, stopping before her.

" Bah ! " she answered, smiling, " you are not clever enough to cheat at play."

" Yes, I cheated, Gabrielle ; I cheated, like the wretch I am."

She knew from his emotion that what he said was only too true :

she sat down on a sofa, and stayed some time without speaking.

" I would rather," she said at last in a voice deeply moved, " I would rather you had killed ten men than cheated at play."

There was a mortal silence for half an hour. The two of them were seated on the same sofa, and did not look at each other a single time. Roger rose first, and said " Good-night " to her, in a fairly calm voice.

" Good-night," she replied, drily and coldly.

Roger told me afterwards that he would have killed himself that very day, if he had not feared that our comrades would guess the reason of his suicide. He did not wish his memory sullied.

The next day Gabrielle was as gay as usual ; you would have said she had already forgotten the confidences of the night before. As for Roger, he had become sombre, fanciful, morose ; he scarcely left his room, avoided his friends, and often spent whole days without saying a word to his mistress. I attributed his unhappiness to an honourable but excessive sensibility, and I made several attempts to console him. but he drily repulsed me, affecting a great indifference towards his unfortunate partner. One day he even made a violent attack on the Dutch nation, and wanted to persuade me that there was not a single respectable man in Holland. Secretly, however, he tried to find out the family of the Dutch lieutenant ; but no one could give him any information about them.

Six weeks after that unhappy game of backgammon, Roger found a note in Gabrielle's room, written by a midshipman, who seemed to be thanking her for favours she had shown him. Gabrielle was untidiness itself, and the note in question had been left by her upon her mantelpiece. I do not know if she had been unfaithful, but Roger thought so, and his rage was terrific. His love and a remnant of pride were the only sentiments that could still attach him to life, and the stronger of them was about to be thus suddenly destroyed. He overwhelmed the proud actress with insults, and, violent as he was, I do not know how he kept himself from striking her.

" Doubtless," he said, " this puppy has given you plenty of money ? It is the only thing you care for, and you would grant yours favours to the dirtiest common sailor, provided he could pay for them."

" Why not ? " the actress coldly replied. " Yes : I would take pay from a sailor, but . . . *I would not steal from him.*"

Roger uttered a cry of rage. He drew his dagger, trembling, and for a moment looked with wild eyes at Gabrielle ; then, pulling himself together, he threw the weapon at his feet, and left the room so as not to yield to the temptation that obsessed him.

The same evening I passed very late by his lodgings, and seeing a light in his windows, I went in to borrow a book from him. I found him very busy writing. He did not disturb himself, and seemed scarcely to perceive my presence in his room. I sat down by his desk and observed his features: they were so altered that any other than I would have had difficulty in recognising him. Suddenly I saw on the desk a letter already sealed and addressed to myself. I instantly opened it. Roger told me that he was about to put an end to his days, and entrusted me with various commissions. While I read, he went on writing without taking any notice of me ; he was making his farewells to Gabrielle. . . . You can guess my astonishment, and what I had to say to him, overwhelmed as I was by his resolve.

" What, you mean to kill yourself, you who are so happy ? "

" My friend," said he, sealing his letter, " you know nothing ; you do not know me ; I am a rogue : I am so despicable that a courtesan insults me ; and I am so sensible of my baseness that I have not the strength to fight against it."

Then he told me the story of the game of backgammon, and all that you know already. As I listened, I was at least as moved as he ; I did not know what to say to him ; I gripped his hands, I had tears in my eyes, but I could not speak. At last I had the idea of suggesting that he could not reproach himself with having voluntarily been the Dutchman's undoing, and that after all he had made him lose by his . . . cheating . . . only twenty-five napoleons.

" Then," he cried, with bitter irony, " I am a little thief and not a great one. And, with all my ambition, to be no more than a pick-pocket ! "

And he shouted with laughter.

I wept.

Suddenly the door opened ; a woman came in and threw herself in his arms ; it was Gabrielle.

" Forgive me," she cried, straining him to herself. " Forgive me. I know well I love no one but you. I love you better now than if you had not done the thing for which you reproach yourself. If you like, I will steal ; I have already stolen. . . . Yes, I have stolen, I stole a gold watch . . . . What worse could one do ? "

Roger shook his head with an air of incredulity ; but his forehead seemed to lighten.

" No, my poor child," he said, gently repulsing her, " there is no help for it ; I must kill myself. I suffer too much ; I cannot bear up against my misery."

" Eh, well ! if you mean to die, Roger, I shall die with you. What is life to me without you ! I am brave, I have fired guns ; I will kill myself just like any one else. Besides I have played in tragedy, I am in the habit of doing it. She had tears in her eyes when she began, but this last idea made her laugh, and Roger himself smiled. " You laugh, my officer," she cried, clapping her hands and kissing him ; " you will not kill yourself ! "

And she went on kissing him, now weeping, now laughing, now swearing like a sailor ; for she was not one of those women who are frightened by a coarse word.

Meanwhile I had got possession of Roger's pistols and dirk, and I said to him :

" My dear Roger, you have a sweetheart and a friend who love you. Believe me, you can yet find some happiness in this world." I went out after embracing him, and left him alone with Gabrielle.

I think we should only have succeeded in postponing his sombre plans, if he had not received a billet from the Minister, appointing him first lieutenant on board a vessel that was to go cruising in the Indies, after passing through the English squadron blockading the port. It was a risky business. I made him see that it was better to die nobly from an English bullet than to put an inglorious end to his days without doing any good to his country. He promised to live. He distributed half the forty thousand francs among disabled seamen and the widows and children of sailors. He gave the rest to Gabrielle, who first swore only to use the money in good works. She had a real intention of keeping her word, poor girl ; but her enthusiasms were of short duration. I learnt afterwards that she gave some thousands of francs to the poor. She bought chiffons with the rest.

We embarked, Roger and I, on a fine frigate, *La Galatée* ; our men were brave, well drilled, well disciplined ; but our commander was an ignoramus who thought himself a Jean Bart, because he swore better than an army captain, because he murdered the French language, and because he had never studied the theory of his profession, whose practice he understood sufficiently badly. However, luck was good to him at first. We got happily off the roads, thanks to a breeze that compelled the blockading squadron to take to the open sea, and we began our cruise by burning an English corvette and one of the Company's vessels off the coast of Portugal.

We sailed slowly towards the Indian seas, set back by contrary winds and the bad navigation of our captain, whose lack of skill added to the dangers of our cruise. Now chased by superior strengths, now pursuing merchant vessels, we did not pass a single day without some new adventure. But neither the hazardous life we were living, nor the troubles of the frigate's routine that fell to his share, could distract Roger from the melancholy thoughts that pursued him without respite. He, who was once the most zealous and brilliant officer in our port, now contented himself with the mere performance of his duty. As soon as his work was done he shut himself up in his cabin, without books and without paper; he spent whole hours lying in his bunk, and the poor wretch could not sleep.

One day, observing his dejection, I bethought myself of saying
to him :

"Great Heavens, my dear fellow, you are grieving over a small
matter. You have tricked a fat Dutchman out of twenty-five
napoleons ; well, and you have remorse enough for a million. Now
tell me, when you were the lover of the Prefect's wife at ——,
were you remorseful then ? Yet she was worth more than twenty-
five napoleons."

He turned over on his mattress without answering.

I went on.

"After all, your crime, since you say it was a crime, had an
honourable motive, and was due to a lofty soul."

He turned his head and looked furiously at me.

"Yes, for anyhow, if you had lost, what would have become of
Gabrielle ? Poor girl, she would have sold her last shirt for you. . . .
If you had lost she would have been reduced to misery. . . . It
was for her, for love, that you cheated. There are men who kill
for love . . . who kill themselves. . . . You, my dear Roger, did
more. For a man of our kind there is more courage in stealing,
to put it clearly, than in suicide."

"Perhaps now," said the captain, breaking off in his story,
"I seem absurd to you. I assure you that in that moment my
friendship for Roger gave me an eloquence I do not possess to-day
and, devil take it if I did not speak in good faith, speaking so to
him, and if I did not believe all I said. Ah ! I was young then ! "

"My friend," he said, seeming to make a great effort to command
himself, "you think me better than I am. I am a low-down
rogue. When I cheated that Dutchman, I thought only of getting
twenty-five napoleons, that was all. I did not think of Gabrielle,
and that is why I scorn myself. . . . For me to value my honour
at less than twenty-five napoleons ! What abasement ! Yes ;
I should be happy if I could say, ' I stole to save Gabrielle from
misery.' . . . No ! . . . No ! I did not think of her. I was not
a lover at that moment. . . . I was a gambler. . . . I was a thief. . . .
I stole money to have it myself . . . and that deed has so brutalised
and debased me that now I have no longer courage or love. . . .
I live, and I no longer think of Gabrielle. . . . I am a done man."

He seemed so wretched that if he had asked me for my pistols
to kill himself, I believe I should have given them him.

A certain Friday—day of ill omen—we sighted a big English
frigate, the *Alcestis*, who gave chase to us. She carried fifty-eight
guns, and we had only eight-and-thirty. We hoisted all sail to
escape her ; but her speed was greater than ours, and she gained
on us every moment ; it was clear that before night we should be
forced into an unequal combat. Our captain called Roger to his

cabin, where they were a good quarter of an hour consulting together. Roger came up on deck again, took me by the arm, and led me aside.

" In two hours from now," he said, " the engagement will begin ; that brave man who is trotting up and down the quarter-deck has lost his head. There were two courses open to him : the first, the more honourable, was to let the enemy catch us up, and then tackle her vigorously, throwing a hundred sturdy rascals aboard her ; the other course, not bad, but rather cowardly, was to lighten ourselves by throwing some of our cannon into the sea. Then we could have closely hugged the African coast that we shall sight over there to larboard. The English, for fear of running aground, would have been forced to let us escape ; but our —— captain is neither a coward nor a hero ; he is going to let himself be destroyed from afar by cannon-shot, and, after some hours of battle, will honourably lower his flag. So much the worse for you ; the hulks of Portsmouth await you. As for me, I have no intention of seeing them."

" Perhaps," I said, " our first shots will do such damage to the enemy that she will be obliged to give up the chase."

" Listen ; I do not mean to be a prisoner, I want to have myself killed ; it is time that I should make an end of things. If by bad luck I am only wounded, give me your word that you will throw me into the sea. That is the proper death-bed for a good sailor like me."

" What madness," I cried, " and what sort of a job are you giving me ? "

" You will be fulfilling the duty of a good friend. You know that I must die. You should remember, I only consented not to kill myself, in the hope of being killed. Come, promise me this : if you refuse, I am going to ask the favour from the boatswain, who will not."

After reflecting a little, I said :

" I give you my word to do what you want, only if you are wounded to death, without hope of recovery. In that case, I agree to spare you your sufferings."

" I shall be wounded to death, or killed."

He offered me his hand, and I gripped it firmly. He was calmer after that, and indeed his face shone with a certain martial gaiety.

Towards three o'clock in the afternoon the enemy's bow guns began to make play in our rigging. We furled some of our sails ; we presented our broadside to the *Alcestis*, and kept up a steady fire to which the English vigorously replied. After about an hour's fighting, our captain who did nothing at the right moment, wanted to try and board. But we had already many dead and wounded, and the rest of our crew had lost their keenness ; finally, we had

suffered sorely in our rigging, and our masts were badly damaged.
At the moment when we spread sail to come up to the English
ship our mainmast, with no longer anything to hold it, fell with a
horrible crash. The *Alcestis* profited by the confusion into which
this accident instantly threw us. She came up by our poop,
giving us her whole broadside at half the range of a pistol; she
raked our unlucky frigate from stern to stem, and we were only
able to reply with two small guns. At this moment I was close
to Roger, who was busy having the shrouds cut that still held the
fallen mast. I felt him forcibly grip my arm; I turned round and
saw him knocked over on the deck, and covered with blood. He
had just received a charge of grape-shot in the stomach.

The captain ran to him.

" What is to be done, lieutenant ? " he cried.

" We must nail our flag to the stump of the mast, and scuttle
the ship."

The captain left him at once, not finding this advice very much
to his taste.

" Come," said Roger, " remember your promise."

" This is nothing," I said. " You can recover from it."

" Throw me overboard," he cried, cursing horribly, and seizing
me by the skirts of my coat; " you can see that I cannot recover;
throw me in the sea; I do not want to see our flag struck."

Two sailors came up to carry him to the cockpit.

" To your guns, you rogues," he shouted; " load with grape-
shot, and aim at the deck. And you, if you do not keep your
word, I curse you, and I hold you the most cowardly and the
vilest of all men ! "

His wound was certainly mortal. I saw the captain call a
midshipman, and command him to strike our colours.

" Give me a hand-shake," I said to Roger.

At the very moment when our flag was lowered——

.   .   .   .

" Captain, a whale to the larboard," an ensign interrupted,
running up.

" A whale ? " cried the captain, transported with joy, leaving his
tale where it was. " Sharp now, lower the long-boat ! lower the
yawl ! lower all the long-boats ! Harpoons, ropes, etc., etc."

I was unable to learn how poor Lieutenant Roger died.

THE ETRUSCAN VASE

PROSPER MÉRIMÉE

AUGUSTE SAINT-CLAIR was not popular in what is called Society ; principally because he only tried to please those who pleased him. He sought them out, and fled the others. Besides, he was absent-minded and indolent. One evening, as he was leaving the Théâtre Italien, the Marquise A—— asked him how Mademoiselle Sontag had sung. " Yes, madame," replied Saint-Clair, smiling pleasantly and thinking of something quite different. It was impossible to attribute this ridiculous reply to timidity ; for he spoke to a great lord, to a great man, or even to a fashionable woman, with the same aplomb with which he would have entertained an equal. The Marquise decided that Saint-Clair was a prodigy of impertinence and stupidity.

Madame B—— asked him to dinner one Monday. She talked a great deal to him ; and, as he left the house, he declared he had never met a more delightful woman. Now Madame B—— was in the habit of collecting wit for a month at other people's houses, and spending it at her own in a single evening. Saint-Clair saw her again on the Thursday of the same week. This time he was a little bored. A third visit decided him never to show himself again in her drawing-room. Madame B—— declared that Saint-Clair was a young man with no manners, and of the worst form.

He had been born with a tender and loving heart ; but, at an age when impressions that last for a lifetime are too easily taken, his too expansive sensibility had made him the butt of his comrades. He was proud, ambitious ; he held to his opinions with childlike tenacity. From that time he studied to hide all the outward signs of what he regarded as an unworthy weakness. He achieved his end ; but his victory cost him dear. He could hide from others the feelings of his too sensitive soul, but in imprisoning them in himself he made them a hundred times more cruel. In Society he won the sad reputation of an indifferent and careless man ; and in solitude his restless imagination made torments for him, the more frightful in that he would confide them to nobody.

It is true that it is difficult to find a friend. Difficult ! Is it possible ? Have two men existed who did not hide a secret from each other ? Saint-Clair scarcely believed in friendship, and the fact was obvious. The young people of Society found him cold and reserved.

He never asked them for their secrets ; and for them, all his thoughts and most of his actions were hidden in mystery. The French love to talk of themselves ; so that Saint-Clair was, in spite of himself, the depositary of plenty of confidences. His friends—and the word means the people he saw twice a week—complained of his distrust of them ; it is a fact that the man who, unasked, shares his secret with us, is usually offended if he does not learn our own. People think there should be reciprocity in indiscretion.

" He is buttoned up to the chin," said one day the handsome Major Alphonse de Thémines. " I could never put the slightest trust in that devil of a Saint-Clair."

" I think him something of a Jesuit," replied Jules Lambert. " Some one told me on his word of honour he had twice met him coming out of Saint-Sulpice. No one knows what he is thinking. I can never be at ease with him."

They separated. Alphonse met Saint-Clair on the Boulevard Italien walking along with bent head, blind to everybody. Alphonse stopped him, took him by the arm, and before they had reached the Rue de la Paix, had told him the whole story of his affair with Madame ——, whose husband was so jealous and so brutal.

The same evening Jules Lambert lost his money at cards. He went and danced. While dancing, he elbowed a man who, having also lost all his money, was in a very bad temper. The result was an exchange of words, and arrangements for a meeting. Jules begged Saint-Clair to be his second, and on the same occasion borrowed money from him, which he has so far forgotten to repay.

After all, Saint-Clair was genial enough. His faults harmed nobody but himself. He was obliging, often delightful, scarcely ever a bore. He had travelled much, read much, and only spoke of his travels and his reading when pressed. Besides, he was big, and well made ; his face was noble and intellectual ; it was almost always too grave, but his smile was open and full of kindness.

I was forgetting an important point. Saint-Clair was attentive to all women, and sought their conversation more than that of men. Did he love ? It was difficult to say. Only, if love did touch this cold being, it was known that the pretty Countess Mathilde de Coursy was the woman he preferred. She was a young widow at whose house he was a regular visitor. There were the following data from which to conclude their intimacy : first, the almost ceremonious politeness of Saint-Clair towards the Countess, and vice versâ ; secondly, his foible of never pronouncing her name in public—or, if he were forced to speak of her, never with the slightest praise ; thirdly, before Saint-Clair had been introduced to her, he had been a passionate lover of music, and the Countess had a similar fondness for painting. Since they had met their tastes had changed.

Lastly, when the Countess had been at a watering-place the year before, Saint-Clair had set off six days after her.

. . . .

My duty as historian compels me to declare that one night in the month of July, a few minutes before dawn, the park-gate of a country-house opened, and a man came out, with all the precautions of a thief afraid of being surprised. The country-house belonged to Madame de Coursy, and the man was Saint-Clair. A woman wrapped in a pelisse accompanied him as far as the gate and leaned through it to see him the longer, as he went off down the path under the park wall. Saint Clair stopped, looked circumspectly about him, and made a sign with his hand for the woman to go in. In the brightness of the summer night he could distinguish her pale face still motionless in the same place. He retraced his steps, came up to her, and took her tenderly in his arms. He wanted to make her promise to go in ; but he had still a hundred things to say to her. Their talk had lasted ten minutes when they heard the voice of a peasant going out to work in the fields. A kiss was taken and returned, the gate was closed, and Saint-Clair, with one bound, was at the end of the path.

He followed a road that seemed well known to him. Sometimes he almost leapt for joy, and ran, striking the bushes with his cane ; sometimes he stopped or walked slowly, looking at the sky, tinting now with purple in the east. Indeed any one who had seen him would have taken him for a lunatic delighted to have broken from his cage. After half an hour's walk he was at the door of a lonely little house he had rented for the season. He unlocked the door and went in, threw himself on a big sofa, and there, with eyes fixed and lips curved in a gentle smile, gave himself up to thoughts and day-dreams. His imagination brought him none but ideas of happiness. " How happy I am ! " he kept saying to himself every moment. " At last I have met a heart that understands my own ! . . . Yes, I have found my ideal. . . . I have at the same time a *friend* and a beloved. . . . What character ! . . . What passion of soul ! . . . No, she has loved no one before me. . . ." Soon, since vanity slips always into the affairs of this world, " she is the most beautiful woman in Paris," he thought. And his imagination went over all her charms at once. " She has chosen me from all. . . . She had the flower of Society for admirers. That Colonel of Hussars, so handsome, so brave—and not too much of a fop . . . that young author who makes such pretty water-colours, and plays ' proverbs ' so well. . . . That Russian Lovelace who was through the Balkan Campaign and served under Diébitch . . . above all, Camille T——, with his undoubted wit, his fine manners, and a handsome sabre-cut on his forehead . . . she has shown the door to the lot of them. And I . . . ! " Then came his refrain : " How happy I am ! How happy

I am ! '' And he got up and opened the window, unable to breathe ; alternately he walked up and down, and tossed upon his sofa.

Happy and unhappy lovers are amost equally dull. One of my friends, who was often in one or other case, found no other way of getting a listener than to give me an excellent luncheon, during which he was free to talk of his loves ; but it was an absolute condition that the conversation should be changed after the coffee.

Since I cannot give a lunch to all my readers, I will spare them the amorous musings of Saint-Clair. Besides, one cannot live for ever in the clouds. Saint-Clair was tired ; he yawned, stretched his arms, and saw that it was full daylight ; he had to think of sleeping. When he woke, he saw from his watch that he had scarcely time to dress and run up to Paris, where he had been invited to a luncheon-dinner with several young fellows of his acquaintance.

.   .   .   .

Another bottle of champagne had just been uncorked ; I leave the reader to decide how many had already been drunk. Let it suffice him to know that the moment had arrived, which comes pretty early at a bachelor luncheon, when everybody wants to speak at the same time, and when the strong heads begin to grow anxious about the weak.

" I wish," said Alphonse de Thémines, who never lost an opportunity of speaking of England, " I wish it were the fashion in Paris as in London, for each man to call a toast to his sweetheart. In that way we should really know whose are the sighs of our friend Saint-Clair." As he spoke he filled his own glass and those of his neighbours.

Saint-Clair, a little embarrassed, was about to reply ; but Jules Lambert was before him.

" I strongly approve of the custom," said he, " and I adopt it." He raised his glass : " To all the milliners of Paris ! I except only those over thirty, the one-eyed, the one-legged, etc."

" Hurrah ! Hurrah!'' shouted the young Anglophiles.

Saint-Clair stood up, his glass in his hand.

" Gentlemen," he said, " my heart is not so comprehensive as that of our friend Jules, but it is more constant. And there is the more merit in my constancy in that I have been separated for a long time from the lady of my thoughts. I am sure you will approve my choice, even if you are not already my rivals. To Judith Pasta, gentlemen ! May we soon see once again the first *tragédienne* of Europe ! "

Thémines wanted to object to this toast, but the applause prevented him. Saint-Clair, having parried the thrust, thought himself quit of the business for the day.

The talk turned on the theatre. Dramatic criticism served as a means of transition to politics. From the Duke of Wellington they passed to English horses, and from English horses to women, by a chain of ideas easy to follow, since young men find, first a fine horse, and secondly a pretty mistress, the two possessions most to be desired.

Then they discussed the methods of obtaining these desirable objects. Horses are bought, and one also buys women ; but we do not speak of that kind. Saint-Clair, after modestly pleading his lack of experience in the delicate subject, observed that the first step towards pleasing a woman was to be singular, and different from the others. But was there a general formula for singularity ? He did not think so.

" According to your view," said Jules, " a lame man or a hunch-back is more likely to please than a straight fellow built like every-body else ? "

" You push things rather far," Saint-Clair replied : " but I accept, if necessary, all the consequences of my proposition. For instance, if I were a hunchback, I should not blow my brains out, and I should decide to make conquests. In the first place, I should pay my addresses to two kinds of women only, to those of a real sensibility, or to those, and there are plenty of them, who pretend to an original character, eccentrics, as they say in England. I should paint for the former the horror of my position, the cruelty of nature towards me ; I should try to set them pitying my lot, and contrive to let them suspect me capable of a passionate love. I should kill a rival in a duel, and poison myself with a feeble dose of laudanum. After a few months they would no longer notice my hump, and then it would be my business to watch for the first access of tenderness. As for the women who pretend to originality, their conquest is easy. You have only to persuade them that it is a firmly established rule that no hunchback can have a love affair, and they will be instantly anxious to prove it by an exception."

" What a Don Juan ! " cried Jules.

" Let us break our legs, gentlemen," said Colonel Beaujeu, " since we have the ill luck not to be born with humpbacks ! "

" I agree absolutely with Saint-Clair," said Hector Roquantin, who was only three and a half feet high. " One sees every day the most beautiful and fashionable women giving themselves to men whom you fine fellows would never suspect."

" Hector, get up, I beg you, and ring for wine," said Thémines with the most natural air imaginable.

The dwarf rose, and every one smiled, remembering the fable of the fox who had lost his tail.

" As for me," said Thémines, taking up the conversation, " the longer I live, the clearer I see that passable looks," and he threw a complacent glance in the mirror that was opposite him, " passable looks, and taste in dress, make the great singularity that conquers the most cruel " ; and he flipped a breadcrumb from the lapel of his coat.

"Bah!" cried the dwarf, "a handsome face and clothes by
Staub win you the women you keep for eight days and are bored by
at the second meeting. But for love, for what is called love, something else is needed. . . . You want——"

"See here," interrupted Thémines, "would you like a decisive
example? You all knew Massigny, and you know what sort of a man
he was. The manners of an English stable-boy, and the conversation
of his horse. But he was as handsome as Adonis, and wore his
cravat like Brummel. Taking him altogether, he was the biggest
bore I have ever known."

"He tried to kill me with dulness," said Colonel Beaujeu.
"Imagine: I had to travel two hundred leagues with him."

"Did you know," asked Saint-Clair, "that he caused the death
of that poor Richard Thornton whom you knew?"

"But surely," replied Jules, "he was killed by brigands near
Fondi?"

"Certainly; but you shall see that Massigny was at least an
accomplice in the crime. Several travellers, Thornton among them,
had arranged to go to Naples, all together, for fear of the brigands.
Massigny wanted to join the party. As soon as Thornton knew it,
he went on, for horror, I suppose, at the idea of having to spend
some days with him. He set out alone, and you know the rest."

"Thornton was right," said Thémines; "of two deaths he chose
the easier. Any one would have done the same in his place." He
paused, and continued: "You grant me then that Massigny was
the most tedious man on earth?"

"Granted!" There was a shout of acclamation.

"Let us not reduce anybody to despair," said Jules; "let us
make an exception of . . . especially when he is expounding his
political plans."

"You will also grant me," pursued Thémines, "that Madame de
Coursy is a woman of brains, if ever there was one."

There was a moment's silence. Saint-Clair bent his head, and
thought that all eyes were upon him.

"Who questions it?" he said at last, still leaning over his plate,
apparently examining with great interest the flowers painted on the
porcelain.

"I maintain," said Jules, raising his voice, "I maintain that she
is one of the three most delightful women in Paris."

"I knew her husband," said the colonel. "He often showed me
charming letters from his wife."

"Auguste," put in Hector Roquantin, "you must introduce me
to the Countess. They say you count for something there."

"At the end of the autumn," murmured Saint-Clair, "when she
comes back to Paris. . . . I . . . I think she does not entertain in
the country."

" Will you listen to me ? " cried Thémines.

There was silence again. Saint-Clair fidgeted on his chair like a prisoner in a Court of Justice.

" You had not seen the Countess three years ago, Saint-Clair ; you were then in Germany," Alphonse de Thémines went on with relentless calm. " You can have no idea of what she was in those days ; beautiful, fresh as a rose, lively too, and gay as a butterfly. Well, among her numerous admirers, who do you think was honoured with her favour ? Massigny ! The stupidest of men, and the dullest, turned the head of the cleverest of women. Do you think a hunchback could have done as much ? No, believe me, have a handsome face and a good tailor, and be bold."

Saint-Clair was in an atrocious position. He was going to give the narrator a formal contradiction ; but fear of compromising the Countess held him back. He would have liked to say something in her favour ; but his tongue was frozen. His lips trembled with rage, and he searched his head in vain for some roundabout means of starting a quarrel.

" What ! " cried Jules with surprise, " Madame de Coursy gave herself to Massigny ! Frailty, thy name is woman ! "

" The reputation of a woman is a thing of such small importance ! " said Saint-Clair, in a dry, scornful voice. " One may pull it to pieces to make a little sport, and——"

As he spoke, he remembered with horror a certain Etruscan vase that he had seen a hundred times on the Countess's maintelpiece in Paris. He knew it had been a present from Massigny on his return from Italy ; and, damning circumstance ! the vase had been brought from Paris to the country. Every evening, when she took off her bouquet, Mathilde placed it in the Etruscan vase.

The words died on his lips : he saw no longer but one thing, thought no longer but of one thing—the Etruscan vase.

" A fine proof ! " a critic will say. " To think of suspecting one's mistress for so small a thing as that ! "

Have you been in love, master Critic ?

Thémines was in too good a temper to be offended at the tone Saint-Clair had taken in speaking to him.

He replied lightly, with an air of good fellowship :

" I only repeat what the world said. It was taken as truth while you were in Germany. But I scarcely know Madame de Coursy ; it is eighteen months since I went to her house. It is possible that people were mistaken, and that Massigny was telling me a yarn. To return to what we were considering : I should be none the less right, even if the example I have just quoted should prove to be false. You all know that France's most brilliant woman, she whose works——"

The door opened, and Théodore Neville came in. He had just returned from Egypt.

"Théodore! Back so soon!" He was overwhelmed with questions.

"Have you brought back a real Turkish costume?" asked Thémines.

"Have you an Arab horse, and an Egyptian groom?"

"What sort of a man is the Pasha?" asked Jules. "When will he make himself independent? Have you seen heads cut off with single sabre blows?"

"And the dancing girls!" said Roquantin. "Are Cairo women beautiful?"

"Did you see General L——?" asked Colonel Beaujeu. "How has he organised the Pasha's army? Did Colonel C—— give you a sword for me?"

"And the Pyramids? And the cataracts of the Nile? And the statue of Memnon? Ibrahim Pasha? etc." All spoke at once; Saint-Clair thought of nothing but the Etruscan vase.

Théodore seated himself cross-legged, for he had taken to the habit in Egypt and had not been able to lose it in France, waited till the questioners had tired themselves out, and spoke as follows, so fast as not to be easily interrupted:

"The Pyramids! I tell you, they are a regular humbug. They are not nearly so high as one thinks. The Minister at Strasbourg is only four metres lower. I am full up with antiquities. Don't speak of them. The mere sight of a hieroglyph would make me faint. There are so many travellers who busy themselves with these things! My object was to study the appearances and manners of all that bizarre crowd that fills the streets of Alexandria and Cairo— Turks, Bedouins, Copts, Fellahs, Megrabis. I made some hurried notes when I was in quarantine. What an infamy that is! I hope none of you believe in contagion. As for me, I calmly smoked my pipe in the midst of three hundred plague-stricken people. Ah! colonel, you would see some fine cavalry there, well mounted. I will show you some superb weapons I brought back. I have a *djerid* that belonged to the famous Mourad Bey. Colonel, I have a *yataghan* for you, and a *khandjar* for Auguste. You shall see my *metchla*, my *burnous*, my *haick*. Do you know, I could have brought some women back if I had wanted. Ibrahim Pasha sent so many from Greece, that they are to be had for the asking . . . but on account of my mother. . . . I talked a lot with the Pasha. He is a clever man, my word, and no bigot. You would scarcely believe how learned he is in our affairs. I tell you he knows of the slightest mysteries of our Cabinet. I drew from his conversation the most precious information as to the state of the parties in France. . . . At present he is much busied with statistics. He subscribes to all

our newspapers. Do you know, he is a determined Bonapartist !
He talks of nothing but Napoleon. ' Ah,' he said to me, ' what a
great man was Bounabardo ! ' *Bounabardo*, that is their name for
Bonaparte."

" Giourdina, that is to say, Jordan," mumured Thémines beneath
his breath.

" At first," Théodore went on, " Mohammed Ali was very reserved
with me. You know all Turks are very mistrustful. He took me
for a spy, damme ! or a Jesuit. He has a horror of Jesuits. But,
after a visit or two, he saw that I was a traveller, unprejudiced, and
curious to learn on the spot the customs, manners, and politics
of the Orient. Then he unbent and spoke to me with an open heart.
At my last audience, which was the third he gave me, I took the
liberty of saying, ' I do not understand why your Highness does not
make himself independent of the Porte.' ' My God ! ' said he,
' I should like to ; but I am afraid that the Liberal papers, which
govern everything in your country, would not support me when
once I had proclaimed the independence of Egypt.' He is a handsome old man, with a fine white beard and never a laugh. He gave
me some excellent preserves ; but, of all I gave him, what pleased
him most was the collection of uniforms of the Imperial Guard,
by Charlet."

" Is the Pasha romantic ? " asked Thémines.

" He bothers himself little with books ; but you know that
Arabian literature is wholly romantic. They have a poet called
Melek Ayatalne-fous-Ebn-Esraf, who recently published some
Meditations beside which those of Lamartine would seem to be
classical prose. On my arrival in Cairo I hired a teacher of Arabic,
with whom I set myself to read the Koran. Although I had only
a few lessons I learnt enough to understand the sublime beauties
of the Prophet's style, and to realise how bad are all our translations.
Look, would you like to see Arabic writing ? This word in gold
letters is *Allah*, that is to say, God."

He showed as he spoke a very dirty letter that he had taken from
a purse of perfumed silk.

" How long did you stay in Egypt ? " asked Thémines.

" Six weeks."

And the traveller went on, describing everything, from cedar to
hyssop.

Saint-Clair went out almost immediately after his arrival, and
took the road to his country house. The impetuous gallop of his
horse prevented him from following out his ideas. But he knew
vaguely that his happiness in this world had been destroyed for
ever, and that he could blame nothing for it but a dead man and
an Etruscan vase.

Arriving home, he threw himself on the sofa where, the night before, he had made that lingering and delicious analysis of his happiness. The idea he had most lovingly caressed had been that his mistress was not a woman like another, that she had not loved, and could never love, but him alone. And now this beautiful dream disappeared before the mournful, cruel reality. " I possess a fine woman ; that is all. She is clever. Then she is the more to blame, for being able to love Massigny ! . . . It is true, she loves me now . . . with all her soul . . . as she can love. To be loved like Massigny ! . . . She has submitted to my attentions, my whims, my importunities. But I have been mistaken. There was no sympathy between our hearts. Massigny or me, it is all one to her. He was handsome, she loved him for his good looks. I sometimes amuse her. ' Well, we will love Saint-Clair,' she says to herself, ' since the other is dead. And if Saint-Clair dies, or grows wearisome, we shall see.' "

I firmly believe the devil watches invisible by an unhappy wretch so torturing himself. It is an amusing sight for the enemy of mankind, and when the victim feels his wounds are closing, Satan is there to open them again.

Saint-Clair thought he heard a voice that murmured in his ears,

    " The singular honour
       of being successor . . ."

He sat up and looked wildly about him. How happy he would have been to find some one in his room. He would undoubtedly have torn him to pieces.

The clock struck eight. The Countess expected him at half-past. What if he were to miss the appointment ! " Indeed, why see Massigny's mistress again ? " He lay down again on the sofa, and closed his eyes. " I want to sleep," he said. He lay still for half a minute, and then jumped to his feet and ran to the clock to see how the time was going. " How I wish it were half-past eight," he thought, " then it would be too late to set out." In his heart, he did not feel he had the courage to stay at home ; he wanted a pretext. He would have been glad to be very ill. He walked up and down in his room, sat down, took a book, but could not read a syllable. He set himself before his piano, and had not the energy to open it. He whistled, looked at the clouds, and wanted to count the poplars before his windows. Finally he returned to consult the clock, and saw that he had not succeeded in passing three minutes. " I cannot help loving her," he said, grinding his teeth and stamping his foot. " She rules me, and I am her slave, as Massigny was before me. Ah well, wretched fellow, obey, since you have not the heart to break a chain you hate ! "

He took his hat and went hurriedly out.

When we are carried away by a passion, we find some consolation for our self-esteem, in contemplating our weakness from the height of our pride. " It is true, I am feeble," one says, " but if I wished ! "

He went leisurely up the path that led to the park-gate, and from a long way off saw a white figure that showed against the deep colour of the trees. She fluttered a handkerchief in her hand, as if to signal to him. His heart beat violently, and his knees trembled ; he had not the strength to speak, and had become so timid that he feared lest the Countess should read his ill-humour in his face.

He took the hand she offered him, kissed her forehead, because she threw herself in his arms, and followed her to her rooms, mute, stifling with difficulty the sighs that seemed ready to burst his chest.

A single candle lit the Countess's boudoir. They sat down. Saint-Clair noticed his friend's coiffure ; a single rose in her hair. He had brought her the day before a fine English engraving, after Leslie's " Duchess of Portland " (her hair is dressed in this way), and had said but these words, " I like that simple rose better than all your elaborate coiffures." He did not like jewellery, and thought like that lord who brutally said : " With decked-out women and caparisoned horses the devil himself would have nothing to do."

Last night, playing with a pearl necklace belonging to the Countess (for he always wanted something in his hands while talking), he had said : " Jewels are only good to hide defects. You, Mathilde, are too pretty to wear them." This evening, the Countess, who remembered his lightest words, had put off rings, necklaces, earrings, and bracelets. He noticed footgear first in a woman's dress, and, like many men, he was a little mad on this point. A heavy shower had fallen before sundown. The grass was still drenched ; yet the Countess had walked across the wet lawn in silk stockings and black satin slippers. . . . What if she were to be ill ?

" She loves me," said Saint-Clair to himself.

And he sighed over his folly, and looked at Mathilde, smiling in spite of himself, divided between his ill-humour and the pleasure of seeing a pretty woman trying to please him by all those little nothings that lovers hold so valuable.

As for the Countess, her radiant face expressed a mixture of love and playful mischief that made her still more lovable. She took something that was in a Japanese lacquer box, and offering her little hand closed, hiding the thing it held.

" The other evening," she said, " I broke your watch. Here it is, mended."

She gave him the watch, and looked at him tenderly, mischievously, biting her lower lip, as if to keep from laughing. Great God, but how beautiful her teeth were ! How they shone white on the vivid red of her lips! (A man looks very foolish when he takes coldly a pretty woman's coaxings.)

Saint-Clair thanked her, took the watch, and was going to put it in his pocket.

"Look now," she went on, "open it, and see if it is properly mended. You who are so learned, and have been to the Poly-technic School, ought to see that."

"I did not learn very much there," said Saint-Clair.

And he absently opened the watch-case. What was his surprise! A miniature portrait of Madame de Coursy had been painted on the inside of the case. How could he sulk further? His forehead lightened. He thought no more of Massigny; he remembered only that he was with a charming woman and that this woman adored him.

.   .   .   .

"The lark, that harbinger of dawn," began to sing, and long strips of pale light furrowed the eastern clouds. It was the hour when Romeo said farewell to Juliet; the classic parting hour of lovers.

Saint-Clair was standing by a mantelpiece, the key of the park in his hand, his eyes fixed attentively on the Etruscan vase of which we have already spoken. He still felt spiteful towards it, in the bottom of his heart. But he was in a good-humour, and the very simple idea that Thémines might have lied began to come into his head. While the Countess, who meant to accompany him as far as the park-gate, was wrapping a shawl round her head, he lightly struck the odious vase with the key, gradually increasing the force of the blows, until it seemed likely he would soon be making it fly to pieces.

"Oh! take care! take care!" cried Mathilde, "you are going to break my beautiful Etruscan vase!"

And she snatched the key from his hands.

Saint-Clair was very dissatisfied, but patient. He turned his back on the mantelpiece, so as not to succumb to the temptation, and, opening his watch, set himself to examine the portrait he had just been given.

"Who is the painter?" he asked.

"Monsieur R——. Massigny introduced him to me. (Massigny discovered after his journey to Rome that he had an exquisite taste for the Fine Arts, and became the Mæcenas of all the young artists.) Really, I think the portrait is like me, though a little flattering."

Saint-Clair would have liked to hurl the watch against the wall, which would have made mending a difficult matter. He restrained himself, however, and put it in his pocket; then, observing that it was already day, he begged Mathilde not to accompany him, crossed the park with long strides, and in a moment, was alone in the fields.

" Massigny ! Massigny ! " he cried with concentrated rage,
" shall I always be meeting you ! . . . Doubtless the painter who
made the portrait, painted another for Massigny ! . . . Fool that
I was ! I believed for a moment that I was loved with a passion
like my own . . . and that because she dresses her hair with a rose,
and wears no jewels. . . . She has a cabinet full of them. . . .
Massigny, who only saw the dress of women, was so fond of jewels !
Yes, she is good-natured, it must be admitted. She knows how to
accommodate herself to the tastes of her lovers. Curse it ! I would
a hundred times rather she were a courtesan, and sold herself for
money. Then at least I should be able to believe that she loves me,
since she is my mistress, and I do not pay her."

Presently a still more painful idea occurred to him. In a few weeks
the Countess would be out of mourning. Saint-Clair was to marry
her as soon as her year of widowhood should be over. He had
promised. Promised ? No. He had never spoken of it. But that
had been his intention, and the Countess had known it. For him,
that was as good as an oath. Yesterday he would have given a
throne to hasten the moment when he should be able publicly to
acknowledge his affection ; now, he trembled at the bare idea of
uniting his lot with that of Massigny's old mistress.

" And yet, I owe it to her," he said, " and it shall be. No doubt
she thought, poor woman, that I knew of her old intrigue. They say
it was public property. And then, too, she does not know me. . . .
She cannot understand me. She thinks I only love her as Massigny
loved her.

Then, not without pride, he said :

" For three months she has made me the happiest of men. That
happiness is well worth the sacrifice of my whole life."

He did not go to bed, but rode all morning in the woods. In a
pathway of the wood of Verrières he saw a man on a fine English
horse who called him by name from a distance and came instantly
up to him. It was Alphonse de Thémines. To one in Saint-Clair's
state of mind solitude was particularly agreeable ; and the meeting
with Thémines turned his ill-humour into choking rage. Thémines
either did not notice it, or else took a roguish pleasure in provoking
him. He talked, laughed and joked, without noticing that he met
with no response. Saint-Clair, seeing a narrow byway, instantly
turned his horse into it, hoping the tormentor would not follow him :
but he was mistaken ; tormentors do not so readily leave their prey.
Thémines turned, and quickened his pace to draw level with Saint-
Clair, and to go on more comfortably with the conversation.

I said the byway was narrow. The horses could scarcely walk
abreast ; it was not surprising that Thémines, excellent horseman as
he was, should graze Saint-Clair's feet in passing beside him.
Saint-Clair, whose rage had reached its utmost limit, could no longer

control himself. He rose in his stirrups and smartly switched
Thémines' horse over the nose.

"What the devil is the matter with you, Auguste?" shouted
Thémines. "Why do you hit my horse?"

"Why do you follow me?" replied Saint-Clair in a terrible voice.

"Are you out of your senses, Saint-Clair? Do you forget that
you are talking to me?"

"I know very well I am talking to a coxcomb."

"Saint-Clair! . . . I think you are mad. . . . Listen: to-
morrow you will apologise to me or pay for your impertinence."

"Till to-morrow, then, sir."

Thémines pulled up his horse; Saint-Clair urged his, and soon
disappeared in the wood.

At that moment he felt calmer. He had the weakness of believing
in presentiments. He thought he would be killed next morning, and
that that was a proper solution of his difficulty. One more day to
spend; to-morrow no more anxieties, no more torments. He went
home, sent his servant with a note to Colonel Beaujeu, wrote some
letters, then dined with a good appetite, and punctually at half-past
eight was at the little gate of the park.

"What is the matter with you to-day, Auguste?" said the
Countess. "You are strangely gay, and yet, with all your jokes,
you cannot make me laugh. Yesterday you were just a little dull,
and I, I was gay. To-day we have changed parts. . . . I have a
frightful headache."

"Dearest, I admit it; yes, I was very tedious yesterday. But
to-day I have had fresh air and exercise; I am marvellously well."

"As for me, I got up late; I slept on this morning, and had
tiresome dreams."

"Ah! Dreams? Do you believe in dreams?"

"What folly!"

"I believe in them: I guess you had a dream announcing some
tragic event."

"Heavens! I never remember my dreams. However, I recollect.
. . . I saw Massigny in my dreams; so you see it was nothing very
amusing."

"Massigny! I should have thought, on the contrary, you would
have been delighted to see him again."

"Poor Massigny!"

"Poor Massigny?"

"Auguste, tell me, I beg you, what is the matter with you
to-night? There is something fiendish in your smile. You look as
if you were laughing at yourself."

"Ah! Now you are treating me as badly as the old dowagers
treat me, your friends."

"Yes, Auguste, to-day you are wearing the expression

you have with people you do not like."

" Naughty one ! Come, give me you hand."

He kissed her hand with ironic gallantry, and they looked stead-fastly at each other for a minute. Saint-Clair lowered his eyes first, and cried :

" How difficult it is to live in this world without getting a reputa-tion for wickedness. . . . One would have to talk of nothing but the weather, or sport, or else discuss with your old friends the reports of their charitable committees."

He took a paper from the table.

" See, here is your laundress's bill. Let us talk of this, my angel, and then you will not say I am wicked."

" Really, Auguste, you astonish me——"

" This spelling reminds me of a letter I found this morning. I must tell you that I set my papers in order, for I am tidy now and again. And so I came across a love-letter from a dressmaker, with whom I was in love when I was sixteen. She had her own way of writing each word, and always the most complicated. Her style is worthy of her spelling. Well, since in those days I was something of a coxcomb, I did not think it suited my dignity to have a mistress who could not write like a Sévigné. I left her abruptly. To-day, re-reading the letter, I perceived that this dressmaker must have been very much in love with me."

" Indeed ! a woman whom you kept ? "

" In great magnificence : on fifty francs a month. But my guardian did not make me too generous an allowance, for he used to say that a young man with money ruins himself and ruins others."

" And the woman ? What became of her ? "

" How do I know ? . . . She probably died in a hospital."

" Auguste. . . . If that were so, you would not speak so carelessly."

" If you must know the truth, she married a respectable man ; and I gave her a little dowry when I came of age."

" How good you are ! . . . But why do you like to seem wicked ? "

" Oh yes, I am very good. . . . The more I think of it, the more I am persuaded that this woman really loved me. . . . But in those days I did not know how to distinguish a true feeling under a ridiculous form."

" You should have brought me your letter. I should not have been jealous. We women have more intuition than you, and we see at once from the style of a letter whether the author is speaking honestly or is pretending a passion he does not feel."

" And yet how often you let yourselves be duped by fools and coxcombs ! "

As he spoke he was looking at the Etruscan vase, and his eyes and voice had a sinister expression that Mathilde did not notice.

" Come now ! You men, you all want to pass as Don Juans. You

imagine you are making dupes when often you are only meeting
Doña Juana, still wilier than yourselves."

" I understand that, with your fine intellects, you ladies tell a fool
a league away. At the same time, I have no doubt that our friend
Massigny, a fool and a coxcomb, died blameless and a martyr."

" Massigny ? He was not too much of a fool ; and then, there are
foolish women. I must tell you a story about Massigny. . . . But,
tell me, have I not told you it before ? "

" Never," replied Saint-Clair in a trembling voice.

" Massigny fell in love with me on his return from Italy. My
husband knew him, and introduced him to me as a man of wit and
taste. They were made for each other. Massigny was very attentive
from the first ; he gave me, as his own, water-colours he had bought
at Schroth's, and talked music and painting to me with a tone of the
most diverting superiority. One day he sent me an amazing letter.
He told me, among other things, that I was the most respectable
woman in Paris ; for which reason he wanted to be my lover.
I showed the letter to my cousin Julie. We were both mad in those
days, and we resolved to play him a trick. One evening we had some
visitors, among others Massigny. My cousin said to me : " I am
going to read you a declaration of love I received this morning."
She took the letter and read it amidst bursts of laughter. . . . Poor
Massigny ! "

Saint-Clair fell on his knees with a cry of joy. He seized the
Countess's hand, and covered it with kisses and tears. Mathilde was
surprised to the last degree, and thought at first that he was ill.
Saint-Clair could say nothing but " Forgive me ! Forgive me ! " At
last he rose. He was radiant. At that moment he was happier than on
the day when for the first time Mathilde had said to him, " I love you."

" I am the most idiotic and most culpable of men," he cried ;
" for the last two days I have suspected you . . . and I did not ask
you for an explanation——"

" You suspected me ! . . . And of what ? "

" I am a wretch ! . . . They told me you had loved Massigny,
and——"

" Massigny ! " and she began to laugh ; then, becoming instantly
grave again, " Auguste," she said, " you can be mad enough to have
such suspicions, and hypocrite enough to hide them from me ! "

There were tears in her eyes.

" I implore you, forgive me."

" How should I not forgive you, dearest ? But first let me swear
to you——"

" Oh ! I believe you, I believe you. Tell me nothing."

" But, in Heaven's name, what motive could make you suspect
such an improbability ? "

" Nothing, nothing at all but my cursed head . . . and . . . you see, that Etruscan vase that I knew Massigny had given you."

The Countess clasped her hands with astonishment ; then, laughing aloud, she cried :

" My Etruscan vase ! My Etruscan vase ! "

Saint-Clair could not help laughing himself, while big tears ran down his cheeks. He seized Mathilde in his arms and said :

" I will not loose you till you have forgiven me."

" Yes, I forgive you, madman that you are ! " said she, kissing him tenderly. " You make me very happy to-day : this is the first time I have seen you weep, and I believed you had no tears."

Then, escaping from his arms, she seized the Etruscan vase, and broke it in a thousand pieces on the floor. (It was a rare and irreplaceable specimen. There was a painting on it in three colours of a fight between a Lapithe and a Centaur.)

For some hours Saint-Clair was the most ashamed of men, and the happiest.

. . . .

" Well," said Roquantin to Colonel Beaujeu, whom he met in the evening at Tortoni's, " the news is true ? "

" Too true, my friend," replied the Colonel sadly.

" Tell me how it happened."

" Oh ! Very properly. Saint-Clair began by telling me he was in the wrong, but that he wished to draw Thémines' fire before apologising. I could but think he was right. Thémines wished it decided by lot who should fire first. Saint-Clair demanded that it should be Thémines. Thémines fired : I saw Saint-Clair turn round where he stood, and fall stone-dead. I have noticed before in many soldiers struck by a bullet this strange twisting round before death."

" It is very odd," said Roquantin. " And what did Thémines do ? "

" Oh ! What must be done on such occasions. He threw his pistol on the ground with an air of regret. He threw it with such force that he smashed the hammer. It was an English pistol, by Manton ; I doubt if there is a gunsmith in Paris who could make him another."

. . . .

The Countess saw nobody for three years ; winter and summer, alike, she stayed in her country-house, scarcely leaving her room, and waited on by a mulatto woman who knew of her relations with Saint-Clair, and to whom she did not say two words a day. At the end of three years her cousin Julie came back from a long journey ; she forced her way in, and found poor Mathilde so thin and pale that she thought she was looking on the corpse of the the woman she had left beautiful and full of life. She succeeded with difficulty in drawing her from her retreat, and in taking her to Hyères. The Countess languished there for three or four months, and then died of a consumption caused by domestic trouble ; so Doctor M—— said, who attended her.

ALEXANDRE DUMAS
1803-1870

ZODOMIRSKY'S DUEL

I

AT the time of this story our regiment was stationed in the dirty little village of Valins, on the frontier of Austria.

It was the 4th of May in the year 182–, and I, with several other officers, had been breakfasting with the Aide-de-Camp in honour of his birthday, and discussing the various topics of the garrison.

" Can you tell us without being indiscreet," asked Sub-Lieutenant Stamm of Andrew Michaelovitch, the aide-de-camp, " what the Colonel was so eager to say to you this morning ? "

" A new officer," he replied, " is to fill the vacancy of captain."

" His name ? " demanded two or three voices.

" Lieutenant Zodomirsky, who is betrothed to the beautiful Mariana Ravensky."

" And when does he arrive ? " asked Major Belayef.

" He *has* arrived. I have been presented to him at the Colonel's house. He is very anxious to make your acquaintance, gentlemen, and I have therefore invited him to dine with us. But that reminds me, Captain, you must know him," he continued, turning to me, " you were both in the same regiment at St. Petersburg."

" It is true," I replied. " We studied there together. He was then a brave, handsome youth, adored by his comrades, in every one's good graces, but of a fiery and irritable temper."

" Mademoiselle Ravensky informed me that he was a skilful duellist," said Stamm. " Well, he will do very well here ; a duel is a family affair with us. You are welcome, Monsieur Zodomirsky. However quick your temper, you must be careful of it before me, or I shall take upon myself to cool it."

And Stamm pronounced these words with a visible sneer.

" How is it that he leaves the Guards ? Is he ruined ? " asked Cornet Naletoff.

" I have been informed," replied Stamm, " that he has just inherited from an old aunt about twenty thousand roubles. No, poor devil ! he is consumptive."

" Come, gentlemen," said the Aide-de-Camp, rising, " let us

pass to the saloon and have a game of cards. Koloff will serve dinner whilst we play."

We had been seated some time, and Stamm, who was far from rich, was in the act of losing sixty roubles, when Koloff announced :
" Captain Zodomirsky."

" Here you are, at last ! " cried Michaelovitch, jumping from his chair. " You are welcome."

Then turning to us, he continued : " These are your new comrades, Captain Zodomirsky ; all good fellows and brave soldiers."

" Gentlemen," said Zodomirsky, " I am proud and happy to have joined your regiment. To do so has been my greatest desire for some time, and if I am welcome, as you courteously say, I shall be the happiest man in the world."

" Ah ! good day, Captain," he continued, turning to me and holding out his hand, " We meet again. You have not forgotten an old friend, I hope ! "

As he smilingly uttered these words, Stamm, to whom his back was turned, darted at him a glance full of bitter hatred. Stamm was not liked in the regiment ; his cold and taciturn nature had formed no friendship with any of us. I could not understand his apparent hostility towards Zodomirsky, whom I believed he had never seen before.

Some one offered Zodomirsky a cigar. He accepted it, lit it at the cigar of an officer near him, and began to talk gaily to his new comrades.

' Do you stay here long ? " asked Major Belayef.

" Yes, monsieur," replied Zodomirsky. " I wish to stay with you as long as possible," and as he pronounced these words he saluted us all round with a smile. He continued : " I have taken a house near that of my old friend Ravensky, whom I knew at St. Petersburg. I have my horses there, an excellent cook, a passable library, a little garden, and a target ; and there I shall be quite as a hermit, and happy as a king. It is the life that suits me."

" Ha ! you practise shooting ! " said Stamm, in such a strange voice, accompanied by a smile so sardonic, that Zodomirsky regarded him in astonishment.

" It is my custom every morning to fire twelve balls," he replied.

" You are very fond of that amusement, then ? " demanded Stamm, in a voice without any trace of emotion ; adding, " I do not understand the use of shooting, unless it is to hunt with."

Zodomirsky's pale face was flushed with a sudden flame. He turned to Stamm, and replied in a quiet but firm boice, " I think monsieur, that you are wrong in calling it lost time to learn to shoot with a pistol ; in our garrison life an imprudent word often leads to a meeting between comrades, in which case he who is known for a good shot inspires respect among those indiscreet persons who amuse themselves in asking useless questions."

"Oh! that is not a reason, Captain. In duels, as in everything else, something should be left to chance. I maintain my first opinion, and say that an honourable man ought not to take too many precautions."

"And why?" asked Zodomirsky.

"I will explain to you," replied Stamm. "Do you play at cards, Captain?"

"Why do you ask that question?"

"I will try to render my explanation clear, so that all will understand it. Every one knows that there are certain players who have an enviable knack, whilst shuffling the pack, of adroitly making themselves master of the winning card. Now, I see no difference myself, between the man who robs his neighbour of his money and the one who robs him of his life." Then he added, in a way to take nothing from the insolence of his observation, "I do not say this to you, in particular, Captain, I speak in general terms."

"It is too much as it is, monsieur!" cried Zodomirsky. "I beg Captain Alexis Stephanovitch to terminate this affair with you." Then, turning to me, he said, "You will not refuse me this request?"

"So be it, Captain," replied Stamm quickly. "You have told me yourself you practise shooting every day, whilst I practise only on the day I fight. We will equalise the chances. I will settle details with Monsieur Stephanovitch."

Then he rose and turned to our host.

"*Au revoir*, Michaelovitch," he said. "I will dine at the Colonel's." And with these words he left the room.

The most profound silence had been kept during this altercation; but as soon as Stamm disappeared, Captain Pravdine, an old officer, addressed himself to us all.

"We cannot let them fight, gentlemen," he said.

Zodomirsky touched him gently on the arm.

"Captain," he said, "I am a new-comer amongst you; none of you know me. I have yet, as it were, to win my spurs; it is impossible for me to let this quarrel pass without fighting. I do not know what I have done to annoy this gentleman, but it is evident that he has some spite against me."

"The truth of the matter is that Stamm is jealous of you, Zodomirsky," said Cornet Naletoff. "It is well known that he is in love with Mademoiselle Ravensky."

"That, indeed, explains all," he replied. "However, gentlemen, I thank you for your kind sympathy in this affair from the bottom of my heart."

"And now to dinner, gentlemen!" cried Michaelovitch. "Place yourselves as you choose. The soup, Koloff; the soup!"

Everybody was very animated. Stamm seemed forgotten; only Zodomirsky appeared a little sad. Zodomirsky's health was drunk; he seemed touched with this significant attention, and thanked the officers with a broken voice.

"Stephanovitch," said Zodomirsky to me, when dinner was over, and all had risen, "since M. Stamm knows you are my second and has accepted you as such, see him, and arrange everything with him; accept all his conditions; then meet Captain Pravdine and me at my rooms. The first who arrives will wait for the other. We are now going to Monsieur Ravensky's house."

"You will let us know the hour of combat?" said several voices.

"Certainly, gentlemen. Come and bid a last farewell to one of us."

We all parted at the Ravensky's door, each officer shaking hands with Zodomirsky as with an old friend.

II

Stamm was waiting for me when I arrived at his house. His conditions were these—Two sabres were to be planted at a distance of one pace apart; each opponent to extend his arm at full length and fire at the word "*Three.*" One pistol alone was to be loaded.

I endeavoured in vain to obtain another mode of combat.

"It is not a victim I offer to M. Zodomirsky," said Stamm, "but an adversary. He will fight as I propose, or I will not fight at all; but in that case I shall prove that M. Zodomirsky is brave only when sure of his own safety."

Zodomirsky's orders were imperative. I accepted.

When I entered Zodomirsky's rooms they were vacant; he had not arrived. I looked round with curiosity. They were furnished in a rich but simple manner, and with evident taste. I drew a chair near the balcony and looked out over the plain. A storm was brewing; some drops of rain fell already, and thunder moaned.

At this instant the door opened, and Zodomirsky and Pravdine entered. I advanced to meet them.

"We are late, Captain," said Zodomirsky, "but it was unavoidable."

"And what says Stamm?" he continued.

I gave him his adversary's conditions. When I had ended, a sad smile passed over his face; he drew his hand across his forehead and his eyes glittered with feverish lustre.

"I had forseen this," he murmured. "You have accepted, I presume?"

"Did you not give me the order yourself?"

"Absolutely," he replied.

Zodomirsky threw himself in a chair by the table, in which position he faced the door. Pravdine placed himself near the window, and I near the fire. A presentiment weighed down our spirits. A mournful silence reigned.

Suddenly the door opened and a woman muffled in a mantle which streamed with water, and with the hood drawn over her face, pushed past the servant, and stood before us. She threw back the hood, and we recognised Mariana Ravensky!

Pravdine and I stood motionless with astonishment. Zodomirsky sprang towards her.

" Great Heavens! what has happened, and why are you here? "

" Why am I here, George? " she cried. " Is it *you* who ask me, when this night is perhaps the last of your life? Why am I here? To say farewell to you. It is only two hours since I saw you, and not one word passed between us of to-morrow. Was that well, George? "

" But I am not alone here," said Zodomirsky in a low voice. " Think, Mariana. Your reputation—your fair fame—— "

" Are you not all in all to me, George? And in such a time as this, what matters anything else? "

She threw her arm about his neck and pressed her head against his breast.

Pravdine and I made some steps to quit the room.

" Stay, gentlemen," she said, lifting her head. " Since you have seen me here, I have nothing more to hide from you, and perhaps you may be able to help me in what I am about to say." Then, suddenly flinging herself at his feet—

" I implore you, I command you, George," she cried, " not to fight this duel with Monsieur Stamm. You will not end two lives by such a useless act! Your life belongs to me; it is no longer yours. George, do you hear? You will not do this."

" Mariana! Mariana! in the name of heaven do not torture me thus! Can I refuse to fight? I should be dishonoured—lost! If I could do so cowardly an act, shame would kill me more surely than Stamm's pistol."

" Captain," she said to Pravdine, " you are esteemed in the regiment as a man of honour; you can, then, judge about affairs of honour. Have pity on me Captain, and tell him he *can* refuse such a duel as this. Make him understand that it is not a duel, but an assassination; speak, speak, Captain, and if he will not listen to me, he will to you."

Pravdine was moved. His lips trembled and his eyes were dimmed with tears. He rose, and, approaching Mariana, respectfully kissed her hand, and said with a trembling voice:

" To spare you any sorrow, Mademoiselle, I would lay down my life; but to counsel M. Zodomirsky to be unworthy of his uniform by refusing this duel is impossible. Each adversary, your betrothed as well as Stamm, has a right to propose his conditions.

But whatever be the conditions, the Captain is in circumstances which render this duel absolutely necessary. He is known as a skilful duellist ; to refuse Stamm's conditions were to indicate that he counts upon his skill."

" Enough, Mariana, enough," cried George. " Unhappy girl ! you do not know what you demand. Do you wish me, then, to fall so low that you yourself would be ashamed of me ? I ask you, are you capable of loving a dishonoured man ? "

Mariana had let herself fall upon a chair. She rose, pale as a corpse, and began to put her mantle on.

" You are right, George, it is not I who would love you no more, but you who would hate me. We must resign ourselves to our fate. Give me you hand, George ; perhaps we shall never see each other again. To-morrow ! to-morrow ! my love."

She threw herself upon his breast, without tears, without sobs, but with a profound despair.

She wished to depart alone, but Zodomirsky insisted on leading her home.

Midnight was stroking when he returned.

" You had better both retire," said Zodomirsky as he entered. " I have several letters to write before sleeping. At five we must be at the rendezvous."

I felt so wearied that I did not want telling twice. Pravdine passed into the saloon, I into Zodomirsky's bedroom, and the master of the house into his study.

The cool air of the morning woke me. I cast my eyes upon the window, where the dawn commenced to appear. I heard Pravdine also stirring. I passed into the saloon, where Zodomirsky immediately joined us. His face was pale but serene.

" Are the horses ready ? " he inquired.

I made a sign in the affirmative.

" Then let us start," he said.

We mounted into the carriage and drove off.

III

" Ah," said Pravdine all at once, " there is Michaelovitch's carriage. Yes, yes, it is he with one of ours, and there is Naletoff, on his Circassian horse. Good ! the others are coming behind. It is well we started so soon."

The carriage had to pass the house of the Ravenskys. I could not refrain from looking up ; the poor girl was at her window, motionless as a statue. She did not even nod to us.

" Quicker ! quicker ! " cried Zodomirsky to the coachman. It was the only sign by which I knew that he had seen Mariana.

Soon we distanced the other carriages, and arrived upon the place of combat—a plain where two great pyramids rose, passing in this

district by the name of the " Tomb of the Two Brothers." The first
rays of the sun darting through the trees began to dissipate the mists
of night.

Michaelovitch arrived immediately after us, and in a few minutes
we formed a group of nearly twenty persons. Then we heard the
crunch of other steps upon the gravel. They were those of our
opponents. Stamm walked first, holding in his hand a box of pistols.
He bowed to Zodomirsky and the officers.

" Who gives the word to fire, gentlemen ? " he asked.

The two adversaries and the seconds turned towards the officers,
who regarded them with perplexity.

No one offered. No one wished to pronounce that terrible
" *Three*," which would sign the fate of a comrade.

" Major," said Zodomirsky to Belayef, " will you render me this
service ? "

Thus asked, the Major could not refuse, and he made a sign that
he accepted.

" Be good enough to indicate our places, gentlemen," continued
Zodomirsky, giving me his sabre and taking off his coat, " then load,
if you please."

" That is useless," said Stamm, " I have brought the pistols ; one
of the two is loaded, the other has only a gun-cap."

" Do you know which is which ? " said Pravdine.

" What does it matter ? " replied Stamm, " Monsieur Zodomirsky
will choose."

" It is well," said Zodomirsky.

Belayef drew his sabre and thrust it in the ground midway
between the two pyramids. Then he took another sabre and planted
it before the first. One pace alone separated the two blades. Each
adversary was to stand behind a sabre, extending his arm at full
length. In this way each had the muzzle of his opponent's pistol
at six inches from his heart. Whilst Belayef made these preparations
Stamm unbuckled his sabre, and divested himself of his coat. His
seconds opened his box of pistols, and Zodomirsky, approaching,
took without hesitation the nearest to him. Then he placed himself
behind one of the sabres.

Stamm regarded him closely ; not a muscle of Zodomirsky's face
moved, and there was not about him the least appearance of bravado,
but of the calmness of courage.

" He is brave," murmured Stamm.

And taking the pistol left by Zodomirsky he took up his position
behind the other sabre, in front of his adversary.

They were both pale, but whilst the eyes of Zodomirsky burned
with implacable resolution, those of Stamm were uneasy and
shifting. I felt my heart beat loudly.

Belayef advanced. All eyes were fixed on him.

" Are you ready, gentlemen ? " he asked.

" We are waiting, Major," replied Zodomirsky and Stamm together, and each lifted his pistol before the breast of the other.

A death-like silence reigned. Only the birds sang in the bushes near the place of combat. In the midst of his silence the Major's voice resounding made every one tremble.

" One."

" Two."

" *Three.*"

Then we heard the sound of the hammer falling on the cap of Zodomirsky's pistol. There was a flash, but no sound followed it.

Stamm had not fired, and continued to hold the mouth of his pistol against the breast of his adversary.

" Fire ! " said Zodomirsky, in a voice perfectly calm.

" It is not for you to command, Monsieur," said Stamm, " it is I who must decide whether to fire or not, and that depends on how you answer what I am about to say."

" Speak, then ; but in the name of heaven speak quickly."

" Never fear, I will not abuse your patience."

We were all ears.

" I have not come to kill you, Monsieur," continued Stamm, " I have come with the carelessness of a man to whom life holds nothing, whilst it has kept none of the promises it has made to him. You, Monsieur, are rich, you are beloved, you have a promising future before you : life must be dear to you. But fate has decided against you : it is you who must die and not I. Well Monsieur Zodomirsky, give me your word not to be so prompt in the future to fight duels, and I will not fire."

" I have not been prompt to call you out, Monsieur," replied Zodomirsky in the same calm voice ; " you have wounded me by an outrageous comparison, and I have been compelled to challenge you. Fire, then ; I have nothing to say to you."

" My conditions cannot wound your honour," insisted Stamm. Be our judge, Major," he added, turning to Belayef. " I will abide by your opinion ; perhaps M. Zodomirsky will follow my example."

" M. Zodomirsky has conducted himself as bravely as possible ; if he is not killed, it is not his fault." Then, turning to the officers round, he said :

" Can M. Zodomirsky accept the imposed condition ? "

" He can ! he can ! " they cried, " and without staining his honour in the slightest."

Zodomirsky stood motionless.

" The Captain consents," said old Pravdine, advancing. " Yes, in the future he will be less prompt."

" It is you who speak, Captain, and not M. Zodomirsky," said Stamm.

" Will you affirm my words, Monsieur Zodomirsky ? " asked
Pravdine, almost supplicating in his eagerness.

" I consent," said Zodomirsky, in a voice scarcely intelligible.

" Hurrah ! hurrah ! " cried all the officers enchanted with this
termination. Two or three threw up their caps.

" I am more charmed than any one," said Stamm, " that all has
ended as I desired. Now, Captain, I have shown you that before a
resolute man the art of shooting is nothing in a duel, and that if the
chances are equal a good shot is on the same level as a bad one.
I did not wish in any case to kill you. Only I had a great desire to
see how you would look death in the face. You are a man of courage ;
accept my compliments. The pistols were not loaded." Stamm, as
he said these words, fired off his pistol. There was no report !

Zodomirsky uttered a cry which resembled the roar of a wounded
lion.

" By my father's soul ! " he cried, " this is a new offence, and more
insulting than the first. Ah ! it is ended, you say ? No, Monsieur,
it must recommence, and this time the pistols shall be loaded, if
I have to load them myself."

" No, Captain," replied Stamm tranquilly, " I have given you
your life, I will not take it back. Insult me if you wish, I will not
fight with you."

" Then it is with me whom you will fight, Monsieur Stamm,"
cried Pravdine, pulling off his coat. " You have acted like a
scoundrel ; you have deceived Zodomirsky and his seconds, and,
in five minutes if your dead body is not lying at my feet, there is no
such thing as justice."

Stamm was visibly confused. He had not bargained for this.

" And if the Captain does not kill you, I will ! " said Naletoff.

" Or I ! " " Or I ! " cried with one voice all the officers.

" The devil ! I cannot fight with you all," replied Stamm.
" Choose one amongst you, and I will fight with him, though it will
not be a duel, but an assassination."

" Reassure yourself, Monsieur," replied Major Belayef, " we will
do nothing that the most scrupulous honour can complain of. All
our officers are insulted, for under their uniform you have conducted
yourself like a rascal. You cannot fight with all ; it is even probable
you will fight with none. Hold yourself in readiness, then. You
are to be judged. Gentlemen, will you approach ? "

We surrounded the Major, and the fiat went forth without
discussion. Every one was of the same opinion.

Then the Major, who had played the *rôle* of president, approached
Stamm, and said to him :

" Monsieur, you are lost to all the laws of honour. Your crime
was premeditated in cold blood. You have made M. Zodomirsky
pass through all the sensations of a man condemned to death, whilst

you were perfectly at ease, you who knew that the pistols were not loaded. Finally, you have refused to fight with the man whom you have doubly insulted."

"Load the pistols! load them!" cried Stamm, exasperated. "I will fight with any one!"

But the Major shook his head with a smile of contempt.

"No, Monsieur Lieutenant," he said, "you will fight no more with your comrades. You have stained your uniform. We can no longer serve with you. The officers have charged me to say that, not wishing to make your deficiencies known to the Government, they ask you to give in your resignation on the cause of bad health. The surgeon will sign all necessary certificates. To-day is the 3rd of May: you have from now to the 3rd of June to quit the regiment."

"I will quit it, certainly; not because it is your desire, but mine," said Stamm, picking up his sabre and putting on his coat.

Then he leapt upon his horse, and galloped off towards the village, casting a last malediction to us all.

We all pressed round Zodomirsky. He was sad; more than sad, gloomy.

"Why did you force me to consent to this scoundrel's conditions, gentlemen?" he said. "Without you, I should never have accepted them."

"My comrades and I," said the Major, "will take all the responsibility. You have acted nobly, and I must tell you in the name of us all, M. Zodomirsky, that you are a man of honour." Then turning to the officers: "Let us go, gentlemen, we must inform the Colonel of what has passed."

"We mounted into the carriages. As we did so we saw Stamm in the distance galloping up the mountain side from the village upon his horse. Zodomirsky's eyes followed him.

"I know not what presentiment torments me," he said, "but I wish his pistol had been loaded, and that he had fired."

He uttered a deep sigh, then shook his head, as if with that he could disperse his gloomy thoughts.

"Home," he called to the driver.

We took the same route that we had come by, and consequently again passed Mariana Ravensky's window. Each of us looked up, but Mariana was no longer there.

"Captain," said Zodomirsky, "will you render me a service?"

"Whatever you wish," I replied.

"I count upon you to tell my poor Mariana the result of this miserable affair."

"I will do so. And when?"

"Now. The sooner the better. Stop!" cried Zodomirsky to the coachman. He stopped and I descended, and the carriage drove on.

Zodomirsky had hardly entered when he saw me appear in the

doorway of the saloon. Without doubt my face was pale, and wore a look of consternation, for Zodomirsky sprang towards me, crying :

" Great heavens, Captain ! What has happened ? "

I drew him from the saloon.

" My poor friend, haste, if you wish to see Mariana alive. She was at her window ; she saw Stamm gallop past. Stamm being alive, it followed that you were dead. She uttered a cry, and fell. From that moment she has never opened her eyes."

" Oh, my presentiments ! " cried Zodomirsky, " my presentiments ! " and he rushed, hatless and without his sabre, into the street.

On the staircase of Mlle. Ravensky's house he met the doctor, who was coming down.

" Doctor," he cried, stopping him, " she is better, is she not ? "

" Yes," he answered, " better, because she suffers no more."

" Dead ! " murmured Zodomirsky, growing white, and supporting himself against the wall. " Dead ! "

" I always told her, poor girl ! that, having a weak heart, she must avoid all emotion——"

But Zodomirsky had ceased to listen. He sprang up the steps, crossed the hall and the saloon, calling like a madman :

" Mariana ! Mariana ! "

At the door of the sleeping chamber stood Mariana's old nurse, who tried to bar his progress. He pushed by her, and entered the room.

Mariana was lying motionless and pale upon her bed. Her face was calm as if she slept. Zodomirsky threw himself upon his knees by the bedside, and seized her hand. It was cold, and in it was clenched a curl of black hair.

" My hair ! " cried Zodomirsky, bursting into sobs.

" Yes, yours," said the old nurse, " your hair that she cut off herself on quitting you at St. Petersburg. I have often told her it would bring misfortune to one of you."

If any one desires to learn what became of Zodomirsky, let him inquire for Brother Vassili, at the Monastery of Troitza.

The holy brothers will show the visitor his tomb. They know neither his real name, nor the causes which, at twenty-six, had made him take the robe of a monk. Only they say, vaguely, that it was after a great sorrow, caused by the death of a woman whom he loved.

MARCEAU'S PRISONER

ALEXANDRE DUMAS

I

ON the evening of the 15th of December 1793 a traveller, pausing on the summit of the mountain at the foot of which rolls the river Moine, near the village of Saint-Crépin, would have looked down upon a strange spectacle.

He would have perceived thick volumes of smoke rising from the roofs and windows of cottages, succeeded by fierce tongues of flame, and in the crimson glare of the increasing conflagration the glitter of arms. A Republican brigade of twelve or fifteen hundred men had found the village of Saint-Crépin abandoned, and had set it in a blaze. Apart from the rest stood a cottage, which had been left untouched by the flames. At the door were stationed two sentinels. Inside, sitting at a table, was a young man, who appeared to be from twenty to twenty-two years old. His long fair hair waved round his clear-cut features, and his blue mantle, but half concealing his figure, left revealed the epaulettes of a general. He was tracing on a map by the light of a lamp the route his soldiers must follow. This man was General Marceau.

" Alexandre," he said, turning to his sleeping companion, " wake up ; an order has arrived from General Westermann," and he handed the despatch to his colleague.

" Who brought the order ? "

" Delmar, the people's representative."

" Very good. Where do these poor devils assemble ? "

" In a wood a league and a half from this place. It is here upon the map."

Then orders, given in a low voice, broke up the group of soldiers extended round the ashes which had once been a village. The line of soldiers descended the roadway which separates Saint-Crépin from Montfaucon, and when, some seconds after, the moon shone forth between two clouds upon the long lines of bayonets, they seemed to resemble a great black serpent with scales of steel gliding away into the darkness.

They marched thus for half an hour, Marceau at their head. The study he had made of the localities prevented him from missing the route, and after a quarter of an hour's further march they perceived before them the black mass of the forest. According to their instructions, it was there that the inhabitants of some villages and the remnants of several armies were to assemble to hear mass ; altogether about eighteen hundred Royalists.

The two generals separated their little troop into several parties, with orders to surround the forest. As they advanced thus in a circle, it seemed that the glade which formed the centre of the forest was lighted up. Still approaching, they could distinguish the glare of torches, and soon, as objects became more distinct, a strange scene burst upon their sight.

Upon an altar, roughly represented by some piles of stones, stood the *curé* of the village of Sainte-Marie-de-Rhé, chanting the mass ; grouped around him was a circle of old men grasping torches, and, upon their knees, women and children were praying. Between the Republicans and this group a wall of soldiers was placed. It was evident that the Royalists had been warned.

They did not wait to be attacked, but opened fire at once upon their assailants, who advanced without firing a single shot. The priest still continued chanting the mass. When the Republicans were thirty paces from their enemies the first rank knelt down ; three lines of barrels were lowered like corn before the wind ; the volley burst forth. The light gleamed upon the lines of the Royalists and some shots struck the women and children kneeling at the foot of the altar. For an instant wails of distress arose. Then the priest held up his crucifix, and all was silent again.

The Republicans, still advancing, fired their second discharge, and now neither side had time to load ; it was a hand-to-hand fight with bayonets, and all advantage was on the side of the well-armed Republicans. The Royalists gave way ; entire ranks fell. The priest, perceiving this, made a sign. The torches were extinguished, and all was darkness. Then followed a scene of disorder and carnage, where each man struck with blind fury, and died without asking for pity.

"Mercy ! mercy ! " cried a heartrending voice, suddenly, at Marceau's feet, as he was about to strike. It was a young boy without weapons. " Save me, in the name of Heaven ! " he cried.

The General stooped and dragged him some paces from the affray, but as he did so the youth fainted. Such excess of terror in a soldier astonished Marceau ; but, notwithstanding, he loosened his collar to give him air. His captive was a girl !

There was not an instant to lose. The Convention's orders were imperative ; all Royalists taken with or without weapons, whatever their age or sex, must perish upon the scaffold. He placed the young girl at the foot of a tree, and ran towards the skirmish. Amongst the dead he perceived a young Republican officer, whose figure appeared to him about the same as that of his prisoner. He stripped him quickly of his coat and hat, and returned with them to the girl. The freshness of the night had revived her.

"My father! my father!" were her first words. "I have abandoned him; he will be killed!"

"Mademoiselle Blanche!" suddenly whispered a voice behind the tree, "the Marquis de Beaulieu lives; he is saved." And he who had said these words disappeared like a shadow.

"Tinguy, Tinguy!" cried the girl, extending her arms towards the spot where he had stood.

"Silence! a word will denounce you," said Marceau; "and I wish to save you. Put on this coat and hat and wait here."

He returned to his soldiers, gave orders for them to retire upon Chollet, left his companion in command, and came back to his prisoner. Finding her ready to follow him, he directed their steps to the road where his servant waited with horses. The young girl sprang into the saddle with all the grace of a practised rider. Three-quarters of an hour after they galloped into Chollet. Marceau, with his little escort, took his way to the Hôtel Sans Culotte. He engaged two rooms, and conducted the young girl to one of them, advising her, at the same time, to take some rest after the fearful night she had endured. Whilst she slept, Marceau determined on the course he would take to save her. He would take her himself to Nantes, where his mother lived. He had not seen her for three years, and it would be natural enough for him to ask permission for leave of absence. As dawn began to break he entered General Westermann's house. His demand was accorded at once, but it was necessary that his permission should be signed by Delmar. The General promised to send him with the certificate, and Marceau returned to the hotel to snatch a few moments of repose.

Marceau and Blanche were about to sit down to breakfast when Delmar appeared in the doorway. He was one of Robespierre's agents, in whose hands the guillotine was more active than intelligent.

"Ah!" he said to Marceau, "you wish to leave us already, citizen, but you have done this night's work so well I can refuse you nothing. My only regret is that the Marquis de Beaulieu escaped. I had promised the Convention to send them his head."

Blanche stood erect and pale like a statue of terror. Marceau placed himself before her.

"But we will follow his track. Here is your permission," he added; "you can start when you choose. But I cannot quit you without drinking to the health of the Republic." And he sat down at the table by the side of Blanche.

They were beginning to feel more at ease, when a discharge of musketry burst upon their ears. The General leapt to his feet and rushed to his arms, but Delmar stopped him.

"What noise is that?" asked Marceau.

"Oh, nothing!" replied Delmar. "Last night's prisoners being

shot." Blanche uttered a cry of terror. Delmar turned slowly and
looked at her.

"Here is a fine thing," he said. "If soldiers tremble like women,
we shall have to dress up our women as soldiers. It is true you are
very young," he continued, catching hold of her and scanning her
closely, "you will get used to it in time."

"Never, never!" cried Blanche, without dreaming how dangerous
it was for her to manifest her feelings before such a witness. "I
could never get used to such horrors."

"Boy," he replied, loosing her, "do you think a nation can be
regenerated without spilling blood? Listen to my advice; keep
your reflections to yourself. If ever you fall into the hands of the
Royalists they will give you no more mercy than I have done to
their soldiers." And saying these words he went out.

"Blanche," said Marceau, "do you know, if that man had given
one gesture, one sign, that he recognised you, I would have blown
his brains out?"

"My God!" she said, hiding her face in her hands, "when I
think that my father might fall into the hands of this tiger, that if
he had been made a prisoner, this night, before my eyes—— It is
atrocious. Is there no longer pity in this world? Oh! pardon,
pardon," she said, turning to Marceau, "who should know that
better than I?"

At this instant a servant entered and announced that the horses
were ready.

"Let us start, in the name of Heaven!" she cried; "there is
blood in the air we breathe here."

"Yes, let us go," replied Marceau, and they descended together.

II

Marceau found at the door a troop of thirty men whom the
General-in-Chief had ordered to escort them to Nantes.

As they galloped along the high-road, Blanche told him her
history: how, her mother being dead, she had been brought up
by her father; how her education, given by a man, had accustomed
her to exercises which, on the insurrection breaking out, had become
so useful to her in following her father.

As she finished her story, they saw twinkling before them in the
mist the lights of Nantes. The little troop crossed the Loire, and
some seconds after Marceau was in the arms of his mother. A few
words sufficed to interest his mother and sisters in his young companion. No sooner had Blanche manifested a desire to change her
dress than the two young girls led her away, each disputing which
should have the pleasure of serving her as lady's-maid. When
Blanche re-entered, Marceau stared in astonishment. In her first
costume he had hardly noticed her extreme beauty and graceful-

ness, which she had now resumed with her woman's dress. It is true, she had taken the greatest pains to make herself as pretty as possible ; for one instant before her glass she had forgotten war, insurrection, and carnage. The most innocent soul has its coquetry when it first begins to love.

Marceau could not utter a word, and Blanche smiled joyously, for she saw that she appeared as beautiful to him as she had desired.

In the evening the young *fiancé* of Marceau's sister came, and there was one house in Nantes—one only, perhaps—where all was happiness and love, surrounded, as it was, by tears and sorrow.

And now, from this time forth, a new life began for Marceau and Blanche. Marceau saw a happier future before him, and it was not strange that Blanche should desire the presence of the man who had saved her life. Only from time to time as she thought of her father tears would pour from her eyes, and Marceau would reassure her, and to distract her thoughts would tell her of his first campaign ; how the school-boy had become a soldier at fifteen, an officer at seventeen, a colonel at nineteen, and a general at twenty-one.

Nantes at this time writhed under the yoke of Carrier. Its streets ran with blood, and Carrier, who was to Robespierre what the hyæna is to the tiger, and the jackal to the lion, gorged himself with the purest of this blood. No one bore a reputation more blameless than that of the young general, Marceau, and no suspicion had as yet attacked his mother or sisters. And now the day fixed for the marriage of one of these young girls arrived.

Amongst the jewels that Marceau had sent for, he chose a necklace of precious stones, which he offered to Blanche.

She looked at it first with all the coquetry of a young girl ; then she closed the box.

" Jewels are out of place in my situation," she said. " I cannot accept it whilst my father, hunted from place to place, perhaps begs a morsel of bread for his food and a granary for his shelter."

Marceau pressed her in vain. She would accept nothing but an artificial red rose which was amongst the jewels.

The churches being closed, the ceremony took place at the village hotel. At the door of the hotel a dèputation of sailors awaited the young couple. One of these men, whose face appeared familiar to Marceau, held in his hand two bouquets. One he gave to the young bride, and, advancing towards Blanche, who regarded him fixedly, he presented her with the other.

" Tinguy, where is my father ? " said Blanche, growing very pale.

" At Saint-Florent," replied the sailor. " Take this bouquet. There is a letter inside."

Blanche wished to stop him, to speak to him, but he had disappeared. She read the letter with anxiety. The Royalists had suffered defeat after defeat, giving way before devastation and

famine. The Marquis had learnt everything through the watchfulness of Tinguy. Blanche was sad. This letter had cast her back
again into all the horrors of war. During the ceremony a stranger
who had, he said, affairs of the utmost importance to communicate
to Marceau had been ushered into the saloon. As Marceau entered
the room, his head bent towards Blanche, who leant upon his arm,
he did not perceive him. Suddenly he felt her tremble. He looked
up. Blanche and he were face to face with Delmar. He approached
them slowly, his eyes fixed on Blanche, a smile upon his lips. With
his forehead beaded with cold sweat, Marceau regarded him as
Don Juan regarded the statue of the commandant.

"You have a brother, citizeness ? " he said to Blanche.   She
stammered. Delmar continued :

"If my memory and your face do not deceive me, we breakfasted
together at Chollet. How is it I have not seen you since in the ranks
of the Republican army ? "

Blanche felt as if she were going to fall, for the eye of Delmar
pierced her through and through. Then he turned to Marceau ; it
was Delmar's turn to tremble. The young general had his hand
upon the hilt of his sword, which he gripped convulsively. Delmar's
face resumed its habitual expression ; he appeared to have totally
forgotten what he was about to say, and taking Marceau by the arm
he drew him into the niche of a window, and talked to him a few
minutes about the situation in La Vendée, and told him he had come
to consult with Carrier on certain rigorous measures about to be
inflicted on the Royalists. Then he quitted the room, passing
Blanche, who had fallen cold and white into a chair, with a bow and
a smile.

Two hours after Marceau received orders to rejoin his army,
though his leave of absence did not expire for fifteen days. He
believed this to have some connection with the scene which had just
passed. He must obey, however ; to hesitate were to be lost.

Marceau presented the order to Blanche. He regarded her sadly.
Two tears rolled down her pale cheeks, but she was silent.

"Blanche," he said, "war makes us murderous and cruel ; it is
possible that we shall see each other no more." He took her hand.
"Promise me, if I fall, that you will remember me sometimes, and
I promise you, Blanche, that if between my life and death I have the
time to pronounce one name—one alone—it shall be yours."
Blanche was speechless for tears, but in her eyes were a thousand
promises more tender than that which Marceau demanded. With
one hand she pressed Marceau's, and pointed with the other to his
rose, which she wore in her hair.

"It shall never leave me," she said.

An hour after he was on the road to rejoin his army. Each step
he took on the road they had journeyed together recalled her to his

mind, and the danger she ran appeared more menacing now that he was away from her side. Each instant he felt ready to rein in his horse and gallop back to Nantes. If Marceau had not been so intent upon his own thoughts he would have perceived at the extremity of the road and coming towards him a horseman who, after stopping an instant to assure himself he was not mistaken, had put his horse at a gallop and joined him. He recognised General Dumas. The two friends leapt from their horses and cast themselves into each other's arms. At the same instant a man, his hair streaming with perspiration, his face bleeding, his clothing rent, sprang over the hedge and, half fainting, fell at the feet of the two friends, exclaiming :

" She is arrested ! "

It was Tinguy.

" Arrested ! Who ? Blanche ! " cried Marceau.

The peasant made an affirmative sign. He could no longer speak. He had run five leagues, crossing fields and hedges in his flight to join Marceau.

Marceau stared at him stupidly.

" Arrested ! Blanche arrested ! " he repeated continually, whilst his friend applied his gourd full of wine to the clenched teeth of the peasant.

" Alexandre," cried Marceau, " I shall return to Nantes ; I must follow her, for my life, my future, my happiness, all is with her ! " His teeth chattered violently, and his body trembled convulsively.

" Let him beware who has dared to put his hand on Blanche, I love her with all the strength of my soul ; existence is no longer possible for me without her. Oh, fool that I was to leave her ! Blanche arrested ! And where has she been taken ? "

Tinguy, to whom this question was addressed, commenced to recover. " To the prison of Bouffays," he answered.

The words were hardly out of his mouth when the two friends were galloping back to Nantes.

Marceau knew he had not an instant to lose : he directed his steps at once to Carrier's house. But neither menaces nor prayers could obtain an interview from the deputy of the " Mountain."

Marceau turned away quietly ; he appeared in the interval to have adopted a new project, and he prayed his companion to await him at the gate of the prison with horses and a carriage.

Before Marceau's name and rank the prison gates were soon opened, and he commanded the gaoler to conduct him to the cell where Blanche was enclosed. The man hesitated ; but, on Marceau repeating his desire in a more imperative tone, he obeyed, making him a sign to follow him.

" She is not alone," said his guide, as he unlocked the low-arched door of a cell whose sombre gloom made Marceau shudder, " but she will not be troubled long with her companion ; he is to be guillotined to-day." Saying these words he closed the door on Marceau, and determined to keep as quiet as possible concerning an interview which would be so compromising to him.

Still dazzled from his sudden passage from day to darkness, Marceau groped his way into the cell like a man in a dream. Then he heard a cry, and the young girl flung herself into his arms. She clung to him with inarticulate sobs and convulsive embraces.

" You have not abandoned me, then," she cried. " They arrested me, dragged me here ; in the crowd which followed I recognised Tinguy. I cried out ' Marceau ! Marceau ! ' and he disappeared. Now you have come, you will take me away, you will not leave me here ? "

" I wish I could tear you away this moment, if it were at the price of my life ; but it is impossible. Give me two days, Blanche, but two days. Now I wish you to answer me a question on which your life and mine depend. Answer me as you would answer to God. Blanche, do you love me ? "

" Is this the time and place for such a question ? Do you think these walls are used to vows of love ? "

" This *is* the moment, for we are between life and death. Blanche, be quick and answer me ; each instant robs us of a day, each hour, of a year. Do you love me ? "

" Oh ! yes, yes ! " These words escaped from the young girl's heart, who, forgetting that no one could see her blushes, hid her head upon his breast.

" Well ! Blanche, you must accept me at once for your husband."

The young girl trembled.

" What can be your design ? "

" My motive is to tear you from death ; we will see if they will send to the scaffold the wife of a Republican general."

Then Blanche understood it all ; but she trembled at the danger to which he must expose himself to save her. Her love for him increased, and with it her courage rose.

" It is impossible," she said firmly.

" Impossible ! " interrupted Marceau ; " what can rise between us and happiness, since you have avowed you love me ? Listen, then, to the reason which has made you reject your only way of escape. Listen, Blanche ! I saw you and loved you ; that love has become a passion. My life is yours, your fate is mine ; happiness or death, I will share either with you ; no human power can separate us, and if I quitted you, I have only to cry ' *Vive le roi !* ' and your prison gates will reopen, and we will come out no more except together. Death upon the same scaffold, that will be enough for me."

" Oh, no, no ; leave me, in the name of Heaven, leave me ! "

" Leave you ! Take heed what you say, for if I quit this prison without having the right to defend you, I shall seek out your father—your father whom you have forgotten, and who weeps for you—and I shall say to him : ' Old man, she could have saved herself, but she has not done so ; she has wished your last days to be passed in mourning, and her blood to be upon your white hair. Weep, old man, not because your daughter is dead, but because she did not love you well enough to live.' "

Marceau had repulsed her, and she had fallen on her knees beside him, and he, with his teeth clenched, strode to and fro with a bitter laugh ; then he heard her sob, the tears leapt to his eyes, and he knelt before her.

" Blanche, by all that is most sacred in the world, consent to become my wife ! "

" You must, young girl," interrupted a strange voice, which made them tremble and rise together. " It is the only way to preserve your life. Religion commands you, and I am ready to bless your union." Marceau turned astonished, and recognised the *curé* of Sainte-Marie-de-Rhé, who had made part of the gathering which he had attacked on the night when Blanche became his prisoner.

" Oh, my father," he cried, seizing his hand, " obtain her consent ! "

" Blanche de Beaulieu," replied the priest, with solemn accents, " in the name of your father, whom my age and friendship give me the right of representing, I command you to obey this young man."

Blanche seemed agitated with a thousand different emotions ; at last she threw herself into Marceau's arms.

" I cannot resist any longer," she said. " Marceau, I love you, and I will be your wife." Their lips joined ; Marceau was at the height of joy ; he seemed to have forgotten everything. The priest's voice broke in upon their ecstasy.

" We must be quick," he said, " for my moments are numbered."

The two lovers trembled ; this voice recalled them to earth. Blanche glanced around the cell with apprehension.

" What a moment," she said, " to unite our destinies ! Can you think a union consecrated under vaults so sombre and lugubrious can be fortunate and happy ? "

Marceau shuddered, for he himself was touched with superstitious terror. He drew Blanche to that part of the cell where the daylight struggling through the crossed bars of a narrow air-hole rendered the shadows less thick, and there, falling on their knees, they awaited the priest's blessing. As he extended his arms above them and pronounced the sacred words, the clash of arms and the tread of soldiers was heard in the corridor.

Blanche cast herself in terror into Marceau's arms.

" Can they have come to seek me already ? " she cried. " Oh, my love, how frightful death is at this moment ! " The young General threw himself before the door, a pistol in each hand. The astonished soldiers drew back.

" Reassure yourselves," said the priest ; " it is I whom they seek. It is I who must die."

The soldiers surrounded him.

" My children," he cried, in a loud voice, addressing himself to the young pair. " On your knees ; for with one foot in the tomb I give you my last benediction, and that of a dying person is sacred." He drew, as he spoke, a crucifix from his breast, and extended it towards them ; himself about to die, it was for them he prayed.

There was a solemn silence.

Then the soldiers surrounded him, the door closed, and all disappeared.

Blanche threw her arms about Marceau's neck.

" Oh, if you leave me, and they come to seek me, and you are not here to aid me ! Oh, Marceau, think of me upon the scaffold far from you, weeping, and calling you, without response ! Oh, do not go ! do not go ! I will cast myself at their feet : I will tell them I am not guilty, that, if they will leave me in prison with you all my life, I will bless them ! "

" I am sure to save you, Blanche ; I answer for your life. In less than two days I shall be here with your pardon, and then, instead of a prison and a cell, a life of happiness, a life of liberty and love ! "

The door opened, the gaoler appeared. Blanche clung more closely to her lover's breast, but each instant was precious, and he gently unwound her arms from about him, and promised to return before the close of the second day.

" Love me for ever," he said, rushing out of the cell.

" For ever," said Blanche, half fainting, and showing him in her hair the red rose that he had given her. Then the door closed upon him like the gate of the Inferno.

III

Marceau found his companion waiting for him at the porter's lodge. He called for ink and paper.

" What are you about to do ? " asked his friend.

" I am going to write to Carrier, to demand a respite of two days, and to tell him his own life depends on Blanche's."

" Wretched man ! " cried his friend, snatching the unfinished letter away from him. " You threaten him, you who are in his

power, you who have set his orders to rejoin your army at defiance.
Before an hour passes you will be arrested, and what then can you
do for yourself or her ? "

Marceau let his head fall between his hands, and appeared to
reflect deeply.

" You are right," he cried, rising suddenly ; and he drew his
friend into the street.

A group of people were gathered round a post-chaise.

" If this evening is hazy," whispered a voice at Marceau's ear,
" I do not know what would prevent twenty strong fellows from
entering the town and freeing the prisoners. It is a pity that
Nantes is so badly guarded."

Marceau trembled, turned, and recognised Tinguy, darted a
glance of intelligence at him, and sprang into the carriage.

" Paris ! " he called to the postilion, and the horses darted
forward with the rapidity of lightning. At eight o'clock the carriage
entered Paris.

Marceau and his friend separated at the square of the Palais
Egalité, and Marceau took his way alone on foot through the
Rue Saint-Honoré, descended at the side of Saint-Roch, stopped
at No. 366, and asked for Robespierre. He was informed that he
had gone to the Théâtre de la Nation. Marceau proceeded there,
astonished to have to seek in such a place the austere member of
the Committee of Public Welfare. He entered, and recognised
Robespierre half hidden in the shadow of a box. As he arrived
outside the door he met him coming out. Marceau presented himself, and gave him his name.

" What can I do for you ? " said Robespierre.

" I desire an interview with you."

" Here, or at my house ? "

" At your house."

" Come, then."

And these two men, moved by feelings so opposite, walked along
side by side, Robespierre indifferent and calm, Marceau passionate
and excited. This was the man who held within his hands the
fate of Blanche.

They arrived at Robespierre's house, entered, and ascended a
narrow staircase, which led them to a chamber on the third floor.
A bust of Rousseau, a table, on which lay open the *Contrat Social*
and *Emile*, a chest of drawers, and some chairs, completed the
furniture of the apartment.

" Here is Cæsar's palace," said Robespierre, smiling ; " what have
you to demand from its president ? "

" The pardon of my wife, who is condemned to death by
Carrier."

" Your wife condemned to death by Carrier ! The wife of

Marceau, the well-known Republican! the Spartan soldier! What is Carrier then doing at Nantes? "

Marceau gave him an account of the atrocities which Carrier was superintending at Nantes.

" See how I am always misunderstood," cried Robespierre, with a hoarse voice, broken by emotion. " Above all, where my eyes cannot see, nor my hand arrest. There is enough blood being spilt that we cannot avoid, and we are not at the end of it yet."

" Then give me my wife's pardon."

Robespierre took a leaf of white paper.

" What was her name? "

" Why do you wish to know that? "

" It is necessary in cases of identity."

" Blanche de Beaulieu."

Robespierre let his pen fall.

" What? The daughter of the Marquis de Beaulieu, the chief of the Royalists of La Vendée. How is it that she is *your* wife? "

Marceau told him all.

" Young fool and madman! " he said. " Must you——"

Marceau interrupted him : " I ask from you neither insults nor abuse. I ask for her life. Will you give it me? "

" Will family ties, love's influence, never lead you to betray the Republic? "

" Never."

" If you find yourself armed, face to face with the Marquis de Beaulieu? "

" I will fight against him as I have already done."

" And if he falls into your hands? "

Marceau reflected an instant :

" I will bring him to you, and you shall be his judge."

" You swear it to me? "

" Upon my honour."

Robespierre took up his pen and finished writing.

" There is your wife's pardon," he said. " You can depart."

Marceau took his hand and wrung it with force. He wished to speak, but tears choked his utterance ; and it was Robespierre who said to him :

" Go! there is not an instant to lose. *Au revoir!* "

Marceau sprang down the stairs and into the street, and ran toward the Palais-Egalité, where his carriage waited.

From what a weight his heart was freed! What happiness awaited him! What joy after so much grief! His imagination plunged into the future, and he saw the moment when, appearing on the threshold of the prison-cell, he would cry :

" Blanche, you are saved ! You are free ! Before us lies a life of love and happiness."

Yet from time to time a vague uneasiness tormented him ; a sudden chill struck cold upon his heart. He spurred on the postilions by lavish promises of gold, and the horses flew along the road. Everything seemed to partake of the feverish agitation of his blood. In a few hours he had left Versailles, Chartres, Le Mans, La Flèche behind him. They were nearing Angers, when suddenly, with a terrible crash, the carriage heeled over on its side, and he fell. He rose hurt and bleeding, separated with his sabre the traces which bound one of the horses, and, leaping on its back, reached the next post ; and, taking a fresh horse, rapidly continued his course.

And now he has crossed Angers, he perceives Nigrande, reaches Varade, passes Ancenis ; his horse streams with foam and blood. He gains Saint-Donatien, then Nantes—Nantes, which encloses his life, his happiness ! Some seconds after he passes the gates, he is in the town, he reins in his horse before the prison of Bouffays. He has arrived. What matters all their troubles now ? He calls :

" Blanche, Blanche ! "

The gaoler appears and replies :

" Two carts have just left the prison. Mademoiselle de Beaulieu was in the first."

With a curse upon his lips, Marceau springs to the ground, and rushes with the hustling crowd towards the great square. He comes up with the last of the two carts ; one of the prisoners inside recognises him. It is Tinguy.

" Save her ! save her ! " he cries out, " for I have failed ! "

Marceau pushes on through the crowd ; they hustle him, they press around him, but he hurls them out of his path. He arrives upon the place of execution. Before him is the scaffold. He flourishes aloft the scrap of paper, crying :

" A pardon ! a pardon ! "

At that instant the executioner, seizing by its long, fair hair the head of a young girl, held it up before the terrified crowd.

Suddenly from the midst of that silent crowd a cry was heard— a cry of anguish, in which there seemed to have been gathered all the forces of human agony. Marceau had recognised between the teeth of this uplifted head the red rose which he had given to his young bride.

A BAL MASQUÉ
ALEXANDRE DUMAS

I SAID that I was in to no one ; one of my friends forced admission. My servant announced Mr. Anthony R——. Behind Joseph's livery I saw the corner of a black frock-coat ; it is probable that the wearer of the frock-coat, from his side, saw a flap of my dressing-gown ; impossible to conceal myself.

"Very well ! Let him enter," I said out loud. " Let him go to the devil," I said to myself.

While working it is only the woman you love who can disturb you with impunity, for she is always at bottom interested in what you are doing.

I went up to him, therefore, with the half-bored face of an author interrupted in one of those moments of sorest self-mistrust, while I found him so pale and haggard that the first words I addressed to him were these :

" What is the matter ? What has happened to you ? "

" Oh ! Let me take breath," said he. " I'm going to tell you all about it, besides, it's a dream perhaps, or perhaps I am mad."

He threw himself into an arm-chair, and let his head drop between his hands.

I looked at him in astonishment ; his hair was dripping with rain ; his shoes, his knees, and the bottom of his trousers were covered with mud. I went to the window ; I saw at the door his servant and his cabriolet ; I could make nothing out of it all.

He saw my surprise.

" I have been to the cemetery of Père-Lachaise," said he.

" At ten o'clock in the morning ? "

" I was there at seven—a cursed bal masqué ! "

I could not imagine what a bal masqué and Père-Lachaise had to do with one another. I resigned myself, and turning my back to the mantelpiece began to roll a cigarette for him between my fingers with the phlegm and the patience of a Spaniard.

While he was coming to the point I hinted to Anthony that I, for my part, was commonly very susceptible to attentions of that kind.

He made me a sign of thanks, but pushed my hand away.

Finally, I bent over to light the cigarette for myself : Anthony stopped me.

" Alexandre," he said to me, " listen, I beg of you."

"But you have been already a quarter of an hour and have not told me anything."

"Oh! it is a most strange adventure."

I got up, placed my cigarette on the mantelpiece, and crossed my arms like a man resigned ; only I began to believe, as he did, that he was fast becoming mad.

"You remember the ball at the Opéra, where I met you ? " he said to me after a moment's silence.

"The last one, where there were at least two hundred people ? "

"The very same. I left you with the intention of abandoning myself to one of those varieties of which they spoke to me as being a curiosity even in the midst of our curious times ; you wished to dissuade me from going ; a fatality drove me on. Oh! you, why did you not see it all, you who have the knack of observation ? Why were not Hoffman or Callot there to paint the picture as the fantastic burlesque thing kept unrolling itself beneath my eyes ? Unsatisfied and in melancholy mood I walked away, about to quit the Opéra ; I came to a hall that was overflowing and in high spirits : corridors, boxes, parterre. Everything was obstructed. I made a tour of the room ; twenty masks called me by name and told me theirs.

"These were all leaders—aristocrats and merchants—in the undignified disguise of pierrots, of postilions, of merry-andrews, or of fishwives. They were all young people of family, of culture, of talent ; and there, forgetful of family, talent, breeding, they were resurrecting in the midst of our sedate and serious times a soirée of the Regency. They had told me about it, and yet I could not have believed it !—I mounted a few steps, and leaning against a pillar, half hidden by it, I fixed my eyes on that sea of human beings surging beneath me. Their dominoes, of all colours, their motley costumes, their grotesque disguises formed a spectacle resembling nothing human. The music began to play. Oh, it was then these gargoyle creatures stirred themselves to the sound of that orchestra whose harmony reached me only in the midst of cries, of laughs, of hootings ; they hung on to each other by their hands, by their arms, by their necks ; a long coil formed itself, beginning with a circular motion, the dancers, men and women, stamping with their feet, made the dust break forth with a noise, the atoms of which were rendered visible by the wan light of the lustres ; turning at ever-increasing speed with bizarre postures, with unseemly gestures, with cries full of abandonment ; turning always faster and still faster, swaying and swinging like drunken men, yelling like lost women, with more delirium than delight, with more passion than pleasure ; resembling a coil of the damned doing infernal penance under the scourge of demons !

"All this passed beneath my eyes, at my feet. I felt the wind

of their whirling past ; as they rushed by each one whom I knew
flung a word at me that made me blush. All this noise, all this
humming, all this confusion, all this music went on in my brain as
well as in the room ! I soon came to the point of no longer knowing
whether that which I had before my eyes was a dream or reality ;
I came to the point of asking myself whether it was not I who was
mad and they who were sane ; I was seized with a weird temptation
to throw myself into the midst of this pandemonium, like Faust
through the Witches' Sabbath, and I felt that I, too, would then
have cries, postures, laughs like theirs. Oh ! from that to madness
there is but one step. I was appalled ; I flung myself out of the
room, followed even to the street door by shrieks that were like
those cries of passion that come out of the caverns of the fallow deer.

" I stopped a moment under the portico to collect myself ; I did
not wish to venture into the street ; with such confusion still in my
soul I might not be able to find my way ; I might, perhaps, be thrown
under the wheels of some carriage I had not seen coming. I was
as a drunken man might be who begins to recover sufficient reason
in his clouded brain to recognise his condition, and who, feeling the
will return but not the power, with fixed eyes and staring, leans
motionless against some street post or some tree on the public
promenade.

" At that moment a carriage stopped before the door, a woman
alighted or rather shot herself from the doorway.

" She entered beneath the peristyle, turning her head from right
to left like one who had lost her way ; she was dressed in a black
domino, had her face covered by a velvet mask. She presented
herself at the door.

" ' Your ticket,' said the door-keeper.

" ' My ticket ? ' she replied. ' I have none.'

" ' Then get one at the box-office.'

" The domino came back under the peristyle, fumbled nervously
about in all her pockets.

" ' No money ! ' she cried. ' Ah ! this ring—a ticket of admission
for this ring,' she said.

" ' Impossible,' replied the woman who was distributing the
cards ; ' we do not make bargains of that kind.'

" And she pushed away the brilliant, which fell to the ground and
rolled to my side.

" The domino remained still without moving, forgetting the ring,
sunk in thought.

" I picked up the ring and handed it to her.

" Through her mask I saw her eyes fixed on mine.

" ' You must help me to get in,' she said to me ; ' you must, for
pity's sake.'

" ' But I am going out, madame,' I said to her.

" ' Then give me six francs for this ring, and you will render me a service for which I shall bless you my life long.'

" I replaced the ring on her finger ; I went to the box-office, I took two tickets. We re-entered together.

" As we arrived within the corridor I felt that she was tottering. Then with her second hand she made a kind of ring around my arm.

" ' Are you in pain ? ' I asked her.

" ' No, no, it is nothing,' she replied, ' a dizziness, that is all.'

" She hurried me into the hall.

" We re-entered into that giddy madhouse.

" Three times we made the tour, breaking our way with great difficulty through the waves of masks that were hurling themselves one upon the other ; she trembling at every unseemly word that came to her ear ; I blushing to be seen giving my arm to a woman who would thus put herself in the way of such words ; then we returned to the end of the hall.

" She fell upon a sofa. I remained standing in front of her, my hand leaning on the back of her seat.

" ' Oh ! this must seem to you very bizarre,' she said, ' but not more so than to me, I swear to you. I have not the slightest idea of all this ' (she looked at the ball), ' for even in my dreams I could not imagine such things. But they wrote me, you see, that he would be here with a woman, and what sort of a woman should it be who could come to a place like this ? '

" I made a gesture of surprise ; she understood.

" ' But *I* am here, you wish to ask, do you not ? Oh ! but for me that is another thing : I, I am looking for him ; I, I am his wife. As for these people, it is madness and dissipation that drives them hither. But I, I, it is jealousy infernal ! I have been everywhere looking for him ; I have been all night in a cemetery ; I have been to a public execution ; and yet, I swear to you, as a young girl I have never once gone into the street without my mother ; as a wife I have never taken one step out of doors without being followed by a lackey ; and yet here I am, the same as all these women who are so familiar with the way ; here I am giving my arm to a man whom I do not know, blushing under my mask at the opinion he ought to have of me ! I know all this !—Have you ever been jealous, monsieur ? '

" ' Unhappily,' I replied to her.

" ' Then you will forgive me, for you understand. You know that voice that cries out to you " Do ! " as in the ear of a madman ; you have felt that arm that pushes one into shame and crime, like the arm of fate. You know that at such a moment one is capable of everything, if one can only get vengeance.'

" I was about to reply ; all at once she rose, her eyes fastened on two dominoes that were passing in front of us at that moment.

" ' Silence ! ' she said.

" And she hurried me on following in their footsteps. I was thrown into the middle of an intrigue of which I understood nothing ; I could feel all the threads vibrating, but could take hold of none of them by the end ; but this poor wife seemed so troubled that she became interesting. I obeyed like a child, so imperious is real feeling, and we set ourselves to follow the two masks, one of which was evidently a man, the other a woman. They spoke in a low voice ; the sounds reached our ears with difficulty.

" ' It is he ! ' she murmured ; ' it is his voice ; yes, yes, that is his figure——'

" The latter of the two dominoes began to laugh.

" ' That is his laugh,' said she ; ' it is he, monsieur, it is he ! The letter said true, O, mon Dieu, mon Dieu ! '

" In the meanwhile the two masks kept on, and we followed them always. They went out of the hall, and we went out after them ; they took the stairs leading to the boxes, and we ascended in their footsteps ; they did not stop till they came to the boxes in the centre ; we were like their two shadows. A little closed box was opened ; they entered it ; the door again closed upon them.

" The poor creature I was supporting on my arm frightened me by her excitement. I could not see her face, but crushed against me as she was, I could feel her heart beating, her body shivering, her limbs trembling. There was something uncanny in the way there came to me such knowledge of unheard of suffering, the spectacle of which I had before my very eyes, of whose victim I knew nothing, and of the cause of which I was completely ignorant. Nevertheless, for nothing in this world would I have abandoned that woman at such a moment.

" As she saw the two masks enter the box and the box close upon them, she stopped still a moment, motionless, and as if overwhelmed. Then she sprang forward to the door to listen. Placed as she was, her slightest movement would betray her presence and ruin her ; I dragged her back violently by the arm, I lifted the latch of the adjoining box, I drew her in after me, I lowered the grille and pulled the door to.

" ' If you wish to listen,' I said to her, ' at least listen from here.'

" She fell upon one knee and flattened her ear against the partition, and I—I held myself erect on the opposite side, my arms crossed, my head bent and thoughtful.

" All that I had been able to observe of that woman seemed to me to indicate a type of beauty. The lower part of her face, which was not concealed by her mask, was youthful, velvety, and round ; her lips were scarlet and delicate ; her teeth, which the black velvet mask falling just above them made appear still whiter, were small, separated, and glistening ; her hand was one to be modelled, her figure to be held between the fingers ; her black hair, silky, escaped in profusion from beneath the hood of her domino, and the foot of a child, that played in and out under her skirt, looked as if it should have trouble in balancing her body, all lithe, all graceful, all airy as it was.

" Oh ! what a marvellous piece of perfection must she be ! Oh ! he that should hold her in his arms, that should see every faculty of that spirit absorbed in loving him, that should feel the beating of her heart against his, her tremblings, her nervous palpitations, and that should be able to say, ' All of this, all of this, comes of love, of love for me, for me alone among all the millions of men, for me, angel predestined ! Oh ! that man !—that man ! '

" Such were my thoughts, when all at once I saw that woman rise, turn toward me, and say to me in a voice broken and fierce :

" ' Monsieur, I am beautiful, I swear it ; I am young, I am but nineteen. Until now I have been white as an angel of the Creation—ah, well—' she threw both arms about my neck, ' —ah, well, I am yours—take me ! '

" At the same instant I felt her lips pressed close to mine, and the effect of a bite, rather than that of a kiss, ran shuddering and dismayed through my whole body ; over my eyes passed a cloud of flame.

" Ten minutes later I was holding her in my arms, in a swoon, half dead and sobbing.

" Slowly she came to herself ; through her mask I made out how haggard were her eyes ; I saw the lower part of her pale face, I heard her teeth chatter one upon the other, as in the chill of a fever. I see it all once more.

" She remembered all that had taken place, and fell at my feet.

" ' If you have any compassion,' she said to me, sobbing, ' any pity, turn away your eyes from me, never seek to know me ; let me go and forget me. I will remember for two ! '

" At these words she rose again ; quickly, like a thought that escapes us, she darted toward the door, opened it, and coming back again, ' Do not follow me, in heaven's name, monsieur, do not follow me ! ' she said.

" The door pushed violently open, closed again between her and me, stole her from my sight, like an apparition. I have never seen her more !

" I have never seen her more ! And ever since, ever since the six months that have glided by, I have sought her everywhere, at balls, at spectacles, at promenades. Every time I have seen from a distance a woman with a lithe figure, with a foot like a child's, with black hair, I have followed her, I have drawn near to her, I have looked into her face, hoping that her blushes would betray her. Nowhere have I found her again, in no place have I seen her again

—except at night, except in my dreams! Oh! there, there she reappears; there I feel her, I feel her embraces, her biting caresses so ardent, as if she had something of the devil in her; then the mask has fallen and a face more grotesque appeared to me at times blurred as if veiled in a cloud; sometimes brilliant, as if circled by an aureole; sometimes pale, with a skull white and naked, with eyes vanished from the orbits, with teeth chattering and few.

"In short, ever since that night, I have ceased to live; burning with mad passion for a woman I do not know, hoping always, and always disappointed at my hopes. Jealous without the right to be so, without knowing of whom to be jealous, not daring to avow such madness, and all the time pursued, preyed upon, wasted away, consumed by her."

As he finished these words he tore a letter from his breast.

"Now that I have told you everything," he said to me, "take this letter and read it."

I took the letter and read:

"Have you perhaps forgotten a poor woman who has forgotten nothing and who dies because she cannot forget?

"When you receive this letter I shall be no more. Then go to the cemetery of Père-Lachaise, tell the concierge to let you see among the newest graves one that bears on its stone the simple name 'Marie,' and when you are face to face with that grave, fall on your knees and pray."

"Ah, well!" continued Anthony, "I received that letter yesterday, and I went there this morning. The concierge conducted me to the grave, and I remained two hours on my knees there, praying and weeping. Do you understand? She was there, that woman. Her flaming spirit had stolen away; the body consumed by it had bowed, even to breaking, beneath the burden of jealousy and of remorse; she was there, under my feet, and she had lived, and she had died for me unknown; unknown!—and taking a place in my life as she had taken one in the grave: unknown!—and burying in my heart a corpse, cold and lifeless, as she had buried one in the sepulchre—Oh! Do you know anything to equal it? Do you know any event so appalling? Therefore, now, no more hope. I will see her again never. I would dig up her grave that I might recover, perhaps, some traces wherewithal to reconstruct her face; and I love her always! Do you understand, Alexandre? I love her like a madman; and I would kill myself this instant in order to rejoin her, if she were not to remain unknown to me for eternity, as she was unknown to me in this world."

With these words he snatched the letter from my hands, kissed it over and over again, and began to weep like a little child.

I took him in my arms, and not knowing what to say to him, I wept with him.